DANGERS TO SOCIETY

A NOVEL

MATTHEW ROLLINS

DANGERS TO SOCIETY

Book 1 of the Dangers to Society Series

Copyright © 2024 by Matthew Rollins.

First printing edition 2024.

Cover art by Matthew Rollins.

Book design by Matthew Rollins.

Published by Building Worlds Books.

For permission requests, contact info@buildingworldsbooks.com.

ISBN: 979-8-9890606-2-7 (Paperback)

ISBN: 979-8-9890606-3-4 (Hardcover)

Library of Congress Control Number: 2024916251

Names, characters, and places are products of the author's imagination. Any similarities to real world people, places, or things are purely coincidental. References to historical events, real people, or real places are used fictitiously.

www.buildingworldsbooks.com

A few cautionary words from the author: This story features lots of swearing, a little bit of what the kids these days call 'spice', and a few bursts of graphic violence. It is an adult story and is not appropriate for children (of any age). It is also meant for entertainment purposes only, and should not be used as an instructional tool in any measure, or taken seriously except in assessment of its previously stated purpose. I hope you enjoy it. If you do, then great minds think alike. If not, then read it again. Took me a few tries too. Thanks! M

DANGERS TO SOCIETY

MATTHEW ROLLINS

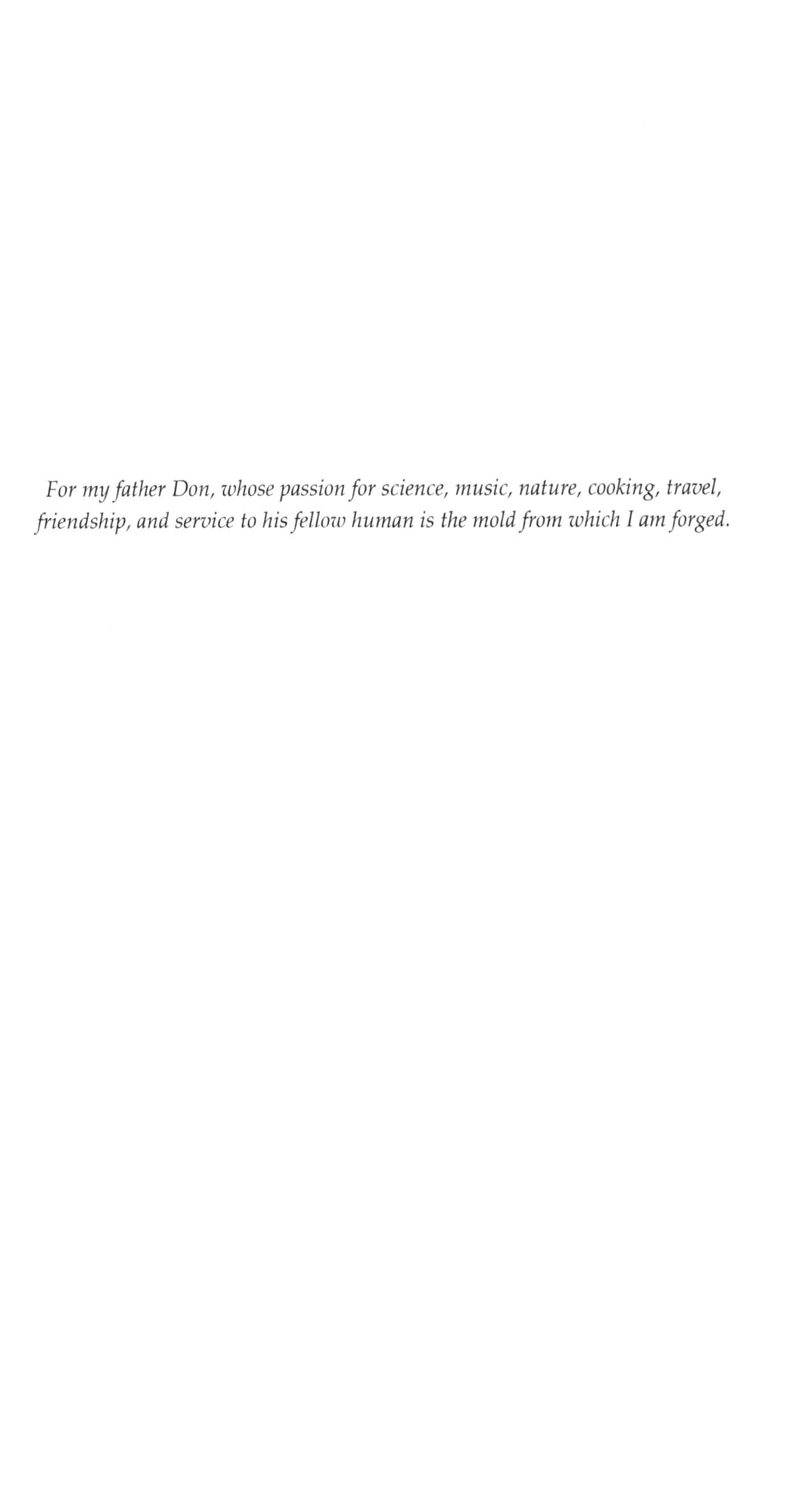

For my father Don, whose passion for science, music, nature, cooking, travel, friendship, and service to his fellow human is the mold from which I am forged.

PROLOGUE. LUCKY

"GOOD MORNING, EVERYONE," the president said to a new world. He took a sip of water from the glass waiting on his podium and offered a grim smile. The press room was packed. Nervous faces filled the chairs and lined the walls in a standing-room-only crowd. Today would be remembered as the day things changed. The course of his presidency, and that of all humankind. The withering stagnation of human progress would not be tolerated anymore. Not after this. He would lead the way.

"Before I begin, let me say that I will tell you everything I know. By the end, any questions I am able to answer will be answered. We'll make time for Q&A tomorrow if we can." He cleared his throat and took another drink of water. It was frigid. Just how he liked it. How he needed it. Every eyeball in the crowd was fixed on him. Each hand held a pen, notepad, or recorder. His legacy was about to be written.

"So, here's what we know at this hour. The UDO - the Unidentified Dark Object as we are presently calling it, has impacted around ten miles north of Pyongyang, North Korea. It was approximately half a mile wide. Satellite images show wide-ranging destruction from the impact, from inside the Chinese border, all the way to Seoul, a diameter of approximately three hundred miles. It is unclear why we were unable to detect the object earlier, but our best guess is that its composition is vastly different from a classic rocky meteor.

"At this time, the long-term impacts to the United States and the entire

Earth are unknown. The object was not large enough to create an extinction-level event. Which, I don't have to tell you, is the best possible news to arise from this tragedy. This catastrophe. Indeed, much of the Korean peninsula has been demolished. The death toll is expected to approach twenty million." The press corps could not contain their gasps and whispers. "Yes. A sad day for humankind."

He paused for more water, and to take in the stunned faces. Just as they should be. "To complicate matters, as expected, minutes before impact, North Korea launched a nuclear weapon at the UDO. It was an understandable decision, given the certain destruction of the country without intervention. Unfortunately, the nuclear explosion appears to have had little effect on the UDO's mass or trajectory, based on the limited data available. We do not yet know why. Our understanding of exactly what the object is composed of and where it came from will undoubtedly improve in the days ahead."

A number of hands shot into the air. *On cue,* he thought. The president masked his enthusiasm with a furrowed brow and covered his smile with a hand. Then, another sip of water. This thirst was unlike anything he'd experienced so far. "I see your hands, and I know what you want to ask. We just survived a potential planet-killing impact with a mysterious object from space we've only known about for a couple hours. But now we have to cope with the fallout of a half-megaton nuclear detonation in the lower atmosphere. What will that impact be?"

The raised hands dropped as the president paused again for water. So cold. Delicious. "The honest answer is we don't know. But I'm hopeful. Preliminary sensor readings from aircraft in the region indicate the UDO may have somehow absorbed or altered a significant portion of the radiation from the blast. We won't know definitively until the impact site is inspected and the object can be dissected and analyzed. But again, I think there's reason to hope that the classic radioactive fallout from the detonation will be negligible." More water. So thirsty.

"And that's what we know right now. I am going to get back to the situation room to observe the developments. Our U.N. Ambassador, Liv MacIntosh, will be at the council's emergency session tomorrow to discuss rescue operations for survivors, environmental cleanup, and development of a plan to study the UDO. I am sure I speak for every American when I say we will provide whatever assistance we can. I'll have another update tomorrow. May God bless you. May God bless America. And may God bless the entire world in the days ahead." The crowd stood as the president stepped away from the podium. They had no idea what was coming. He couldn't wait.

CHAPTER 1
THE JUGGLER

TYSON BURROWS CLOSED the door to his boss' dust-covered white and orange office trailer and squinted as the hot North Texas sun hit his face again. A huge grin gleamed on his face. He pulled his phone out and texted his best friend.

"Guess what! IT HAPPENED!! You won't believe what I can do! On my way to show you now!"

He put his phone back in his pocket, stooped to pick up several pieces of broken concrete off the ground, then began to toss them in the air as he walked. One, two, three, four, five - he stopped counting after a dozen. More and more went into the air. He could juggle! Not just juggle, but manage any number of objects in the air; he hadn't found a limit. Hands and arms shuttled back and forth in a blur, as fast as needed to keep everything aloft. He could even do it with his eyes closed. It probably wasn't going to make him rich and famous or anything, but finally, after over a year of waiting, he was one of them. An Adapted!

Tyson rounded the corner of the office trailer and walked past an open dumpster, half full of construction debris. Then his head was knocked clean off his shoulders.

CHAPTER 2
GARBAGE GIRL

ABBY ALSTROM BOUNCED her knees up and down as she sat in an uncomfortable, mid-1970s vintage teal plastic chair, complete with four skinny chrome legs, and three wide, parallel slots in the back of the seat, good for who-knows-what. The space around her seemed like an ordinary interior office. Windowless and small, it was the kind of space she imagined first-time managers got starting out on their long and arduous climb from the ranks of mop closet peons to the echelons of absurd stock options and torrid affairs with executive assistants. The space screamed bland: barely off-white walls, inexpensive mottled gray carpet tiles that camouflaged dirt and stains, acoustic tile ceiling grid, and a brilliant LED light that shone like a rectangular star over the cheap black Formica table in front of her. A metal shelf in one corner held pencils, clipboards, and pads of yellow paper. A small trash can sat in the opposite corner by the lone door. Her nose twitched as a peculiar, oversweet scent wafted through the air.

"Almond extract? What's that about?"

She looked around, but could not determine where the aroma was coming from. Aside from the disappointing lack of freshly-baked cookies in the room, the only thing unusual about the space was that she was in it at all; she couldn't remember ever stepping foot in a proper office building in her nineteen years. That, and the very obvious fact that it was moving. Every few seconds, the dull vibrations in the floor would turn into a lurch or bump as whatever vehicle she was in met a variation in the road. She hadn't been waiting there for long. At least she didn't think she had, but she couldn't quite remember how she got there, or why her stomach was in knots. The circumstances should have made her apprehensive, but she wasn't and was unsure why. The only thing she was fairly certain of was that she came voluntarily. Which didn't sound like her at all. Wondering what the time was, she checked her back pocket for her phone, but found it wasn't there. *That* made her nervous.

"Where's my phone?" She said to no one, then attempted to jog her memory by taking her blue Texas Rangers hat off and running her fingers through her short, spiky blonde hair. It didn't help.

On cue, the door across the room opened to reveal two men in navy suits and black ties, one in his mid-thirties, one not much older than her, maybe twenty-five. Both cute. The shorter, younger of the pair sat down at the table across from her, so she sized him up first. He was slight, fair-skinned but tan, probably in his early to mid-twenties. His wavy brown hair was cut military-short on the sides, and he had rich Dr Pepper brown eyes that pleaded apologetically like he was either begging to leave, or begging forgiveness. Abby loved Dr Pepper. Her gaze settled on the taller, more distinguished man in back and had to swallow to keep her jaw from dropping. His muscles bulged up and down his sports coat. His brown skin was radiant and flawless. Just the right amount of salt-and-pepper scruff dabbled his angled cheekbones, and he topped it off with an impeccably-cut fade of black hair christened with short curls. The man was underwear model gorgeous. As close to physical perfection she had ever shared space with, male or female. She swallowed again.

Mr. Universe grabbed a clipboard off the shelf and spoke first. "Good afternoon, Ms. Alstrom. Thank you for meeting with us today. I am Agent Rice, this is Agent Palmer." He tipped his head at the man at the table, who nodded and pursed his delicious lips just a little. Rice oozed confidence and authority, and probably a ton of pheromones. Hell. They both did. She cursed her hormones as she bit her lip.

"Why, exactly, am I here?" Abby asked. "I don't even remember coming here." While waiting, she wasn't nervous. Then the two suited men entered the room and announced they were 'agents' and the jitters finally arrived. *Agents for whom?* she wondered. What kind of trouble was she in? How long had she been there? Her trim nails tapped on the table, causing a haphazard array of shallow clicks.

"Yes, I apologize for the gas," Rice said. "It's a standard RADSA safety procedure these days. Ensures these interviews we do with Adapted go as smoothly as possible." He scanned whatever was on the clipboard.

Abby's eyes bulged. "You're RADSA?" A surge of adrenaline rushed into her bloodstream. In the close confines of the office they were in, interrogation seemed a more apt choice of words. She gauged Rice with a wary eye. What exactly did that gas do to her?

The Radiologically Adapted Dangers to Society Administration was the least popular (at least social media-wise) of President Lawrence "Lucky" Phelps' sweeping progressive reforms after the still poorly named Unidentified Dark Object obliterated much of the Korean Peninsula last year. President Phelps was quick to push through bi-partisan legislation to cope with the new normal of random people being able to do random things. Lucky was right. If President We-Don't-Like-To-Talk-About-Him was still in charge, every single Adapted would get rounded up like a criminal or terrorist and abruptly shipped to an inescapable tropical island somewhere in the Atlantic. Even little old grandmas that just happened to develop toxic sweat.

Despite the small room's comfortable temperature, beads of sweat raced down the back of Abby's neck. She grasped the edge of the table, bracing for the news that she would have to pack her bags for a one-way trip to Island-A.

"What do you want with me? My R-Skill isn't something on the Dangers to Society list." Abby reclined in her chair, but found no comfort in the unyielding plastic.

Rice held out an open palm. "No need for alarm, we're the good guys. We're hoping to help you."

"Help… me?" Abby smirked and pushed back from the table. "Listen, I'm doing just fine, Mister - uh, Agent Rice."

Expressionless up to that point, Agent Palmer winced. Then he spoke across folded arms with a calm baritone. "Don't lie, Abby."

Amid the sweat, the short hairs on the back of her neck stood on end. She scoffed and glared at Palmer across the table. "Screw you, I'm not lying!"

He calmly blinked and shook his head.

The lust in her heart now beaten out by fresh palpitations, Abby shot Rice a quizzical look with raised eyebrows. "Is this where you two play good cop, bad cop?" She turned her head. "Which one are you supposed to be, shorty?" Abby was an inch or two taller than Palmer, who deflected her comment without a verbal or physical response.

Rice had a small chuckle. "No, that's Agent Palmer's R-Skill. He can sense when people are telling the truth. He's like you."

"The hell he is!" Abby jumped out of her seat. Her blood frothed with instant rage. "Whoever heard of an Adapted working for RADSA?" She wanted to deck the guy, then give him a big hug. The chat group she started on the hugely popular A-Space social media platform with other Adapted she knew around Dallas was woefully small. And boring. No one wanted to talk or hang out. She wished she knew more people with R-Skills. But even if she knew a thousand Adapted, none of them would ever support the organization that sent their kind to the island.

The island! Abby's heart raced. She glowered at Palmer. "Is this where you tell me to pack my bags for a tropical vacation, traitor? I've won the big prize! An all-expenses-paid lifelong trip, relaxing on beaches, eating three square United Nations-approved meals a day, sleeping in a proverbial human shoebox with no air conditioning, and eventually dying of utter boredom? Sign me up!" She flashed a toothy smile, then glared at the turncoat across the table.

Palmer winced again and exchanged a look with Rice. Abby paced along the edge of her side of the table.

What a shitty fate, she thought. Word was that Island-A was already overcrowded, which was an issue, given its new guests tended to be the type that could shoot bullets from their fingers or belch stomach acid twenty feet on demand. Indeed, part of RADSA's charter was to separate (and ship off) the irreversibly dangerous from those Adapted that could blend into society without too much disruption. But with no trial or tribunal? No advocate to argue the Adapted's case? The process was sheer cruelty, pure and simple, even if done under the guise of keeping everyone else safe.

Rice cleared his throat. "Abby, I think you've misinterpreted why we're here."

She made fake furtive looks at the corners of the room. "This isn't one of those gross amateur Internet video setups, is it? I don't see a sticky black leather sofa here. C'mon. You're RADSA. You're here to ship me off."

Palmer closed his eyes and rubbed his forehead. "No, we're not."

Abby wasn't buying it. RADSA had celebrity-laden commercials regularly promoting their role in promoting tolerance and mediating grievances, but most Adapted assumed the agency was primarily focused on the separating/shipping part. Internet rumors ran rampant that they didn't always adhere to the official Dangers to Society list which defined who had to go to Island-A, and who got to keep their lives intact. Of course, most normies assumed each and every Adapted on the planet was a lurking mutant flesh-eating zombie predator, awaiting the most inopportune moment to interrupt their Sunday afternoon football party and consume everyone not fast enough to escape. That happens one time and the whole planet freaks.

Shit, what do I do? Abby asked herself. She pulled her cap off and tousled her hair as she paced.

Palmer leaned back in his chair. He massaged his chin in analysis of Abby.

Rice sighed and set his clipboard down, then adjusted the joints in his neck with audible pops. "Ms. Alstrom, please relax. As I said, we're the good guys. We want to help you. Have a seat, this won't take long."

Abby sat back down, surprised that she did with zero resistance. "Right. Because a couple of government jackboots gassing and interrogating teenagers in a windowless mobile command center is all on the up-and-up. I'd like to go now, please."

"It's all for your own protection." Rice motioned with his hands that she should stay put and retrieved his clipboard again. "Now, I've shown you mine." He gestured to Palmer. "If you'd be so kind as to show me yours."

"My what — tits?" Abby scoffed.

Rice's chiseled cheeks turned red under his stubble. "Uh, no, Abby. Your gift. Your R-Skill. I already know what it is from your file, but I'd like to see it all the same."

Abby groaned. Of course they had a file on her. They probably had a file on everyone. Why did she volunteer to come here? Had she volunteered? She couldn't remember. She looked at Palmer and pointed. "Is that why Benedict Arnold is here, so I can't just blow you off and say I don't have one?"

Rice shrugged and smiled a little. "He does make my job easier."

Slumping in her already uncomfortable seat, Abby conceded, ready to skip to the end. "I can throw garbage into trash cans. Any size and weight, any distance." She paused. "As long as I know where the trash can is."

"Remarkable." Agent Rice picked his clipboard back up and scribbled something on the second page, then turned to Abby with a smile. "Is that it? Any side effects or limitations?"

She shook her head. "The only side effect is I play with construction garbage all day for my job. Yay for me." She twirled a finger in the air and rolled her eyes.

"You should feel proud. I've interviewed close to a thousand Adapted. The variety of R-Skills is endless. There are some pretty unfortunate ones out there."

Abby scoffed and began to play with her array of earrings. "Yeah, I bet. Did you get to interview that madam in Las Vegas that can make dudes' dicks bigger by fucking them? She makes a million a pop! Maybe she gave you a free demonstration? Or did you talk to the Pope before he realized that his ability to fly was actually an irreversible immunity to gravity? Do you think he suffocated, or froze to death first before he floated off the planet?" She smirked at Rice.

Rice cleared his throat and adjusted his tie. Palmer continued to stare at Abby, with just a hint of a frown. The shiny film of sweat on his forehead made his skin appear more reptilian than human under the bright LED light. He was almost cute, but also approaching creepy.

While she was never one to celebrate the death of anyone, let alone an Adapted, the Pope's televised ascent to the heavens was comically ironic. Up until that point, the conservative religious response to the Adapted was that their emergence was the work of the Devil, and that they should be shunned, captured, experimented on, and ultimately killed. Once the Pontiff publicly showed off his R-Skill and accidentally booked a one-way trip to see the Man upstairs, Christianity (and many other religions) saw it as a sign from God that the Adapted were His children as much as everyone else. The new Pope elected weeks later ushered in a much more welcoming stance. Having President Lucky in office of course helped a great deal as well. Man, that guy could give a speech. Also, easy on the eyes, which helped his popularity, even when his policies weren't complete successes.

Agent Rice stooped to pick a paper coffee cup out of the trash can, then set it on the table. "If you wouldn't mind."

Abby groaned and snatched the cup off the table. She backed into the farthest corner of the room, then blinked at the trash can, turned her head, and flicked the cup towards the receptacle without looking. It tumbled through the air in a graceful arc and reentered the trash can, dead center.

"Nice shot. Ever miss?" Rice asked.

She cocked her head in mock appreciation and scrunched her nose. "Nope, due to my adaptability to UDO-altered radiation." She flourished her fingers in the air, sprinkling imaginary glitter on her head. "Can you get me a WNBA contract?"

Palmer stifled a laugh and rubbed his forehead.

Rice smiled. "You know, if R-Skills were allowed in professional leagues, and they played with basketballs made from trash, I could probably make that happen."

Abby dropped back into her chair and folded her arms. "And I suppose that's your R-Skill, Agent Rice — contract negotiation?"

He chuckled and cracked his knuckles. "Er, no. I don't have one."

She looked at Palmer, who continued to gaze at her like he was playing the world's longest game of Don't Blink. He didn't flinch, so she figured Rice must be a normie. Her shoulders slumped. She had a sneaking suspicion that this wouldn't be the last time RADSA would come calling. If the impossibly good-looking guy running the show here was an Adapted as well, that would go a long way towards calming her nerves. *Give it time,* she hoped. *Anyone can be an Adapted.* Still, she had a hard time rationalizing the idea that the organization that sent some Adapted to live in tropical isolation for the rest of their lives would be staffed by other Adapted willing to carry out that mission.

As she returned to her seat, the stiff molded plastic chair reminded Abby that her phone was not in her back pocket. No doubt the agents had taken it, which rankled her last bits of patience away. She huffed in exasperation. "Right. So, again, where's my phone? And why exactly am I here?"

Rice put his hands behind his back and drew his eyebrows together into a flat line, his dreamy countenance now dead serious. "Because, Ms. Alstrom, you killed someone."

CHAPTER 3
BOUNCY

GIGI CONLAN WATCHED her screen and harrumphed. "I don't like her."

Ben and Steve's interview with the trash girl was playing out on a monitor at her station inside "Bessie", the North Texas regional RADSA team's mobile command center. The name was Ben's idea, as the exterior of the over-long, extra-wide semi-trailer was constructed to look like a large, innocuous cattle carrier. The interior was anything but rustic: modern, sleek, state-of-the-art, complete with military-grade surveillance, tactical ops equipment, and two Keurig coffee makers. She sat at her station at the center of Bessie's Bay, where a handful of workstations for various purposes lined the side wall between the interview room and media lounge. Around her, dozens of screens followed news and camera feeds all over the Dallas/Fort Worth region. She kept her ear on the interview as she checked the news ticker on CNN on a separate screen, then flicked through the social media streams on her phone. She frowned at the paltry total of mentions and likes on her accounts today.

Eddie Carrasco looked up from his desk, where he was working on Gigi's new uniform. "Come on, *chica*. She's not that bad. How would you feel if you had accidentally killed someone?"

She glanced at him and shrugged. "I'd probably get more followers. Maybe I *should* kill someone."

Eddie rolled his eyes and hissed in disapproval.

"You know I'm not here to save the world, *girlfriend*," Gigi said. "I just want to get famous."

"Your family's money couldn't buy that?" He huffed and stroked his dyed-black goatee. The graying ponytail tied to the rear of his balding head shook back and forth. "Maybe you could try getting famous by saving the world? Rice must have seen something in you for you to be here." He gave her a wink.

She shrugged again and turned her attention back to the dozen screens in front of her, then groaned. Rice had just offered the snarky girl a job. Abby cackled on screen, and Gigi smiled. Though Abby was sitting down, Gigi could tell the new recruit was tall - much taller than her. That snarky attitude would be a pain in her ass if she joined the team, and Gigi didn't like being looked down on, physically or metaphorically. Plus, she didn't need anyone else stealing the limelight on the team, if there was indeed any to be had.

Eddie was too old to understand. Social capital was mandatory at this point. Society moved past anyone that still eschewed it. Whatever it was that Rice saw in her three months ago, he hadn't shared it yet. Still, the offer to join the team was too good an opportunity to pass up. A social media darling inside RADSA? That would be a first! She just had to get footage of doing something more important than exercising in a sports bra and yoga pants, or interviewing the latest person that could fill empty bottles with orange Gatorade with a touch, force squirrels to fall asleep, or something else equally bizarre.

Gigi stole glances at Eddie while he worked. There was a man of contradictions. A middle-aged Latino from El Paso, former leader of a motorcycle gang, tubby, balding, all manner of tattoos on his arms and neck — one with three dots below his right eye — and craggy wrinkles all over his sunbaked face. His was the look of a hard life lived. The kind of person decent folk would avoid walking past on the same sidewalk. But he was actually friendly as hell. Always saw the best in people, rarely said anything negative. Also recently out of the closet and pleased as punch for it. Plus, he could stitch things together with a swipe of his finger. Paper, fabric, metal - he could make any seam. He could even mend cuts on skin (which felt incredible). Now that was an R-Skill with clear utility.

On the other hand, Gigi was still searching for her purpose in RADSA. She tapped her feet, feeling the familiar tingle approaching. She stood up and walked over to the rear door.

"I'm going out for a run. Mind filming me a little?" she asked.

Eddie turned just in time to catch her phone. "Uh, sure. Just for a couple minutes, I'm almost done with your uniform." He held up a steel blue jumpsuit, with narrow electric pink inlays up the sides and across the chest. And pockets. Had to have pockets.

"Nice. I like the colors." The addition of pink was her idea. "Make sure it's tight. I don't need any drag out there."

She opened the door, and high winds whipped her face as she tied her blonde hair back and pulled goggles over her eyes. A six-lane, man-made canyon stretched as far as she could see. Bessie was humming along the rarely used toll express lanes of I-635 in north Dallas - the perfect place to hop out for a dramatic run. Gigi stooped to pull her shoes and socks off, dangling her bare feet out the door so they didn't touch the floor of the trailer. She waited for the only oncoming car in sight to pass them, then turned to Eddie and winked. "See ya in a few!" she yelled, then jumped off the trailer.

CHAPTER 4
THE ADJUSTER

AGENT BENJAMIN RICE poked his head out of the interview room to check that Gigi and Eddie were not watching the monitors in the Bay, then stepped back inside and shut the door. Abby was practically hysterical at this point, the Truex gas having worn away her defensive inhibitions.

"How am I going to live with this? I killed my best friend. Up until last week, my boyfriend! I'm a killer." Abby covered her face with her hands and sobbed.

Steve sat with folded arms, showing no sign of empathy with only a half scowl on his typically impassive face.

"Steve," Ben said. "I think we're finished here. Go ask Bailey to head to Abby's apartment."

Abby cried.

"Sure," Steve said as he rose from the table and tugged at his sports coat. He gave a slight shrug of his shoulders and raised an eyebrow as he met Ben's eyes, passing him to the door.

Ben knew Steve wouldn't bother watching Gigi's station with the president's press conference coming up. He'd head straight for the lounge and flip on CNN. Even if he did catch what was about to happen, Ben could just clean it up later.

"Abby," he said, barely above a whisper.

Between spurts of crying, coughing, and sniffling, Abby continued her existential wail. "Oh my God, what am I going to do? Tyson's dead! I'll be fired! Sued! Thrown in jail!"

A large sigh escaped his lips. He didn't have to do this. No one would bat an eye if Abby was served whatever justice a court of law saw fit to deliver. But he could tell she was special. He didn't know why, but his gut urged him to help her.

"Everything is going to be alright, Abby."

She slumped her hands to the table with a messy splat and looked at him with red, tear-filled eyes. "How in the world is it going to be alright?"

He popped the joints in his neck and shoulders freeing their tension and whatever stored energy they contained that his R-Skill required to activate. Then he went to work. "It will be considered an unfortunate workplace accident. Construction sites are dangerous places, and he wasn't wearing a hardhat."

Abby rolled her eyes, either in disbelief or a haze from the Truex.

"It's true. When you get home, you're not going to feel bad about what happened with Tyson. You didn't know he was going to be there." He wasn't sure that last bit was true, but for Abby it would be her truth. "Life will go on. You will be your usual self."

"Ugh." She lightly shook her head in disagreement.

"We're going to take you home. Put your head down here for a bit and relax. You'll feel better. When Steve comes back in, he'll walk you to your apartment."

Without protest, she laid her forearms across one another on the table, then dropped her head down.

Ben let loose a contented exhale and bent each knee inward towards the other until each joint popped. He finished his work with a final thought, then left the room.

CHAPTER 5
BOUNCY

IN A SPLIT SECOND, Gigi's feet hit the ground. Soft, smooth, spongy, welcoming. The concrete flexed like a super-trampoline around her. The pliant surface absorbed the momentum from her jump, then rebounded and flung her into the air. The unnaturally flexible road wobbled back to normalcy as she flew twenty feet skyward, nearing the underside of the toll-free interstate decking above her. She executed a triple flip with a half twist mid-air, then with little effort caught her momentum with bent knees as she hit the ground and it became pliable beneath her again. Her gymnastic prowess developed over nearly twenty years of training was well-matched to her R-Skill. Bit of a stroke of luck, she had to admit. Olympic dreams had faded, but after becoming an Adapted, she had doubled down on practice. Gigi still had the form of an elite competitor and knew it was just a matter of time before her ability made her a household name. She just had to keep pushing, getting better, stronger, faster - more amazing than anyone else on A-Space. The social media network chronicling the exploits and affairs of the Adapted had already passed TMZ in viewership, with a firm eye towards reaching for the YouTube and Facebook stratospheres. She had to be a part of it. She wanted to lead it.

Gigi bobbed up and down to a gentle stop in the middle of the empty highway. Bessie was nearly a half mile ahead of her already. She took a huge breath, then began a full sprint after the semi-truck. With each step, her stride became longer as the suddenly springy concrete propelled her forward faster and faster. Step, bounce. Step, bounce. After half a minute she was easily closing distance on Bessie. The wind whipped at her face, the noise in her ears was deafening, but the thrill was still there. She could run - well, bounce - over 100 miles per hour!

Eddie whooped and hollered as she approached. He held her phone out of the rear door of the trailer with one hand, the other holding for dear life to a handhold inside. The half smile/half grimace on his face made him look like he was either having the time of his life, or about to lose his grip. As his cheers reached earshot, Bessie rolled over a patch of gravel left on the highway and flung a swarm of small rocks into the air.

Gigi tried to duck, but a sharp stinging pain whipped across her cheek. "Fuck!" she yelled, losing her rhythm.

Bessie began to pull away. Gigi executed a forward double-flip to reset her timing, then bounded after the truck again. Eddie backed into the trailer to make space for her to land. She caught up, made one last powerful bounce, lurched up to grab the chrome ladder on the side of the trailer with one hand, then swung herself to a seated stop in the doorway.

"Woo!" Gigi exclaimed. She gulped down air as she put her socks and shoes back on, then slammed the door shut. The thrill of the run was outpaced by her anticipation of how good the footage would look. "How'd I do?"

"Dang, Gigi! You had to be going at least a hundred!"

She smiled in half-appreciation as she pulled her goggles off. "Yeah, but look." She wiped her hand on her smarting cheek and showed Eddie a smear of blood on her fingers. "I gotta get a protective mask or something."

"Tsk." He smiled. "Or, you could not do your bouncy thing on the highway? Just a thought."

Eddie walked over to her and held his hand out. She winced at the pain from the gash in her cheek until he ran his thumb over it. In an instant, pain was replaced by a localized euphoria, as if the cells in her cheek were each orgasming in unison. She shuddered in pleasure.

"There," Eddie said with a smile as he tossed her a towel from a nearby shelf.

"Thanks." She caught the towel and wiped the blood off her cheek, then poked at the spot where the gash used to be. The skin felt perfectly normal. She would of course check it in a mirror later, but as in times past, she figured there wouldn't be a mark. She rubbed the side of her face and smiled at him. "God, I don't think I will get used to how that feels. Do you ever…" She motioned her finger in a line down her chest towards her waist. "You know, do it to yourself?"

"Nah." He turned to walk back to his workstation. "It doesn't work on me. Quirky, right?"

"Yeah, it's funny how the R-Skills have their limitations. Still, that might be for the best. I'm not sure I could resist the temptation." She heaved a contented sigh after catching her breath, then sat back down at her station.

Ben and Steve were chatting by the lounge. Her boss gave her a pair of acknowledging nods, and Steve smiled slightly, but otherwise looked as anodyne as he usually did.

Gigi swiveled in her chair, unable to hide the scowl on her face as her euphoria from the run mingled with trepidation over the trash girl. "Well, did she sign up?"

Ben scratched his head as he went to a locker and hung up his coat. "She politely declined."

That drew a laugh from Steve. "She gave us an open invitation to walk by any dumpster at her worksite. What a bitch!"

"Keep your opinions to yourself, *mentiroso*!" Eddie snapped. "There's no truth to that! She was bawling when you brought her here."

Steve's face turned red.

Ben stepped between Eddie and Steve. "Enough of that. We'll take her home and let her think about it. Once the gas wears off and she remembers, I think she'll have a change of heart. Give her one more dose so we can take her home."

Gigi hit the button on her station that released the Truex gas into the meeting room. After Ben went into his office and Steve turned his focus back to the TV in the lounge area, Gigi hit the button again and hoped Abby wouldn't remember a thing. Eddie caught it and just shook his head with a frown.

CHAPTER 6
THE ADJUSTER

THE CRISP SNAP of popped knuckles bounced off the walls in Ben's office. He stretched his neck from one side to the other, eliciting audible pops as he moved in each direction, then shrugged each shoulder until his collar bones popped. His RADSA-approved, government-issue, black executive leather chair, provided limited luxury to his stiff back as he popped his lower vertebrae. Then came his knees. Finally, he stretched his toes and rolled his ankles, releasing the tension stored in his joints. Ben breathed a sigh of relief, then sucked air back in through his teeth knowing he'd have to do it all over again soon enough.

He reached for an oversized bottle of Advil from the top desk drawer and took three pills out. Almost empty. Again. No doubt the pace at which he consumed painkillers was ill-advised, but he didn't know of another way to deal with the constant discomfort in his joints. He forced the three pills down with a slug of cold coffee and cleared his mind of his own predicament for a moment. Until he saw the face looking back at him in the mirror on the wall by his office door.

The face that he saw was his. His true face. A scar dominated the left side, from his forehead to his chin. Most of the damaged tissue had settled into a creamy purple, interspersed with striations of browner skin randomly interwoven like a spider web. It looked like the rind of a sickly, alien cantaloupe. Of course, that's not what other people saw, at least anyone he interacted with.

He pressed a large sigh through pursed lips. Being an Adapted was remarkable, but many R-Skills came with drawbacks. Unfortunately, his did, manifesting in joint pain. An orthopedist called it early arthritis and pointed to Ben's rigorous workout regimen as the cause. But Ben knew better. His joints drew in tension from everyone around him, building into painful pressure. It was also the source of strength for his R-Skill. When he popped a joint, relieving the tension, he was able to lower the tension in someone, giving them a sort of micro-amnesia — enough to coerce the individual to forget things and leave them open to suggestion. Essentially permanent hypnosis. After telling just one person he had become an Adapted, Ben had decided to keep it a secret from everyone else.

Beneath the bottle of Advil sat a silver photo frame containing the only memento he still kept of his ex-fiancée. Staring back up at him were two perfect faces, his, and Rachel's. They were smiling for a selfie on the beach outside the Hotel Del in San Diego where he had proposed over a year ago. He closed his eyes to remember that moment, and instead felt a searing jolt on his face. Only two weeks after she had said "yes", she threw a pot of boiling water at him the night he told her he had changed. Become Adapted. He had been one of the first he knew to change, and at the time, public fear of any Adapted was rampant. A lot of that had to do with the unfortunate woman from New York City who had emerged while on a bus on the Brooklyn Bridge. Her R-Skill hyper-accelerated the oxidation of metals around her. The bus and section of bridge she was on disintegrated in moments, hundreds were killed, including the Adapted that caused the collapse. Were it not for a kid on the bus who happened to be live streaming his first trip to the Big Apple, the cause may have never been found. Paranoia and fear spread like wildfire across the globe. Protests raged outside the White House and every capitol building in the country, where tensions were especially high. Most of the early Adapted — and all of the dangerous ones — emerged from the United States. Scientists had attributed this to the prevailing air currents in the lower atmosphere where the North Korean missile hit the Dark Object. More and more Adapted were beginning to appear in other parts of the world, but to the surprise of the scientific community, most were still in the United States.

"Shit." Ben blinked and shook his head. He remembered asking Rachel if they should go to a protest at the Dallas City Hall only a couple of days before he changed.

Despite developing an R-Skill listed in the top five of RADSA's list of Island-A-worthy dangerous abilities (4. Mind control and/or the ability to alter/deny others' free will.), the moment he emerged, he felt ashamed for his fear. He knew having an R-Skill didn't make him any worse of a person. Then pride washed over him like a warm summer ocean wave. He could prove people wrong. He would. But before he had a chance to explain the sensation to Rachel, she had ruined his face with the scalding contents of their pasta pot. For all the regret he still had over that entire incident, he was eternally grateful the water had missed his left eye. It hadn't missed much else on that side of his face.

After discovering his R-Skill could alter the mental image of how his face was perceived by others, his depression over the disfigurement lessened. But it wasn't gone completely, because he himself saw it a dozen times a day or more. The hope that someday RADSA would come across an Adapted that could repair damaged tissue kept him going. *Only a matter of time,* he thought. After he had recruited Eddie to the team, the biker got to see the real Ben Rice for a fleeting moment and was characteristically sympathetic and polite, calling Rachel what Ben assumed was all manner of unkind things in Spanish. Ultimately, Eddie's R-Skill was limited to joining seams of things very close together and was ineffective at improving Ben's scar. Eddie didn't remember a thing about it now and only saw Ben's formerly flawless face.

Ben closed the drawer and shifted his gaze to the photo sitting on the shelf next to his desk. It showed him and RADSA Director Francine Gustafson shaking hands outside the RADSA HQ building in Maryland as he accepted his post of regional manager. A strange picture. He towered over the short, middle-aged woman, he in his typical navy sports coat with black tie, and she in a bright sky-blue power suit with a graying bob of permanent curls.

"Well, Frannie, I'm building my team. Trying to do it the right way," he told the photo. He'd meet with Abby's boss at the construction site and the investigators assigned to the incident with Tyson Burrows. Abby wouldn't face charges. It was an accident, after all. If a crane cable snapped and a heavy load had crushed Tyson instead, would the crane operator be blamed? Of course not.

Ben wondered how Abby would feel about joining the team in the morning. She was blunt in voicing her distaste for Island-A. He hadn't used his R-Skill to coerce anyone to join the team. Yet. He thought after Abby had calmed down, they'd hear from her. If they didn't, he might consider changing her mind.

As he looked with nostalgia at the months-old photo, he had no remorse over doing a little work on the director in order to obtain his job.

The irony was, Director Gustafson was Rachel's mother, someone who had never balked at her daughter dating a Black man. Instead, she welcomed him with open arms into their family. He still felt a bit of that kinship for Frannie, though he let go of his feelings for Rachel. Orchestrating a sustainable tangle of new truths between ex-fiancée and ex-future-mother-in-law regarding the end of the engagement was painful, but necessary, and it taught him the extent of his ability. He hated himself for it every time he thought about Rachel or saw Frannie.

A calendar appointment on his computer popped up with a polite "bing bong" chime, reminding him the president's latest press conference was about to start. He clicked on the link to the livestream, then as it loaded looked at his face once more in the mirror. Not for the first time, he wished he could use his R-Skill on himself as he could anyone else, hide the scar from himself, and forget Rachel ever happened.

CHAPTER 7
LUCKY

"YES, CHARLIZE." President Lawrence "Lucky" Phelps pointed to a member of the media in a bright red blazer, press credentials dangling from a CNN lanyard around her neck.

"Thank you, Mr. President. You've stated recently that the rate of Adapted converting appears to be increasing. How are you measuring this, and can you account for it?" the reporter asked.

"Well..." The president drew in some air between closed teeth. "We don't know why, yet. We measure this simply by the number of contacts RADSA has been able to make on a weekly basis, news reports, social media trends, etcetera. More or less, the same as you would at CNN, or your friends do at the other media outlets. We are keeping tabs on every Adapted we find, as best we can." He gestured around the room and pointed to the rear with a smile. "I see you there in the back, Mr. Schwartz. *Love* the flowers." Heads in the room turned, looking at the middle-aged reporter from YouTube in the last row, with white flowers growing out of his head instead of hair and beet red color flushing his cheeks. "As far as the acceleration," said the president, calling attention back to himself. "So far, I'm afraid there is no accounting for the increase. The study of the effect of the interaction of extraterrestrial materials with domestic radiological sources is nascent. We are still in the early throes of new research contracts with top universities to quantify the short and long-term effects of what happened." He rubbed the buzz-short hair on his balding head. "If President Kim could have seen the non-result of the nuclear strike against the UDO, perhaps that order wouldn't have been made. Maybe." He drew a long breath. "Then again, maybe not. Given the near-certain destruction of North Korea from the asteroid's projected impact, we can all understand the desperation that led to the first atmospheric nuclear weapon detonation in decades. Unfortunately for the millions of lives lost that day, that desperation didn't change their fate, but did irreversibly alter ours."

The White House press room became awkwardly still as the deaths of over twenty million people on and around the Korean peninsula were made fresh once more.

"I know I speak on this topic often. Seems it's more popular than football these days. But I'm happy to — it will define the period in which we live. The world was forever changed that day, and all we can do is move on." The president paused for effect, then grasped the sides of the podium with a loud slap. "No. Not just move on. Grow! This event — this *change* — in the course of humanity is an opportunity for us as a nation, and we as a species, to come together and grow closer than we have in recent times. We can once again be a nation and world our children can be proud of."

A number of hands thrust up in the air as he stopped for a drink of water. He waved them down.

"And yes, I followed the news out of San Francisco this morning and called the mayor, congratulating her and the police chief for controlling the situation with that dangerous Adapted quickly, without loss of life. I'm thankful for that." He paused, every hand in the room shot up again. President Phelps quelled the audience, waving his hands. "It's obvious you seek answers. I'm afraid there are none more to be had. *Yet*. What I can offer, no, promise, is more access to information. I will request the director of RADSA to begin a weekly press briefing to give you more to fill your Twitter feeds with. Sound good?" He rapped the sides of the podium with his hands. "Thanks everyone."

The president smiled and waved as he left the briefing room, leaving behind a few nods and quizzical grimaces.

His press secretary, Angel Bretstock, stepped up to the podium in a white pantsuit with navy blue trim, sunset red lipstick, and her trademark brown, no-hair-out-of-place ponytail. She pointed at thirsty, curious reporters and provided uninformative non-answers, smiling eyes, and a bleached white grin to each.

CHAPTER 8
THE SLEUTH

"THAT GUY IS SO full of shit," Eddie said, muting the post-press conference dissection on CNN. He tossed the TV remote in the empty seat next to him.

Steve groaned from the adjacent sofa in Bessie's lounge, rubbing his forehead. "Like you know him."

"And you do?"

Political discussions were discouraged in RADSA's training videos, and usually weren't a problem as the entire agency owed its existence to President Phelps' leadership through the Korean UDO crisis and emergence of the Adapted. But for whatever reason, Eddie disliked the president and made no qualms about mentioning it at any opportunity. This, despite the man's status as an Adapted clearly lining up with President Phelps' political views.

"Actually, yes. I met him twice while he was still a senator. We talked for a bit. He's as genuine as they come." The circumstances surrounding his two meetings with then-Senator Phelps weren't something Steve cared to share, but he was confident in his assessment of the man. One he was always ready to defend.

"Bah. That was before you got your whole truth thing," Eddie said, waving his hand in the direction of Steve's head. "You don't really know him. I've got a sixth sense about people. I can tell. *El presidente ojete!*"

Steve got to his feet. He didn't know much Spanish, but knew an insult when he heard one. "None of that! Phelps has been nothing but good for our country. And for *us*."

Eddie scoffed. "You'll see. He's making money on the side or somethin'."

"You would know all about making money on the side."

Surprisingly nimble for a middle-aged man with a tubby gut, Eddie sprang to his feet and got right in Steve's face. "You got a problem, jarhead?"

Steve clenched his teeth and balled his fists, ready to trade blows. It had been a while since he'd been in a good brawl. His time in the corps had come and gone, but he was still fit, and he had no doubt had far more physical combat training than Eddie. His opponent did have a couple of decades more life experience, including a few years of hard time for smuggling counterfeit electronics with his motorcycle gang. Pride claimed that Steve had the advantage. His R-Skill wouldn't let him say it though, which held his fists in check.

Gigi barked at them from her station, eyebrows raised. "Guys. Seriously? Phelps is like the biggest supporter of Adapted there could be. Can you imagine our lives if we had a President that hated us? Think how hard it would be for us to get a job if Adapted could be discriminated against. Eddie, who's hiring a gay, ex-con, former motorcycle gang leader these days?"

Steve smirked at Eddie and raised an open palm in Gigi's direction.

"And he's a politician, Steve. He's not a saint; none of them are," Gigi said.

"Ten lies for every truth," Eddie said, shrugging. He backed down from Steve and moved back to his station.

"That's true." Gigi stood and stretched. "But he can't be as bad as... *you know*."

Eddie clicked his teeth and fiddled with some fabric on his table.

Steve sighed and slumped back into the sofa. "Yeah. Thank God that guy was out of office before all this started. I would have to live off the grid if he was still president."

Gigi offered a fake retch. "No Internet? No thanks. I'd rather gouge out my eyeballs." She sat back down and turned her attention to several screens displaying social media accounts.

Steve rubbed his face and sighed again. Watching the news in general gave him a headache. Depending on which left- or right-leaning station was on, even factual stories were delivered with such a bend that they came off as untruths. Usually, Phelps' press conferences were safe to watch, but Eddie wasn't exactly wrong when he questioned if the president was telling the truth. Phelps had several facts wrong. Steve's head was still throbbing. At times like this, he truly wanted to leave the world behind and go off-grid in some secluded mountain cabin. Politicians had hidden agendas. People spoke while misinformed. Everyone lied. Even Gigi had just lied about preferring to blind herself over doing without the Internet. But the president was probably just reading someone else's remarks off the teleprompter, and they had gotten their facts mixed up. Steve massaged his temples as the pain from his R-Skill slowly subsided.

"Well, that wasn't very informative, was it?" Ben said as he entered the Bay from the hallway to his office. "Let's get back to work. We're almost to Ms. Alstrom's apartment complex. Steve, please escort her home and make sure she's okay."

Steve shrugged and nodded.

"Gigi, check the local social media feeds for trends. I want to pounce on the next potential local recruit as soon as we see one."

"Sure," she answered, face already focused on her screens, but a slight scowl creasing her lips.

"Eddie," Ben paused. Everyone turned to look as Eddie raised his eyebrows.

"You do you."

The tattooed biker answered with a playful salute. "*Si, patrón.*" He winked at their boss, then turned his attention back to the uniform on his station.

Ben coughed politely, then turned back down the hall to his office.

Steve rolled his eyes. The attraction there was obvious. And obviously one-way. Eddie was barking up the wrong tree. He pressed the intercom button at his station to call Bessie's driver. "Hey Bailey, how long 'til we reach Ms. Alstrom's apartment?"

"Uhhhh," a brusque female voice returned. "About five minutes to Richardson."

The words, even electronic, brought comfort to Steve's tense body. His attunement to the truth was so fine that even estimations spoken with the intent of truth would hurt if the speaker was wrong. Bailey was familiar enough with Steve's R-Skill to provide truthful answers that only partially answered any questions raised. He stood and smoothed his sports coat.

Gigi offered disdain. "Do you think Abby's gonna join us?"

Steve shook his head. "I don't see her fitting in."

"Oh, that's too bad," Gigi said. "I think she'd be fun to have on the team."

Steve sank back into the sofa and rubbed his throbbing forehead. The day couldn't end fast enough. The sooner they were done with Abby Alstrom, the better.

———

The joint viewing for the bodies of Lance Corporals Milo Phelps and Quentin Fargo was a twisted affair of mourning and political posturing. The sons of a popular Senator and the CEO of a cutting-edge pharmaceutical company had been killed in action, and people had come to pay their respects, be photographed, and bend some ears. Dozens of high-ranking brass from the Marines and other armed services dotted the large room, which was lined with American flags. The two elaborate mahogany caskets were separated by thirty feet to allow ample room for mourners to view the deceased.

Corporal Steve Palmer stood by himself in his dress blues next to Milo's casket, the crowds having finally cleared enough for the less prominent invitees to get close enough to pay their respects. The handful of marines from his unit that were still there had gathered around Quentin's coffin. The commander of the marine security guard detachment, Master Gunnery Sergeant McNamara was there as well. Far too many of the marines' faces were smiling.

Milo was also fitted in dress blues, hands resting atop a white barracks cover over his midsection. Steve barely recognized his best friend's face; the skin was pallid and drawn thin, hair combed all wrong, and his lips were eerily flat as if pressed up against glass. No traces of the explosion.

At the other end of Milo's casket was his mother, Olivia Phelps. She maintained the spot she had staked for most of the evening. She dabbed at her eyes with a black cloth and spoke softly with another mourner.

While he waited his turn to stand before the casket, Steve ruminated on the many profound things he could say to his dead best friend. Now with the chance to utter his goodbyes, his lips were glued together with shame. His mind drifted back to the fateful evening when Milo had died, and Steve again bemoaned missing almost the entire thing.

Nearing footsteps snapped him out of his brooding. Senator Phelps approached his son's casket, hand outstretched. Steve looked up at the tall man and swallowed. Phelps was certainly photogenic on-camera, but in person he was magnetic. Despite approaching sixty, he was in good shape and had only a few distinguishing lines on his forehead. His hair still had most of its sandy blond color, and a deep cleft chin complemented his angled jaw. Phelps wore a black suit and white shirt, accented by a dark blue tie with white stripes. A smile peeked through his pursed lips and his hazel eyes were wide and bright. The senator's communications director, Angel Bretstock, followed a respectable distance behind in a sharp navy business suit and hair pulled back tight. Her attention was buried in her phone. Steve fought down the lump in his throat and raised his hand to shake.

"Lawrence Phelps," the senator said as he gripped Steve's hand.

"Corporal Steve Palmer, sir. I'm so sorry for your loss. I wish I could have—"

"No need to trouble yourself, son. I was in the debrief with Sergeant McNamara. Thank you for your service to America. You got Ambassador Gustafson out. You served your country well." Senator Phelps looked over at the boisterous crowd surrounding the casket of Corporal Fargo and shook his head as he looked down at the body of his only son. "Milo did too. He never really fit in though, did he?"

"Sir?"

"Scrawny, shy. Not exactly the prototypical marine." Phelps nodded in the direction of Quentin's casket twenty yards away. "He only ever mentioned you when discussing friends in the corps."

Steve studied the senator and kept a frown at bay. "Milo was the best shot in our unit. He worked hard at it. And he didn't really care about fitting in. Said that he was there to do his job, and trying to be popular wasn't part of it."

Phelps smiled. "That was Milo, wasn't it? Always saying the right thing."

Peals of laughter erupted from the marines standing by Quentin's casket. Steve watched as several of them elbowed each other, and Sergeant McNamara bent over in laughter. *Probably discussing all the dirty pranks Quentin played on Milo,* Steve thought.

A pair of men in suits with American flag lapel pins — senators, Steve guessed — approached Senator Phelps from behind and clapped him on the shoulder. He turned and graciously thanked them for coming to pay their respects.

"Call me tomorrow, Lucky," one of them said. He had a monarch butterfly pin on his lapel, beneath a Gold Star. "Your nickname truly fits."

"Sure thing Tom. Can't wait," Phelps said with a wide grin.

Steve realized the man was Tom Fargo, Quentin's father. He wasn't the hulking brute his son had been, but he was still built like he mainlined protein shakes and walked with the same off-putting swagger that Quentin had. Steve turned toward Milo to hide his scowl.

The senator said his goodbyes to the men, then cast his gaze back to his son's body. But the smile had yet to leave his face.

More laughter came from the crowd surrounding Quentin. A brief groan slipped from Steve's lips.

"Something on your mind, son?"

"A lot of people here seem to be in a better mood than one would expect."

"Don't mind those jokers over there. They're just retelling stories of Quentin's greatest exploits in the service."

Steve raised an eyebrow. "And you?"

Phelps chuckled. "Don't miss much, do you? I'm in mourning, fear not. I have been since I got that phone call from your sergeant." He clicked his tongue and thumbed the glinting gold-on-purple Gold Star pin on his lapel opposite the one with an American flag. "I would give this back in a nanosecond if it meant Milo could still be with us. But the winds of fate can fill your sails when you least expect."

"Sir?"

The senator looked over Steve's shoulder and waved at his wife, who was turning to walk away. He gestured for Steve to step closer and smiled. "What would you call a parent that takes advantage of an opportunity created by their child's death?"

"Uh..."

"Callous? Cold-hearted? Unscrupulous?"

Steve swallowed. "Sure."

"Well, I'm going to go for tenacious. I will honor Milo's memory by pushing for lasting change that will mean something for our country and our planet. I want to free the world from the kinds of vectors that led to the attack on the embassy. To his death. I'm talking education, health care, sustainable agriculture, climate change, economic growth, home and abroad — big ideas. I'm going to get them done." Phelps ran his thumb over the Gold Star pin again.

"Sounds great, sir, but how are you going to accomplish that kind of meaningful change?"

Phelps leaned over and whispered into Steve's ear. "After the next election, I'm going to be President of the United States."

Steve nodded and forced a slim smile. Phelps would make a great president. But as he gazed at his friend's body again, his heart sank and the smile vanished.

Milo could have been the son of the president.

———

"We're here," Bailey said over the intercom.

Steve took a moment to rub the shame from his eyes, then retrieved Abby from the interview room and led her down the rear stairs of the trailer. Though able to stand on her own, after a second helping of the gas, she was barely conscious enough to lead him to her apartment, stumbling over several of the steps up to the second floor of her building. It was a three-story structure, with slightly peeling, grayish-green paint on the faux wood siding, and air conditioners rattling on the ground in between poorly trimmed Indian hawthorn bushes.

Steve didn't like that RADSA used the gas; it was just more dishonesty, but at least it usually led to less pain from his R-Skill during interviews. At times, the gas was a necessity for safety, and he supposed the introductory meeting with a killer, even an accidental one, would be as appropriate a time as any. He watched Abby dig in her pocket for her keys and could envision her future. She'd have to live with the consequences of that accident for the rest of her life and would probably develop a thick layer of deception to armor her public image. He could imagine the lies she would have to sling and could feel the Adapted cells in his body doing their worst. As a rule, he avoided deceptive people like the plague, and regardless of how honest she was before, Abby would have to be a liar now.

Her apartment complex was in an older neighborhood of the Dallas suburb Richardson — not falling apart, but nothing to write home about either. Steve folded his arms as she fumbled with the three keys on her key ring for a good thirty seconds before managing to unlock the door. Out of courtesy, he offered an elbow for stability which she took in silence as they crossed the threshold into a sparsely decorated room, featuring an open living room/kitchen area and a hallway leading presumably to the bedroom and bath. She absentmindedly pulled her Converse sneakers off as they entered. Steve elected to keep his shoes on — he didn't plan on staying long. Inside, the walls were painted an uninspiring beige, paired with a similarly bland shade of rental-grade tan carpet on the floors.

The kitchen wasn't much to speak of. Formica and linoleum. Inexpensive, apartment-grade appliances. The sink was full of dirty dishes, and the trash can at the edge of the counter was in desperate need of emptying. Several wadded-up Taco Bell wrappers lay neglected on the floor. Evidently her R-Skill didn't help to keep thrown garbage in the can if it was already full.

Abby wobbled into the living space next to the kitchen and plopped onto a fatigued blue leather sofa. It sat against one wall, adjacent to a modest television and older generation Xbox. Two game controllers were splayed on a stained laminate coffee table in front of the sofa. Abby sniffed and picked up a broken picture frame from the floor.

"I don't know why," she said as her head wobbled.

"Why, what?"

"Why I don't feel bad." She caressed her fingers over the fractured glass, then tossed the frame on the floor. "I should feel bad, right?"

Steve found the statement puzzling. She was telling the truth. And, she should be laden with remorse having just killed her only recently ex-boyfriend. Maybe she was sociopathic? It was odd, but he was ready to move on. She wouldn't be joining the team. "Probably the gas. I can't imagine what you were feeling that morning." Steve looked at the picture. It was of Abby, and Tyson Burrows. The very man whose head she knocked off with a casually tossed four hundred fifty-pound scrap block of reinforced concrete. Her arms were draped around his neck, and their smiles were wide. "You were close?"

"Yeah, if you count him-wanting-to-move-in-with-me as close. I just wasn't ready, ya know?"

Steve watched as she talked to no one in particular.

"It's not like I loved him. I mean, don't get me wrong, he was fun, we fucked and all, and he let me kick his ass in Call of Duty, but I don't need to commit to anything right now. I've only been on my own out of my foster home for half a year. If it weren't for my turning Adapted and finding a job, I'd still be there with the Kims, pretending not to help my sister Mary with her homework."

Some truths, some lies. "I see," Steve uttered through clenched teeth. He paced over to her balcony window in an attempt to stem the swells of pain in his body from boiling his temper. It was hard. His head spun like an out-of-balance washing machine.

Abby sniffed and attempted to turn it into a polite cough, then spread out on the couch, still looking at the picture as she propped her feet up on a cushion.

Steve rubbed his chin as he looked her over, five-o-clock stubble already poking through his cheeks despite his watch only reading 2:30pm. Her black Radiohead T-shirt and faded, torn jeans matched her attitude. But even with the gas, she was deceptive during the interview. He didn't like that. RADSA could do better. Her R-Skill wasn't so fantastic that the team — fledgling and understaffed as it was — couldn't live without it. Resigned to wait for the next recruit, he moved to the door. "Are you feeling alright? The gas should wear off in an hour or two and you'll be back to normal. Give us a call if you want to talk." He had neglected to leave her a business card.

Her eyes were half-closed as she responded, the unpredictable drowsiness of the gas apparently kicking in. "Of course I'm not alright, Palmer. You can see the truth." She looked up at him with surprisingly stark lucidity. Her pale blue gaze pierced him for a silent moment before floating up to the ceiling.

A tranquil wave of honesty washed over him like the refreshing first blast of cool air after the AC turns on. Steve drew in his first pain-free breath in her company. Her drifting eyes were on the verge of tears, and now, with her armor removed, he found her not entirely unattractive. But the memory of her combative attitude on Bessie snuffed any idea of her being compatible with him.

Abby sighed, then dropped the picture frame to the floor, dislodging shards of broken glass. Then she turned her back to him and fell asleep on the couch. Steve huffed a half laugh and put a hand on the doorknob to leave. A corkboard next to the door was dotted with a few dozen collectors pins, some from the Texas Rangers, and a few Disney characters — Rey, Hawkeye, the Frozen princesses, and Stitch. A large Phelps for President button pinned to the middle of the board brought a slight smile to his face.

Unable to resist curiosity, he looked down the hallway toward Abby's bedroom and saw a number of other pictures simply tacked to the wall. Most were pictures of Abby and Tyson — a Texas Rangers game, Dave and Busters, the Dallas Zoo, handing out plates of food at a rock concert of some kind — each was of the two of them out enjoying life, as young adults do. The images built a mote of pity within him, and he knew they would do far worse to her. Another couple pictures were of Abby arm-in-arm with a young Korean girl in mouse ears at Disneyland. He guessed that was her foster sister, Mary.

The bedroom was a mess: bed unmade, various undergarments — men's and women's — on the floor, an open box of condoms on one night-stand next to some beer bottles, and two pairs of large Nike basketball shoes leaning neatly against a haphazard pile of hand-colored canvas sneakers. The bathroom sink featured two toothbrushes, one mechanical, featuring My Little Pony characters, the other a masculine blue Oral-B model. Tyson wasn't an occasional visitor. The accident at the construction site would no doubt claw at her insides for some time.

On his way out, Steve saw a lone picture in the bedroom that featured Abby cheering at a political rally for Phelps' election campaign three years ago. She wasn't even old enough to vote then. Steve smiled at the thought of her carrying her sharp tongue into a political debate with Eddie.

Abby snored softly as he returned to her living room. Steve looked at her sleeping form on the sofa and smiled, then took a business card out and put it on the table. "No Abby, I don't think you're alright. But… you're alright." He glanced between her and the little paper rectangle, and he wondered if he'd regret leaving the door open for her to get in touch. He locked the door as he left, rubbing his forehead in anticipation of the pain she could cause him.

Out on the landing of her apartment, he spoke softly. "I hope you call." It was the truth. That's all he could speak.

CHAPTER 9
GARBAGE GIRL

A HUGE LUMP formed in the back of Abby's throat as she digested the news her supervisor, Carl Bolton, had just delivered.

"Sorry Abby, but I think it's best for all of us."

She fought off tears. "Carl, I have to have this job. It was an accident."

The haughty man, dressed in what looked like a 70s-era plaid brown short-sleeve shirt, leaned back in his chair, fondled his thick, graying moustache, and attempted to fold his hirsute arms over his ample belly with limited success. He scoffed. "You couldn't even show up to being fired on time! Look. This decision comes from way above me. I'm just the messenger. You're a sweet kid and do good work when you feel like it, but I've defended your slacking off enough and the developers won't stand for bad publicity. They're still fighting with the city for all the tax breaks they were promised and if the PR surrounding this goes the wrong way they'll lose support. An injury can get swept under the rug, but a death, caused by an Adapted? You were gone before Tyson's head hit the bottom of the dumpster."

Her stomach convulsed, threatening to erupt breakfast tacos all over her now former boss. The mental dams willing her tear ducts to stay closed gave way and she bawled, covering her eyes.

Carl held out his hands. "Jesus, sorry. That was, uh, crude. I just never liked that guy. Too lazy."

Abby wailed.

Checking the time on a wrist with no watch, Carl stood. "Listen, I have to run to a meeting. They're gonna give you four months' severance for agreeing to say nothing. Monique outside has the document for you to sign. That'll give you some time to find a new gig." He moved to the door. "I know a guy that manages a recycling sorting center not too far from here. He'd probably love to have someone with your… talent. I'll send him your info."

She said nothing, just cried. Carl excused himself from the room with a fake cough, and Abby was left alone in his shabby, cluttered office.

Minutes passed, full of sobbing, frothing self-pity, and a cavern where her remorse should be — all unfamiliar, all scary. Her head slowly shook side to side as she whimpered. "I'm so sorry Tyson. This isn't what I…"

Two loud knocks on the door interrupted her solitude, and the door opened. Carl's assistant Monique walked in, folder and pen in hand. Abby attempted to stifle her tears with a series of sniffs up her nose, to little avail. Her eyes stung. She wiped at them with some tissues from the desk, trying to clear away her ruined makeup. It didn't help. She carelessly flung the tissues at the corner of the room where they hurtled straight into the trash can.

Monique offered a meaningless "tsk tsk" noise as she pulled a document from the folder and plopped it and the pen on the desk. "Tough break honey." She paused as Abby looked up at the piece of paper still sniffling. "Take the money and run. If I got offered four months' pay, I'd be outta here in a heartbeat. Carl sucks. This whole place sucks."

Were it not for the crushing weight at her temples and chest, Abby would call Monique on her assessment of Charles & Munck Construction. Carl's assistant had the cushiest job at the worksite, rarely having to leave the air-conditioned comfort of the office trailer. She was asked to do something even less often.

"Fuck that guy," Abby muttered, shaking her head.

"Ew, no."

The two women had only a passing familiarity with each other, but in that moment, Abby knew they shared a common bond: Carl Bolton was unequivocally the least sexually attractive person either of them knew. Abby looked up at Monique, who sported a Cheshire-wide grin. They both laughed, but briefly. The need to blink away the sting in her eyes forced new tears down Abby's face, and she continued to sniff at the relentless stream of mucous from her nose. She scrawled her signature on the page without even reading it and stood to leave.

"Is Tyson… his family…" She couldn't finish her question.

"They'll be taken care of, don't you fret. The company has insurance for this sort of thing. You just worry about you. You're young and cute, I'm sure you'll find a new job right away."

The monotone delivery of the words revealed how much they had been practiced. For an instant, Abby wished Agent Palmer was there to offer his opinion on their veracity, but as soon as that thought entered her mind, she reminded herself that he was a dick for working for RADSA. A curt "ahem" rolled into Carl's office from the next room.

"I'm afraid it's time to go. Get your things." Monique collected the paper and pen off the desk as Abby stood and picked up her purse, reflective orange vest, and hard hat that was covered in more random stickers than the back of a Volkswagen Microbus. Monique politely, but firmly, placed a hand on Abby's shoulder and turned her toward the door. "Now don't get upset or anything, but security is here to walk you out."

"Ugh. Whatever." Abby wiped at her eyes with her forearms. Under ordinary circumstances, she would have protested the indignity of an escort to the curb. Instead, she was almost glad to have someone to lean on in case she needed to vomit. She left Carl's office, then slammed the door as she exited the trailer, knocking one of the many coats of dust off the orange and white paint. She hurried down the steps Tyson had used a few minutes after he told her he had found someone else. The same ones he'd also used just moments before she killed him. As she dwelled on the graceful arc of the concrete block on its fatal collision course with his head, she figured her breakfast would be coming back up any second. But her stomach was calm. Her sneakers hit the dirt of the yard, and an inexplicable wave of relief came over her.

The nameless security guard pulled at her elbow. "The exit is this way, Ms. Alstrom."

Abby said nothing, just turned and followed, noticing a second security guard had joined the scene watching from behind. A third waited at the gate, putting on as serious a face as he could muster, looking ridiculous for the effort.

Nameless pulled at her elbow again as they left the yard and headed to the bus stop a block away. "Per the terms of your agreement, Ms. Alstrom, you are not to be seen within five hundred feet of this, or any Charles & Munck worksite," he said.

Abby mulled over his statement for a moment and attempted to visualize exactly how far five hundred feet extended from the fence. She then realized that outside of the job, she had no reason to be anywhere near that close. "Don't worry, you're probably never going to see me again."

"That's too bad. I was hoping to get your number."

She looked at him again and knew she didn't know his name. There was a reason for that. He had an inauthentic smile on his face whenever she saw him and his eyes had the dull, Neanderthalish look of a recent high school dropout that couldn't make the military. "Uh, why?"

"I've always wanted to fuck an Adapted!"

She scoffed in disgust.

He laughed and stopped walking to form a triangle around his crotch with his thumbs and index fingers, then thrust his pelvis at her a few times. "Too bad, I'm packin'!"

"Gross. Get lost, or I'll find a clump of cement around here with your name on it." She looked around on the ground, only half faking her interest in finding something to throw.

The guard's eyes grew wide. He turned tail and walked in silent, unmasculine fashion back towards the worksite like a scared rat.

Abby shook her head and allowed herself half a smile as she walked away. As she rounded the corner of the street toward the bus stop, she looked back at the coward. He had returned to the gate and was now watching her again with folded arms, sharing with his guard mates what she presumed were unflattering obscene comments about her. A sliver of gratitude eased her insides. She wasn't going to miss the construction crew.

———

Back home, Abby wasted no time collecting every remnant of Tyson Burrows from her apartment. Each memory felt like a dagger to her chest. The pictures, clothes, even his My Little Pony toothbrush — everything went into a large trash bag, which she hefted off her second floor patio into the dumpster two hundred feet across the parking lot. As she watched it float in defiance of Sir Isaac Newton, she wished she could have thrown up the heavy pit in her stomach and put it in the bag as well. A brief guitar riff from a Styx song floated into her ears from inside, informing her someone was calling. She didn't recognize the number.

"Hello?" she answered, putting the phone on speaker.

"Uh, hi. Abby Alstrom?" The man's voice sounded weak, almost trembling.

"Yeah. You are?"

"My name is Elliott Jennings. I work for ACES - Advanced Clean Environmental Services. I got your name from Carl Bolton. He said you might be looking for work?"

"Wow. You don't waste any time, do you? I just got canned two hours ago." She plopped onto the sofa and swept everything on top of the coffee table onto the floor with her feet.

"Yeah, well. Carl told me you were special. Could do things with garbage?"

Abby chuckled with remorse. "Yeah, I guess you could call it that." The pit in her stomach had not changed, but the weight in her mind had lessened a little. At least it seemed she wouldn't be out of work long.

"Well, I'm always looking for help at the recycling center if you're interested."

"And what is it you'd have me doing?"

"North Texas isn't exactly a hotbed of environmentally conscious consumers. Most people use their recycling bins as a second trash can. We separate the recyclables from the garbage."

"Ah." The thought of sifting through an endless stream of refuse was not exactly appealing. "Does it pay well?"

"Sure does. I can start you out at twenty bucks an hour, since you're, well, special."

Abby groaned. "I'm making almost twice that at C&M." She paused. "Well, *was*."

"Yeah, well, that's far more than we can offer." He sounded annoyed. "Look, Carl described what you can do, you would really help out around here. You'd be helping the environment!"

"Golly gee, Mr. Jennings," Abby replied in her worst fake southern accent. "That sure sounds like it'd be worth a fifty percent pay cut." She was all for environmental causes, but not at the expense of her ability to pay rent.

Elliott laughed on the other line. "Carl said you had a mouth too."

Abby sighed. "Does it smell like trash?"

"Sure does. But after a while you don't notice it."

Her nostrils preemptively protested. She closed her eyes and slumped her head down, not relishing the idea of sulking in her apartment for weeks looking for another job. Even with all physical objects related to Tyson laying in the dumpster outside, the space was full of memories of him. Sitting on the sofa, she could practically feel his large hands deftly massaging her shoulders, caressing her arms, then groping her ass as they passionately kissed. She opened her eyes and saw their picture, his wide, cheesy grin gleaming back at her through the fractured glass. An unfamiliar blue card was pinned underneath the frame. She pulled it off the floor. On one side, it had a large, white seal of the Department of Homeland Security on it, and prominently featured the acronym RADSA and its definition. She couldn't believe she would even consider taking Rice up on his offer, but desperation has a way of changing things.

"Well, I appreciate the call, Elliott. I think I'll look around first to see what's out there before I decide."

"Yeah sure, I get it. Let me know soon, okay? I've gotta keep the line moving." He hung up, sounding completely indifferent whether she took the job or not.

Abby looked at the business card and realized she could not remember how it came to be in her apartment. She flipped it over, revealing a phone number, an email address of seemingly random letters and numbers, and instead of the person's name, a codename. THE SLEUTH. She frowned.

"Palmer."

CHAPTER 10
THE ADJUSTER

ON BEN'S MONITOR, a couple dozen other regional RADSA managers fiddled about their desks through their webcam feeds, all waiting for the director to appear and begin her briefing. She was late, per usual. Idle moments passed. A number of the other managers toyed with their phones, one paged through a magazine on boats, some seemed to be texting each other based on the timing of laughs from one video box to the next. *Probably gossiping about R-Skills,* Ben thought with a frown. Ben busied himself studying the mannerisms of his peers. It was a fairly diverse collection of women and men across various ethnic groups. Where RADSA leadership fell short was in being represented by those they championed — the Adapted. Most of the managers' video feeds were rimmed in a silver frame in the telecon. Just five of the thirty-eight boxes had bright blue outlines, indicating that those regional managers were Adapted themselves. His frame was not outlined. Pride and shame battled inside him. He was proud of his R-Skill. It was a good one. Powerful even. Why shouldn't he be proud of it? That would be like asking LeBron James to be ashamed to be awesome at basketball.

And yet, he was ashamed when he used his ability. It was one deemed too dangerous for the public. Which, on the surface, was silly. But in the hands of someone with less restraint than he, a Number Four R-Skill could cause significant harm. If word got out that an Adapted could manipulate others' minds, riots would soon follow. He didn't feel bad about using it to get his job, because he felt uniquely qualified for it, and at the time wanted to help the Adapted cause. And, in a way, it was compensation for what the Director's daughter, his ex-fiancé, had done to him. Plus, Frannie had already promised him the position.

He used it on anyone he met — hell, anyone that looked at him. To hide his scar. His secret shame. But that he used it on his team distressed him. He had to, he thought, to keep them motivated. Who would want to go to work every day looking at his ugly, disfigured mug? Recruitment would be impossible. Only Eddie would have joined after seeing Ben's real face. He gave himself another reminder of it with a glance at the mirror across the room and grimaced. He had to keep reminding himself.

Finally, Frannie Gustafson, the Director of RADSA, graced the video conference with her presence, straightening several files on her desk before starting the meeting. Ben popped some more Advil pills and chased them down with a swallow of tepid coffee.

"Hello everyone," she said in her thick, cheery Minnesota accent. "I trust you've all seen the president's latest announcement. In keeping with his charge to increase communication to the media regarding the administration's efforts regarding Adapted, I am requiring regional statistics on our four-Cs to be submitted on Wednesdays in preparation for my new weekly press conference." The ultra-high-definition video showed every crease in her face as she smiled. "In addition, I want to see more positive tales of heroism or community outreach from you, your teams, and the unrecruited Adapted in your regions. The president feels maintaining a steady beat of positive communication is vital to avoiding a witch hunt on all Adapted." She drew a deep breath, and an even longer drink of coffee, then looked directly in her camera. "That should bear special significance for a number of you. I expect better productivity."

Though some of Ben's regional manager peers were Adapted, Frannie's words spoke straight to his soul. He knew she didn't know. She couldn't. And though he was looking at a video feed sent to all the regional managers, Frannie's wide-eyed glare seemed specifically meant for him. A war of public opinion over the Adapted still simmered, but President Phelps' deft maneuvering with RADSA and welcoming style with the media had kept the discourse since the UDO mostly civil. But every Adapted knew roiling unrest lurked under the surface. At least the ones that paid attention did. Ignorance, jealousy, anger, loss, religious zealotry - all fueled the rage some extreme individuals felt: that every Adapted should be eliminated, to remove all threat to their own personal existence and preferred parking spot at Walmart.

Frannie continued after another sip of coffee. "Capture, Communicate, Catalog, Collect. I want emphasis this month on collect and capture. You should be growing your teams. Each week. Every new Adapted is a potential resource for you and your region to bring to bear. Every new Adapted is also a potential serious danger to society that needs to be relocated. Do not hesitate to call for reinforcements, should a situation have the chance to get out of hand. The president will not tolerate avoidable catastrophes. Better to ship off anything remotely dangerous to Island-A than risk a fuck-up with an Adapted going viral. It may seem unfair to some, but that's our new reality."

Ben laughed to himself at the director's curse. She didn't do it often, but with her accent and diminutive size, it was like a friendly little garden gnome swearing. The mention of Island-A brought a frown to his face. He hoped the rumors of overcrowding and rampant fighting were untrue, but knew things on the island could get out of hand in a hurry. He hadn't had to ship anyone there yet and was hopeful to keep that streak going as long as he could. Sooner or later some poor sap in DFW would wake up with radioactive sweat and Ben would have to deal with it.

The director closed her call with some recent statistics on new Adapted counts - over two thousand across the country in the past month, and thirty-one relocations to Island-A. More, and less, than Ben had expected. *Two thousand. The rate is increasing.*

With faint disinterest, Frannie began to read a list of newly discovered R-Skills. It was the highlight of the meeting each week for some managers and set the course of conversation abuzz for the following day. The news first traveled inside RADSA, then later in social media circles as details were inevitably leaked. This week, the discoveries included someone that could transmute cellophane tape into an as-yet-unidentified metal, another whose skin repelled water, and a third that could discern the ingredients and ratios for any individual's best-tasting taco possible. Most of the muted faces on his screen smiled or laughed as each new R-Skill was mentioned. The regional managers that were Adapted tended to keep an even keel during this part of her regular briefing, and Ben was no exception. Quirky R-Skills weren't funny. Some were fabulous, others special in their own way, but many were life-changingly unfortunate, such as the man that could no longer make contact with water (the poor, smelly soul). His heart sank when Frannie mentioned the names and their R-Skills that were ultimately shipped to isolation on the island, which included a man that could hurtle jagged spears of a ceramic-like stone from his hands, and a teen that caused a massive traffic jam on the 405 in Los Angeles by intentionally melting the tires of all the vehicles around her. Ben couldn't disagree with the sizable risk that each of them posed and was glad he wasn't the one that had to make those calls.

After the video conference ended, Ben stood and stretched and popped the joints in his neck again, then made a new cup of coffee on his Keurig and walked out into the Bay to talk to the team.

CHAPTER 11
THE SLEUTH

STEVE, Gigi, and Eddie sat in the media room, watching the prior night's A-Space Tonight interview between host Kristen Brently and astrophysicist Dr. Norman Pruett. The scientist's popularity hit the stratosphere shortly after the dark object struck and he started a new Q&A series on YouTube. It was the most-watched program on the Internet so far that year. Practically any discovery, discussion, or news about the UDO strike and the Adapted was must-see viewing, and Steve already felt behind the curve for missing it in favor of a good night's sleep. It was the new global pastime: to devour, decipher, interpret, and predict what the incredible turn in the course of human history meant on an individual and global scale.

"Thanks for joining us, Dr. Pruett," the host opened.

"Glad to be here, Kristen."

"Are there any new developments about the meteor you can share with us?"

"Absolutely. But don't call it a meteor. This was something completely new to us." The large man clapped his hands together, and the audience followed suit. "Let's get to it."

Kristen feigned a fake surprise at the crowd's enthusiasm, then smiled and gestured for Norman to continue.

"First, it seems that the composition of the dark object as we've come to call it was of primarily organic elements - you know, carbon, nitrogen, oxygen. This came as a huge shock to the scientific community when first discovered, as these elements are not typically observed in great amounts in the bodies found in space — asteroids, comets, etcetera. Even more peculiar, from the few pure samples that have been recovered, we've been able to determine the molecular composition of the object was somewhat similar to that of Vantablack."

Kristen spoke up. "The super-dark material that absorbs practically all light?"

Norman nodded. "The very same. Vantablack and the other ultra-black materials like it are essentially a forest of nanotubes - very tiny tubes made from carbon. Light goes into a tube and cannot escape. It bounces around until it is ultimately transformed into heat."

"And if the object was like that, I'm guessing it would have been very hard to detect?"

"Precisely. We had no idea it was out there."

"Has there been any determination as to why the radiation from the nuclear missile was altered by the dark object, and why the Adapted phenomenon began?"

Norman paused for a moment. The studio was dead silent. Then he grinned. "That's the big question, isn't it? The scientific community is still baffled by the lack of detectable radiation from the warhead, and the emergence of the Adapted. It's a complete mystery."

"Well, whoever figures it out has a Nobel prize waiting for them, right?"

Norman smiled with wide eyes and nodded. "At least one."

"So many questions!" Kristen blurted with her trademark frazzled enthusiasm. "Do we know where it came from? Could it happen again? Could we stop the next one?"

Norman laughed. "No. Yes. Probably not."

Hushed murmurs descended from the studio audience, and those watching inside Bessie exchanged concerned looks.

Kristen rolled her hands in circles. "Could you elaborate?"

The aged scientist folded his hands on his ample tummy. "Well, due to our lack of data on the path it traveled to reach us, we honestly have no idea. Though, based on its composition, I can say with confidence that it did not originate within our solar system."

And that's when the pain began. Steve felt a twinge on the side of his forehead - just enough to know that what the scientist just said was wrong.

"Could it happen again? Sure. It's already happened once, so another impact is within the realm of possibility. But we have almost every telescope on the planet at our disposal looking at the sky for patterns of missing starlight." He gestured to the cameras. "A big thanks to all you intrepid astronomers out there keeping watch!"

The crowd raucously applauded at the host's insistence.

"We have better search algorithms now, ones specifically tailored to detect a similar phenomenon. I think we'd see another one coming, hopefully months to years in advance since we know what to look for. There aren't any other bodies like the dark object out there right now."

Wrong again. Steve winced as the other side of his forehead erupted. He made an audible noise as he sucked in a tense breath. Gigi and Eddie turned to look at him, all four eyebrows raised.

"Are you okay, Steve?" Gigi asked.

Steve rubbed his face. "He's..."

On the screen, Norman continued. "And as far as stopping the next one, we'll have to hope NASA and the other space programs around the world can come up with a solution. Unfortunately, given the difficulty in detecting something like this, we may not have much time to react if another is in Earth's path.

Kristen clenched her teeth in a pseudo-smile and hammed for the audience.

"But I think such an event is exceptionally unlikely. I can say with confidence, in the four-and-a-half billion-year history of the Earth, the dark object that struck last year was the first of its kind." Norman said.

Steve gasped in pain again.

"Well, that's good. I've gotta go to a Bar Mitzvah next week."

The audience roared with laughter; Norman chuckled.

"I think you'll make it. But I'd just like to say that our thoughts and prayers continue to be with the Korean community around the world, as well as those in China, Russia, and Japan affected by the impact."

"Indeed. It's a tragedy I don't think any of us will ever forget." Kristen shook her head.

Norman nodded in agreement, though the smile on his face betrayed the fact that the scientist was tickled pink at the sheer scale of discovery at hand.

Kristen clapped her hands to pick up the suddenly somber mood. "Alright, coming up, my *favorite* segment of the show. Amazing Adaptations! We've got a guy that can change his beard color on command, and a 10-year-old girl that can speak to beetles! How cool is that? They'll tell you their stories, and we'll vote on the guests for my Double-A segment next week. Can you stick around Dr. Pruett?"

Norman smiled. "Oh, I wouldn't miss it."

Eddie muted the screen, and placed a hand on Steve's shoulder, giving it a little squeeze. "You okay Stevie?"

The pain was abating, but his head still hurt like it had just been hit with a cast-iron pan on both sides. "He's… he's wrong."

Gigi spoke up. "Wrong? About what?"

"The dark object. There are more out there. There have been others."

"How can you possibly know that?" she asked, incredulous.

"Because it hurt when he said it was the only one. There's no other explanation."

Gigi and Eddie exchanged concerned glances.

"Oh God," she said. Then she sat back and ran her hands over her hair. "Oh my God! Should… should we tell someone?"

Steve rubbed his forehead and nodded. "I'll talk to Ben. Doesn't sound like there's much that can be done."

CHAPTER 12
LUCKY

"CAN you tell us a little more about what's happening on Island-A?"

President Phelps smiled at the preposterously young reporter. "Of course." *It would be the A-Space reporter that asks about the island*, he thought, holding back a groan. He motioned to Frannie. "Let's have Director Gustafson field this one."

"Thank you, Mr. President," Frannie said after stepping up to the podium. She looked at the reporter and gave her one of those grandmotherly *You're so naive* smiles that gently wobbled her graying curls.

"Island-A is… a work in progress," she said. "We currently have two hundred fifty-seven residents, and sixty-five full-time staff from RADSA. That does not include the security detail that the marines have provided."

Nearly every hand in the media pool shot up as she paused for a breath. Phelps smiled as he watched from behind, sipping his water.

"Not quite a tenth of a percent of the three hundred thousand-plus known Adapted we have information on possess R-Skills on the Dangers to Society list. This distribution, roughly eight in ten thousand Adapted, has been fairly steady, even as RADSA's cataloguing efforts approach full steam."

Frannie paused for some water and pointed at a reporter from Fox News.

The reporter stood and asked his question across folded arms. "Thank you, Director. What, exactly, are all these guests of the administration doing day-in and day-out on the taxpayers' dollar? Is there any hope of rehabilitation or reintegration, or a plan to develop some kind of… antidote to R-Skills?"

Phelps gnawed his cheeks. He resisted the urge to take over the podium and lambaste the reporter for his rudeness. Instead, he nursed his water and glowered at the reporter.

"All good questions, Mr. Stokker, thank you. The honest answer is we don't know yet. There is no 'antidote' to becoming Adapted. As far as we have been able to determine, the physiological change is permanent and irreversible. We are studying ways to suppress dangerous R-Skills in a meaningful way that would allow for the possibility of reintegration at some point in the future. There is, at present, no timeline on the availability of such a treatment. As far as what the guests do with their time—"

Stokker interrupted. "What about the considerable cost RADSA and Island-A pose to taxpayers? What is your long-term plan? You are the head of another enormous government program, the likes of which we haven't seen since the advent of the Department of Homeland Security. Could the functions RADSA performs not have been carried out by DHS or the FBI or ICE or any other number of existing programs? Surely you can see how your department sponsoring free lifetime tropical vacations for whomever it deems worthy would be seen as ridiculously frivolous and wasteful?"

Blood now at full boil, Phelps had enough. It was one thing to disagree with the policy. But being a dick about it would not be tolerated. He jumped up to the podium and patted Frannie on the arm. "I'll take this one," he told her.

"Sit down, John," Phelps growled at the reporter, who did as he was told.

"What is so wasteful about wanting to protect our neighbors? What is so frivolous about showing compassion to our fellow Americans, who, through no fault of their own, have to be ripped away from their American Dreams — their careers, their homes, their *families* — so that the rest of us may pursue our own dreams in safety?"

The reporter shrank in his chair, where he received more than one incredulous look from others in the media pool.

"I understand the conservative viewpoint here. I do. Especially since a significant portion of the RADSA budget came from the defense budget. And yes, the loss of jobs in the sector — from the Boeings, the Raytheons, the Lockheeds — was spectacularly news-worthy. But answer me this: would you rather have those private sector jobs still on the government payroll, or a balanced budget? Job growth in the private sector is booming.

Booming. The emergence of the Adapted has created an entirely new facet to our economy. We've not seen that since the rise of the Internet and dot-com era. Far more jobs have been created in the advent of the post-UDO era than have been lost from defense cuts." Phelps stopped to drain his water glass, then held it out for someone to fill.

A sigh slipped from his lips at the tired, old arguments from the conservative critics. Despite towing a centrist line, balancing the budget, and handling a spectacularly large global crisis with aplomb, the fact he ran on the Democratic ticket meant Republicans would oppose anything he did. There was no longer any political discourse between parties. Only immobile contrarianism. Could he be the one to knit some civility back into American politics?

Time to put on a show, he thought. He grasped the podium with trembling hands and shook his head, staring straight at Stokker. "RADSA's charter will continue, and the department will grow. It must. I intend to pursue even more funding for Frannie next year. I am passionate about this. We all should be. Out of the ashes of a terrible catastrophe, America and the world were presented with the incredible opportunity to come together. To change the course of progress. To improve humanity. Part of that is showing compassion to those that must go to Island-A. The lifelong tropical vacation as you put it is the *very least* we can do."

The blood drained from John Stokker's face.

"Alright, let's have Director Gustafson take some more questions," Phelps said, turning away from the podium with a smirk on his face.

CHAPTER 13
BOUNCY

THE ALARM RANG at its usual time: 5:00AM sharp. Gigi sat up and stretched, the socks on her feet dutifully keeping her R-Skill contained. The haze of getting not-quite-enough sleep slowly lifted, and she looked through the wood slats covering her window to her early morning companion, the streetlamp. Even the birds were still asleep. The notion of being lumped in with the 'early riser' camp was vexing. It tended to connote a less-than-social mindset. For her, the social media climb was omnipresent in her mind.

As she nursed a glass of water, she checked her social feeds for new followers, direct messages, or something trending to comment on. A tinge of disappointment creased her lips. Not much happened overnight. She reviewed the video she made from the footage Eddie captured. Everything was on point. *Time to be a star*, she thought as she uploaded it to YouTube and broadcast it out to her few thousand followers, adding the requisite request for everyone to like, share, comment, and subscribe.

"All it takes is one video. Today's the day," she sighed.

She shook the final cobwebs from her head, then commenced with stretching, followed by three sets of bodyweight strength training. Gigi was still committed to maintaining her physique and athletic ability. A responsibility. And an opportunity. She had released a video of the same exercise routine last month. It had brought in a few hundred new subscribers, but it wasn't the smash success she had hoped. The Internet was replete with videos of good-looking exercise enthusiasts trying to earn a living on social media, each one featuring gratuitous six-pack abs, cleavage, and ass shots. Hers had all those as well but lacked whatever 'It Factor' the anonymous consumers online demanded to make such videos a success. If only she could use working for RADSA to her advantage. The agency wasn't shy about employing Adapted, even internally stressing the need for it. But it sure was adamant its employees didn't use their positions to make themselves famous. Ben's attitude towards that rule was that it was written by someone who wasn't an Adapted. Should a video of her in action 'accidentally' end up going viral, the publicity and community outreach would be worth whatever admonishment came from the director. But it had to happen naturally.

After exercise was done, she went to the kitchen to whip up another almond butter-lemon-kale yogurt smoothie, still not happy enough with the flavor to post the recipe yet. She tossed in some chia and flax seeds and topped this version off with just a touch of local honey. It wasn't bad, but it wouldn't win any awards either. Perhaps her mom would have some suggestions; Gigi was overdue for a call home.

After showering, brushing and teeth whitening, she did her makeup and smiled at the mirror. The same, half-satisfied, half-disgusted smile she gave herself every morning. Her sandy hair, tied back in a ponytail was neat and tidy. Tan looked good, great muscle tone, abs well-defined. In fact, she liked nearly everything about her body, except her face. Her eyebrows were unnaturally thick, and her eye color was a dull, unsatisfying hazel. Nothing to write home about. The topography of her cheekbones was always a little too pudgy, and she was resigned to the fact it would always be like that until Father Time began to have his way with her. All of that she could live with. But she absolutely hated her nose. It was small, cute, and turned up at the tip so much that her nostrils pointed almost straight out. Her best friend on the gymnastics team had once called it a pig's nose, and Gigi couldn't disagree. Others had far less kind words to describe her face. She sighed at the reflection.

"Alright, let's get to work."

Bailey had texted where the pickup point would be that morning. "Richardson, Belt Line and Central." It showed no specific address, but usually there was no need. The giant faux cattle trailer stood out like a sore thumb almost anywhere in town. The biggest parking lot at that intersection was the one with the Alamo Drafthouse movie theater. Bessie would likely be parked in plain view, waiting for everyone to arrive to begin the day's adventure.

Gigi dressed in her usual attire of colorful yoga pants and matching top. Today's was a mélange of blue shades. She hopped up to reach her light jacket from the too-high coat hanger by the door, then grabbed her phone and left the condo to continue her quest for fame.

———

Per usual, traffic in Dallas sucked in all directions that morning. She had less than ten miles to drive to get to Richardson, but needed nearly an hour to work her way through a cavalcade of semi-trucks, heavy construction equipment, and pickups towing uncovered trailers filled with all manner of landscaping machinery. Between the large vehicles meandered an endless parade of distracted highway drivers on their phones. She was, of course, on her phone too, but the bright red Tesla was doing all of the work for her. When going through the morning news headlines didn't quell gridlock boredom, she checked how the new upload was faring. Her heart sank. Not even a hundred views yet and it had already been up for nearly two hours. If only she could add *#RADSA* to her hashtags. No matter. After the morning team meeting, she'd park at her station, look busy, and spend the day promoting her video.

The Tesla wheeled into the parking lot where Bessie stood waiting only five minutes late. Ben was a stickler on most things, particularly so for timeliness, but he rarely admonished her for being tardy. She preferred being the last one to walk in. Gigi bounded up the steps at the back of the trailer, punched in the code to the door, and went inside. Then her jaw dropped. Huddled around the Bay was the whole team, plus another head wearing a baseball cap, ripped jeans, and a Foo Fighters t-shirt. The trash girl.

"Wow, that was fast," Gigi said.

"Ah, and here's the other member of our team, Gigi." Ben waved in her direction. "Gigi, this is Abby Alstrom."

Abby walked over to shake hands, a tentative smile on her face. She was even taller in person than on camera. Up close, Gigi practically had to crane her neck to make eye contact. "Hi," she managed with all the politeness of a furloughed worker training their replacement.

To her credit, Abby picked up on the tone. "Uh, yeah. Nice to meet you."

With a loose grip and disengaging mid-first bounce, Gigi left no doubt in her participation of the handshake that she wasn't interested in cordiality.

"I still can't believe you're all Adapted," Abby said. "I mean, most people think RADSA just relocates every Adapted they get their hands on to the island.

"Yeah," Ben said. "Though, it's a lightly held secret. The director has a vision of regional response teams, but so far, we have been mostly working on developing our contact list, if you will. Alright, here's the list of potentials we'll visit today," he said, handing a sheet of information to everyone.

Gigi looked at the list with disinterest; recruitment runs were her least favorite part of the job, though it's what they all spent most of their time doing.

"Steve, I'd like you and Gigi out on these assignments today, Abby can go with you to see how we do things."

Steve looked at Gigi, smiled, and nodded.

Gigi clenched her teeth.

Abby spoke up. "So, we just cruise around town looking for Adapted to abduct, gas them, then do an interview for potential to join our team? And we get paid for this, Agent Rice?"

Ben chuckled. "Call me Ben. If you want to distill it down to the bare essence, that's not too far off. We try not to use the gas too much."

Gigi giggled.

Abby folded her arms and slouched to one side. "Uh huh."

"If there's a situation where we can lend a hand, we will offer our assistance to first responders in the area. But our involvement is up to them. We've been at this for a few months, and no one's taken us up on the offer yet." Ben shrugged. "It's not like we have superhero-level R-Skills, those are very rare, and usually end up on the island. I'm sure we'll get a call sooner or later."

"Months in, and you only have half a dozen people to show for it?" Abby asked.

Ben popped his neck and shrugged again. "What can I say? I'm picky."

Gigi checked her phone again and frowned at the meager progress of her video. "Are you sure you want me to go recruit? Might be better if I stayed to monitor the feeds."

Ben nodded. "Eddie and Bailey will handle it while you're out. As the team grows, I need to rely on everyone to be able to represent us and RADSA in the field."

"But if something happens, I may be best suited to assist with… something," Gigi said.

"I'm sure we'll be fine. If we need your talents, I'll let you know." Ben patted her on the shoulder.

Gigi tried to hold back a groan. Maybe she'd be able to work on her video while her car drove to the interviews.

"And what is your R-Skill, Gigi?" Abby asked, eyebrows raised.

Always glad to be made the center of attention, Gigi stood a little straighter and smiled. "Well, my bare feet turn any surface pliable, kind of like a smooth trampoline. Only much springier. I can use it to jump really high or run very fast. Just yesterday I was up to almost a hundred miles per hour."

"Wow," Abby said, eyes wide. "That's pretty cool!"

Gigi smiled back. It was more than pretty cool. "It's pretty disruptive to complex surfaces, like the floor here." She tapped her foot on the shiny metal deck plating. "So, I've gotta keep at least socks on pretty much all the time. Even in the shower or sleeping."

"Huh," Abby said. "I guess you get used to that."

Gigi faked a yawn. "Yeah, it's no big deal." She hated wearing socks in the shower.

Eddie piped up. "Hey Bouncy, I've got your uniform ready. Found you some goggles that match." He tossed her the blue-and-pink suit.

She giggled at the use of her code name. They rarely did that. "Thanks, Stitch."

Abby looked horrified. "Bouncy? Stitch? We have code names?"

Steve spoke up. "Yes, but we don't typically use them. The RADSA database assigns them using AI."

"You let a computer make up names for all of you? What has it come up with for me?" Abby asked.

Steve and Ben looked at each other.

"Garbage Girl." Gigi stifled a laugh through her nose.

Abby scrunched her face. "Eh, yeah. I think I'll stick with Abby."

Eddie gestured to Gigi. "Well come on, show us how it looks!"

Gigi shrugged, then walked over to the lockers a few feet away, pulled hers open, and began to disrobe. From the corner of her eye, she could tell Steve and Ben were watching. She smiled.

Ever the neophyte, Abby spoke again. "Woah, you all just drop trou like that?"

"I'm not shy. Being a gymnast, you're used to being more or less naked in front of random people after a while. If you've got it, flaunt it!"

She left her black sports bra and thong on, then stepped into the blue-gray suit. It clung to her form just right - snug, not loose anywhere. The pink stripes Gigi had suggested waved back and forth up the sides of the legs and torso, fanning along the outer curve of her breasts up to the collar in a tapering fashion not unlike the lapping tip of a flame. The suit had a couple of slim pockets on either side of each hip for her phone, and a zipper up the front ending low enough for not too much cleavage, but enough to attract attention. Gigi drew in a satisfied breath; it looked good. Ben and Steve were smiling, obviously ready to devour her. Eddie looked more proud than salivating, but Gigi suspected he wasn't all gay in there.

Abby cringed. "What, are we all going to wear this? Like the X-Men? Don't you think that's a bit ridiculous?"

Ben shrugged. "Given Eddie's talents, we've volunteered as a test case of sorts. But management thinks it could be a good idea for the future."

"Great. I can't wait," Abby said.

Steve winced and glared at Abby.

Ben cleared his throat. "Anyway, I'm going to take Bessie towards Arlington today." He looked at Steve, Abby, then Gigi. "Does one of you have a car to go out recruiting in?"

Steve shook his head. "Mine's at the dealer getting serviced."

"I walked," Abby said.

Gigi rolled her eyes. "Ugh, fine. We'll take my car."

CHAPTER 14
GARBAGE GIRL

"NICE CAR," Abby said as she got into the rear seat of Gigi's Tesla.

"Thanks," Gigi replied, in as polite a way as a subliminal "fuck you, peasant" could be delivered.

Abby brushed it off and tapped Steve on the shoulder. "This is so weird, just going around to do interviews with other Adapted. We get paid to do this?"

"We do, provided you show up on time." Steve shot Abby a glance over his shoulder. "It does seem a little frivolous. Especially considering what we have on the list today. But if we come across someone that truly is a danger to public safety, that's where we'll earn our keep."

Gigi programmed the team's first destination into the Tesla's computer and set it to auto-drive. Then she picked up her phone and put her earbuds in.

A sickening lurch in Abby's stomach stirred her cold pizza breakfast as the car put itself into motion. She had not yet been in a self-driving car, and the experience was unsettling. Even more so since Gigi seemed intent to pay no attention to what the car was doing. "Is this safe?"

The *thump-thump-thump* of dance music crept from the backsides of Gigi's earbuds — a clear indication that she had completely tuned out Abby, Steve, and the rest of the world.

"First time in a self-driving car?" Steve asked.

"Oh, no. I've been lots of times. I *love* having the progenitor to the Matrix in charge of my safety," Abby said.

Steve winced and clicked his tongue. "Right." He looked over his shoulder at Abby. "Can I ask something of you?"

Gigi peered at him through the corner of her eye, before going back to her phone.

"Uh, sure?" Abby said.

"Cut out the sarcastic wiseass routine. At least with me." He rubbed his forehead and turned around. "I know it's your thing, but it fucking hurts."

Abby folded her arms and shrank in her seat a little. "Oh. Sorry. I didn't—"

He cut her off with a wave of his hand.

They sat in silence for several minutes as the car maneuvered itself onto the highway with the accuracy and defensive posture of a driving instructor. Steve read through several pages on his tablet, then held it back to Abby. "Here's our list of interviewees today. Wanna read up on them?"

"Yeah, sure," Abby said, then realized as she took the tablet she wasn't entirely certain she meant what she said or not. Steve didn't flinch, leaving Abby to guess if she actually did. *Will be walking on eggshells with this guy,* she thought. He had busied himself with his phone, so Abby allowed herself a moment to study his profile. She still hadn't quite gotten past her initial reaction the first day they met, erupting in Bessie's little interview room after learning he was an Adapted working for RADSA. As it turned out, a whole bunch of Adapted worked for RADSA, and now she did too, of all things. Certainly wasn't fair to harbor any resentment toward him for that. But his R-Skill was a bit invasive, in a way. The idea of working with someone she couldn't bullshit was disconcerting.

She scanned the names and R-Skills on the list. Six people, all emerged recently. Nobody she had heard of, and none of the abilities seemed particularly threatening. Or useful. She thought of seeing her own name on the list, and wondered why Agent Rice, Ben, thought she would make for a good addition to the team. It couldn't be her winning attitude, as that seemed to be in direct contradiction to Steve's personal comfort.

The first stop on the list was to visit Rosa Taliveras, a middle-aged school teacher from Garland. She had developed the ability to blow ketchup out her nose. Poor thing. "Are these people expecting us?"

"Ms. Taliveras is," Steve said. "The ones we don't expect to be dangerous I'll call ahead and arrange a time. If they're potentially harmful, we would just drop in on them unannounced."

"That seems like the less-safe approach, for us, at least," Abby said.

Evidently paying attention after all, Gigi jumped into the conversation.

"Yeah, but if it's obvious they would go to the island, they'd just run. We can't let someone with toxic urine slip away."

"Ew, that happened?" Abby asked.

"Yeah, up in Minneapolis a couple months ago," Gigi said. "Took them two weeks to find him after he slipped the RADSA team. Dozens sick."

"I don't remember seeing that in the news." Abby looked at Steve, who raised an eyebrow and nodded.

"It came and went pretty quick," Steve said. "That was the week the identical twins went public with the ability to control the freckles on the other's face. Did you see them on Late Night?"

Abby chuckled. "Oh yeah, I remember that. Imagine waking up one morning and seeing a befreckled 'DORK' on your forehead staring you back in the mirror. I can't imagine the kind of pranks I would play on my sister Mary."

Steve laughed. "I'm an only child, but I can see how that would be an endless supply of torment."

The car drove itself without issue to the proper highway exit. Gigi took over and turned into a modest apartment community right on the access road, the kind with the type of property management company that would spring for fresh paint to keep the outside looking decent but would spend little else on upkeep. The only parking space available to them was between someone doing an oil change on a late-90s yellow Ford Mustang that appeared to be used part time in a demolition derby, and a mostly rust-covered 1970s-era Chevrolet pickup on blocks with all four tires missing. Abby was afraid for the shiny red Tesla, but Gigi showed no concern.

They made their way up to Ms. Taliveras' apartment, and Steve knocked on the door. "Ms. Taliveras?" he asked, when the door opened to reveal a short, stocky woman with graying hair done up in curls, wearing a floral muumuu and a glass of orange juice in her hand.

"Yes," the woman answered, taking a sip of her drink. "Are you the RADSA gentleman I spoke with?"

"Yes ma'am," Steve said. "I'm Agent Palmer, and this is Agent Conlan and Agent Alstrom."

Rosa took in the trebly uncoordinated attire of the three at her door. "Seems the government is lax with its dress code these days. Come on in."

Abby had to agree with the incongruous appearance of her in a t-shirt and jeans next to Palmer in his business suit and Gigi in her silly pink-and-blue jumpsuit. It was even stranger to be referred to as 'Agent Alstrom'.

The three agents sat down together on a well-worn and scratchy brown sofa. Abby looked around. The apartment was more or less the same size as her own, with a bar-style countertop providing a break between the kitchenette and living space. It was definitely older than her unit, but a great deal of meticulous care had been put into its upkeep and flowers-everywhere decor, giving it a well-loved feel. The nearly empty gallon jug of cheap vodka on the bar with its cap off added another dimension to her analysis. The teacher could be drinking simply to relax. Perhaps the stresses of being a grossly underpaid educator had finally pushed her to the brink of reckless alcoholism that would ultimately threaten her livelihood and career. Or, she was drowning her sorrows at developing so ridiculous and impractical an R-Skill.

Rosa sat down in the chair beside the sofa. She set her now half-empty cup of juice and presumably vodka on the coffee table in front of them. "I don't suppose you're here to take me to Island-A, are you? I could use a vacation." She spoke with a mild accent and the steady, controlled pace of a seasoned educator.

Steve offered a polite chuckle. "No, I don't think that's likely." He tapped on his tablet to take notes. "We're mostly here to catalog what you can do, when you discovered your R-Skill, where it happened, etcetera. If you have any questions about RADSA we can answer those as well."

"Ah. A girl can dream, can't she?"

"We try to avoid assigning Adapted to the island except in the most extreme of circumstances."

"And I'm not likely to kill a bunch of innocent people with a splatter of ketchup from my nose?" Rosa asked.

"Do you feel that's likely?" Steve asked.

Rosa snorted, and ketchup shot out from her nose, spraying the carpet and coffee table in a thick red paste, splashing some into her drink, and splattering several drops onto the three agents. "Oh! *Maldición!*" She put a hand to her nose and looked at her ketchup-coated fingers, then found a nearby rag to wipe her face.

Gigi stifled a laugh and earned a swift elbow from Steve. He then ungraciously snapped a photo of the mess with his tablet. Abby quietly sighed at the mess and frustration on the teacher's face. What kind of chaos would ensue should that happen in the middle of class one day? No doubt her foster mother Betty would be squawking a shrill "pitch in around this house!", so Abby naturally resisted helping.

"Eck!" Gigi said after having catalogued the array of splatter on her clothes. "Let me get some paper towels." She found some in the kitchen, addressing her clothes first before helping with the mess.

"How sweet, thank you. I'm sure you agents have better things to do with your time. I'm so sorry about your clothes!"

Despite only knowing her for a short time, Abby thought it odd Gigi would volunteer to assist at all. She didn't seem the type. After the gymnast struggled for several minutes with it, Abby finally got on the floor and helped clean up.

"So," Steve continued without flinching. "Ketchup from the nose. Can you do it on command, or is it just… reflexive, as we've seen?" he asked.

"Bit of both I suppose. I'm sure I'll be a hit at the next hot dog social at school."

Again, Gigi stifled a laugh. Abby too this time.

Steve tapped away at his tablet. "Ketchup only, or any other types of fluids?"

"Just ketchup. Come to think of it, I don't think I have regular, uh, boogies anymore."

"Interesting. Probably worth scheduling an appointment with your doctor, just to see if it could cause some health implications down the road." Palmer said. "When did you first observe the ability?"

"A week ago, Tuesday." Rosa said.

"Where were you?" he asked.

"At school, in the teacher's lounge," Rosa said. "I had just come back from getting burritos with a couple of the other staff. We go to Chipotle once a month to break the monotony of our packed lunches."

"I see," Steve continued. "Did you feel anything else at the time? Nausea, dizziness?"

"Not that I recall," she said.

"Do you know if your coworkers that were with you have developed any abilities? Or anyone else at school?" Steve asked.

"No. To my knowledge, I'm the first there. Lucky me." Rosa said.

"Have you tasted it?" Gigi asked sitting back down, unable to constrain her amusement.

"My girl, it's all I can taste anymore. And I never liked the stuff much to begin with." Rosa sighed.

Abby caught on to the teacher's distress. "Do you have any questions for us? Is there anything we can help you with?"

Steve looked at her with surprised eyes. Gigi's expressed annoyance, as if she were ready to get out of the apartment and never look back.

"Well," Rosa started. "I'm sure you get this all the time, but I'm afraid for my job. Being an Adapted isn't something that's popular everywhere, and I know our principal Mr. Cordday isn't a fan."

"Thom Cordday?" Steve asked, looking at his tablet.

"Yes." Rosa said.

"But he's —" Abby started, but Steve cut her off with a quick shake of his head. "He's so nice."

"You know him?" Rosa asked with surprise.

Abby bit her cheek, needing a plausible lie quick. "Yeah. I don't remember where we met, it was some district function my little sister's school band was playing at. I think he was greeting people at the door. Or something."

Gigi's snort was drowned out by Steve drawing air through his teeth and putting his hand to his head. "Sorry, headache," he said, without looking at Abby.

"Ah. Would you like some Tylenol?"

"No, thank you. I'll be fine." Steve said. He shot a look at Abby that was the equivalent of "shut the fuck up please".

Abby sat on her hands and zipped her lip.

Steve blinked his eyes a few times. "So, with regard to your job. The Adapted Protection Act passed at the end of last year prohibits employers from discriminating against Adapted for purposes of considering employment. Provided said Adapted has been screened and cleared for public safety, which, among other things, was the purpose of today's meeting. I can say with pleasure you are safe to return to work. Should you encounter difficulty with your employment, I would advise contacting a lawyer specializing in Adapted cases. I'm sure you've seen the billboards around town."

"Mmhmm," Rosa said, nodding.

Steve withdrew a pamphlet from his coat pocket. "Here is some information on free counseling services that RADSA is presently offering. There are also a number of links to resources on our website, which is listed on the back."

Rosa took the pamphlet, heaved a sigh, and put it on the sticky coffee table without looking at it. "Thank you."

Abby looked at the teacher and felt her own heart breaking. This woman was clearly not looking forward to going back to work, or living out the rest of her years with ketchup coming out of her nose. She thought it a shame RADSA had no further help to offer.

CHAPTER 15
THE SLEUTH

"WELL, THAT WAS INTERESTING," Abby said as the trio returned to Gigi's car.

Steve allowed himself a laugh after suppressing it for the better part of an hour. "Yeah. The wacky R-skill interviews usually go like that."

Gigi furiously tapped away at her phone, no doubt sharing the experience with her friends.

"Use discretion with what you share, Gigi," Steve said.

"I know, I know," Gigi replied with a roll of her eyes. She put the phone down, looked at the next address on the list, and got the Tesla underway to their next destination.

Steve turned to Abby. "So, some ground rules. You read the non-disclosure we all signed. We don't out Adapted. That's not our job, nor would someone with a sensitive R-Skill appreciate being exposed to ridicule. I'm sure you can appreciate that."

Abby nodded, "Of course. I just thought it odd that two people from the same school should develop R-Skills. Maybe it's not so weird."

"I agree, it's a peculiar coincidence," Steve said. "All of the information we collect from interviews is put into a database, but we don't look for correlations ourselves. That system searches for trends to identify regions of higher radiation exposure or predict future locations of emergence, but so far nothing has been developed." He thought on it again for a moment. "For the two from the middle school, it's probably just a random coincidence."

Abby shrugged. "I guess." She was busy picking dried bits of ketchup from her jeans. "Poor thing. I'm sure that's going to cause her all sorts of problems at school someday."

Steve found Abby's empathy unexpected. It seemed she had a soft spot for the plight of the less-fortunate Adapted, dangerous or wacky. Which made her reaction during the interview to learning of him, an Adapted, working for RADSA, more understandable. RADSA was an easy antagonist to those unaware of the inner workings. "Yeah," he said. "Sometimes it's a curse." He hadn't made up his mind yet how he felt about his own R-Skill.

"So, she's not a candidate to join the team, I guess?" Abby asked.

Gigi tried unsuccessfully to turn a guffaw into a cough.

Steve shook his head. "No. The system identifies recruitment candidates for us ahead of the interviews,"

"And it had identified me?" Abby asked.

"Just so," Steve said, scrolling back through the interview history list, to show her name, address, R-Skill description, and a green checkmark under the column heading 'Recruit?'.

Gigi sighed. "If it hadn't, you wouldn't be here," Gigi said with a resentful air.

Steve sensed the tension coming from Gigi, and while he thought it within her personality to be standoffish to any new addition to the team, her attitude seemed especially forward for Abby's first day. He wondered if Abby had done or said something to Gigi he wasn't aware of.

Abby handed the tablet back to him. "Where are we headed next?"

"A Chick-fil-A, actually. We're meeting one Thom Cordday for lunch," Steve said.

"Ugh, fast food," Gigi said.

"Not a fan of awesome fried chicken, Gigi?" Abby asked.

"I don't do fried anything," Gigi replied, face already back in her phone.

"That's a shame. You must be fun to take to the State Fair." Abby said.

Gigi scoffed with a tone that rebuffed the notion she would ever be found at Dallas' month-long annual celebration of all things fried and unhealthy, mixed in with overpriced midway games and rides, concerts, butter sculptures, livestock shows, the classic Texas-Oklahoma football game, and all manner of people watching.

"I like the State Fair," Steve offered.

"Cool. I hear that someone has deep-fried an entire double bacon cheeseburger this year. Sounds awesome!" Abby said.

Steve looked at Abby and found it hard to believe she could entertain eating such a thing. It was perplexing, and a little cute. More than a little. He wasn't sure he could handle one on his own. Much like had happened at the Texas Rangers' now-retired ballpark during their halcyon years of World Series contention when he was just a kid, the latest trend at the State Fair of Texas was the creation of gigantic food with enormous caloric value. Only the fair's fare was almost all fried. The fair restaurateurs all said their latest behemoths were meant to feed anywhere from four to ten people, but that didn't stop fairgoers from attempting to solo each year's "best giant taste" winner. Last year's winner was the Texas Brushfire, a cardiologist's waking nightmare. The nachos-inspired plate featured five-thousand calories of gooey fried cheese curds on a bed of maple syrup-coated fried bacon 'chips', drizzled with a smoked ghost pepper and Carolina reaper creamy salsa — and dipping cups of ranch dressing, naturally. Steve had tried a single bacon nacho last year, and while the flavors were great, the salsa was so spicy he couldn't taste anything else he ate the rest of that night. "Did you try the Texas Brushfire last year?" he asked.

Abby made a retching sound. "Yeah. Too spicy."

Steve smiled in agreement and felt a tingle of scorching memory on his taste buds.

They pulled into the Chick-fil-A after a short drive.

"I think I'll wait here if you don't mind," Gigi said. "All that grease clogs my pores."

Steve's R-Skill shot a knife of pain behind his eyes. He closed them and tried to shake the pain clear. "Suit yourself, you know what Ben will say," he said as he got out of the car. Gigi's self-importance was annoying enough. This new adversarial dynamic between her and Abby was altogether unwelcome where his efforts to avoid constant lying were concerned. Most days it was a painful, losing battle. He didn't need any more than he already received on a daily basis.

Inside the restaurant, Steve waved at Mr. Cordday, who was already eating at a table. He and Abby ordered their own lunches and sat down. The interviewee was as typical as school principals get: Caucasian, middle-aged, balding brown hair, a well-developed beer belly, and a plaid button-down shirt two decades out of fashion.

"Mr. Cordday, thank you for meeting with us. I'm Agent Palmer." Steve gestured to Abby. "And this is Agent Alstrom."

Abby stifled a giggle.

The principal seemed friendly enough, heartily shaking each of their hands before returning to his food. He picked up a large waffle fry and dunked it into his bowl of chicken noodle soup.

"That's… new." Abby said, staring.

Steve chuckled. "I've not seen that before, either."

Thom shrugged and chomped on the fry. "It's my thing." He offered his tray towards the agents, with a smile. "Try it."

Abby and Steve each took a smallish fry and dunked them in the soup. Steve found the flavor about what he expected.

"Meh," Abby said as she chewed. "I prefer the Honey Roasted Barbeque."

An employee delivered two trays of fried chicken and fries for them.

"Speak of the devil," Abby said, ripping open a packet of the yellowish sauce and squirting it under her sandwich bun.

Steve bit a nugget dipped with Polynesian sauce, then turned his tablet on. "So, tell us about your R-Skill. All it says here is it involves water."

Thom laughed. "Barely. It's the silliest thing. I can make things just a little bit damp. Here." He put his hand on a napkin sitting on the table, then withdrew it. The dry white paper was now slightly translucent and shriveled."

Abby stifled a laugh behind her sandwich.

"Silly, right?" Thom said.

Steve held his own laugh down. "Okay. Anything else? Fully controllable or sometimes involuntary?"

"That's pretty much it. As far as I know I can fully control it."

"When and where did you first notice your ability?"

"Oh," Thom paused to scratch his chin. "I think it was last week after I had lunch with some teachers from the school. We go to Chipotle every so often."

"Huh," Abby said, trading looks with Steve.

"Okay," Steve said. "Any concerns, or questions?"

"Nah, as far as abilities go, mine is pretty benign I'd say. I'm not too worried about it."

"Good." Steve took out an info pamphlet from his coat pocket. "Here's some information from RADSA with counseling resources, should you find yourself looking for someone to talk to." He held out the pamphlet, but Thom put his hand up.

"I'm good, thanks. Gotta get back to my school, have had teachers missing a lot of days lately." Thom said. He stood and shook Steve's hand, then Abby's.

She squirmed in her chair a little, looked startled for a moment, then stood with anger in her eyes. "Dude! Not cool!" She flung her soda at the principal then stormed away from the table.

"Jesus! Shit!" Thom yelped, shaking soda from his shirt.

Steve watched Abby disappear down the restroom hallway, eyebrows raised. "What just happened?" he asked.

"Hell if I know. Women, huh?" Thom looked more sheepish than upset as he flapped his soaked and likely ruined shirt.

Another spike of pain stabbed behind Steve's eyes. He immediately didn't like this guy.

"I'd better go. Need a change of clothes." Thom navigated around the mess on the table and waved. "Nice to meet you, Agent Palmer." He hastily left the restaurant, leaving the RADSA brochure on the table.

Steve assisted a Chick-fil-A employee in mopping up the tossed soda, then stood as Abby returned from the restroom.

"Did he leave?"

"Yeah, right after you tossed your drink on him."

"What a fucking creep!" Abby said, sitting down.

Steve moved around the table to sit opposite Abby. Her face was red with anger, cheeks tinged even darker with a layer of embarrassment. "What happened?" he asked.

"Ugh, nothing. I don't want to talk about it."

The stab of pain behind his eyes told him she was only half lying. He rubbed the bridge of his nose to work the pain away. "Come on Abby."

She rolled her eyes. "Sorry. How do you deal with it?" She drew an imaginary circle on her forehead with a finger. "I'm sure people are lying all day everywhere around you."

"At times, it truly sucks. I spend a lot of time in isolation."

"Sounds lonely," she said looking down at her sandwich.

"What did he do?"

Abby huffed an exasperated sigh. "He… made me… wet."

Steve looked at her hand, wondering what the big deal was.

"Down there," she added.

Then he got it. "Oh. Oh! That's…"

"It's nothing. Let's just finish lunch and move on."

"Are you sure? You don't want to tell the police or someone?"

"No."

Her face was red. And his head hurt again, but he let it drop. Instead, he picked up the tablet and added a note to Thom Cordday's entry: Potential sexual predator, recommend monitoring.

They finished lunch and went outside to find Gigi's car had moved several spaces. She had gone elsewhere and picked up a smoothie.

"Avocado, chia, spinach, and strawberry," she said, holding the cup up as if to offer a taste.

"I'll pass," Abby said.

Steve shook his head.

"How'd it go?" Gigi asked.

"Nothing special. Makes things a little damp," Steve said.

Gigi laughed, then looked at Abby, who merely shrugged with a pissed-off look on her face. "Okay then, who's next?"

CHAPTER 16
THE ADJUSTER

BEN SAT at his desk inside Bessie's trailer, attempting to complete his "Four Cs" report for Director Gustafson ahead of her press conference. He frowned at the numbers he had for the week. Communicate: Gigi had sent out ten tweets per day from the team's official Twitter account, fishing for information on Adapted in the area. They had received a paltry twenty-three likes for those seventy tweets, and a dozen comments that were mostly about irrelevant things (Gigi's latest workout videos). Catalog: Forty-five interviews performed. Collect: One new Adapted (Abby Alstrom) recruited to the team, bringing the group's size to six. Ten short of what was budgeted. Capture: Zero persons discovered with R-Skills on the Dangers to Society list.

He wasn't disappointed in that last one. Or any of them, really. Why would they want to have a team full of people with R-Skills that didn't amount to anything? He wanted a team with impact. A team that mattered. So far, every member of the squad brought something truly special to the table.

Eddie popped his head around the corner of the open office door. "Hey boss. What do you think of this?" He held out a new steel blue uniform like Gigi's. This one featured a wide stripe on either side that stretched from each shoulder down to the cuff of each pant leg, one black and one bright green. "For Abby."

Ben chuckled to himself. "Did she give you that suggestion?"

"I thought I'd surprise her."

Ben shrugged. "She seems pretty locked-in to her wardrobe of rock concert t-shirts and shredded jeans."

Eddie nodded. "I think she'll come around to it eventually."

"Maybe." Ben pointed to his screen. "I gotta finish this."

Eddie zipped out of view and Ben resumed his typing.

"Here's Bailey's." Eddie had returned to the doorway, holding a far-smaller suit with dashed yellow lines, a la road stripes, piped down the sleeves and legs.

"Sure, looks good. I really need to get this done."

"Okay."

Again, Eddie darted out of view, and Ben continued his report, now deep in the middle of the summary of the various R-Skills he and his team had encountered that week. An exchange student from Germany who could recite the current United States Tax Code in its entirety. A teacher that expelled ketchup from her nose. A principal who made things a little damp by touching them. Those last two were co-workers and developed their R-Skills within minutes of each other on the same day. In his comments, Ben proposed the RADSA research division in Washington D.C. investigate the frequency of two unrelated individuals in close proximity developing R-Skills at the same time. Perhaps there was a pattern to be found. Over three million people had developed an R-Skill since the UDO, so there had to be similar occurrences out there.

"Do you think Steve will want one?" Eddie said, again popping his head around the corner.

Ben rolled his eyes. The uniforms were a bit of a pet project he had come up with for Eddie to keep him busy. He'd like to take the biker on more interviews, but his heavily tattooed exterior proved to be intimidating to several people.

"Maybe. Just ask him."

"Okay." Eddie disappeared again.

A sigh slipped his lips. He was looking for something dramatic to include in his report to bolster the optics of his team's efforts, but there just wasn't anything going on.

"How about you?" Eddie asked.

Ben groaned. "No, Eddie." He rolled his neck and joints popped. In that instant, a thought went through his mind: *No more distractions today, Eddie.*

"You got it boss," Eddie said cheerily. He darted out of sight.

The hallway outside his office was well-lit, but dark from the black polycarbonate paneling that lined most of the walls of Bessie's trailer. Ben stared into the empty space, watching the darkness grow pitch black, until his vision was enveloped by the void of his horror. He had just used his ability on Eddie. Instinctively. Without even thinking about it. After cleaning up his failed engagement and netting his job from RADSA, Ben had made rules for himself. Apart from hiding his scar, he had refused to use his R-Skill on anyone for anything. The one exception he had made was when Steve joined the team. Ben allowed himself the leeway to cover up his own lies when he needed to, but rarely did. Such self-control was necessary to demonstrate that he was not a danger to society.

"Damn it," Ben muttered as he stood from his desk and walked out to the Bay.

Eddie was whistling to himself, continuing to cut fabric and ply changes to the uniform he was working on for Abby.

"Eddie, I..." Ben started, but couldn't think of something to say that would ease his conscious and not give something away that he'd have to use his R-Skill to fix.

The biker visibly jerked away from his station at Ben's words. "Uh, sorry boss. Didn't mean to bother you." He was shaking.

Ben swore at himself. *Be better*, he thought. He cracked a few knuckles and undid the adjustment he had made to Eddie moments before. The large man's discomfort eased.

"No, no. I just changed my mind. You can make me one too."

"Oh, okay. Any suggestions for the design?"

Ben almost blurted out 'island-themed' in self-chastising humor, but caught himself. "Something simple. Patriotic or RADSA-themed or something. Artist's choice." He flourished a respectful hand in Eddie's direction, then returned to his office, locking the door behind him.

He sat back down at his desk with a sigh. Instead of resuming his report, he stared at the mirror on the far wall. His horribly scarred visage stared back. Disapproving. Disgusted.

Keep it under control, he thought.

If only he could use his ability on himself.

CHAPTER 17
LUCKY

"I KNOW you're all eager to hear from me regarding the new unidentified dark object detected a few minutes ago. All I'm going to say on the matter is to repeat what the scientific community has already stated. This new object — asteroid, comet fragment, whatever you want to call it — has been determined to be of a size and trajectory that will pose no threat to humanity when it lands."

A number of reporters' hands went up.

"Whiiiiich will be in the southern Pacific Ocean, a thousand miles off the coast of Antarctica in the middle of nowhere. This one is small. It will not impact atmospheric health. A few ships may be in for a rough ride if they choose not to alter course, but all American vessels we're aware of in the area have been notified, and it is my understanding that all will be safely clear of the impact area."

He took a drink of water and closed his eyes to collect his thoughts. Then he checked his watch. *I guess there's time for a question or two,* he thought. He pointed to Derek Schwartz of YouTube, whose seat had recently been moved up to the third row by the White House Correspondents Association. The little white flowers on the reporter's head jiggled ever-so-slightly when he heard his name called.

"Thank you, Mr. President," Schwartz said as he stood. The Adapted was beaming. "Has there been any progress in identifying the source of the UDOs, assuming they originated from the same place?" he asked.

"Thanks Derek," Phelps said. "There's no way for us to know at this point if the UDO that destroyed the Korean Peninsula and the one that will splash into the Pacific today come from the same place. They may, they may not. Right now, our best guess is they are merely another form of interstellar matter that we simply had not come across before last year. They're more or less asteroids that are simply hard to track."

He pointed to another reporter, but Megan Lykos, his Chief of Staff, rushed up to the podium and whispered something in the president's ear. Phelps raised his eyebrows while sipping his water, then put on a serious face.

"Ladies and gentlemen, I apologize for the interruption. Meg has just informed me a second small UDO has just been spotted and will also splash down somewhere in the Pacific soon. I'm afraid I'll have to cut this short and head to the Situation Room. We'll send out an official statement when we know more. Thank you."

CHAPTER 18
GARBAGE GIRL

A SHARP DAGGER of sunlight stabbed Abby in the face, rousing her from a pleasant dream of watching the Foo Fighters perform at Lollapalooza in Chicago. They were playing in panda costumes, each with attire and patterned fur to look like one of the members from the band KISS. Dave Grohl, the Foos' frontman, wore the outfit that looked like the KISS drummer Starman and shot light from his mouth as he sang/screamed.

"I have got to see that concert," Abby said as she rubbed the sleep from her eyes, wondering if the singer actually had an R-Skill.

Her phone buzzed once. She looked at it and caught the time. 7:10AM.

"Shit!"

The text was from Steve. "Wakey, wakey." It was the third he had sent, after "I'm here" and "Ready?".

"Dammit!"

He had driven her home yesterday and offered to give her car-less ass a ride to work today. Steve had said they were 'going to eleven', which seemed code for something cool, plus an excellent reference to *This is Spinal Tap*, the rock band mockumentary and one of Abby's favorite movies. *Watch him leave without me*, she thought. Abby mashed a reply into the screen as she tumbled into the bathroom. "Crap, sorry. Gimme 10 mins." She turned the shower on and groaned when the water barely got past the comfort level of an outdoor swimming pool in summer. The apartment community's boiler was overtaxed every morning, and she was bringing up the rear of the pack today. Despite his protestations, her old boss Carl was fairly lenient on when she showed up, and ordinarily she would have just made breakfast and waited for the water to get enjoyably hot. Today wasn't that kind of day. Her inner self-loathing at oversleeping boiled hot enough for her to tolerate stepping into the tepid stream. Furiously scrubbing, she eked the last dregs of hot water from the pipes, then jumped out. She scrambled into some clothes — yesterday's jeans, a free sponsored-by-Dr Pepper T-shirt she caught at a Rangers game, and her trusty blue Rangers hat.

She raced outside, then caught herself on the steps downstairs, realizing she forgot to lock the door. Why was she hurrying? She didn't think Steve would care much, aside from the potential to make him late, which he could always blame on her. And despite his reputation, Ben seemed so easygoing that Abby thought he wouldn't actually enforce the penalty for being late. Whatever that was. She only knew he was a 'stickler' for people being on time. She turned the key in the deadbolt, looked down the steps, and felt anticipation warm her insides. She was actually looking forward to work. The previous day meeting all those other Adapted was fun — creepy middle school principal aside. Her work for Charles and Munck had never provided such satisfaction, and she had been there for months. Abby bounded down the steps with a wide smile. Steve was waiting in his unassuming, muted gold Toyota Camry with the window down, listening to NPR.

"Hey," she said.

"Hey yourself." He looked up from his phone and smiled.

A small tingle went up her spine. She stopped to take in his smile. It was something. He pointed a thumb behind him, suggesting they should go. She walked around and got in. The car was meticulously clean inside. The basic tan cloth seats and simple radio told her that this was a base model Camry. She smiled as she looked around. "So, did you pick the color to make a low-volume statement, or to avoid standing out too much?"

Steve shot her a raised eyebrow that said, 'That's how we're starting our day?', then put the car in motion and got on the road. "Bit of both I suppose." He said nothing further for a few minutes as he merged into the slow molasses of morning traffic.

They sat in silence, save for the din of engines rumbling on all sides of the car as they inched along. She attempted to find a comfortable position in the seat and hoped to come up with a less insulting way to reintroduce conversation. He beat her to it.

"If we get marked down for being late, you're taking the blame," Steve said. He looked at her, face stoic.

She wanted to think he was just joking, but as she understood his R-Skill, Steve could only tell the truth. Falsifying a statement like that might cause his nose to gush blood or head to explode. She laughed.

"What?" he asked.

"Oh, I was just hoping you might be joking and wondering what would happen if you didn't tell the truth."

"I am incapable of lying, fabrication, or jokes. At least ones that misrepresent the truth for humor."

She shook her head, smiling. "You must be a hit with all the girls."

He shrugged.

"So, you couldn't, like, tell Agent Rice we had to turn around because I forgot something?"

"Did you forget something?"

"Well, yes, but I wasn't going to suggest we turn around."

He raised a curious eyebrow. "What did you forget?"

Abby sat up straight, folded her arms, and looked straight at the traffic ahead. "I am presently riding commando." She made a show of squirming in her seat and stifled a giggle. It was kind of fun being completely honest with someone.

Steve looked her up and down twice. "Well, you aren't lying." He tapped his forehead.

Abby mocked indignation. "Okay, Mr. Psychic Truthteller. If you already knew that, what's with the eye scan? Do you have X-Ray vision too?"

"No, but I do have an imagination." He turned his head back to the road, but then looked back at her with one eye and a wide grin.

She shoved him and covered her smile. "Agent Palmer!"

The car jerked a little in its lane as Steve recovered and held his palms up on the steering wheel. "Only being honest!"

He scanned her up and down again, smiling. This time, Abby felt her cheeks flush. She gazed out her window to hide it.

"What I could say," Steve started, "is that you forgot something. If he asks a follow-up question, you can ad lib it, and I'll try not to wince."

"Eh, don't give yourself an aneurysm. I can take my medicine if Agent Rice is upset about it."

Their destination that morning was the hiding-in-plain-sight headquarters for the North Texas RADSA team. It was a large warehouse sitting in a massive complex in north Irving, about five minutes from DFW airport. Three stories tall, metal sides with a shade of paint that could only be called 'nondescript' on a swatch somewhere. It had one window, placed between its two doors. One door was for people. The other, for Bessie. Above the smaller door, a pair of distressed metal number ones indicated the building number.

"So, Warehouse 11 is just the eleventh building in this complex? I thought that name was code for something."

"Nope. Just a warehouse. The last tenants had a bunch of guitar amplifiers stored here."

Abby realized he wasn't joking and laughed as they got out of his car.

"What?" Steve asked with a confused look on his face.

She put her hands on her hips. "Haven't you seen *This Is Spinal Tap*?"

"Well, sure, like when I was ten," he replied, then chuckled when he got the reference to the up-to-eleven volume knob on the lead guitarist's amplifier in the movie. "Oh. Hah. That's funny." He held the door open for her as they walked in.

Inside, the space was cavernous. Polished concrete floor, a bank of sofas surrounding a TV in one corner, an office on the far wall next to the restrooms, and a workout area with weights, benches, and a padded floor in another corner. Next to them by the front door was a large area covered by rubber mats where Bessie would be parked.

"What's that metal box for?" Abby asked, pointing to what looked like a small shipping container with a door on it and a big red button on a box by the door. It was isolated in the other corner of the space.

"That..." Ben said as he walked up, "...is the isolation tank. In the unfortunate event we come across someone that has to go to Island-A, agency policy is for them to be detained in the tank under effect of the gas until they depart."

Abby scoffed. "That sounds inhumane, Ben."

"It's a little draconian, I know. But in the case of a violent Adapted or an unpredictable R-Skill on the D2S list, it's for our safety, as much as the occupant's. There's a bed, bathroom, and TV in there. We'll do our best to make them comfortable. Hopefully, we'll never have to use it." He flourished his hand to the rest of the warehouse. "Welcome to Warehouse Eleven."

If Ben was upset at Steve and Abby showing up almost an hour late, he gave no sign. He said that he would be heading out to Fort Worth in Bessie for the day, but wanted to see her settled in first and sign her paperwork. The day at the warehouse started with said paperwork, to be followed by a litany of policy, safety, and sensitivity training videos. Abby wasn't looking forward to slogging through all of them, but her mood significantly improved when she found out her salary would be even higher than what Ben had told her over the phone. It was a huge raise from what she had been making at her old job. She even managed to talk her new boss into a signing bonus to start so she could get a car. Ben had shrugged and written her a check on the spot without a second thought. Evidently, budget wasn't a concern. She patted her back pocket every so often to make sure the check was still there, though she resolved to stay on Steve's good side for as long as she could to milk his carpool generosity for as far as it would go. A smile crossed her lips at that thought. Her initial impression of Steve was way off. She smiled even wider when she realized her bank account would soon have a balance over $3,000 for the first time ever. The severance check from C&M would make it even better. Tyson would have been so excited. She bit her tongue again, hoping the pain would obscure the strange not-quite-guilty-feeling gnawing at her gut. It wasn't helping.

She nestled into one of the cushy black leather sofas in the lounge area and got to work watching mind numbing training videos. The TV on the near wall was playing the local morning news on mute. She found her attention pulled away from the videos every few minutes, but each time she looked at the TV, all they were showing was the nothing-but-sun five-day forecast. Not a cloud in the sky, or a daytime high below 100 degrees. She wasn't a huge fan of the heat.

After managing to absorb most of the first training video, she saw the next was something about integrity in government contracting and sighed a huge yawn of disinterest. She pulled her phone out to check out the headlines on A-Space, but saw that the battery was drained. Per usual, she had forgotten to plug it in the night before. "Damn thing," she said as she tossed it to the table. The clatter caught Steve's attention. He said he understood her boredom and offered her a coffee.

"Thanks, but I prefer Dr Pepper."

"Ask Bailey to put some in the fridge," he said. "Right now it's just full of Gigi's Gatorade. How's the training coming? Which video is this?"

She hadn't even been paying attention. "Uh… 'Dangers to Society and Island-A'."

Steve whistled. "That one's a doozy."

"Can you believe they — I mean, *we* — don't even allow family members to say goodbye when someone's going to the island? How inhumane is that?" Abby shook her head.

"Seems cruel on the surface. But it's for everyone's safety."

"It's terrible. I hope we never have to do that."

"You know what's worse? The next training video." Steve smiled as he took a seat on the opposite sofa with his laptop.

Abby looked at the title of the next video. "Department of Homeland Security: Integrity in Defense Contracting?"

Steve pursed his lips and raised his eyebrows at her.

Abby sighed and was about to start the video when Bessie's engine roared to life and drowned the warehouse in a rumbling cacophony. The backing alert beeps came on, and Bessie slowly retreated outside with Bailey, Ben, and Eddie on board. Abby smiled as she wondered how little Bailey could handle such an enormous vehicle. Before leaving for Fort Worth, Ben left instructions that the rest of the team should write their reports for the previous day's interviews, then visit with a probable 'acquisition' target named Jezekiel Thomas after lunch.

It didn't take long for Abby's eyes to glaze over while watching the defense contracting video. "Ugh, this sucks," Abby said. "I can't wait to do a super-fun and exciting report!"

He grimaced. "Actually, they're rather detailed and tedious. But it's the only way the RADSA database gets its data."

Abby saw him rubbing his forehead and could feel the rapport they had built in the car unraveling like a sweater. She frowned.

"Shit. Sorry."

He raised a hand. "It's okay." A forced smile creased his lips. "It's a rare conversation when that doesn't happen. I'm mostly used to the small stuff by now."

As Steve had described it, each falsehood he heard caused a stabbing sensation behind his eyes. She couldn't imagine dealing with that on a constant basis.

She shook her head and smiled, patting him on the shoulder. "That just sucks."

He looked down. "Yeah, sometimes."

"Wanna show me how to do a report?"

"Sure." He got up and sat next to Abby.

"Did you get your account set up and all that?" Steve asked.

"Yeah, I did that yesterday. Surprisingly fast turnaround. Took like a month to get an email address at Charles & Munck."

"RADSA is well-funded at the behest of the president, it seems."

"Yeah, I can see that."

Between all the gadgets on Bessie, her signing bonus, and the enormous headquarters, her team seemed beyond well-funded. She wondered if all the regional teams were so lucky.

"Are you good with computers? Or are you more of a work-with-your-hands type?" Steve asked.

Abby raised an eyebrow and scoffed. "I'm better at computers than you, pencil pusher."

He stretched back from her in surprise. "Evidently you are, according to my R-Skill."

The primary system and database were called RADSAnet, of course. Steve showed her how to request a secure key fob to log in from remote locations, the interview report process, and where to go to search and view submitted information. None of it seemed out of the ordinary.

"Ooh, can I see what you wrote about me?"

"No, we're restricted from viewing our own record. And I'd rather that you didn't. You're turning out to be quite different than what I put down in my report."

"Agent Palmer, I'm crushed! You mean to tell me I'm more complicated than what an hour-long interview revealed while I was gassed into a stupor? I thought I was shallower than that!"

He winced again.

Abby loosed an exasperated groan. "Fuck! You're gonna hate me in short order."

"Maybe you'll pelt me with so much sarcasm that I'll become fully desensitized to the minor pain."

"Well, if you want me to give it a shot…"

He held up his hands. "No." Then softer, "No." His face had the look of resignation.

Abby had it pretty good, as far as R-Skills went. Hers had its limits, but didn't have any negative drawbacks. Steve's definitely did, and it grated at her that she would be a routine source of headaches for him. She resolved to attempt to reign in her tongue and forced an apologetic smile. "Okay then, show me this report business."

True to form, the interview report process was dry and tedious. Steve showed her where to pull up his notes from the prior day's interviews, then opened up the report form. First up were dozens of text boxes for easy things like various physical characteristics and mannerisms. Abby thought she'd need a notebook to remember those types of details, and wondered why they were all required fields. Next came a large box for a detailed description of the interviewee's R-Skill with a note to remember to include drawbacks and limitations. After that came more subjective fields for psychological profile, prediction on long term stability, short term needs analysis, and, naturally, the danger to society assessment. Then came an optional box for a suggested code name. She wondered which of the team had the bright idea to call her Garbage Girl. Probably Gigi. Lastly, a lone question at the bottom of the form asked, "Transport to Island-A?" The yes/no radio buttons seemed cruelly insufficient to cast a vote for such a fate.

"That's it?" Abby asked. "Doesn't seem so bad."

"You will be doing these a *lot*. And Ben reviews them before they go to RADSAnet. He is a stickler for editing and grammar and loves to ask for more detail." Steve waved his hand above her head as if anointing her with an imaginary wand. "You have now been forewarned," he uttered in a raspy voice.

Then he smiled. That smile. Another tingle went up Abby's spine. She was really beginning to like this guy. She raised her arms and bowed toward him in exaltation. "Oh, wizened one, I am humbled by your bountiful tutelage." Her movement had the effect of sliding them closer to each other on the sofa. She raised her head back up and they locked eyes for a silent moment.

"Uh, hey you two — whatcha doin?"

They both looked towards the entrance to see Gigi approaching, eyebrows raised, sipping something so bright green it looked radioactive.

"I was showing Abby how to submit an interview report," Steve said.

"Ah. Right." Gigi said, walking up to the lounge. "Those."

Abby caught Gigi's suspicious stare and scooched a little away from Steve. "I'm just about to start with Mrs. Ketchup from Garland. Wanna join us?" she asked.

Gigi laughed, then shook her head slightly, patting a laptop under her arm. "Nah, I did mine last night on the treadmill while listening to podcasts." She plopped her things on a chair. "While you do yours, I'm gonna go workout and make some videos for my channel." Dressed in her usual form-fitting yoga attire — red and black today, Gigi stretched her arms overhead, thrusting her chest out and making a point to look directly at Steve, then jogged over to the workout area at the opposite side of the warehouse.

"High achieve much?" Abby muttered.

"She's fine, once you get to know her." Steve said.

"I'll believe that when I see it, Mr. Honesty," Abby said. She logged into her account and started her first report on one Rosa Taliveras.

CHAPTER 19
BOUNCY

AFTER HER WORKOUT, Gigi sat down in the lounge to review the footage from her cameras. Abby was diligently typing away at a laptop across the table, while Steve had gone out to collect lunch for everyone. She sipped at her smoothie that in the intervening hour had grown unpleasantly warm.

"What are you drinking?" Abby asked. "It looks like the precious drippings from a bunch of glow sticks."

Gigi took a long, deliberate sip, forcing down each swallow with a smile. "Wheatgrass, kale, mango, and a few other things. It's good. Made it myself. Wanna try it?" She held up the cup, already knowing the answer. "You look like you could use a vegetable. Might develop some color in your skin other than sickly white."

"I happen to be allergic to any vegetables that aren't fried or drowning in ranch dressing. And I'm quite proud of my pasty white heritage, thank you very much." Abby folded her arms with a smug smile.

"And what heritage is that? Weren't you adopted by some Koreans?"

Abby shot Gigi an annoyed look. "They're my foster family, not that it's any of your business."

Gigi smiled to herself. This was a sore spot for Abby she could poke at. "Did you know your parents?"

"Again, not that it's your business, but not really. I was five when they died after eating some bad sushi."

Gigi had to stifle a laugh. She loved a good plate of sashimi. "That's… tragic."

Abby shrugged. "I don't dwell on it. I think they were Swedish." She pulled her baseball cap off and ruffled her spiky blonde hair.

A tinge of envy nibbled at Gigi's gut. She went for treatments every month to keep her blonde color perfect.

Abby went back to her reports, and Gigi resumed moving footage from her cameras to her phone for editing. Nothing noteworthy. She had hours upon hours of videos of her going through floor routines, bouncing roof-high off the concrete floor, and running — well, bouncing along — faster than a cheetah. None of it had brought her fame, and not for lack of trying. All the talent agents her parents had managed to connect with suggested Gigi's R-Skill wasn't out of the ordinary enough to achieve the kind of rocket-trajectory stardom Hollywood producers were looking to get out of fresh Adapted faces. One had the audacity to call into question her fitness level and to suggest she simply wasn't pretty enough. He was just bitter because she wouldn't go out on a date with his warty toad ass. She still had a couple agents to whom she sent particularly good videos, but the rest had tuned her out in favor of the latest person that could turn their teeth purple or correctly guess the days of freshness left in a carton of eggs (it was always weeks after the suggested date). Gigi was left to her own devices to build an audience. She followed the social media playbook — lots of videos, bubbly personality, fan interaction, and plenty of T&A. She enjoyed the process but loathed the lack of results. Of her many virtues, patience was not one.

Steve crashed through the door a few minutes later, bearing a large bag from Chipotle. He pulled out two salads and a behemoth of a burrito that was testing the limits of its aluminum wrapping. Abby grabbed the burrito and began chomping away.

Gigi gave a fake retch. "Ugh. How can you eat that? The tortilla is almost an entire day's worth of calories on its own."

Abby shrugged. "I dunno. I poop a lot?"

Steve snorted and choked on his soda.

"Gross," Gigi said, cringing. She pulled the lid off her salad and picked at the chicken. She looked at Steve and Abby sitting next to each other and exchanging smiles. Of course, he would get friendly with the new girl on the team, and of course she would be interested in him. Just like he and Gigi had done a few months back. It didn't take her but a few days to grow tired of Steve's 'truth' act. In her opinion, he plied his own opinions as the truth far too often. Despite his looks, it wouldn't take long for Abby to grow tired of it too. But she didn't see what Steve could see in Abby. Aside from being skinny, the girl brought little to the table. Snarky, average face, wearing the stupid baseball hat and concert T-shirts all the time, and no family or money to speak of. Steve glanced in her direction. Gigi rolled her eyes in return. She then turned her head toward the TV so she didn't have to watch them anymore. She saw the breaking news headline and cocked her head.

"Hey. What was the name of the guy we're supposed to interview this afternoon?" Gigi asked.

"Jezekiel Thomas," Steve said, mouth half full of greens.

"Like, Zeke Thomas?" Gigi pointed at the screen.

"Oh, shit," Abby said.

"Wow. That's…" Steve trailed off.

"Fucked up!" Gigi finished.

On the screen, live video from a news camera drone showed a young man with creamy brown skin sitting on the edge of a highway overpass. The graphics overlaid on the screen said his name was Zeke Thomas. The line beneath his name read 'Suicidal Adapted'.

Steve pulled out his tablet and tapped at it. "Yeah, that's him."

"I guess our afternoon just opened up," Gigi said.

"What?" Abby slapped her hands on the table. "We should go help him!"

"How?" Gigi asked. "It's not like they're going to let us near him."

"We're RADSA. Aren't we, like, supposed to intervene in moments of crisis and shit?" Abby said.

Steve chuckled. "Only when we're asked."

"Fuuuuuuuuuck that," Abby said as she stood up. "He's one of us. Let's go save a life." She motioned towards the door.

"I guess it couldn't hurt, it's ten minutes from here," Steve shrugged.

Gigi yawned and grabbed her salad. "Whatever. You drive. I'm gonna finish lunch."

———

Traffic already moved at a summer turtle's crawl by the time they approached the intersection of the president George H W Bush Turnpike and Interstate 35. The three busied themselves with the sharing of each other's social lives. Steve had a couple buddies from the Marines he saw on occasion. Abby's was mostly her family, and the Tyson guy she killed (which was awkward to listen to). Gigi mentioned her friend Kendra and a few friends from her college sorority at the University of Texas whom she rarely spoke to anymore because they were all off planning extravagant weddings or making babies already.

Steve parked his car to the side of the road ahead of where it turned into a bridge and several police cars had blocked lanes to usher traffic onto an exit. A uniformed officer barked at them with a bullhorn as they got out.

"No spectators! Get back in your car and off the road!"

Steve took the lead, Gigi and Abby following a few steps behind. He approached the officer with one hand in the air holding a business card.

The officer took the business card and looked the three of them over. "RADSA? Here? What do you hope to accomplish?"

"We'd like to talk to him, officer," Steve said.

"He's not talking to anyone. Pretty sure he would jump if you walked over and offer him a trip to Island-A," the officer said.

"Based on his profile, he wouldn't be a candidate to go there," Steve said, matter-of-factly.

"Is that so? Listen, we..." the officer began.

Abby cut him off. "He's Adapted, we're Adapted. He'll talk to us."

The officer's eyes widened. He looked at each of them in turn. "All of you?"

Gigi folded her arms and subtly pushed her breasts up through her tank top, enhancing their cleavage. "Yup. It's kind of our thing. We were actually supposed to interview him this afternoon."

"I see." The officer took the bait and stared at her chest a little too long. "Uh, yeah, why not. But go talk to the chief over there first." He pointed to another man in uniform farther up the highway bridge.

"We should get government badges we can whip out like the FBI or something. Look all official," Abby said as they walked up the bridge.

Steve chuckled.

"Do you want to have to carry that around with you all the time?" Gigi asked. "We already have government IDs."

"Well, no. But still, it'd be cool," Abby said.

"Yes, it would," Steve agreed.

They reached the police chief, and after reciting practically the same spiel they had with the first cop, got a fleet-footed escort through the line of first responders keeping the media at bay. Ahead, they saw

Jezekiel Thomas sitting on the concrete barrier, legs dangling over the side. He was precariously close to a terminus that would undoubtedly leave far more people upset over the disruption to their evening commutes than those distressed over the loss of a life. A crowd of police and firemen had cordoned off the area with traffic cones, yellow caution tape, and stern looks. Some officers were discussing with some guys in plainclothes — probably negotiators — what the best approach would be to talk the subject off the wall. Several media cameras were set up behind the cordon, and a number of news drones hovered in the air nearby.

"What are we even going to say?" Gigi asked, still unsure what they thought they were going to accomplish here.

"I'm probably not the right person to speak," Steve said. "I don't have a filter."

"I'll do it," Abby said eagerly. "I want to."

She took the lead, moving slowly from the side so Zeke could see them approach. Steve and Gigi followed. The police chief and several others trailed behind.

"Hi, uh, Zeke? Jezekiel Thomas?" Abby asked as she got close enough to be heard over the din of the cars zipping by in the northbound lanes. The southbound lanes were empty, diverted to the access road that went under the section of bridge they had already passed. Every few seconds, horns argued over who was at fault for the heavy road congestion.

The shade of a higher overpass brought some relief from the sun's glare, but the summer heat still baked. The young man's dark skin glistened, a likely combination of the heat and nerves. He had a handsome close crop of curly black hair. He wore cheap jeans, a white polo shirt wet with sweat, and a flour-dusted black apron. Sitting mere inches from a fatal fall, his feet dangled over the edge of the tan concrete barrier, streaked with various shades of car paint and tire rubber. One shaking hand gripped a mile marker, the other held onto the barrier. He wobbled slightly, as if swaying in the humid summer breeze. He had been staring off in the distance, and turned in surprise when he heard Abby's voice. "Who are you? Don't come any closer!"

Abby put a hand behind her as if to signal for the others to stay behind, but she approached another three steps. "My name is Abby. This is Steve, and Gigi. We're from RADSA."

"RADSA? Really? You wanna get your interview in before I fall to my death?" Zeke scoffed.

"No," Abby said, "I want you to come off that wall. Forget the interview."

Zeke looked her up and down. "You don't look like a RADSA agent." He looked around her to Steve. "He does." He looked at Gigi. "She looks like a gymnast."

A swell of pride tickled Gigi's stomach.

"All three of us are," Steve called out.

"Gigi *is* a gymnast — very observant by the way, but also an agent. I am too. I'm new, just my second day." Abby said. "We're a relaxed bunch. You look like you could use some relaxation."

Zeke snorted, holding back tears and wiping his face. "I need my girlfriend back. I thought we were gonna get married."

"This is over a girl?" Gigi said under her breath. "Good grief."

Steve elbowed her in the ribs.

Abby stood motionless in thought for a moment with a frown on her face, then took another step. She was just ten feet from him now. "Oh man, that sucks. I, uh, recently lost a boyfriend too."

Zeke rolled his eyes. "You didn't lose yours because you're a damn Adapted."

"Actually," Abby said, "I did."

He looked at her in surprise. "What — really?"

"Yeah. All of us are." Abby pointed back to Steve and Gigi.

"Huh."

Abby stepped closer. "If I tell you what happened, can you keep a secret?"

Zeke recoiled away from her, a dangerous move when sitting on the outside of a bridge safety rail. He looked more concerned that Abby would push him off, than attempt to pull him back.

Abby held up her hands. "I promise I won't try to grab you or anything."

"Uh, okay," Zeke said.

Abby slowly approached, holding her palms out. She got within a foot of Zeke and leaned over to speak to his ear.

Gigi couldn't make out what she said over the noise from the traffic. "What's she saying?"

"I don't know," Steve said.

Zeke turned his head and looked at Abby in surprise. "Oh shit!"

Abby nodded with a grim frown on her face. She took one step back, then changed course and stepped closer to him.

Zeke began talking to her in a low voice, shaking his head every few sentences. Abby reached out and put a hand on his shoulder, talking softly.

"She's got him," Gigi whispered. "All she has to do is pull him back and it's over."

"That's not the outcome she's hoping to get," Steve said.

Zeke laughed, suddenly. Abby patted his shoulder. "Can I sit down next to you?" she said, loud enough to be heard.

"What?" Steve asked, alarmed. "Abby —" He took a step forward, then stopped to hold back the first responders that had gathered around.

Abby turned and looked at Steve and winked, waving him back.

"Girl's got a death wish," Gigi said. She didn't exactly hope that Abby would fall over the side, but the thought did pass through her head.

"She knows what she's doing," Steve said, far louder than necessary.

Gigi looked at him, surprised he would say something so silly. She saw the painless look of focus on his face and realized he wasn't joking. But the furtive look in his eyes said that he didn't quite believe what he said, despite his rock-solid faith in his R-Skill. He really did like this girl. Stupid. Gigi pulled her phone out and started recording for posterity. She wanted to be able to show this to him later after he came to his senses about their latest teammate.

Abby sat down next to Zeke. She then swung her legs up and over the railing and turned around to face the same direction Zeke was. Her hands clutched the top of the barrier; her knuckles were white. They continued to talk. Abby edged herself closer, and closer still, until they were touching. She put her arm around his back, and after a moment, Zeke did the same around hers.

Steve had a worried look on his face. "What are you doing, Abby?" He asked under his breath, toeing closer towards the pair on the rail.

Gigi followed. "Is she… seducing him?" she asked.

Steve looked at her with wide eyes, mouth agape and eyebrows reaching for his hairline.

Abby stroked the back of Zeke's neck. He shuddered. She had a purposeful smile, and he looked like he was enjoying the physical attention way too much. Abby giggled as she continued to talk below the noise of the highway below. Zeke laughed. She reached around him and gave him a big hug, then waved at Steve for help in getting back over the railing. Zeke waved too.

The crisis was over. At Abby's gesture, Steve and several firemen walked purposefully up to the concrete rail and delicately pulled her over, followed by Zeke. He hugged Abby, then accepted an escort into the back of a police cruiser. Steve handed the officer a business card.

Gigi stopped filming. While Steve and Abby shook hands and clapped backs with the first responders, Gigi stared over the edge of the highway and marveled at what had just happened. *What a coup for the team*, she thought. They would certainly receive commendations from Ben and probably Director Gustafson not long after. Steve motioned for them to walk back to his car, and Gigi took up position behind the other two, playing back the footage she recorded. The audio was fairly useless due to the background noise, but Abby's bravery was there front and center. And then it occurred to Gigi that she herself wasn't. The North Texas RADSA team would make the evening news, and she wasn't the star. Abby would get the praise. Abby would be interviewed. Abby would get the likes and mentions.

At once, Gigi felt drained, like she did in her final U.S. Olympic trials a few years ago. Her body had gone cold sitting on the bench too long waiting for her turn, but worse, her mind was out of it. She recalled the last vault she ever did in competition. The gymnast right before her turn had attempted a Produnova. The difficult move requires a front handspring and two tucked somersaults, something Gigi had never even attempted in practice, much less considered bringing to a meet. The other competitor had over-rotated and landed on her face, stunning Gigi and silencing the crowd. It took nearly fifteen minutes for the medical team to escort the poor girl from the floor, the event staff to clean up the blood from her broken nose, and the competition to resume. Despite jogging around to keep limber and doing her best to push the scene from her mind, Gigi's head focused on a freeze frame of the blood splatter fanned out from the girl's mangled face. Her brain was mush as she did her Amanar vault — a difficult maneuver on its own with two-and-a-half twists after a backflip, but no Produnova. She got off the center line too far and took a giant step after landing. After placing tenth, more than one coach told her to give up the dream. She was too old, and just not getting any better. Gigi knew it too, but still bawled her eyes out the rest of the afternoon. The following day, she resolved to never let someone else take her dream away from her, whatever that ended up being.

As she stared off over the side of the bridge at the highway below, Gigi realized Abby had nailed a proverbial Produnova on just her second day on the job.

CHAPTER 20
THE SLEUTH

"I MUST SAY ABBY, I didn't expect that from you," Steve said.

"Why not?" Abby replied, not looking up from her phone.

He stared at the parking lot of cars in front of them as they sat in traffic. "Well," he paused, trying to form his impression into words. "You were very, uh, friendly with him, for a stranger. You didn't strike me as someone who cared that much. I guess." He looked over at her.

She shrugged, then met his eyes. "I don't care."

A wave of unexpected calm came over his brain. He wouldn't have expected such an answer to ring true. "I don't understand. What you did for Zeke…"

"On a macro level, I don't care. What good can a foster kid barely attached to a squarely middle-class family do on a large scale? I'm not going to be a celebrity, nor do I want to be one like Gigi does. I don't have the personal network to get into politics or be a CEO. I don't care to try to change the world because I know I don't possess the raw materials necessary. And I'm at peace with that. All I want is to not worry about next month's rent and eat better than microwave ramen seven days a week."

Steve laughed. "So say we all. That still doesn't explain—"

"Wait. Was that a Battlestar Galactica reference? Nerd much?"

Steve nodded with a smile.

She smiled back, then sighed. "At a personal level, sure I care. It would be inhumane not to, right? To see someone suffering right in front of you and not be compelled to do something if it's within your power? Plus, despite the positive spin A-Space puts on all things Adapted, it's hard out there for a lot of us still."

Steve had to agree. He knew it without his R-Skill telling him it was true.

"Zeke seemed like a nice enough guy. Put yourself in his shoes. Think about how you'd feel about never being able to kiss anyone again."

"Yeah. I guess that would be disappointing."

"Disappointing?" She mimicked his tone. "To me, that's the first step to full-on depression. Kissing is like the best part of a new relationship!"

Steve could sense her veracity. "You must really like kissing."

"You don't?"

"Well sure I do. But I guess I always felt it was just the first step on the path to, uh… better things."

Abby rolled her eyes. "Ugh. Always thinking with your pants, huh?"

Steve raised an eyebrow. Knowing he couldn't say anything but the truth, he played his answer off as sarcastically as possible. "Always."

She eyed him up and down. "That's not such a bad thing."

His pulse jumped. He looked at her in surprise as again her words felt true.

"Sometimes."

"Is that so?" he asked, already knowing her answer.

She gave a wry smile and turned back to her phone.

Blood rushed to his head. He turned up the A/C one notch and loosened his tie.

Abby scoffed. "Why do you even wear the suit? It's not like we have a dress code."

"I don't know. I think it's professional."

She wiggled her fingers in air quotes and mimed one of the RADSA training videos. "Choose an appearance that you believe will put your interview subjects at ease." She scoffed. "*You* don't even look at ease."

Steve shrugged. "I think it looks good."

"You *do* look good," Abby's face turned red. "In the suit, I mean." She looked out her window. "Seems to me they'd be uncomfortable in the heat."

"It's not too bad. I guess I could go casual more often."

"Hell. I'd wear shorts every day if I wasn't so pasty white."

Steve chuckled. "You could just stay indoors."

"And miss all this beautiful traffic?"

He hit the brakes as a box truck swerved in front of them just as traffic came to yet another halt. The truck had a decorative, anatomically correct penis scrawled into the grime on its rear door. Steve pointed. "Are you into modern art?"

Abby looked up from her phone and laughed. "Wow. Nice detail. I'm more into movies, though."

Steve reveled in the wash of calm from her honest words and baffled at the ease of their conversation. For the first time since he had come to grips with the good and bad of his R-Skill, he found himself looking forward to talking with someone. "I like movies, they don't trigger my R-Skill."

"Have you seen the new Termin8or yet?" Abby asked.

"Nah, I'm not interested," Steve said. "The last couple weren't great. And it's not like Arnold Schwarzenegger needs the work."

"Aw, c'mon. He's an Adapted like us. That's pretty cool."

"Yeah, but how many more of his movies can we take? He puts out three a year! Great for him his R-Skill de-aged him back to his 30-year-old prime. But after so many sequels, prequels, and spinoffs to his back catalogue, he's almost a prop in his own movies."

Abby shrugged. "I still think they're fun."

"Wanna go?"

She looked at him and raised a surprised eyebrow. "I think we're obligated — for work purposes, of course."

"Of course," he said with a grin.

The anatomically correct truck swerved again, cutting off another driver in the next lane as traffic slowly inched forward. Steve moved his Camry ahead to get past the grimy visual.

"Hmm," Abby said, tapping away at her phone. "Says here you were in the marines."

He raised an eyebrow at her. "That was a few years ago. Reading up on me?"

"Just trying to get to know my chauffeur better, Corporal Palmer. So, what was that like?"

A long-ignored knot in his stomach churned. "I... don't really like to talk about it."

"Oh. Okay then. What'd you do between that and joining RADSA?"

———

Pandemonium. Chaos. Louder than the twin rotors of a hovering V-22 Osprey. The jubilant crowd had only just begun to quiet in its third hour of celebrating Lawrence Phelps' decisive victory in the presidential election. Stray rectangles of red, white, and blue tissue confetti occasionally flitted down from the rafters in the PPG Paints arena. The air was thick and warm, and Steve tugged at his tie and shirt collar as he stared longingly at the Stanley Cup champion banners for the Pittsburgh Penguins, wishing the temperature was down at ice hockey levels. He had been excited, and surprised, to receive an invitation to attend the possible victory speech in Phelps' hometown of Pittsburgh. Now, after hours of cheering and smiling, his face hurt, and his enthusiasm had ebbed as his exhaustion increased.

The other discharged marines from Steve's unit at the embassy had all been invited to attend. Only a handful did, as most did not align their political views with Phelps. That suited Steve fine. The only marine Steve really ever cared to talk to was buried in a small plot in Arlington National Cemetery nearly a year ago.

After accepting his honorable discharge, Steve did his best to honor Milo's memory by joining the local campaign for Lawrence Phelps in Dallas. No amount of hand shaking, door knocking, or phone calling could fill the void of a dead best friend. But it at least put a little spackle over the hole.

The victory speeches ran dry, and the giant video board behind the stage settled into the image of a billowing American flag overlaid with the flashing words 'PRESIDENT-ELECT LAWRENCE PHELPS!'. Steve smiled in satisfaction that he had a part, albeit an immeasurably small one, in making this night happen. Milo would have been thrilled. He also would have hated to mingle in this crowd, and Steve was ready to bail too. He had shaken enough hands for one night.

"Palmer!"

Steve nearly choked on his beer and straightened his back as he turned to see his former commander, Lamont McNamara, now too a civilian and working security for Quentin Fargo's father's company. He had kept his short haircut, but the Oreo cookies the man loved were making an impact on his waistline. The two had crossed paths three times during the celebration, and Steve had turned down three offers of employment. Now the man was coming in for apparently a fourth handshake.

"Oh, hi gunnie," Steve said, raising his weary hand for another shake. He checked his three and nine for an easy escape route if McNamara wanted anything more than a brief goodbye.

"Hey Mr. President! He's over here," McNamara shouted over his shoulder.

Steve's eyes grew wide when the crowd behind McNamara parted and newly minted President-elect Phelps strode through, followed by his wife Olivia, Angel Bretstock, several other hangers-on, and half a dozen burly Secret Servicemen, all with matching suits and earpieces.

"So glad you made it, Mr. Palmer," Phelps said, extending his hand. He still wore the Gold Star pin on his lapel, opposite the one with the American flag.

"Thank you, sir. And congratulations. Milo would have been proud."

Phelps smiled and clapped Steve on the shoulder. "The work in honoring my son is just beginning. I understand you helped the local campaign office in Dallas?"

Steve nodded.

"I'm humbled. Thank you. What are your plans now? I'm sure we could find something in the new administration for an upstanding young citizen."

A jolt of excitement raced up Steve's spine. The next leader of the free world had just offered him a job. Then he saw a familiar tuft of graying curls bobbing up and down in the group behind Phelps.

"Ambassador Gustafson?" he asked.

Frannie Gustafson brushed aside a few nameless faces to step forward. She held out her hand to Steve. "Why hello again, Corporal Palmer. So good to see you. Quite the night we're having here, isn't it?"

"Yes… ma'am."

Steve's stomach swirled. A flood of closeted memories washed over him. The ambassador's sun-withered face and lopsided smile were exactly the same as they were on the aircraft the last time he saw her. She was a stained-glass mural, full of history and calls for introspection, and that was before the attack on the embassy. No doubt Frannie Gustafson would find her way into the new Phelps administration, and the roiling storm in his stomach pleaded for Steve to keep his distance. Seeing her and McNamara here together was too much.

He forced down the lump in his throat and summoned his courage to turn down the president-elect's offer. "Thank you, sir. But I think I need to spend some time back in Dallas with my family. I worked so much on the campaign; I've hardly seen them since I left the marines."

Phelps patted him on the shoulder. "Completely understand. Don't be afraid to get in touch. I'm sure you're going to turn out great."

And with that, the president-elect was off to shake more hands and thank more faces. His entourage followed closely behind, save for Angel Bretstock, who stepped up to Steve and handed him a business card and a bleached-white smile.

"You're on his friends list, and he remembers his friends," she said. "If you need a job or help — anything really, give me a call."

She smiled and shook his hand, then strode off to join the entourage and no doubt chase her career.

McNamara stood there with a smirk on his face, gazing at Angel's backside as she walked away.

Without saying goodbye, Steve turned and raced to the exit to chase a breath of fresh, cold November air.

———

After dropping Abby off, Steve went home to watch the president's press conference and make dinner. Milo was on his mind. Abby's inadvertent questioning had prodded at his years-old, calloused-over sore spot. Steve had come to some semblance of peace with losing his best friend since joining RADSA, considering he ended up working for Gustafson in the end anyway. At least he didn't see her face regularly. Every time he did, he was reminded of his friend, just as Abby had accidentally done.

But tonight, Milo would have been on his mind anyway. Since the last time he saw the president speak, Steve couldn't shake the notion that something was amiss. The back of his neck prickled. He wondered what his friend would have thought of the UDO, the Adapted, and a father turned president that was either misinformed, or lying to the American people.

He reheated some casserole leftovers from a recipe he got from Ben, who said it was his mother's creation. Chicken, broccoli, cheese, plus a handful of spices in a creamy sauce. At first, Steve was skeptical, but was persuaded by his boss to try it. To his surprise, it tasted great out of the oven over rice, but was even better as leftovers. He settled in with his plate and a local beer called Velvet Hammer and pulled up the press conference on his laptop.

The president spoke.

"Ow. Fuck." Steve rubbed his forehead.

The president spoke some more.

"Damn it!" He paused the playback and went to the cupboard for some

Excedrin. It didn't seem to help much, but as his R-Skill was already firing off so much, he figured he would need any help he could get to abate the stabbing sensation behind his eyes. Especially since his plan was to review the footage several times and he didn't want to pass out from the pain. He recalled the night that had happened once at a bar and remembered waking up the next morning on a friend's sofa with a crude marker drawing on his forehead.

He finished dinner and a couple more beers waiting for the painkiller and alcohol to kick in. Then he started the playback over. As the president spoke, Steve highlighted the transcript each time his R-Skill sent pain shooting behind his eyes.

"Ow. Ow. Jesus! Fuck! What? Ow!"

After the speech was over, he looked over the transcript. Not much wasn't highlighted.

"Dark object… threat… loss of life… United States will help with recovery."

It painted a picture that the president knew far more about the objects than he let on. Or he had been misled, either intentionally or accidentally. Steve thought the latter a far more likely scenario. This was Milo's father, after all. But who could do that? And why? Was the scientific community so unable to provide reliable information on the dark objects? If not, what purpose would it serve for them to lie to the president about potentially cataclysmic rogue objects from space? Steve's imagination wandered to visions of the Earth under siege by aliens hurtling the dark objects from a distant world.

Steve texted Ben. "What'd you think of the press conference today?" He drummed his fingers on the table, waiting for a response.

Minutes later, his phone buzzed. "Wild. You?"

"I don't know," Steve texted back. "It didn't make me feel good, if you catch my meaning. Something's not right."

CHAPTER 21
GARBAGE GIRL

"HOW OFTEN DO we meet at the Eleven warehouse? This is a bit of a commute during rush hour." Abby resisted the urge to bury herself in her phone as they waited in traffic and instead forced small talk with Steve.

"Every Wednesday for training. Other days when we have a light interview schedule," he replied.

She recalled her sleep-inducing first day at Charles and Munck spent watching boring out-of-date videos in a tiny cubicle. "Like the workplace sensitivity and government contracting integrity stuff? We do those every week?"

He laughed. "Those are just once a year. Bailey gives us hand-to-hand combat training every week, more often if we're not busy."

Abby gulped. "Hand-to-hand combat?"

"RADSA has not condoned the use of firearms by agents, but they do promote self-defense training in the event we come up against a difficult Adapted."

"Fat lot that'll do you if you piss a guy off that can boil your blood with a whistle. Did you see that story from Arizona last night?" Abby's stomach turned a fresh flip as she recalled the evening news footage showing an Adapted's estranged girlfriend on the floor of an apartment, cooked alive from the inside. The footage then showed the perpetrator's self-same suicide.

"I did." Steve's tone was unchanged. If he was affected by the story, he didn't let on. "Our goal," he said, giving Abby a serious look, "is to not piss such people off."

"Damn, you're calm about it. Do we come across Adapted with D2S R-Skills often?"

"No. Those seem to be fairly rare. Like one in ten thousand or less. I don't think anyone from our area has ever been sent to the island. I've not interviewed one yet."

The mention of Island-A sent a shiver up Abby's spine. From everything she had heard about the process before joining RADSA, Adapted were sent there merely at the whiff of potential hint of danger. There was no trial, no appeal, no choice. The entire concept of Island-A was an affront to what she thought America stood for. Instead, now it was liberty and justice for those lucky enough to not develop a randomly dangerous R-Skill.

The Camry picked up speed as traffic passed a slowdown next to a stalled car. Cars came and went. Every minute or so, a pickup truck with a lift kit and too-large tires changed lanes with little regard to their blind spots. Some drew honks from behind. No one cared. Abby warmed to the idea of buying a car but hated the idea of sitting by herself in traffic. She figured Steve would eventually tire of carpooling with her. Not many could withstand her attitude long-term. Tyson was one. "Damn," she muttered under her breath. She bit her tongue hard enough to head off a flood of memories that would have otherwise ruined her morning. Memories, but few emotions, which still had her unsettled.

Steve looked at her. "You alright?"

"I'm fine."

He gasped and the car lurched to the side briefly. "Abby…"

"Shit. Sorry!" She saw the wince obscuring his deep brown eyes. The lie had hurt him, and she began to develop an understanding for his mannerisms. Her cheeks flushed with heat. She clenched her fists. "I just thought of Tyson there for a moment." The admission seemed to calm Steve, for which she was unexpectedly glad. But speaking Tyson's name cracked her emotional dam a bit. She held a hand over her mouth to hide her grimace.

Steve did her the courtesy of not drawing out the conversation, but she felt compelled to say something. "It's weird. I remember it happening. I remember feeling bad. But I don't feel bad about it now. I haven't since I met you guys. I should, right?"

His face contorted with confusion. "I suppose. But it was an accident, after all. It's okay to move on."

Steve coughed and kept his eyes on the road. The corner of his eye glistened for a moment until he wiped at it with his sleeve. Abby didn't know what to say. Evidently, Steve didn't either as several uncomfortable minutes of silence passed. Finally, he poked at the radio.

"Uh, you want some music?"

"I'll pass on your goofy jazz, thanks. Tell me more about this combat training."

———

Abby began her morning at Warehouse 11 with the training videos still in her queue, while Steve chatted with Ben about something. The videos were as interesting as the ones she had already watched, somewhere on the spectrum between paint drying and congressional subcommittee procedural debates on C-SPAN.

She wiped her palms on her jeans. Her mind was iterating the possibilities of what hand-to-hand combat training could entail. A few short, bare-knuckled scraps in high school were all Abby had to go on for experience.

The first video finished without her registering a word. She checked the title — The Productive Workplace for Government Employees — and figured it would be the typical spiel about diversity, inclusion, and open-mindedness towards coworkers' viewpoints. Abby had seen a similar video when she started at Charles & Munck, and agreed in general with the sentiment, if not fully understanding how it actually improved productivity. Even after she wasn't as distracted with the prospect of sparring on the mat in the opposite corner, the video wouldn't be worth watching again.

She was about to start something from OSHA on workplace safety when the warehouse's huge garage door rolled open, and Bessie rumbled inside. The commotion was deafening. Deep bass rumbled throughout the cavernous metal structure, drowning out the video just inches from Abby's face. Through the open door, she spied a red Tesla parked outside. Gigi was in it, talking on her phone. *I guess she just shows up whenever she feels like it,* Abby thought. The garage door rolled shut, far faster than the trainers on the OSHA video would have considered safe. Bessie's raucous engine came to a halt, and the driver's door swung open.

"Hi Bailey," Abby said as she walked up to the truck, thankful for the distraction.

"Yeah, hi," a voice called out in a thick southern drawl.

A small hand reached for the steel ladder that was bolted to the side of the cab. In a practiced move that went by in a blur, Bailey swung her body out of the cab, slid down the rails of the ladder, then hopped to the floor. She was so small! Abby had met her in the trailer briefly on her first day, but hadn't seen her since, and hadn't gotten used to the idea that she actually knew a little person — or whatever the proper word was for someone so diminutive.

Bailey's skin was a leathery tan, and her highlighted brown hair was cut in an asymmetrical line from her right ear to her left shoulder. She wore a steel blue jumpsuit — one of Eddie's — with a vertical line of dashes the color of yellow road stripes from each shoulder to each foot.

"Welcome to Warehouse 11," Bailey said. She reached out a short arm and small hand to shake.

"Thanks. But I was here yesterday," Abby replied, extending a hand and stepping closer to reach for the shake.

"Today will feel like your first day, guaranteed." Bailey grasped mostly Abby's fingers, but had quite the grip. Abby needed all of her resolve not to jerk her hand back as she felt several knuckles pop as Bailey bounced her hand up and down.

"I still can't believe you drive that." Abby pointed at the door of the glossy black semi-truck.

"You've been ridin' around with us, haven't you?"

"Well, yeah."

"That's me drivin'. I don't let anyone else touch Bessie. Got me a neural network interface to run the controls."

Abby raised her eyebrows. Bessie was evidently brimming with cutting edge tech. "Wow, cool."

"Pfft, dummy. That's Star Trek. I use the wheel and pedals like anyone else. They're just… closer."

The idea of this country bumpkin-sounding little person watching Star Trek was too much to take. "Ah," she said, laughing.

The smaller of the warehouse's front doors clanked open, drawing their attention. Gigi strolled in, wearing another skin-tight yoga ensemble — today's was sea green — and expensive headphones perched on her neat, pulled-back hair. She waved. Bailey waved back. Abby waved. Gigi rolled her eyes.

Great, Abby thought. *I hope I can smooth things over with her today.*

"C'mon," Bailey said. "Let's get started." She led Abby toward the exercise area at the far corner of the space and motioned for Gigi to join.

Abby shrank away from Bailey as they crossed the expanse. The sensitivity video she had just watched was having an effect; she didn't know how to refer to someone of smaller stature.

Bailey chuckled. "You're not going to break me. Don't be shy."

"Sorry," Abby swallowed. "I've never known a… uh…" She swallowed again. "I don't know the right word."

Equality movements raged non-stop across the Internet. From gender and sexuality to ethnicity and ageism (and throw in the Adapted), everyone now felt entitled to their own personal self-defining and affirming categorization. Defending one's entitlement to be offended by the malice, ignorance, or indifference of another was the new national pastime.

"Vertically challenged? Little person? Dwarf? The 'M' word?"

"Uh, yeah." Abby looked at her feet. She couldn't help but notice they were twice the size of Bailey's.

"I am a human. I have dwarfism. You may refer to me as Bailey." She smiled.

"Okay then."

"And I am *not* vertically challenged!" Bailey took one step, then jumped in the air towards Abby and slugged her in the shoulder as if the full force of Bessie were behind the blow. Abby's soft tissues screamed in pain.

"Ow! Jesus!" she yelped, grabbing her shoulder.

Bailey then slapped Abby on the back. Hard. "Buckle up, kiddo. There's a lot more of that on the way today." She pointed to a red plastic crate sitting on a bench by the wall. "Get your pads on."

Gigi snickered as she arrived at the black mat-covered area. "Nice one, Bailey."

"I got one for you too if you slack off, Bouncy." Bailey waved a small, balled fist and glared at her with eyes that said she would enjoy the opportunity.

"Uh huh," Gigi said as she started to put on her own set of pads. "You know, I've always wanted to see a dwarf fly." She engaged in a showy analysis of the warehouse rafters. "I think the ceiling is high enough."

Bailey switched her fist to a pointed finger. "You keep those socks on, missy!"

Abby fished through the crate and pulled out what appeared to be a padded leather vest. "How do I put this on? I've never done... what are we doing?"

"Sparrin'," Bailey said. She assisted Abby in donning her padded gear, which the personal protective equipment video had failed to mention as standard issue. "Okay, you two have fun. No hits to the unpadded areas. I'm gonna go talk to the boss."

From head to toe, Abby armored herself — at least on her front side — in various pads and plastic plates. In the mirror on the wall, she looked like a scared adult about to go out on her first skateboard lesson, aside from the proper helmet. Dumbstruck, Abby felt adrenaline begin to tickle at her cells in anticipation of what was about to happen.

"What? We just fight? I don't know what to do."

Bailey had already turned her back and was on her way to Rice's office at the other end of the warehouse. Abby turned to face Gigi, only to see her opponent now mere inches away. Gigi parted her lips in a smile, revealing a pink mouthguard. She then cocked her head slightly and slammed a gloved fist into Abby's padded stomach. Abby doubled over to one knee in pain, coughing in shock.

"Pretty much," Gigi said. "Better put your mouthguard in." She pointed to a cabinet against the mirror. "I wouldn't want to concuss you."

Panic tickled the hairs on the back of Abby's neck. She looked up at Gigi, mouth agape.

"At least, not on your first day of sparring. Would be a shame for it to be your last too."

Abby stumbled over to the cabinet and fumbled with the drawers through padded gloves. She had hoped to smooth out any frayed feelings with Gigi today, having been the center of the praise the team received after rescuing Zeke Thomas from himself. Instead, Gigi seemed intent on working out her frustrations using Abby as a training dummy.

Abby extracted a new mouthguard, neon green on one half, black on the other. She slammed it in and turned to analyze her assailant. Gigi was short — gymnast short, no more than five feet tall in shoes, but dense and muscular through and through. Her taut skin was the type that screamed, "I do cardio every day." Abby was naturally lean, but had done the bare minimum of physical activity possible through high school. A few pre-teens were harassing her sister Mary a while back and Abby had used her sheer height advantage to bop them on the heads a few times until they renounced their evil. But this was going to be an actual fight, and Abby was about to pee her pants.

She closed her eyes and could hear her foster parents Walter and Betty chastising her for staying indoors all the time. The construction job had at least gotten her outside; she had a decent farmer's tan going. Unfortunately, though she could lift giant hunks of discarded concrete, she didn't have the muscles to show for it. That capacity was granted through her R-Skill, which evidently affected her in some way other than building gargantuan upper body musculature. Abby suspected she had an advantage of reach - she was nearly a foot taller than Gigi. She just needed to figure out how to put that to use.

"Let's see what ya got!" With another pink mouthguard smile, Gigi motioned for Abby to move in, fists raised in defense.

Abby approached and raised her own fists, completely at a loss with how to proceed. She gauged the closing speed and threw a downward-angled punch aimed for her target's face. Gigi ducked beneath it easily, countered with a heavy blow to Abby's thigh, then swept a leg under Abby's feet in lightning-fast combination. Abby toppled to the mat and grasped at her thigh. The pain radiated up and down her quadricep. "Fuck!" she mumbled through the mouthguard. Either Gigi was quite the fighter, or the pads weren't doing their job. Abby stared into the rafters and started counting the bright LED lights, hoping to avoid further contact.

"Get up," Gigi taunted. "You're not gonna learn anything down on the mat."

"Geez! Take it easy." She shot Gigi a derisive look.

"The world doesn't take it easy on us. We need to be prepared."

"Whatever."

Abby harrumphed into the mat, then stood and shook her leg. The pain subsided a little. She immediately swore at herself for staring up at the lights, because she now had blots of black all over her vision. She held her forearms and fists out in defense as she caught an obscured view of Gigi moving in. Her hands were knocked down by a phantom swing, which cleared the way for a swift left hook to her chin. Again, Abby tumbled to the mat. And again. And again. Each time she was knocked down, Abby forced herself to not give up, to not give in to Gigi's taunting. After a solid thirty minutes of getting her ass kicked, Abby was panting for breath, aching all over, and ready to shred Gigi to pieces if she could ever land a blow. If this passed for a weekly routine, Abby didn't think it would take long for her to begin reconsidering the importance of that handsome new paycheck over her own structural integrity.

"Alright, take five ladies." Bailey called as she returned to the scene.

Gigi grabbed a blue Gatorade from a small refrigerator by the wall, sat on the bench and picked up her phone. She had hardly broken a sweat.

Abby collapsed on the opposing wall's bench and spit out her mouthguard, ready for a trauma helicopter to evacuate her to the nearest hospital. Bailey spared her the trip to the fridge and brought a Gatorade over.

"Thanks." Abby took a sip of the cool blue liquid. All she could taste was her own blood.

Bailey patted her on the shoulder. "Told ya. Now, listen'," she looked over at Gigi. "You're no physical match for her - none of us are. She's kicked the tail of every single person that's stepped into a fracas with her, with effort to spare. Rice and Palmer included. You're gonna have to think outside the box if you want to make a dent in her bravado."

Another swig of Gatorade helped clear the blood from Abby's mouth. "What exactly am I supposed to be learning here?"

"To think on your feet! You don't always have to win to survive. Observe. Endure. Wait for the right opportunity."

With that, Bailey pulled Abby up and robbed her of her cold drink. Abby chomped down on her mouthguard and slapped her gloved hands together.

Gigi seemed amused at this show of determination and hopped to her feet. She charged right in, as she had done before. Abby recognized the approach, and dodged the attack, shoving Gigi aside as she lunged. It was hard to smile with the mouthguard in, but Abby could feel the corners of her mouth stretch upward ever so slightly. Gigi turned and huffed a laugh, then moved in again. Abby made show of an offensive attempt, then instead dodged to the opposite direction as Gigi moved to counter and lunged past again, then groaned in frustration.

"Are you gonna fight, or what?"

"Eh," Abby shrugged, feeling a bit more herself. "If you can't hit me, you're not really fighting either. Just vigorously pursuing with an occasional dramatic lunge."

That set her off. Gigi growled and rushed in, jumping with the intent to introduce a knee to Abby's face. Abby had her next move already planned, and ducked as soon as Gigi left the mat. She whirled around and gave Gigi a bear hug from behind when she landed, then pushed forward with all her might until they crashed together into the supplies cabinet. Abby's wrists took a solid blow from the metal drawers, but having the upper hand for once washed away all the pain.

"Christ! Ow!" Gigi exclaimed, clearly unused to being on the receiving end. "That's against the rules! No hitting unpadded areas."

"I didn't hit you, I *hugged* you." Abby said. "You were looking a little frustrated. Thought I'd be a good teammate." She craned her neck over and gave Gigi a peck on the nose. "Feel better yet?" She snickered when she realized she hadn't gotten to the sexual harassment video yet.

"Ugh! Get off me!"

Gigi elbowed herself free, then swung wildly with one hand then the next, landing two blows to Abby's padded head. Abby collapsed in a heap again, and couldn't stifle her laughter, though the pain was doing its best to try. She sat up, and Gigi slammed into her forehead with a knee. It was padded, but the knee may as well have been a sledgehammer. The pain was blinding. Actually, it was the fresh blood pouring into her eyes that was blinding. Abby was cut. Bad. She crumpled to the mat, barely able to think.

"Hey!" Bailey yelled. "None of that! You're done Gigi, go make yourself useful somewhere else!"

Gigi huffed but did not argue. She tossed her pads to the floor next to Abby and stomped off.

"Well, I hope you're satisfied." Bailey said to Abby.

Abby touched her forehead, feeling a large gash. Her fingers were now coated in blood. "Oh yeah, that was worth it."

Bailey laughed. "Damn right it was." She patted Abby on the back. "And today's lesson was?"

"Hugs are better than punches," Abby said as she spit out her bloody mouthguard and winced.

"That they are. She'll be more cautious next time." Bailey pulled Abby to her feet as best as her small fame could manage.

Abby's spent legs needed a few moments to collect their balance. She pulled off her gloves and headgear and propped herself up over the disheveled supply cabinet. The mirror reflected an ugly wound dead center in her forehead, blood oozing down one side of her nose and smeared all over her face. She was no surgeon, but figured she'd need stitches. "I guess there goes my modeling career."

Bailey shook her head. "I've seen worse. Let's go see Eddie. He'll fix you up. You're gonna enjoy this."

Abby raised her eyebrows, then winced as fresh blood stung her eyes.

She wiped it away and looked around the mostly empty warehouse. Gigi was standing by some lockers, pretending to look at her phone, but eyeing Abby all the way. As they walked past, Abby resigned herself to not being on everyone's good side. At least Bailey seemed to be in her corner. She had thought that with practically everyone on the team being an Adapted, there would be a tighter bond. But, instead, it was just another workplace full of humans that disliked each other for various petty reasons. A workplace where coworkers beat each other senseless on a weekly basis. *That* was not covered in the training videos.

CHAPTER 22
THE ADJUSTER

SOMEWHERE IN THE PACIFIC OCEAN, approximately ninety kilometers east of Taiwan, the *Guangdong* sailed amidst the six ships of its support group. A massive quartet of propellers carved calm blue waters into a roiling froth, pushing the massive aircraft carrier at a breakneck thirty-five knots. The pride of China's navy, the new Yue Fei class behemoth housed four nuclear reactors, good for nearly three hundred megawatts of power supplied to the steam engines. The ship's state-of-the-art systems had triple-redundant fail-safes to safely control and contain the nuclear fission reactions.

None of that mattered. The UDO screamed from the sky like a smoldering coal, flung from a far-off star. It smashed into the *Guangdong*, squarely in the middle of the deck. Instantly, the trillion-yuan vessel was reduced to sinking scrap metal, and the final resting place for over a thousand Chinese sailors.

Ben watched the replay of the video footage, shot from one of the *Guangdong's* support frigates. The visual was straight out of a summer Hollywood blockbuster. The two jagged halves of the ship flung enormous fireballs a hundred feet into the air in the scant seconds before the ocean claimed her prize.

Two new UDOs had fallen into the Pacific Ocean today. One harmlessly splashed into open water. The second, somehow, scored a direct hit on China's newest, and most expensive military apparatus, while it was moving at top speed. According to the news cast, not a soul on board survived.

The loss of life was indeed tragic, but paled in comparison to the colossal destruction reaped by the first UDO on the Korean Peninsula. The United Nations-led cleanup effort was still ongoing. They unearthed new, greatly decomposed bodies every day. Each was catalogued, identified if possible, then cremated. The ashes were collected to be interred at an enormous Korean memorial that would be erected at the site of impact in the future.

Ben's laptop chirped, indicating a video chat request. It was Director Gustafson. He attempted to shake free of the shock the news footage had wrapped around his mind.

"Good morning, Director," Ben said after accepting the chat.

The director had her usual stern, grandmotherly look affixed to her face: flattened eyebrows hovered over dull hazel eyes, and a craggy face framed by a high pile of graying curls. Ben thought she might be hiding a kitten up there. Or a hand grenade.

"Hi Ben. You look flushed. Everything alright?" Frannie asked.

He popped a couple Advil and chased them down with cold coffee. "Yeah. I was just watching the footage of the Chinese aircraft carrier."

"Incredible," she said with disinterest.

"That's… one way to describe it. What can I do for you?"

Frannie clicked her tongue. "Well, I went through your weekly report, and we need to chat about your numbers. You need to grow your team, Ben. I've relayed the president's desires on our ability to address each community's needs, and… well, to be frank, your team is bringing up the rear."

"I understand, Frannie. I'm trying. *We're* trying. I don't want to add just anyone."

"You need more people on your team, Ben. Plain and simple. I see your team's reports coming in. You have plenty to choose from."

Yeah, if I wanted an endless supply of ketchup, he thought. Ben disagreed with the president on this. The best way to represent RADSA, and to help the Adapted in his community, was to build a team that mattered. Simply checking boxes and filing reports would not matter to anyone. But a team filled with the likes of Eddie, Gigi, and Abby could actually make a difference. They were just less common.

The itchy pressure between his vertebrae urged Ben to change Frannie's mind on this. He had already used his ability on her before and was reminded of such every time he saw her. But, he suppressed the temptation. He could play ball.

"I know I've been picky, Frannie. I apologize if it's making waves. We've just been focused on recruiting those with impactful R-Skills."

"Your region's backlog is growing. We need to get every Adapted out there catalogued the second they are found. Any *listers* have to be sent to the island as soon as humanly possible."

"I know, I know." He couldn't hide his frown at the thought of sending someone off to a lifetime sentence.

She shook her head. "Forget that. Ben, first and foremost, you and your team are ambassadors between the Adapted and the rest of your community. You need to be *seen* to keep the president's narrative in the public eye."

"I know, it's just—"

"Stop blabbing and just listen. Find some bodies and put them in your chairs. Friendly bodies. Good-looking bodies. Doesn't matter if they can lift a building, remove rust with their spit, or simply turn heads in a bikini. You can't do the job with less than half the team you're supposed to have. Either get it done, or I'll find someone who can be more effective."

Ben held his tongue. The idea of hiring non-Adapted people for the team had never crossed his mind.

"There were a lot of raised eyebrows over here when I gave you that position after you left my daughter. I'm past that, just like she is. But I thought you could do this, Ben, and you're not getting it done."

The mention of his ex-fiancée stirred motes of fury in his blood. He didn't leave Rachel, that was just the lie he had constructed. She had scarred him for life, and he had fallen on the sword, taking the blame for the end to their relationship. Rachel got to move on. Ben got to hold on to all of his memories of their time together, right up to the final moment when he had altered her mind. That was a thousand times more painful than the boiling water that had maimed his face.

But he hadn't forced Frannie to give him anything more than what she had already promised. Of course, she didn't know the truth either, but her comment dug up his emotional wounds and peeled them fresh again. He rolled his shoulders until they popped, then growled through clenched teeth. "You don't need to mention Rachel to me again. We are done with that chapter of our lives."

Frannie blinked at the camera on the other end, then reclined in her chair and scratched her head. "Um, where was I?"

Ben popped his knees under his desk. "You were saying how we had done a good job in selecting an impressive team for DFW."

After a moment, she nodded. "That's right. You've done a good job with your team, Ben."

Every word she parroted back was a stab in his gut. He was treading dangerous ground. No doubt, using any ability on the Director of RADSA without her knowledge would be grounds for dismissal, or worse. But his was on the list. Every time he used it the lid to his own personal Pandora's Box opened just a little bit more. If he wasn't careful, the web he was weaving would begin to look like a one-way ticket to Island-A.

"Keep up the good work, Ben. But do try to get a few more on your team if you find some you like."

"Thanks, Frannie. I'll see you on the staff call tomorrow."

She nodded and ended the video chat.

Ben rubbed his face in an attempt to wipe away his shame. He glared at the mirror on the wall. It sternly swayed back and forth in disapproval as Bessie rumbled along. The dark brown eye surrounded by scar tissue looked back at him through the mirror and scolded him. *One of these days, your whole ship will sink too.*

CHAPTER 23

BOUNCY

SHE KNEW THIS WOULD HAPPEN. Just by looking at her, Gigi could tell that Abby would be a Texas-sized obstacle. The newcomer had saved the boy from himself on the bridge, and had been showered with accolades from Ben, and RADSA leadership. It was Saturday, and Gigi was glad to have the day off. She needed to unwind. To reassess. And to make another smoothie, because the first one she made tasted like the sweaty drippings from a gym towel.

But what to do about her situation? Stick it out, or look for something better? Of course, she always had an eye out for new opportunities, but since starting with RADSA, she had been pretty content about how things were going. Then Abby walks in and obliterates the apple cart without even knowing there was one. No. Gigi didn't need to share the stage with Ms. Naturally-Swedish-Blonde.

She calmed her mind with an extra half hour of yoga, then made another smoothie, falling back on a safer concoction of spinach, celery, strawberries, Greek yogurt, and lemon juice. She eased into her sofa, ready to enjoy the thirty minutes she gave herself each day to do nothing but veg. Then her phone buzzed.

"Hey Gigi," the text read. It was from her best friend, Kendra Hunt. A second text quickly followed. "Busy today?"

Gigi smiled. Best friend. Best rival. Best shoulder to cry on. Best leech of Gigi's goodwill. Kendra's picture-perfect face would be featured in a whole-page dictionary pullout of the word 'frenemy'. She was also the sister Gigi never had. Her parents gave her pretty much everything she asked for growing up, except a sibling.

So that's how Gigi found herself spending her precious Saturday watching Kendra shop and try on outfits for an audition. "Something big," Kendra had called it. Gigi couldn't refuse.

A tinge — okay, several tinges — of jealousy curdled under Gigi's skin. Kendra had everything Gigi wanted, but didn't have to work for any of it. Her mom had dragged an unwilling, uninterested thirteen-year-old Kendra to an open talent audition, and an agent took an immediate liking to her. Now, she was regularly offered small roles in local productions, was the on-air spokeswoman for a car dealership (Kendra's fake southern twang *was* the best), and made a considerable income as a hand model, of all things. Kendra had a big enough social media following to reach even higher strata of career and connections if she wanted, but she seemed satisfied enough to let her accounts coast on the laurels of her acting and modeling content alone.

"What do you think of this?" Kendra asked, stepping out of the changing room on the second floor of Nordstrom. She wore a white floral crop top that showed off an ample amount of her well-toned and tanned midriff. *How the hell does she get her skin so perfect?* Gigi mused to herself.

As Kendra ogled herself in the mirror, flipping her perfectly curled, platinum blonde hair back and forth, Gigi wondered why Kendra had never pushed further into a full modeling career. She had the required trifecta: face, physique, and complexion, plus great hair, tan, and brilliant blue eyes.

Gigi forced back a yawn and smiled. "I like the top. Not so sure about the nuclear pink miniskirt though."

Kendra frowned at the mirror with her hands on her hips. "Yeah. Maybe denim?"

Gigi shrugged her disinterest, which could coincidentally be interpreted as "Sure, try that."

Somewhere between the third and thirty-third outfit tried, Gigi's boredom conquered her manners and she pulled out her phone. Her eyes widened as she scanned through her new emails. Buried in the sea of promotional spam and social media notifications was a lone message from Lon Smiley. He was one of only a handful of talent agents that would still give her the time of day on occasion. The subject line of the email simply read: Potential A-Space Opportunity.

Gigi couldn't contain her squeal of excitement.

"Oh, you like this one?" Kendra asked.

Gigi looked up to see Kendra in a hideous, skin-tight, metallic purple minidress. The shape of the dress was fine, nice really, but the color was all wrong. Kendra was radiant. She needed to be in silvers, yellows, and golds.

"Yeah, it's good. Not sure about the color. Does it come in silver?"

Kendra raised her eyebrows and frowned at Gigi, then saw the phone in her hand.

"Something else got your attention Geeg?"

"Sorry, one of my old agent contacts sent me something about an A-Space reality show to be filmed here in Dallas."

"Huh." Kendra's disinterest was plain as she sorted through which outfit to try on next.

"This could be a big opportunity," Gigi protested.

"I hear those things are pretty tough to get into. Every Adapted and their sister wants to get in on the A-Space fame train."

"Well, yeah."

Gigi dreamed of the celebutante life. Adoring fans. Eyeballs drawn to her anywhere she went. Her pick of eligible bachelors. She couldn't understand why Kendra didn't pursue it.

"Silver, huh?" Kendra looked back and forth between her reflection and Gigi several times. "I was thinking of a color with more contrast. To stand out."

A stifled chuckle slipped from Gigi's lips. Kendra stood out without even trying. Gigi wasn't invested in the fashion show enough to argue the point. "Maybe go back to the flower crop top, with the denim skirt? I liked that one." She didn't really.

Kendra tried that ensemble on again and, somehow, agreed with Gigi's false assessment. "C'mon, I'll buy you lunch," she said. "Then I want to look at shoes."

———

Kendra could not have shown less interest when Gigi read over the details of the A-Space All-Stars reality competition. "That's interesting," she said, with less enthusiasm than she showed for her salad.

By contrast, Gigi was ready to burst. A competition on social media exclusively for Adapted? Sign her up. "Says here the open audition is just a couple weeks away. This is so cool!"

Kendra shrugged. "You'd probably have an easier time getting in if you had an agent. I bet they only fill one or two spots from the open audition."

Gigi grumbled to herself. She had tried for years to get an agent to represent her. "Do you think your agent would rep me?" she asked Kendra, for at least the fifth time in as many years.

"No." Kendra laughed. "LeAnne is so particular now. Back when she took me on as a client? Maybe. But she's not as thirsty as she once was. The Adapted thing is still pretty fresh, and since she isn't one, she just says it's not her forte."

"Maybe after I win the open audition?"

"Yeah, maybe. She likes talent that's ruthless. Willing to do what it takes to succeed in the business. Ya know?"

"They're all like that." Gigi poked with disinterest at the veggies on her plate that had been steamed to mushy oblivion. Her mind raced with all the possibilities even a bit of exposure on the A-Space show could create. But forget all that - she was going to win the damn thing!

"I bet you'll do great at the audition," Kendra said after a quiet moment. "It's not like every Adapted that's trying out will have been a former Olympic hopeful. You'll be the most fit contestant there."

Gigi rolled her eyes. Kendra didn't really believe that. "Thanks. Want to come with me for moral support?"

"Sure."

That was not the answer Gigi expected. She hid her surprise by forcing down a forkful of flavorless zucchini.

"As long as my schedule is open."

Gigi nodded in appreciation, and the understanding that with that qualifying statement, Kendra was as likely to come to the audition as Gigi was to finish her lunch. She pushed her plate away.

"Hey, I saw you on TV the other day," Kendra said.

"Oh yeah?" A tickle of excitement danced across Gigi's skin.

"Yeah… for like a second. You and that Steve guy you told me about were in the background. They mostly showed the boy you rescued and your new girl."

"Ugh. Abby."

"What's wrong with her? From what the news said, she sat down with that Zeke guy right on the edge of the bridge and talked him down herself."

"Pretty much. She's just, I don't know. Annoying. All happy-go-lucky, take life as it comes. Wears stupid rock T-shirts all the time like she's still in middle school or something."

"Funny."

Gigi considered spilling the beans on Abby's construction site mishap that eventually led her to join the RADSA team. But she figured if word got back around to Ben, she would be fired on the spot. He was a tight ass about the rules, and chief among them was the non-disclosure agreement that everyone signed. It forbade the discussion of personal details about teammates or Adapted interviews to outsiders. Actually, he was a tight ass about almost everything, including his workout dedication. She caught herself daydreaming about the sculpted physique he hid beneath a coat and tie and chomped down on the lemon in her Stevia-sweetened iced tea to shake her brain cells free.

"She's just so annoying. Has a powerful R-Skill and doesn't do much of anything with it. Then she lands a job with the team and saves that Zeke guy's life on her second day. Life comes too easy for her." Gigi left out the part where Abby bounced around like a pinball in the foster care system for nearly a decade.

"What's her ability?"

Gigi chuckled. "Her code name is Garbage Girl. She can throw garbage into garbage cans."

"That doesn't sound too impressive."

"Any size of garbage, any distance, to any trash container she can see. Like she used to work in construction and would toss huge chunks of concrete into dumpsters like they were nothing."

Kendra's eyes widened. "Wow. I wish I had an R-Skill like that."

A wry smile creased Gigi's lips. Could this be something she had Kendra was actually jealous of? That would be a first. "You actually want to be an Adapted? It's not a great club to join if you don't get a good ability. And most people without an R-Skill don't trust those that have one."

Kendra sighed and shrugged, poking around at the food on her plate. "Yeah, I guess."

Gigi took a sip of her tea and drank in her friend's expression. Slumped shoulders, averted eyes, flush cheeks. Something was on Kendra's mind. A hidden cherry tomato rolled out from under a leaf of spinach as Kendra played with her salad, and as Gigi watched it tumble to the center of the plate next to a larger, plumper, juicier, without-a-doubt better tomato, her mouth opened into a wide grin.

"Holy crap, Kendra! You *are* Adapted, aren't you?"

"What? No."

Gigi craned her head forward with a slight tilt. A predator ready to pounce. "I can tell."

Kendra scoffed. "No, you can't. Nobody can."

The slight pause in Kendra's response gave away the truth before she even spoke. Gigi didn't need Steve around to suss this out. "You know, RADSA will find out sooner or later." Gigi leaned back in her chair, as if trying to goad a suspect into a confession. "We have our ways."

Kendra's eyes widened at Gigi. She stole quick looks at the well-to-dos at the tables on either side of them and crouched over her plate. "Keep it down. Shit."

Gigi lowered her voice. "This is so cool! What can you do?"

"I'm not telling you. I was trying to keep it secret. Damn it!"

"Hey, I won't tell anyone. It's not on the Dangers to Society list, is it?"

"What? No. It's just… lame."

Twin ropes of empathy and superiority pulled at Gigi from opposite directions. Superiority was crushing her empathy. She finally had something her one-upping best friend would be forever jealous of.

"Listen, I meet dozens of Adapted every week. Nearly all of them have lame abilities, some are pretty awful."

Kendra rolled her eyes.

"I'm serious." Gigi crouched lower over the table. "Since you gave up your secret, kinda, I'll tell you one. But you can't tell another soul. I interviewed a guy the other day who started growing hair on his tongue. Like sasquatch hairy. He's gotta trim it daily or he'll choke."

"Ew, gross."

"See? Whatever your R-Skill is, it can't be that bad."

"It's not. I just wish it was… useful." Kendra quickly wiped at her eye to prevent a tear from falling.

The empathy rope jerked hard at Gigi, pulling her down from her internal pedestal. "You seem upset over the ability you got. Why does it matter to you so much?"

"I don't know. I think if you had told fifteen-year-old me I'd end up a model, slinging hand creams and pickup trucks, I'd be pretty disappointed in myself. That Kendra wanted to actually do something with her life. Help people. Or something." More tears welled in her eyes.

Gigi hadn't used her sympathy muscles in so long, she was at a loss as for something meaningful to say. She reached across the table and cupped Kendra's arm. "So what if your R-Skill isn't world-changing? I think mine's pretty great, and it hasn't gotten me more than a few thousand followers. If you care that much, you've got the money and social capital to make a difference if you wanted. Start a foundation for underfed albino squirrels or something."

Kendra wiped at her eyes again and attempted a half smile. "Yeah, maybe I will. It's just— I saw what your team did for that guy on the bridge and thought it would be awesome to be a part of something like that."

I hardly had anything to do with it. And it had nothing to do with our R-Skills, Gigi thought, gnawing at her cheek.

"If you like, I can ask my boss about you. You'd have to give up your R-Skill secret though."

"Thanks. Not ready for that yet."

"Okay. Just remember, not everyone wins the genetic lottery like you did. Most people would kill to have your looks and sling hand creams for a living."

Kendra's cheeks flushed anew.

Ugh, caring is hard, Gigi thought. She smiled to herself. This revelation added much more weight to the friend side of the frenemy scales of their relationship. She reached the bottom of her tea glass with a gurgling slurp. "What do you say we take your mind off R-Skills for a while and get back to shopping?"

"Yeah, I think I'm ready to look for the perfect pair of shoes," Kendra said. Relief washed over her face.

Remembering the hideous floral top and mismatched skirt Kendra had settled for, Gigi smiled and shook her head. "Actually, I think we should look at some more outfits first."

CHAPTER 24
GARBAGE GIRL

THE INTERVIEW LIST backlog had grown from seven to forty-five names overnight. Abby hadn't seen it out of the single digits in the ten days she had been on the team. She fidgeted with Steve's tablet in excitement as the pair cruised down the highway in Steve's Camry. What at first had seemed like the most mundane part of the job had turned out to be her favorite. Well, outside of spending time with Steve. But today the two went hand in hand, and it was all Abby could do to maintain her composure.

"Why do you think the list got so big last night?" she asked.

Steve shrugged. "Beats me. A little unusual. But then RADSA doesn't share what goes on under the hood inside the RADSAnet database."

Abby wiggled her fingers like she was tickling the air. "Big Brother is watching!"

Steve looked at her with a wide wry smile. He tapped his forehead and gently nodded.

Abby flung her eyes open wide and made an audible gulp. They both laughed.

"Okay then. Abby, and RADSAnet if you're listening, any potential new teammates on the list?" Steve asked.

"Hmm." Abby grinned and scrolled through the list of Adapted, tapping into each to read what the database had managed to collect on their R-Skills. Most were sparsely populated, or uselessly vague. "Here's one that can renew the adhesive on the back of Post-It Notes. Another one says they can exhale helium."

Steve chuckled. "I bet they'd be a hit at Party City in a clown costume."

"Yeah. Ooh! This one simply says 'auditory assault'. Maybe that's like a banshee screech or something? That'd be cool!"

"Dunno. Sounds interesting. Who's our first appointment?"

Abby switched to the calendar display. "Hamad Behram, a software programmer from Plano."

"What's his R-Skill?"

Abby giggled. "He can walk on milk."

Steve contorted a moment, swallowing his laughter. "Wow. Sign him up."

The day's first R-Skill interviews (as they were officially called) were a fun, if not compelling affair. Zany ones usually went quickly because there wasn't much to uncover. The Milkwalker was no danger to society, nor a particularly compelling candidate to add to the team. Certainly personable, but his R-Skill didn't meet Ben's criteria for an invitation (needs to be in some way useful to the team in a crisis).

The Post-It Note refresher didn't fit the bill either. Steve suggested they call him the Fresh Prince of Post-Its. Abby thought Freshum P.I. was better (and shorter). In the end, it would be RADSAnet that would select the codenames, and it could choose something submitted in the agents' reports, or another name that the artificially intelligent toaster oven found most suitable.

"Alright. Time for Banshee, and then some lunch, I think," Abby said, getting back into Steve's car after Freshum's interview.

"Banshee, huh? You're pretty gung-ho on this one. What's his name?"

"*Her* name is Yu-ji Tsai."

"Oops. Okay. What's her story?"

"Let's see…" Abby paged down the profile. "She's a… seventy-six-year-old grandmother, originally from Taiwan."

Steve chuckled. "Wow. I can just imagine her sprinting across the street with a walker, screeching down a crew of hardened bank robbers with her banshee wail."

Abby raised an eyebrow. "You just said that. Does that make it true?"

"I said I could *imagine* it. Which I can. I can't will imaginary nightmares like crime-fighting sonic screaming grandmas into existence like that."

She tweaked him on the chin. "Good thing too. That's number six on the D2S list. Unwelcome and unavoidable torments to others' quality of life. How nondescript is that?"

"Necessarily so, I suspect, in order to give broad latitude to the regional teams to make the hard judgement call when they have to."

"Ugh. Island-A is so awful. I still can't believe we, well not *we*," Abby paused to gesture between Steve and herself, "send innocent people to an island jail with practically no due process. It's like a stupid superpower Alcatraz for people who've done nothing wrong except win the bad luck lottery."

Steve shook his head a little. "Everything changed after the UDO. Society got, I dunno… tighter. I mean, things globally are actually better if you think about it. The economy is good, conflict is down, scientific influence on policy is way up, and the United Nations is as relevant as it's ever been."

Abby had to agree. Since the UDO destroyed the Korean Peninsula, a lot of the adversarial regimes around the world had stepped up to play nice with the United States. Hell, even Israel and Palestine had enjoyed over a year of unprecedented peace, which had led to greatly reduced — if not entirely eliminated — hostility across the Middle East.

"Still doesn't excuse sending innocents to tropical life-sentences. Who knows what's even happening at Island-A? It's not like we're told. The press conference the other day with the president and Frannie wasn't exactly forthcoming with the details. It could be complete anarchy."

Steve simply nodded and shrugged.

They had a half-hour drive to get to the interview with Mrs. Tsai, which was to be done at her boba tea shop called Mystertea in Rockwall. Abby read through the rest of the interview backlog, eyeing ones she was particularly keen on meeting. The leading candidate was a student from the University of Texas at Dallas that could listen to a song once and play it back on guitar with exact precision.

"That sounds pretty well-suited to a career on A-Space or YouTube," Steve said.

"Yeah, or a boyfriend. Just imagine having the equivalent of Eddie Van Halen or David Gilmour or Matt Bellamy in your living room any time you wanted."

Steve shot her a look. "Sounds dreamy."

"Right? We have got to do that interview! Think we can trade with Eddie and Bailey?"

"We do as RADSAnet commands," Steve deadpanned.

"Ooh, the big bad AI in the sky is going to send in the drones if we don't do our assigned interviews!"

Steve shook his head.

With as much time as the two had spent together since she had joined the team, she figured her snark would have worn him down. But it hadn't. She could tell by the little twinge in his forehead that what she had said hurt him a little bit. And he hid it. He didn't complain. What's more, his impassive, brutal honesty schtick hadn't put her off either. She liked that she could trust him. And she was looking for any excuse to make physical contact, so she pinched his arm.

"Ow! I suppose what the AI doesn't know won't hurt it. Geez."

He gave her a wide grin after a moment to recover, and it was all she could do to not leap out of her seat and mash her lips into his while they sped down the highway.

———

Mystertea was situated in one of DFW's myriad testaments to modern architectural practicalism: a rectangular mixed-use strip mall with residences on the second and third floors, and retail shops on the ground level. It was covered in red bricks, faux-limestone façades, and absolutely zero personality. All the units close to Mystertea were suspiciously vacant.

A pleasant heavy bell announced their arrival as Steve opened the door. The interior of Mrs. Tsai's store was decorated with stark contrast to the outside: a genial, pastel mélange of tropical trees, ocean waves, and floating plastic cups with little spheres and straws inside. The menu offered hot and iced teas, and a wide variety of tapioca pearls and other gooey objects that could be slurped up through bright red, half-inch wide straws. There wasn't a soul inside, save the proprietor, sitting behind the counter watching something on her phone.

"Hello, welcome to Mystertea," Mrs. Tsai said with just a hint of a Mandarin accent. "What would you like?"

Abby scanned the quiet room. All of the chairs were neat and square against their tables. They might be her first customers of the day. "Yes, thanks. I'd like a chai milk tea with classic bubbles, please."

"You drink this stuff?" Steve asked.

"Yes," Abby said, glancing around the empty room. "And so do you."

"Oh." Steve contemplated the menu. His eyebrows drew into a narrowed line. "Uh, I'll have what she's having."

Abby giggled and paid for the drinks after shooing away Steve's credit card, and Mrs. Tsai began preparing the order.

"Mrs. Tsai, we're actually from RADSA. I'm Abby — er, Agent Alstrom, this is Agent Palmer. We're here to do your interview."

"Oh, that's ni—"

A loud smattering of applause came over unseen speakers.

"THANK Y'ALL, THANK Y'ALL," a throaty male voice boomed in a deep southern accent.

Mrs. Tsai's mouth hung open as she worked on the drinks. The strum of a few chords on an acoustic guitar came out of nowhere, followed by more applause.

"Oh, I know this song," Steve said.

Abby groaned, glancing around for the speakers.

"WHEN YOU LEFT ME, I COULDN'T SLEEP."

She winced at the volume of the star country singer Brad Brickenbrack belting out his hit 'Dry as Late July'. "Uh, Mrs. Tsai, could you turn down the radio volume so we can talk?"

Mrs. Tsai straightened up, shaking two plastic cups full of a creamy, orange-colored tea and ice, sealed on top with plastic film sporting the magnifying glass-in-a-cup logo of Mystertea. She faced Steve and Abby, and the volume increased as she stepped up to the counter. Her mouth was still wide open.

"CHECKED YOUR SOCIALS, LIKE A CREEP."

Steve looked at Abby, wide-eyed. She returned his concern. The full force of the bass and drums entered the song.

"THE MEMORY, STILL EXCITIN'."

Mrs. Tsai, mouth still gaped open, set the bubble teas and two straws on the counter and gestured at a table. She turned around and began cleaning something. The volume decreased only slightly.

"BUT I SHOULDA BEEN EXORCISIN'."

Oh my God, Abby mouthed to Steve.

"THEY SAY THE HEART IS A GARDEN."

He nodded in the direction of a table in the far corner.

"THAT GROWS IN GOOD TIME."

Steve moved with mechanical precision to a chair. His eyes were fixed on Mrs. Tsai, and his brow furrowed. Abby flopped into a chair beside him, taking care to use her momentum to scoot it close enough to bump into Steve.

"I hate this song," she said.

"What?" Steve yelled.

"I said, THIS SONG SUCKS!"

"BUT MINE WON'T, CUZ MY GARDEN'S AS DRY AS LATE JULY."

There was a brief reprieve in volume as the acoustic guitar went through a mournful solo.

"What's the matter with it?" Steve asked. "I don't listen to country music and even I know this song. It's super popular."

"Ugh. It's so *twangy*," Abby said, wincing at the steel guitar that just entered the ensemble. "And the chorus doesn't even rhyme." She speared the top of her tea with the straw's pointy end and took a big slurp.

"At least the tea is good." She waggled the cup in front of his face.

Steve pierced the plastic cover on his tea and nursed it, watching the proprietor make herself look busy behind the counter. Abby covered her ears to deaden the song, but it had little effect. Mrs. Tsai's eyes rolled as the song blared from her mouth. The volume waxed and waned as she faced toward or away from the pair at the table.

They just sat there, watching. Drinking their tea. The music dominated the space.

The RADSAnet description had this right, it was an auditory assault. It was all Abby could do to contain her laughter at the absurdity of it. And it was a country song. This poor woman.

The entire song played through. Abby breathed a sigh of relief as Brad Brickenback's final "DRY AS LATE JULY" declaration came, and the store was thick with silence.

"Okay," Mrs. Tsai said, gingerly walking around the counter and approaching the table. "I'm so sorry about that."

Abby wiggled fingers in her ears, attempting to shake free the off-key falsetto Brickenbrack used in the middle of the song.

"So, that's your R-Skill?" Steve asked abruptly.

Mrs. Tsai gave him a confused look.

"Your ability? You play back songs?" he added.

"Ah, yes. But just the one. Dry as Late July. I'm afraid I don't like it very much." Mrs. Tsai sighed and forced a small smile. Her eyebrows contorted with embarrassment.

The bell above the door rang as a college-aged couple walked in.

"Excuse me." Mrs. Tsai shuffled back behind the counter to help her new customers.

Abby looked at Steve. He had a surprisingly dour expression.

"This is," he started.

"About the silliest R-Skill we're ever going to come across." Abby slipped a hand over her mouth to hide her grin. "Worse than ketchup."

The smattering of applause that opened the song tickled through the air again.

Abby gawked at Mrs. Tsai, then back at Steve. "Oh man."

"THANK Y'ALL, THANK Y'ALL," Brickenbrack's voice boomed again.

Steve rubbed his chin, frustration creasing his brow. "I was about to say, not good."

The song played all the way through. And then again. The two college students collected their drinks and left the store like they were fleeing from a wildfire. Steve motioned for Abby to follow, and they stepped outside.

"We'll be right back," Abby yelled to Mrs. Tsai, who did not appear to register the words.

Outside, Abby could still hear the song. It was thankfully not as loud, but it was still inescapable. "No wonder the other stores are vacant. At least she's gonna help kill Brad Brickenbrack's career."

Steve grumbled.

Abby danced around Steve to the tune and grinned at the absurdity of the situation. "I think we're gonna have to send this one to the island."

"I agree," Steve said.

Abby giggled as she shook her hips to the awful lyrics. Then her eyes grew wide when she realized Steve meant it. She grabbed his shoulders and yanked on them like she was starting a lawnmower. "What?!"

"This is a clear number six. I don't like it, but I don't see any way around it."

"Steve," Abby pleaded. "You have got to be joking! You want to send this little old grandma to Island-A? The same place where they sent the killer with spider venom?"

"It's the law, Abby. It's our job."

She walked a few paces away from him and rubbed her face. "I don't believe this. I can't believe *you*. How can you be so cruel?"

"This is what we signed up for, Abby. Our duty. Suppose the landlord of this strip mall comes calling and asks why a number six is still occupying his otherwise vacant building. Vacant because with her here he can't sign anyone else to a new lease. What do we tell him?"

Abby threw her arms to the sky. "Tell him we will compensate him for his lost business. RADSA is well-funded, right? We're supposed to protect Adapted too, you know. Help advance their cause? How is sending

Grandma Brickenbrack to Island-A protecting or advancing anything here except the pocketbook of a property owner?" Her eyes watered. "That hardly seems just. Why can't we find a little stand-alone building where her song won't bother anyone? Make sure she's got sound insulation in her house to keep her neighbors happy?"

Steve rubbed his chin. "That would open a Cowboys stadium-sized can of worms. Think of all the judgement calls every team in RADSA would have to make."

She walked up to him and popped him on the shoulder again. "You just said D2S number six was necessarily vague to allow us to make judgement calls. So, let's make one, Agent Palmer!"

"DRY AS LATE JULY!" Brickenbrack sang as the song finished for the third time.

Steve looked from Abby to Mrs. Tsai inside, then at the cup in his hand as he rubbed his arm. "Well, I think Ben is going to be on the fence with this. But I'm willing to go to bat for her as long as you take the lead on finding her a new place that will work. The tea was good. And she's hardly a danger to anyone."

A thrill of relief tickled Abby's spine. She was about to hug Steve when the song started again. "THANK Y'ALL, THANK Y'ALL."

He groaned. "It sure as hell is annoying."

She stepped in close to his ear and whispered just above the drone of the music. "Yeah, well they say the only sure things in life are death, taxes, and Brad Brickenbrack."

He almost cracked up. Almost. The little twinge of pain written on his forehead indicated that was definitely not what they say about the only sure things in life.

She beamed. He had a heart, she knew it. Hers was racing, first from the fury at the thought of sending Mrs. Tsai to the island. Now it galloped at their closeness. He smiled ever-so-slightly (a huge thing for stoic Steve), and gazed at her with those deep, Dr Pepper eyes of his. Abby wanted to rip her clothes off and swim in those pools.

"I am sure of one other thing," Abby said, whispering in his other ear.

"What's that?" Steve asked, recoiling in preparation for another spike of pain from his R-Skill caused by her relentless wit.

Instead, Abby dropped her cup, reached out with both hands to his cheeks, and kissed him.

CHAPTER 25
LUCKY

"GOOD AFTERNOON, EVERYONE," President Phelps began. "First, I'd like to begin today by again offering our condolences to the Chinese Navy for the loss of their new aircraft carrier in the Pacific Ocean. I understand rescue operations are still ongoing, but no survivors are expected. A terrible loss of more than a thousand souls. Our hearts go out to their families, and their country in this tragedy. The United States will assist with recovery efforts in the weeks ahead."

He paused to sip his water.

"Okay! Now, for the positive news. I am overjoyed to announce that the State Department has signed a significant new trade agreement with China. I participated in some closed-door negotiating myself this week with President Chan to help seal the deal. It will ensure the stability of our economic partnership for years to come and serve to ease tensions between our countries. As you know, having an even playing field between the dollar and yuan has been one of our staunchest complaints for decades, and in exchange for certain import guarantees on our side, they will submit to United Nations monitoring of currency manipulation, and severe fines for infractions. They have also agreed to significant penalties for intellectual property theft and cyber warfare. We will be subject to the same guarantee and penalties, and the FBI will vigorously pursue and prosecute any American entity — private, public, government, or commercial — that violates the tenets of this new agreement."

The well-dressed press corps exchanged a few perplexed looks. One intrepid reporter raised his hand while the president paused for another drink of water.

He pointed to the reporter from the Washington Post. "Yes, Tom?"

"Mr. President, are we to understand that this impromptu press conference is only about the trade agreement, and not the two dark objects that crashed into the Pacific last week?"

Phelps laughed. "That's correct. Please hold further questions until the end, everyone." Many heads in the media exchanged looks and murmurs.

Resigned, the president slapped the sides of the presidential podium. "I get it. I do. But our brightest minds have said there are no UDOs out there we can detect, and we here at the White House will continue business as usual until told otherwise. Of course, the Pentagon is tracking every inch of space they can. Of course we're discussing potential countermeasures. But people far smarter than I have said we're under no immediate threat, and I trust that they can make that determination far, far better than I or anyone else in this building can. To imply otherwise would only serve to incite panic and unrest. Here, and around the world." He paused, and threw stern looks around the room. "Barring new information, we will continue to do our everyday jobs, trying to make things better for all Americans, and provide a shining example of freedom, liberty, and prosperity for the world to follow."

He could sense the audience shifting in their chairs, settling in for a much less headline-grabbing affair.

"And," he shouted.

The press snapped into alert focus.

"This agreement will have a significant material impact on the overall trade deficit. We will be adding and greatly increasing exports to China in a number of areas: produce, livestock, raw metals, all the way to household goods from shampoo to table salt." He grinned. "This is all great stuff."

Various individuals were scribbling notes. Many were not.

"Alright. Here is something for your top web links. This deal will provide opportunities for every working man, woman, cis, trans, gay, straight, Adapted, and unaffected in our country. New businesses. Job security. Huge increases in overall employment. It's GDP growth. Job growth. Salary growth. Attitude growth. Our chief economic partner and rival is finally playing ball by the same rules the rest of the world has been playing by. China will strongly benefit from the import guarantees we're committed to and new access to our own exports that were previously restricted. But we will reap substantial rewards. This growth, combined with our balanced budget, will allow us to pay down the national debt for the first time in over twenty years. I think this agreement will be the achievement my presidency is remembered for, decades after I'm out of office."

He scanned the room. There wasn't an impressed face on the floor. He smiled. *Mission accomplished,* he thought. "Alright. I guess the news-du-jour is elsewhere today. I'll take your questions on the trade agreement, if there are any."

There weren't any.

CHAPTER 26
THE SLEUTH

SHE KISSED HIM!

Steve shoved away his initial shock and reveled in the moment. Her lips pressed into his. A hand gently tugged on his tie. His neck craned at an odd angle, as for the first time in his life, he was kissing someone taller than him.

Two seconds or ten minutes, he could have stayed there forever. But Abby, still in the lead, drew her head back and smiled at him. Her left eyebrow reached skyward to a quizzical height.

Steve stammered. "That was…"

"Weird. You taste like chai tea."

Abby strained to keep a straight face. Her kind eyes were about to pop from holding back her laughter.

"I thought that was you," he said.

"Nope, definitely you. I was drinking a latte."

And then, pain. The familiar knife behind his eye.

"Ow. That one hurt."

"Shit. Sorry." Abby rubbed his forehead with a thumb. "Feels like I'm saying that to you a lot. Guess I don't know my own strength."

Steve gazed into her pale blue eyes and time again slowed to a crawl. Did he want this to go farther? He had so carefully avoided anyone that casually set off his R-Skill. Here was this cute, compassionate girl that actually liked him — him, R-Skill and all — and it was second nature to her to joke and rib falsehoods. Could he handle getting closer to someone like this? Would it be worth all the pain?

He knew the truth without it having to be spoken.

Steve smiled and shook his head slightly, then ran his hand through her hair. He caressed the back of her neck and stepped close to her.

"THANK Y'ALL, THANK Y'ALL!"

Steve broke it off, laughing.

"Oh my God! I can't stand this song!" Abby groaned in protest.

"I think it may be my new favorite." He grinned at her, then pulled her in for another kiss.

———

They suffered through the R-Skill interview with Mrs. Tsai, enduring Brad Brickenbrack's hit song another nine times. Steve had never been so glad to be back in his car as he and Abby each shut their doors, dampening an encore performance.

Clocking in at three minutes and forty seconds (Abby timed it the fifth time through), they had spent well over half an hour sitting and nursing their second and third helpings of boba chai tea waiting for each replay to finish. In order to keep to their schedule, they had to opt for drive-thru cheeseburgers for lunch. Abby happily munched away as Steve drove them towards their next interview appointment.

"So… do you want to talk?" Steve asked.

Abby chomped down on a french fry. "About what?"

Steve stumbled with a response. "About… you know."

"The interview? No thanks. I'm still trying to get that song out of my brain." She wiggled her head and twisted a pinky finger in her ear. "I need some heavy metal or something."

"No, that's not what I—"

"Oh." Abby stopped to deliberately slurp on her soda. "You mean the part in the middle where we kissed? You're not gonna make it weird, are you?"

Steve shook his head.

She smiled. "Good. So, let's see. I liked it. Did you like it?"

"Yeah."

"Well then, I'd say that it's likely to happen again at some point. Does that sound alright with you?"

He chuckled. "It does."

"Cool."

Abby seemed unexpectedly casual about the whole thing. Any time Steve had concluded a 'first kiss moment' with a girl in the past, it felt more… momentous. The two brief kisses he and Abby shared seemed more like the first stepping stones on a winding path through an unknown forest. He had absolutely no idea where it was going. Maybe he could just chalk the difference up to youthful inexperience. She seemed content to enjoy the moment they had as much as she was presently enjoying her fries. But some sense of obligation compelled Steve to press forward.

"How about tonight? Wanna grab dinner?"

"I'm actually more a fan of the part of the experience where we actually consume the food, instead of merely acquiring it."

"Huh?"

"But I can't tonight. I have a date."

Date? Her words were true. His grip tightened on the steering wheel.

"What?"

"Mary's got an algebra test tomorrow and I promised I'd help her study."

More honest words. "Oh." Steve let a sigh of relief slip out and hoped she hadn't caught him tensing up.

"How about Termin8tor tomorrow?" she asked.

———

Steve gnawed on a fingernail as he waited on hold. It took over a week to find the business card Angel Bretstock, now President Phelps' press secretary, had given him the night of the election victory. He almost didn't call, but his head hurt so damn much he was desperate for any kind of help.

Doctors were no use. The Adapted phenomenon was too new. Not enough research. Take some Excedrin and drink lots of water. Each time a doctor or nurse fed him some bullshit to get him out the door, Steve's head thundered in pain. He had already burned through his sick days staying home and away from people at the mall where he worked as a security guard. Pretty soon they would just let him go. He would need to find a new job anyway, something where he wouldn't be around so many people.

A chipper voice finally answered. "Mr. Palmer, so nice to hear from you. How is everything?"

"Hi, uh, Secretary Bretstock. I'm—

"We're friends, Steve. You can call me Angel."

"Oh, well Angel, I'm Adapted. It happened a couple weeks ago. I was hoping you might put me in touch with someone at RADSA that could help. I'm having… problems. I tried their hotline, but there are so many new Adapted emerging right now they said I may not get their attention for a while. I need help."

"I see. What kind of problems? Your ability isn't on the Dangers to Society list, is it?"

"No, no. It's just… painful."

"What does your R-Skill do?"

"I can tell when people are speaking the truth. When they don't, it hurts. A lot."

"Wow. Well, that's interesting. All these abilities are so unexpected. But that's the first one like that I've ever heard of. I'll be sure to tell the president, he'll get a kick out of it."

Steve rubbed his head. Something she said wasn't right. He blew it off, hoping she may have a lead that could help him. "Do you know if RADSA has any kind of solution, or cure, or something? I'm not sure I can handle living with this."

"Not that I know of," she said. "But I hear a lot of people feel that way when they become Adapted. We had an intern become Adapted last month and she was suddenly able to see in the infrared spectrum. Poor thing. She screamed and screamed when it happened. It took her a while to adjust, but she's got the hang of it now. It takes time. RADSA is just getting going, but they're doing lots of research, and working on providing resources to new Adapted like yourself. And it just so happens that an old friend of yours, Frannie Gustafson, is going to be taking over at RADSA. Maybe she could even get you a job, if you're interested. Let me find her number."

Steve hadn't seen that in the RADSA news, but the wave of tranquility that followed Angels' words told Steve it was true. But it was truth he could have done without.

———

The rectangular abyss on the living room wall beckoned to Steve as he entered his apartment. He knew the result of that siren's song: pain, pain, and more pain. The president's latest press conference waited. It called to him.

"You don't have to watch it," Steve told himself as he hung up his coat and tie and changed into shorts and a T-shirt.

It was the truth. He didn't have to watch it. He was under no obligation to torture himself with a politician's falsehoods.

But in this case, there were two truths. The other was that Steve absolutely *had* to watch the press conference. He couldn't leave a mystery unsolved, and in the past few weeks, a disturbing pattern had emerged: President Phelps knew far more about the UDOs than he let on.

Steve sighed as he admitted to himself that his course for the evening was set, and would no doubt be a painful one. He wished Abby had been free to go out tonight, so he could have at least delayed the stabbing sensations by a day. He preemptively downed some Excedrin, and enjoyed a couple beers with his leftovers, hoping the needle-sharp gouge his R-Skill wielded with relentless constancy would be dulled, if only slightly.

"Alright, let's get it over with," he said after tidying up the kitchen. He grabbed a pen and notebook, and pulled up a replay of the press conference on the TV.

The president strolled up to his podium in front of the press corps, wearing his slightly too-happy-for-grim-news smile he usually carried. Steve had checked the headlines for most of the afternoon, so he knew today's announcement wasn't about a new UDO. Steve braced himself as the president began to speak.

Waves of truth washed over him. As welcome as they were surprising, Steve stopped the replay and started it over. Rescue operations - true. No survivors - true. Thousand souls - true. Recovery efforts - true.

The president paused to sip on his water. He did that an awful lot when he spoke for whatever reason. Steve rubbed the sharp stubble on his cheeks, still shocked at the uncharacteristic chain of truths. Then Phelps made his big announcement: a new trade deal with China.

"Big whoop!" Steve barked at the TV, then laughed. The reactions from the press corps were as unenthusiastic as his. "Talk about the UDOs or the Adapted already!"

But the president was apparently only there to talk about the trade deal. Which he did with zeal. And truth. Every. Single. Word. Steve watched in bewilderment. Not once since he had become Adapted had he seen a politician speak with perfect honesty.

The press corps became a little antsy as the president scolded them on their lack of interest in the trade deal. He waxed prophetic about the riveting impact to the trade deficit.

And then the pain came. Lie. Lie. Lie. Truth. Lie. Steve's eyes watered, ready to burst from the shooting pain. Then relief as the president continued to talk. More truths. Job opportunities, economic growth, yada yada.

Steve paused the feed and rubbed his head as he retrieved another beer from the fridge. He was hesitant to replay the speech again, but what had just transpired was too incongruous to ignore. The ratio of truths to lies was inverse to that of Phelps' typical orations.

He restarted the feed, this time studying the president's facial expressions. Besides appearing far too chipper when mentioning the destroyed aircraft carrier, Steve couldn't discern anything out of the ordinary. As the brief string of lies approached, Steve braced for the pain. Produce - lie. Livestock - lie. Raw materials - lie. Table salt - true. Shampoo - lie. He paused the playback again and took a long pull from his beer. It didn't help with the pain. He played through the list of erroneous export goods, then shut the TV off and laid back on his sofa to collect his thoughts and calm the screaming pain behind his eyes.

"What the hell is going on?"

These falsehoods were peculiar. Different from the business with the UDOs. The president was wrong about the types of goods the trade deal included. But he had to be lying — he was involved in the negotiation.

Why had Steve not followed the other Steve's advice from a few minutes prior and avoided the press conference? That Steve's truth involved a lot less pain.

He texted Abby to see if she was free to chat, but she said she would be busy with her sister for a while. Something about an existential teenage crisis.

Steve tossed his phone down next to his notebook and was about to head to his bathroom for a shower when he observed a new pattern from the president written down in his notebook: truth, hidden amidst the lies. Table salt. It was most definitely part of the trade deal. But why lie about the rest? To make it sound more interesting or impactful? He growled as he turned the TV back on to suffer through another replay of the speech.

This time through, he picked up on a new nuance to the pain: deception. Aside from salt, Phelps was intentionally lying about the export goods. But, again, to what end? It was a strange thing to try to cover up, especially when presented amongst so many truths.

A second nagging itch began to tickle the back of Steve's neck. Now he had two mysteries involving the president to work through. At least this new one would be easier to research. He pulled out his laptop and prepared for a long night spent learning everything he could about table salt.

CHAPTER 27
GARBAGE GIRL

ABBY ARRIVED AT THE KIMS' house at precisely 7:47PM. Far too late to endure her foster mother's home cooking, and hopefully after her foster father would have finished the dishes so Abby wouldn't have to do them. She rang once, then let herself in. She knew the Kims could see her through the video doorbell and wouldn't come. She instinctively pulled her shoes off and placed them neatly next to the other three pairs that rested in a line by the front door. The no-shoes-in-the-house rule had irked her the first few months she lived there, but now she had the same rule at her own apartment.

The heady aroma of the family rice cooker in action filled the air, punctuated with the bite of strong coffee brewing, and a less pleasant odor of fish. The Kims lived in a classic Plano McMansion, complete with vaulted ceilings, well-appointed tile-and-granite kitchen and bathrooms, hand-scraped hardwood floors, and non-committal gray wall paint. The house was too big for four people when she lived there. Now with just three, it was cavernous. She rounded the corner into the kitchen and put on her smile.

"Hi Mom, hi Dad."

"Abby!" Walter Kim said, looking up from the sink, arms up to his elbows in suds. His graying mop of black hair was neatly combed, and he wore a sharply pressed blue checkered shirt with the sleeves rolled up and dark slacks.

Her foster mother, Betty, continued fiddling with a game on her tablet for several moments, then turned to look at Abby with a raised eyebrow and half-smile. Betty's favorite coffee mug sat on the table. It was white, with the famous I-Heart-N-Y graphic, except the mug said I-Heart-S-K and replaced the heart with the red and blue *Taegeuk* circle from the South Korean flag. Her hair had had some recent work done, looking unusually curly and dyed black as night. She wore a modest white bathrobe with a hotel logo on it. Her face said, "I told you you'd be back here begging for help," but Betty simply mumbled something unintelligible into her coffee cup as an acknowledgement.

"Where's Mary?" Abby asked.

"Studying in her room," Betty said, somehow emitting the words without her lips moving.

Both her foster parents were second-generation Americans and spoke flawless English, but each had a slight accent from growing up speaking Korean at home. They had attempted to keep that tradition alive with Mary, but gave it up when her grades started slipping behind her English-only speaking peers. After all four of Mary's grandparents were killed when the UDO struck, Walter and Betty doubled down on speaking Korean at home, and attempted to bring much of the culture that had been lost into their daily lives. Most of that took the form of Betty's home cooking, which had been primarily Western fare when Abby had arrived at their house, but was now exclusively Korean. Abby had developed a tolerance for most of it, but her tongue absolutely feared Betty's lava-hot kimchi.

"Oops!" Walter clanked a pot into the dishwasher and splashed sudsy water all over his shirt. "You missed dinner. There are leftovers in the fridge."

"I'm good, thanks." She greatly preferred eating things with four legs. The oily stench of oven-roasted fish painted the room, and Abby was ready to flee upstairs.

"You're not here for money, are you?" Betty quipped between chimes of whatever game she had going on her tablet.

"Nope, I'm good," Abby said. "Just here to see Mary."

Betty scoffed. "That's a first."

Ah, the familiar cold shoulder from her foster mom. Over the years, Walter had done his best to make Abby feel welcome, as taking her in was primarily his idea. But he was often out of the house and as much a klutz with his words as he was with the dishes. So, Abby had to navigate the unpredictable minefield of her foster mom, Betty. Making fun of Abby's habits was the routine. Betty kept her digs small, but Abby suspected she secretly kept a list of every transgression, large or small, to present to Walter at some point and demand Abby be kicked to the curb. Betty had always seemed to think that Abby was moments away from brainwashing Mary into a suicide-pact cult and took years to get at least outwardly comfortable with the idea of leaving them alone together. All this, despite the fact that Abby had pretty much behaved herself for the three-plus years she had lived with them. The most trouble she had gotten into was getting suspended two days for getting physical with Mary's bullies. Betty found nothing but fault in Abby's actions, but Walter was eternally grateful for Abby's intervention. She knew he would go to bat for her on that score alone. Plus, he knew Abby was also the primary reason Mary was passing her math classes.

Until the Kims, Abby had always been the youngest sibling of her various foster families. But being the older sister for a change had been good for Abby, as well as Mary. Sure, the hail-resistant, 30-year warranty roof over her head and presumably safe food to eat were nice, but she was truly grateful for the relationship that had blossomed with Mary. Who knew being a big sis would be so much fun? If not for Mary, Abby wouldn't have been compelled to stick around.

Abby put her hands on her hips, broadened her shoulders, and attempted to radiate pride at Betty. "I'll have you know, I started a new job, thankyouverymuch."

Walter beamed at her while desperately scouring a pot. "Congratulations!"

"Couldn't keep your old job, huh?" Betty mocked, then went back to tapping on her tablet.

Abby folded her arms, annoyed that her foster mom couldn't be bothered to show at least a little enthusiasm. "Actually, I got a better offer. Something with the government."

Walter's eyebrows almost launched off his forehead. "Oh yeah? Helping troubled kids like you used to be?"

Abby couldn't quite swallow her chuckle. "Not exactly."

Betty scoffed again. "Still throwing garbage for a living?"

"Nope. Well, not yet at least. I imagine I will at some point," Abby said with a shrug.

A tender teen-aged voice called from upstairs. "Abby, is that you?"

Betty slipped a "woop" as her game showered her with tinkly winning noises. "Don't stay too long, she has homework."

"I know, just here to say hi." Abby gave Walter a wink and headed upstairs. Abby knew he understood the reason she was here. She bounded up the stairs, knocked three times on Mary's door, and let herself in.

"Hey Mary-K, whaddya say?" Abby said, smiling.

"A-double-B-Y, lookin' fly!" Mary said, completing their secret sisterly greeting, though without her usual gusto. The math must be getting to her.

Abby nodded and brushed imaginary dust off the sleeve of her black Killers t-shirt. Mary had grown a bit this year, but would likely end up short like her parents. She was still wearing her school uniform: a white polo shirt and maroon plaid skirt. Her neck-length hair was jet black, save for a new, inch-wide band of pale purple that framed the left side of her face.

Abby poked at the purple hair. "I like the color."

Mary smiled at the compliment, then went back to scribbling on her homework sheet.

The bedroom was locked in time; Mary was firmly ensconced in teenage fandom. Her tastes shifted every year or so, but her latest passion — K-Pop — had not yet been supplanted. Korean bands that had survived the UDO disaster saw their popularity skyrocket, chief of which was Pop-Wing-Flight, Mary's favorite. Over a dozen K-Pop posters adorned the walls, featuring girl and boy band members in tight clothes, gender-bending makeup, and all manner of hairstyle and color. One had a black cloth band pinned across the front with RIP marked on it with white shoe polish. At one point, Abby had made an attempt to develop an appreciation for what her sister listened to so they could chat about the bands. But that was short lived. Not enough distorted guitars, and she didn't speak a lick of Korean.

Mary's desk was cluttered with textbooks, notebooks, pencils, and a bulbous Texas Instruments graphing calculator decorated with pink electrical tape.

"Whatcha workin' on?" Abby asked.

Mary frowned. "Oh, you know, the usual. Me and my old friend the quadratic equation were debating which one of us is stupider."

"Well, you do love an endless debate. Can I help?"

"That depends. Did you bring a cheat sheet to get me through the test tomorrow?"

Abby shrugged the backpack off her shoulder and plopped it on the desk. "Better. I brought Dr Pepper."

After an hour of reviewing the finer points of variables, coefficients, and parabolas, Abby was convinced Mary had the topic down, but her sister's mood hadn't improved. Something else was going on. She drained the last drops from her can of Dr Pepper and absentmindedly attempted to throw it into Mary's trash bin across the room. The can unceremoniously sailed past the bin and smacked into the mirror above Mary's pink dresser, falling to the hardwood floor with a judgmental clatter.

"Aluminum is still your kryptonite, super-sis?"

Abby retrieved the can and walked it over to a smaller blue bin reserved for recyclables.

"I have vanquished my eternal foe, the recyclable!" Abby trumpeted.

Mary sighed. A frown tugged at her lips.

"Okay, MK, what's up?"

"I hate algebra."

Abby slid up to Mary's side and bumped into her shoulder. "That's not it," she said in a melodiously mocking tone.

Mary eyed the trash can. "It's nothing."

"Is it boys? It's boys."

"No."

"A girl?"

"No."

"Walter and Betty?"

"No!" Mary grumbled. Abby knew referring to their parents by their first names annoyed her sister.

"Um… The existential dread of being a teenager and realizing your window of opportunity for shirking the responsibility of adulthood is closing soon?"

Mary drew in a quick breath. "Responsibility?"

"You're growing up. You've got big changes coming. College. Independence. Womanhood. Laundry detergent."

"Something like that." Another sigh.

"Fine, keep your mysterious dark secret to yourself." Abby slapped Mary on the back. "Being an adult isn't all bad. You get to do taxes and mind your fiber intake. Oh! And they do this little thing to your brain that makes NPR actually interesting."

Mary gagged. "Gee, I can't wait."

This was uncharacteristically moody for her little sister, and almost certainly had nothing to do with the math in front of them. Usually, run-of-the-mill teenage problems rolled off Mary's back. She needed to figure out what was going on. Abby scratched her head and shouldered up to Mary.

"C'mon, tell me. You're not getting bullied again, are you? I don't mind cracking some more skulls. It's not like they can suspend me from school again."

"No, they'll just toss you in jail instead."

With the mention of jail, Abby's thoughts turned to the accident with Tyson, and the fact that she somehow evaded any kind of trouble for knocking his head off with a block of cement. Just a severance package and a quick walk to the front fence. The police didn't even interview her. Outside of an external prompt, she never dwelled on him either, which struck her as borderline sociopathic. A small knot of guilt worked itself into her throat. Not over what happened with Tyson, but the confusion over her lack of emotional response to it. She swallowed it down and pressed on.

"What are big sisters for? I'm happy to club a few Internet trolls for you. Though I may have already used my get out of jail free card."

Mary raised her eyebrows. "Huh?"

"Oh. Never mind. I'll tell you some other time when you're not brooding."

"I'm fine."

Abby remembered saying the same thing not long ago and how Steve reacted. At the time, he knew she wasn't fine, though she seemed more or less perfectly fine about what happened to Tyson now. So strange. Steve would be able to cut to the issue with Mary. Maybe with Abby too. She began to daydream about his eyes, his smile, and that little speck of compassion she had unearthed under that mountain of stoicism.

"Mmm." Mary hummed and scribbled an answer on her homework sheet.

"Hah!" Abby whooped and elbowed her sister in the ribs. "You can do this stuff. Don't worry about your test."

"I know. It's just… do you ever get the feeling that going through all this effort isn't going to make a difference in your life at all?"

"Ah, the quintessential crisis. I guarantee you that every single kid has that feeling about math at some point."

Mary scoffed. "Math? I mean *everything*, Abby. What's the point of any of it?"

"I… don't follow," Abby said, hoping Mary would volunteer some accidental details that would direct the conversation.

"We could have another global pandemic. I could get hit by a car. Another mysterious dark thing from space could come down and wipe us all out tomorrow. Why bother with any of it?" Tears welled in her eyes.

Damn, Abby thought. This was a full-on existential meltdown of Chernobyl proportions. What could she possibly say? She pulled another can of Dr Pepper out of the cooler bag in her backpack and cracked it open. The sweet symphony danced on her tongue — cola, cherry, spices, bath water, unicorn dust, and whatever the heck else made it taste so good. Instantly, she had an answer for Mary.

"Drink this," she said, handing the can to her sister.

Mary wiped her eyes and took a sip.

"You like it?"

Mary nodded.

"You want more of it?"

Mary nodded again with raised eyebrows.

"There you go."

Mary groaned and pushed Abby off her chair. "That's your answer? Life is worth living because of Dr Pepper?"

Abby pulled herself off the floor. "First, ouch. Second, yes."

"Ugh." Mary rolled her eyes. "I thought you were gonna drop some worldly wisdom on me there for a second, not carbonation and corn syrup. Shouldn't you tell me it's friends and family or some other bullshit like that?"

"Those are correct answers too, my young Padawan learner."

"Star Wars?"

"Also correct. Star Wars, friends, family, and Dr Pepper. The reasons life is worth all the crap we have to shovel."

"For you, maybe."

"So that's my answer. You have to know yours. You've got your violin. And…" Abby looked around the room. "You love the K-Pop bands. You've got Walt— Dad and Mom. They'll bend over backwards for you. Me too."

"All of those things can get taken away."

"There are always more. I just… uh, broke up with my boyfriend." Thoughts of Tyson drifted into her mind once more. Abby had to focus to keep the trembles out of her voice. "But I got a new job and there's another guy there I'm into. He's a little weird, but he's cute, and I think he likes me."

"You got a new job?"

Abby brushed off the question. "Yeah. I'll tell you about it some other time." She opened another can of Dr Pepper and took a big slurp. "My point is, already in front of you there are any number of small things you enjoy that make life worth the effort. When one is taken away, another will always come along soon enough."

Mary sighed.

"Don't forget, you've got a badass older sis that'll beat up your bullies for you."

Nothing.

"How about a badass older sis that'll let you pick the color of her new car?"

A small chuckle slipped from Mary's frown. "I think bright orange, so pedestrians can see you coming and run away. Like a giant warning sign."

"Maybe a light bar and siren too?"

Mary nodded and smiled, but the smile was short-lived. She sipped at the Dr Pepper and went back to drawing squiggles on her homework sheet.

Though pumped at the pep talk she had just improvised, Abby wasn't certain it had helped. That Mary wasn't immediately buoyed by it was disappointing. But then, what did Abby know about psychotherapy? Her own experience as a teen was far from smooth, and done mostly without guidance. Mary had a loving family that would do just about anything for her. She'd turn out just fine.

"You know your folks and I would do anything for you. I can speak from experience when I say not everyone gets that growing up. All you need to do is call me. We can solve anything together. Including quadratic equations."

Mary nursed her drink and looked up, shifting her gaze between each of the five Pop-Wing-Flight posters on her wall (one for each dreamy, heavily-airbrushed band member). After the fifth little sip, a small smile stretched out from her lips. "Thanks. I guess I can live with that."

"Good. Now let's get back to studying. Unless you'd like to take a crack at my taxes?"

CHAPTER 28
BOUNCY

THE GOLDEN EMBRACE of the sun continued its summer onslaught upon the comfort of North Texans everywhere as Gigi strolled from her car over to Bessie's trailer. She didn't mind the heat. Get out of the kitchen and all that. She checked the time on her phone. *Twenty minutes late. Right on time,* she thought.

Gigi considered it the mark of superiority to have the appearance that she always had socially significant obligations outside work, and that her job wasn't the most important thing in her life. It was, in fact, the most important thing in her life, insomuch as she saw it as her best available launch pad to greater things. The visibility she could get working for RADSA could be the thing that propelled her to celebrity status. If not of the full-on Hollywood variety, at least that of a well-known social media personality. Something sustainable. Once she had a wide enough viewership, she knew she'd be able to easily maintain the celebrity status quo. Any number of videos of her showing off the fantastic feats she could perform with her R-Skill would be worth that payoff. Hell, she'd settle for daily videos of her working out in tight clothes if they kept the views coming.

"Hey Gigi," Eddie called from across the parking lot.

He was sitting on his motorcycle, an absurd Harley or Victory something or other with the ridiculously high handlebars. Gigi didn't know much about motorcycles. All she knew was they were loud. Eddie's was *fucking loud.*

"Fashionably late, Eddie?" she asked, sipping on her morning smoothie. She had experimented with some root veggies in today's formula: parsnip, jicama, and purple carrots, plus persimmon, lemon, yogurt, and of course the requisite kale. It tasted like Eddie's filthy bike tire, after it had rolled through mud, parking lot oil stains, and a grassy spot a dog had done its business in last week. She forced it down.

"You know it, *chica*. I'm following your example."

Gigi blinked at him and put on a saccharine smile as Eddie joined her on approach to the trailer's rear door.

"New teammate today, huh?" he asked.

"What?" She gawked at him and almost dropped her smoothie. Which wouldn't be that great a loss. It really did taste awful. But another teammate to deal with? Someone else to vie against for the spotlight? Gigi pinched the crown of her nose and sucked in a breath of hot, humid morning air. Bessie's giant stainless steel trailer was beginning to feel inadequately small.

"*Sí*," Eddie replied.

"Who is it?"

Eddie shrugged. "All I saw was Ben's email this morning."

Gigi rolled her eyes. She had a habit of not paying attention to work-related communications when she wasn't on the job. *Couldn't be any worse than Abby*, she thought.

She opened the trailer's back door and saw the team standing in the Bay. They surrounded a tall, handsome young man in a white shirt with a patterned blue tie. He had creamy dark skin and neat, short black hair. All smiles, he was buddied up next to Abby and had his arm around her shoulder. Gigi was wrong. This was worse than Abby.

"Zeke?" she said, far louder than she had intended.

Jezekiel Thomas. Zeke. A walking, talking testament to Abby's greatness. Her compassion. Her make-a-difference attitude toward the Adapted. The young man mere moments from ending his life, pulled back from the brink by Abby. He was now on the team? Gigi wanted to slam the trailer door shut, run back to her car as fast as her legs would carry her, and once inside, scream until her eyes bled. In her stomach, she felt the same rancid stew brewing she had every time an inferior gymnast scored better than her in a competition.

Instead, Eddie shoveled her inside with his beer belly and closed the door behind him. "Hot out there, girl. Oh cool! Zeke!"

Gigi shot annoyed daggers at him, noting the large man's balding head was already slick with sweat beneath the few strands of hair he had left. He wiped his face and waved at the cheery crowd ahead.

"Eddie, Gigi. Come in and say hi to our newest family member, Zeke Thomas," Ben called.

Gigi found her bravest, friendliest face, and put it on. She wouldn't let Abby continue to hog the spotlight.

"Hey Zeke, so glad you're here. I'm Gigi. I was… there on the bridge last week." She shook his hand, and let the contact of their skin linger just a little bit longer than it needed to. After all, he was just coming off a breakup, and had already proven himself to be susceptible to physical attention. Plus, he was pretty cute. "Are you feeling alright? It's only been a few days since the bridge. I would have thought you'd be in rehab or something."

Zeke nodded, still smiling wide. "I remember you. Thanks for helping me. I did end up in rehab, but they ran some blood tests and found I was critically low in Vitamin D. To the point where it could cause severe depression and suicidal thoughts. I knew my R-Skill depended on Vitamin D, but didn't realize to what degree. They got me on some supplements and I was feeling like myself in no time. It takes sixteen pills a day now to stay well, but I feel amazing."

"Wow," Gigi said, batting her eyes. "Well, it's great you're here. It's a fun group." She looked around the team, skipping past Abby.

Zeke squeezed Abby with a big shoulder hug. "I know! I feel like I know everyone already. Abby's told me so much."

Abby blushed. Gigi nearly barfed. The two towered over her, and she felt as small as Bailey in that moment. She glanced down at Bailey to make herself feel better and received a nod hello in return.

"Well," Ben said. "We've got a number of interviews to do today—"

"Why don't I walk Zeke through the training and help him get his bearings?" Gigi blurted. "The others can knock out a few this morning and we'll catch up with them after lunch."

The whole team looked at Gigi with surprise.

"What? I need to catch up on some reports and he can watch me do those too," she said.

Ben shrugged with a furrowed brow and smirk on his face. "Okay then."

Zeke said his goodbyes as Steve and Abby left together, followed by Eddie and Bailey, who were going out on their own interview run today. That was an odd pairing. Eddie, the burly, aging, gay biker dude with gloriously magic fingers, and Bailey, the sweet southern belle that wasn't even four feet tall and drove a semi-truck with impossible precision.

"I'll be in my office if you have any questions Zeke," Ben said, giving him a pat on the back and heading down the hall.

"Okay, so what's first — reports, or training?" Zeke asked.

Gigi peered down the hallway, lined with bright LED lights down each corner, floor and ceiling. When Ben's office door closed, she snapped her head towards Zeke with a wry smile. "Nah, fuck that shit. You can do it later. We're gonna have some fun." She walked over to the lockers. "First, I'm gonna change. Time to show off my new uniform." Gigi kicked her shoes off towards the rear door, then whipped her shirt off and pulled off her leggings just as quickly. She turned to Zeke and gave him a flirty wink. "We're not modest around here, better get used to it."

The new recruit was doing an admirable job keeping the drool inside his mouth despite it hanging open as he gawked at her in just her socks, bra, and thong. Zeke stammered, failing to utter any actual words.

As if attempting to perform the phrase 'slow-motion' for a game of charades, Gigi pulled her new jumpsuit from her locker and slid into it like a greased python. *So easy*, she thought, eyeing Zeke's astonishment and laughing to herself. Gigi turned and studied how the snug uniform clung to her in all the right places. *We should have called Eddie 'the tailor'. This is good work*, she thought. She pulled up the zipper, leaving it a couple inches short of the electric pink hem at the top so the bridge of her neon blue bra showed. Then, as if she hadn't just been nearly naked in front of a practical stranger, she waltzed over to Zeke with a smile and slapped him on the arm with a cupped hand. "C'mon, let's go make some videos."

"Okay." Zeke struggled to blurt even that out, still wide eyed and failing to keep his gaze away from her jumpsuit-enhanced cleavage.

Gigi tapped some buttons on her console to start recording on the trailer's external cameras, then grabbed Zeke's hand and led him outside.

"Don't you want your shoes?" he asked.

"Nope."

Gigi flung open the back door and did a handstand in the door frame. "This might sound weird, but would you take my socks off?"

"Woah." Zeke hesitated, and he looked kind of confused, but she couldn't quite tell. The expression on his face was upside-down after all. After a moment's thought, he walked over and pulled her socks off one at a time, grasping her bare ankle as he did. He had big, strong hands she wouldn't mind getting to know a little better.

"Thanks." She pushed off of the deck plating and did a double-backflip into the parking lot. Her feet came down onto the concrete and her R-Skill transformed the rock-hard conglomerate into the familiar soft, rubbery cushion. She bounced up and down, arms akimbo, and grinning ear to ear at Zeke, who stared at her like she was the first Adapted he'd ever met.

"That's so cool!" he said, clambering down the steps to the ground.

She cocked her head and nodded, "Thanks. I wanna see yours now." She halted her momentum by bending her knees and flexing her quads, and her upward bouncing settled into a gentle wobble on the parking lot. "I admit I haven't read your file, so I don't even know what it is you can do."

"Oh," Zeke said, looking at the ground. His amazed smile collapsed into a frown. "When I kiss something I radiate this kind of wave. It pushes everything away. Hard."

"Wow, that's kinda… awesome," Gigi said, not entirely patronizing him.

"I guess. Except for the not being able to kiss anything again part."

"Wait. How do you eat? Don't you do the same kind of motion with your lips to eat off a fork or sip a drink?"

He shook his head. "It's not the same. Kissing has a bit of a forward 'push' with the lips, if you think about it. That's the only difference." He thought a moment and chuckled. "I suppose if I'm not careful, I'd blast my lunch all over someone like a food cannon. But it hasn't happened yet."

She gave him a come-hither finger. "Show me."

"You want me to… kiss you?"

"Sure, why not?"

"Well, for one, I think it'd hurt. I've never hit anyone with my wave. And two, we kinda just met."

She started bouncing on her springy concrete a little harder, just to make Zeke watch her. "Pfft, don't think of it like that. Think of it like… sparring, except with our R-Skills."

"Oh." He scratched his head. "I dunno. It's pretty strong. I could probably knock the trailer — Bessie — over with it."

Gigi giggled. "Yeah don't do that. You don't want to get on Bailey's bad side. I'll bounce around a little, you try to catch me and use your kiss to blast me into the air."

"But…"

"I'll be fine." She bounced higher on the concrete, and did a few flips and twists in the air. "See? Gymnast."

"Wow. Okay."

She grinned. This was going to be fun. She wasn't going to make it easy for him, but she'd let him catch her eventually. "C'mon."

Gigi led him to an emptier part of the parking lot, but still well in view of the trailer's cameras. She began bouncing around him in a slow circle. At first, he just stood there and ogled in amazement. She couldn't blame him. But after a minute, she started darting toward him and then away, sneaking pokes at his arms — which rippled with stiff muscles when she got in a good stab.

"C'mon, Z! Defend yourself!" She bounded at him again and popped him in the gut with a solid right fist.

"Ow, hey!" He doubled over, holding his stomach.

"Sparring!" she called to him with a sing-songy taunt, bouncing high in the air. "I'm a bad guy! How are you gonna stop me?"

"Do you haze all the new recruits like this?" Zeke looked up at her with a little fury in his eyes finally. Or was that lust? Either would do.

"Nah, just you." She winked at him.

As she started descending from her latest bounce, he dashed towards where she would land, leaped, and tackled her to the concrete.

"Ow! Fuck!" she yelled as she felt the rough hard concrete on her back rip through her new uniform.

Zeke was above her. The weight of his body pressed into hers. She was about to cackle with laughter, but then he grabbed her shoulders and rolled over, flipping her on top. He pulled her to him and kissed her on the lips.

For a split second, she felt the tenderness of his mouth — the need of her own lips to feel the intimate touch of another person. His large hands grasped her waist and gave a delicate squeeze. In that instant, she sympathized with how he felt on that bridge. She wouldn't want to never be able to kiss someone again.

Then her body was flung into the air. She yelped as she began to tumble over backwards, rising above the parking lot. She was high. Really high. A chill of fear struck her spine as she tossed about. *I've gotta land on my feet,* she thought, knowing that only her feet would protect her from this fall. The parking lot and strip mall circled around the horizon as she tumbled out of control. Then her training kicked in, she stopped gaining and started falling, and caught a reference point on the ground where she would hit. It was pretty close to the trailer, but she was confident she wouldn't hit it. And was confident the footage would be stellar with her landing spot coming so close to the cameras. Her adrenaline pumped hard as she focused. She got her body's torque under control and executed a couple twists and a flip before coming down on her feet right behind the trailer's rear door. The concrete gave way in a deep, wide, inverted cone, stretching all the way under the wheels of the trailer, which caused the metal structure to dip down. It then rebounded upward as Gigi bounded off the ground herself. The restorative momentum of the concrete coming back to its normal state pushed the trailer an inch into the air. It crashed down with a resounding thud.

"That was badass!" Zeke yelled. He ran over to her. "Are you okay?"

"Great!" Her neck was indeed a little stiff, but Gigi was beside herself. As giddy as she was the first time she made the US Olympic Team's gymnastics trials. She couldn't wait to see the footage.

Then Ben's angry face popped out of the trailer's back door. "Gigi! What the hell are you doing?"

She looked up at him with a sheepish grin. "Uh, training?"

Ben snapped a finger at Zeke. "The training he needs to be doing is on a laptop. Let's start him on *Integrity for United States Government Employees.*"

Zeke pulled his shoulders in and mumbled, "Sorry."

Ben grumbled, then retreated back into the trailer.

Zeke looked at Gigi with concern.

"Don't sweat it," Gigi said. "He's pricklier than a divorced porcupine when it comes to following RADSA's rules. I guess we should get you going on the laptops. C'mon," she said, motioning to the door. Gigi shook her head, wondering why Ben could be such a stick in the mud sometimes. *Fuck him*, she thought.

CHAPTER 29
THE ADJUSTER

A SHRILL BEEPING JERKED Ben awake. He kept his phone on vibrate, so that it was making noise at all was concerning, let alone at 2:17AM. A series of weather alerts clogged his screen, but a single text message at the top got him out of bed.

"Wake your team, Ben. You've got work to do." It was from Director Gustafson.

He scrolled through the local news. While he slept soundly to the patter of steady rain and roll of distant thunder, a massive supercell had opened a can of meteorological whoop-ass on Collin County to the north. That was just what had been reported by eyewitnesses. The suburbs of Frisco, Allen, and McKinney were particularly hard-hit. An area in Frisco near the Dallas Cowboys' practice facility, The Star, was evidently flattened.

Ben sent out a group text message, advising the team they were going into the storm area to assist first responders. Gustafson had given him a special alert code to trigger all the phones to make an audible alert. He'd have to ask her more about that at some point.

All but Gigi responded within five minutes.

"I'll go get Abby," Steve volunteered in a reply. "She'll need a ride."

Ben jogged to the kitchen to start some coffee brewing, then took a quick hot shower to urge some alertness into his muscles and got dressed. He advised the team to meet at the Galleria Mall to board Bessie; they would enter the disaster area together. As he typed the word 'disaster', his pulse quickened. This would easily be the most important work his local team had ever done, the talking down of new teammate Zeke Thomas notwithstanding. A number of other regional squads across the country had been called in for similar service, but none of them had made a material impact. They were a visual representation of RADSA lending aid for news and social media coverage, but those teams were essentially just extra hands. None of the other regional teams' Adapted possessed particularly impactful R-Skills. Ben hoped his selectiveness was about to pay dividends in a real crisis.

He arrived at the Galleria and was unsurprised to find Bailey already there; Bessie was rumbling and ready. Bailey, the team's de facto quartermaster, was in the trailer preparing the utility vests. Others straggled in over the next half hour. All but Gigi, who was nowhere to be seen. *Way to miss an opportunity*, Ben thought.

"Well, this is exciting," Ben said to the team sitting around the lounge inside Bessie's trailer. "I'll get started, even though Gigi's not here yet."

Abby yawned between gulps of Dr Pepper. The others nursed coffee or energy drinks.

"Thank you all for the prompt response. Director Gustafson called the Frisco police chief and offered our assistance. He's agreed to let us into the disaster area and lend what aid we can." Ben said.

"Which is what, exactly?" Steve asked.

"Well, for one, I think Eddie's R-skill will come in handy here. Given the swath of wreckage, there will undoubtedly be plenty of injuries." He addressed the biker. "Let the paramedics handle anything serious, of course, but you could take some pressure off their workload. "

"Sure thing, boss." Eddie said.

"I want footage of everything we do, so everyone should grab a utility vest." Ben said.

"Gigi's not here yet, so I'll show you how to work the cameras, Zeke" Bailey added.

"Abby, you may be able to assist with clearing rubble and wreckage. There will probably be a number of streets that are impassable," Ben said.

"Well, that sounds like fun for three-in-the-morning, if I can even do it. Is someone going to follow me around with a legion of dumpsters?" Abby rubbed her head, sans hat for the first time he'd known her.

Ben laughed. "I'll see what can be arranged."

"Not everything on the ground qualifies as garbage, ya know," Abby said.

"Zeke may be able to help clear things with his ability too," Ben said.

"I'm game!" Zeke replied.

Ben checked the camera and radio on his vest. "I will coordinate with the emergency response leader and see where else we can make an impact. Let's get rolling."

And with that, Bailey jogged off to the cab to get Bessie in motion. Ben looked over the team to gauge their moods, which were a mix of somnolent and excited. His was entirely the latter.

"Hopefully Gigi will catch up," Ben said. He called and texted her again, with no response.

CHAPTER 30
GARBAGE GIRL

AN EERIE DREAD smothered the ordinarily well-lit streets of nighttime Frisco. In Gigi's absence, Eddie had punched up the camera feeds from around the trailer up on the lounge TV, and the team watched as the pitch black service road of the Dallas North Tollway slowly scrolled by, lit only by the semi's headlamps. Towering highway bridges loomed overhead, their silhouettes barely visible against the light pollution from the parts of DFW still with power that reflected off the clouds. Bailey kept Bessie moving at a slow pace, deftly weaving a path through all manner of debris strewn across the roadway.

A gnarly pit of worry festered in Abby's stomach. Her bones quaked with the fatigue of getting only two hours of sleep. Early reports had stated that the area had sustained a direct hit from an F4 or F5 tornado, and many of the structures, including Stonebriar Mall, were in ruins.

Steve sat next to her as they watched the road crawl by on the screen. As the trailer rolled over chunks of debris, she would bump into his shoulder and long to have him wrap comfort around her with his arm. He didn't shy away from her intermittent contact, but he made no effort to initiate any of his own.

The trailer banked as Bessie turned into the access drive toward the mall, between the local IKEA and Frisco's minor league ballpark. The front camera was well-lit, thanks to Bessie's generous complement of headlights and floodlights. A large object straddled both sides of the drive ahead. The slow scroll of the video feed came to a stop as Bessie's progress was halted.

The massive yellow awning from the front of the IKEA building laid across their path in a twisted heap.

"Looks like we're walking from here," Bailey said over the intercom. "Unless you think you can move it Abby?"

Everyone in the lounge looked at her. Abby wanted to shrink into the sofa. She had no idea if she could move something so large, though she had never come across a piece of debris at the Charles & Munck worksite that she couldn't handle. But this was far, far larger than anything she had ever lifted. "Um, I guess I could try," she said, without a drop of confidence.

"Here," Ben said, handing her a trash can from the floor.

"Aw, you know just what to get a girl," Abby said, hoping the levity would fight off the goosebumps dancing on the back of her neck. It did not, though it did get a chuckle out of Ben. She didn't want the first time using her R-Skill in a meaningful way for the team to be a dud. Right now, she felt like she was about to walk into an exam having partied all night prior. She donned her vest, camera, and radio, then stepped down the rear steps, trash can in hand.

The night air was thick, like walking through uncomfortably warm black pudding. The storm had done little to impact the summer's sweltering oppression. Abby wiped her forehead, only to have the little beads of sweat replaced by twice as many. The trash can wobbled in her shaky hand. She sighed, then tossed the basket into the adjacent parking lot for her target; it clattered onto its side, but didn't have to be standing upright for her R-Skill to work. She walked over to her opponent: a twisted hunk of yellow-painted metal, concrete, and foam at least fifty feet wide, and a dozen feet high in places.

"C'mon, you," Abby said to the hunk of building after turning on her camera. She knelt under the spot that looked like the middle of the heap and pulled up. It lifted as easily as a sheet of paper. She held it up in front of her, triumphant. Then it snapped in half. The structural metal groaned and cracked as the weight of the ends strained the structure apart. One half slipped her grasp and came crashing back down to the ground. A freshly shorn jagged steel edge sliced the palm of her hand as it fell.

"Ow! Fuck!" she yelled.

Blood gushed out. Her heart pounded in her chest. She knew it wasn't a mortal wound — not even close, but the sight of blood brought her still-digesting Taco Bell dinner up to the back of her throat. A stream of crimson red ran down to her wrist and fell to the ground, and a vision of Tyson's headless corpse lying in a pool of blood rushed into her mind. The wet blanket of guilt she had somehow been able to mostly avoid wrapped tight around her. Abby dropped to the ground and slumped her head into her hands.

"Are you okay, Abby?" Bailey called over a speaker. "Come in and get that fixed. We can walk to the mall, it's not far."

Abby hated herself for not being able to compartmentalize. For caring. For killing her friend. What was she even doing here? She should be in jail for manslaughter at the least, or better yet, quarantined to Island-A next to all the other deadly Adapted. Why had she even been given this chance?

Abby stifled a gag at the smell of her own blood and forced her burrito supreme back down from the brink. She stared ahead to where Stonebriar Mall should be and squinted. Through the black veil, beyond the reach of Bessie's bright lights, a faint mountain of rubble rose beneath the inconsistent flashing of police car reds and blues. Despite the early hour of the morning, there could be people in there that needed help. Certainly at the movie theater, and maybe some of the restaurants might have had people inside. Buried under all that. She could get them out. That was why she was there. A tool. A machine. And machines didn't complain when they got hurt, they just did their jobs until they could no longer function.

She stood. Her hand throbbed from the bloody wound, but she was almost numb to the pain as adrenaline coursed through her veins. She re-centered herself on the piece of wreckage to her right. As before, it lifted easily. Without a second thought, she hefted it towards the trash can. The structure floated silently as it flew, bits of foam coating flaking off and wafting in the air like celebratory confetti. It clattered on top of the can with a calamitous crash of screeching metal. Abby hoisted up the other half of the awning and tossed it on top of the first with a similar crash.

"Well. That wasn't so hard," she said, holding her wounded hand as she returned to the trailer. Bessie lurched as Bailey got them in motion again.

"Not bad, Abby," Ben said, smiling.

"Let me see that," Eddie said, pointing at her bloody hand. He grabbed it with one of his hairy, tattooed paws, the exact opposite image of a medical professional's hand. He pressed a thumb down on the edge of the gash in her palm, and a spike of pain shot up her arm. Then pleasure. Waves of pleasure. Incredible pleasure radiated through her body as Eddie ran his thumb over the wound. She gnashed her teeth and shuddered, trying to exude some self-control. But it was hopeless, like trying to swim up Niagara Falls. She lost track of time, the people around her, the room, the mission, even the gentle hand holding hers. All she could sense was the pleasure. Impossible, incredible pleasure. And then it was over. She opened her eyes and Eddie smiled. Abby tried to shake some sense into her head and clenched her shoulders.

Somewhere in the middle of Eddie's ministrations, Steve had grabbed her other hand. "Just enjoy it," he said. "Nothing else you can do."

Abby felt sheepish. "Well, I…"

Eddie handed her a towel to clean her hand and face. "Good as new."

"Thanks," Abby said. "Sorry if I…"

Eddie patted her shoulder. "Steve's right, *amiga*." He shrugged and smiled. "A lot better than lidocaine and stitches, no?"

Abby could feel the heat from her flushed cheeks. She pressed through the team to plop down on the leather sofa so she could resume trying to shrink into the cushions. Their faces beamed at her. Ben's, Zeke's, and — oh, Steve's. His smile. It was the widest of the bunch. Pride straightened her spine. She could feel what they saw: capability. Her R-Skill really could lift any amount of garbage she wanted. She stood and flexed her hands, ready for more. "Get your vests on, people! You're not gonna let me have all the fun, are you?"

CHAPTER 31
THE SLEUTH

BESSIE CAME to a creaking halt not far from the mid-level entrance to the mall, by the entrance to a Barnes & Noble, Dave and Busters, and the AMC movie theater — well, what was left of the movie theater. The metal structure of the building reached out like a skeletal hand through the cloak of darkness, exposed steel protruding from the mound of rubble-like bones through skin. Yesterday a bustling retail experience, the mall was reduced to a future eyesore; it was simply a pile of junk waiting for its inevitably delayed insurance claim to finally come through before being carved up and hauled away.

Steve didn't want to be here. He had stayed up far too late, investigating the history of salt production in America, and was surprised to find that one of the largest salt mines in the country was just east of Dallas. But as he took in the video of commercial carnage in the wide beams of Bessie's headlights on the screen, his thoughts drifted to his service with the Marines.

Two hours of sleep was enough for today — he had done that while deployed on more than one occasion. But this carnage hit close to home. The mall was about twenty times bigger, but the jagged rubble under the full moon here looked eerily similar to that of the new U.S. Embassy in Somalia the last time he had seen it. The last dregs of the terrorist group Al-Shabab made an ill-advised attack on the building in Mogadishu. He was there. The enemy managed to blow a massive hole in the building, right where the ambassador's office was. He had seen her safely away not moments before the explosion. For their troubles, the terrorists got pounded into the dirt by a bunch of pissed off marines itching for a fight. Afterwards, the embassy was temporarily closed, which brought about the end of Steve's final foreign deployment with the Marines Security Guard.

"Testing!" Ben barked through his shoulder mic. Everyone's radio volume was evidently turned to max, as Ben's voice turned to squawky feedback and reverberated through the trailer.

Steve shook off the noise and tried to keep his head in the here and now. He had been discharged nearly three years ago, but he could remember that night like it had just happened. That, and the eerie flat look of Milo's dead face at the viewing before his funeral. Both memories popped up at inopportune moments, like an unwelcome in-law dropping in on Sunday dinner.

"Okay," Ben said. "I want eyes and ears peeled out there. Cameras on. Our primary goal is the location of survivors, and rescue if it can be easily done without endangering the integrity of the wreckage. We don't want to risk crushing anyone on the level below us.

The rear door clattered open. "I hear voices in there!" Bailey yelled from outside. "Let's go, Abby!"

"Me too!" Zeke said.

Abby massaged her recently repaired hand and had yet to clean off the blood from her face. She had steely determination in her eyes. The effect was striking. Abby seemed a completely different person than the one that went out to move the yellow chunk of the IKEA store minutes before. "Can someone find me another trash can or dumpster or something?"

"I will," Steve said.

Abby gave him a slight smile and ran her hand across his stomach, then followed Zeke out the back door. Steve watched them go with a sigh. "In the rear with the gear again, eh?" he asked himself.

"What's that?" Ben asked from behind.

Steve whipped his head around. "Oh. Nothing. Just have my mind on something else."

"Need you focused, Steve. I know we didn't get much sleep. There are smelling salts in the first aid cabinet if you need to wake up."

"I'm fine."

Ben checked his watch. "Have you heard from Gigi?"

Steve shook his head. She wouldn't text him. Not since their ill-fated single date months ago.

"She'll get here on her own schedule."

"Yeah." Ben fretted. He zipped up his utility vest and checked the pockets. "Okay. I'm going to go over to the command tent on the east side. You're in charge here. I'll be on the police band, but will check in with you every fifteen minutes. Stay down here and coordinate. We don't want any more people up in the rubble than necessary."

"Where's my trash can?" Abby yelled from outside.

"Duty calls," Steve said, grabbing the wastebasket under Eddie's station and heading outside behind Ben.

In the wash of headlights from Bessie, Abby and Zeke cut long, dancing shadows up the side of the mountain of debris as they clambered up. Bailey, not as much. Her shorter limbs weren't as capable of spanning the large gaps. She mostly kept to the edge of the parking deck, combing a methodical path and calling for survivors. Eddie walked a similar path on the edge of the building further east.

"Where do you want it?" Steve called to Abby.

"Anywhere away from the trailer," she yelled. "Then get clear!"

He tossed the wire mesh basket as far as he could into the parking lot. It clattered and rolled twenty yards away, just barely visible in the glow from the floodlights on the back corners of the trailer. Seconds later, out of the darkness, a huge chunk of metal roof crashed down on the basket with a calamitous thud. Followed by another, and another, each preceded by a metallic, rending screech as the fragment was pulled free by Abby's R-Skill-enhanced hands.

Wow, Steve thought as he admired her prowess. *She's awesome.*

"What can I do to help?" Steve called.

No one answered. *Not much*, it seems. He figured he at least could walk around the edge of the ruin and listen for voices, if nothing else. Glad to be in jeans and sneakers, he approached the collapsed wall that used to keep all the books and magazines inside the Barnes and Noble protected from the elements. Now it was a splintered heap of shattered glass and disintegrated faux stucco. Pages upon pages were scattered into the darkness in every direction. He reached for an exposed metal stud to pull himself up onto the sloped side of the rubble. A memory from the worst night of his life tried to rise up to the front of his mind, but he pushed it down. He didn't need to be distracted by that right now.

Sweat ran down Steve's face, only half of which was thanks to the swampy post-storm atmosphere. A memory flashed in front of his eyes; the image of his best friend's dead body lying inside a black bag. His stomach convulsed.

He walked away from the destruction to collect his thoughts and find some cleaner air. Another large hunk of twisted metal clanked down into the substantial pile Abby had been building. Steve recoiled, reaching to his shoulder for a rifle that wasn't there. *Calm yourself,* he thought.

He closed his eyes and wrested control of his breathing. Why was he so damn on edge? It's not like he had PTSD; the docs cleared him of that. He just didn't like feeling like such a piece of shit standing around with nothing to do. Like after what happened to Milo.

A buzz in his pocket snapped his attention back to the present. It was a text from Gigi.

"Hey where are you guys at? I'm close to Frisco now."

Fashionably late to an actual emergency, Steve thought, smirking.

"Second level parking lot by south entrance of Stonebriar Mall. Trying to rescue survivors, need your help."

Bailey and Eddie were at opposite ends of the parking lot, canvassing the perimeter of the building. Abby and Zeke had scaled twenty to thirty yards into the mound of rubble. Abby tossed hunks of concrete and metal skyward as if they were paper airplanes.

"Hey, we've got one up here!" Abby yelled.

Steve stifled a chuckle and switched on his shoulder mic. "Abby, we have radios."

"Oops, right," she said over the radio moments later. "We've got a survivor here. He says he's banged up, but not bad. Wants to know where the others of his group are."

"Can you reach him?" Steve asked.

"Not without excavating more debris. He's in a pocket about fifteen feet below me. Should I do it?"

Steve waited for Ben's direction on the radio, then realized it was his call. He pressed the talk button on his radio again. "Can he walk well enough to scale down the debris? If not, we should wait for a crane or a crew with ropes."

"He says he can," Abby replied.

"Okay, go ahead. But start slowly. We don't want to cause a collapse."

A steady stream of debris began to crash into the pile Abby had built onto the poor wastebasket, certainly flattened to a thin mesh pancake by now. *At what point does it cease to be a wastebasket and become trash itself?* Steve wondered. Small chunks. Big chunks. Massive, car-sized chunks. Every few seconds, a twisted mass of clattering steel or concrete smashed into the pile.

"Okay, we've got him. Zeke's gonna help him down. Eddie, he's gonna need your, uh, special services."

"*¡Por supuesto!*" Eddie squawked over the radio. "I'll be right there."

Steve clambered up five yards or so to meet Zeke halfway and aided a teenaged movie goer down to a bench at the edge of the parking lot.

"Thank you," the young man said when he reached the ground. He was caked in muddy grime from head to toe. "I'm Derek," he stuttered.

Steve shook his filthy hand. "Hi Derek, I'm Agent Palmer with RADSA. This is Agent Contreras. He's an Adapted and can heal your cuts with his touch if you'll allow it."

The teen shrunk back and gawked wide eyed at Eddie lumbering closer. He sheepishly nodded.

"Good choice. It feels amazing."

Steve shone his palm flashlight on the young man as Eddie began to work his thumb over the various cuts and scrapes. The teen's eyes rolled into the back of his head and his tongue lolled out of his mouth. As Eddie moved from cut to cut, the young man squirmed.

Eddie shot Steve a glance and they barely avoided laughing.

"We've got another here," Abby said over the radio. "Ooh, two more. This is great!"

Eddie gestured towards the mountain of rubble with his head for Steve to go help. "I'll get him inside the trailer."

Steve nodded.

"Can I get Zeke over here?" Bailey asked over the radio. "I've got a couple survivors I can't quite reach."

Zeke raised his hands, gesturing he needed help finding her.

"That way," Steve said into his mic, pointing west in the direction of Bailey. "Get your flashlight out."

He watched in ceaseless amazement as Abby transferred rubble from one mountainous pile to another. Each hunk soaring gracefully through the air, as if a thousand pounds of mangled steel perfectly belonged murmuring amongst the birds.

The sound of metal scraping on metal ripped through the quiet night and Abby suddenly vanished. She screamed. Instantly, Steve's mind was back in Mogadishu.

———

"This is such a nuisance!" Ambassador Gustafson complained. "All this for a silly threat on Twitter?"

"Yes ma'am," Corporal Steve Palmer said as he picked up the bags on her desk. "Sorry ma'am. We have protocols to follow for this sort of thing. I'm sure it's nothing."

"Palmer!" Gunnie McNamara's booming voice rolled in from the hallway outside the ambassador's office. "The Osprey's waiting. Time to go."

Steve motioned to the door and followed the Ambassador out. He tried to quell his racing heart, but it was no use. After nearly four years of service, and a year and a half with the Marine Security Guard stationed in Mogadishu, he might see some live action. Almost all his time was spent doing administrative work. Day after day of paperwork, training, and meetings. Twelve hundred and seventeen days of nothing out of the ordinary, and now, suddenly, to be tossed in the deep, deep end where the big sharks swim. He couldn't wait to grab his rifle. The odds of a real fight were slim, but his adrenaline was pumping all the same. A half hour-old Tweet from the radical group al-Shabaab (which had been silent for years and was thought to have disbanded) made some cryptic reference to their last attack at the US embassy in Somalia in the 1970s. It could be a hoax, but protocol dictated that the civilians were to be evacuated and the compound locked down.

"Let's go," McNamara said to Steve as he and the ambassador entered the hallway. Beads of sweat trickled down the sides of the master gunnery sergeant's nearly bald head. As the local commander of the security guard detachment, McNamara was an effective leader, but was no more experienced with a hostile encounter than Steve.

"After you," Steve said to the ambassador, gesturing down the hall.

McNamara led them down two flights of stairs and out the rear exit to where the V-22 was waiting inside the expansive, high-walled courtyard. Four marines were stationed just outside the door. Two of them, the huge brute Quentin Fargo, and Steve's best friend Milo Phelps, joined the escort on either side of the ambassador.

The four marines moved in lock step, their boots crunching small rocks in the sunbaked courtyard dirt. Gustafson wore sensible black walking shoes that padded quietly as she shuffled forward with small steps. Steve took stock from his spot at the ambassador's back. Quentin and Milo both had weapons at the ready. Quentin's head darted around at random angles, ready to shoot at the first sign of anything out of the ordinary.

Milo's head was locked facing forward. His skin was slick and pale. The ambassador's curly gray hair bounced around as she walked, as indifferent as she seemed to be at the potential threat to the embassy. McNamara moved in even, practiced steps straight towards the Osprey.

They reached the tiltrotor aircraft in a scant ten seconds. The rear gate was open, and the other dozen or so civilians that were at the embassy today were already inside.

"Oh, sergeant," Gustafson said, stepping up the ramp to the Osprey. "There are a couple of file boxes I'd like to take with me on the floor beneath my desk. Could you have those brought down please?"

"You really need to be off, ambassador," McNamara replied as he motioned to the pilots to spin up the rotors.

The engines roared to life. It would be loud as hell in moments. Steve hoped the sergeant would just send him on his way so they could get on with preparations for an attack.

"It'll just be a minute to get them," Gustafson said, raising her voice to be heard over the rising noise. "This whole thing is just a nuisance anyway."

McNamara shook his head. "Fargo, Phelps. Go grab the ambassador's boxes and get them here on the double," he yelled.

"Yes gunnie," they both replied.

Steve nodded at Milo as his friend shouldered his rifle and turned back toward the embassy behind Quentin. He followed the ambassador into the Osprey and fixed her bags behind the cargo nets, then helped her to her seat and got her buckled in.

"Thank you, corporal," she said with a smile.

"Yes, ma'am. Have a safe trip. See you soon." He smiled back.

A thunderous boom rocked the courtyard. The V-22 shook. The fuselage rattled with metallic clinks from bits of debris. Steve ran to the ramp and looked up to see a huge cloud of smoke and fire filling the courtyard. He pulled his rifle from his shoulder and took a defensive position at the side of the ramp opposite the gunner's seat, craning for a view of where the attack could have come from.

"RPG! Get out of here!" McNamara screamed. He pointed at Steve. "Stay with the ambassador!"

Before Steve could protest, the aircraft began to lift off. The gunner manning the machine gun at the ramp yelled at him. "Take a seat!"

Steve couldn't. He hooked the cargo netting with his elbow and gripped his rifle, scanning the shrinking courtyard for signs of a firefight as the Osprey gained altitude. All he saw was the angry cloud of smoke and flames billowing out of the massive hole where the ambassador's office used to be. They had gotten her out just in time. His pulse raced at their narrow escape, then a massive lump formed in his throat as he realized that Milo was inside when the explosion happened.

Within a minute, the Osprey was out over the ocean. It banked south to head to Manda Bay, Kenya where the East Africa Response Force was based. Steve only took a seat after the smoke from the embassy was too small to see. He rubbed his stubble the entire flight, itching for news from the compound.

After they landed in Manda Bay, Steve stayed with the Osprey as the civilians were rushed out. He accepted the ambassador's well wishes as she departed, but didn't register a single word. Two dozen heavily armed, ready-for-action marines shuffled on board, and they lifted off again and headed straight back to Mogadishu.

Reports leaked in over the radio during the flight that a firefight had taken place not long after the explosion. A couple of rusty trucks full of men with rifles had showed up at the front gate and opened fire, but the terrorists were suppressed in short order. There were no other explosions or signs of damage to the building beyond the first rocket-propelled grenade.

The streets surrounding the embassy flashed with blue lights from local police cars that had blocked off the area. The fire at the back of the embassy had been put out, but the charred ruin of the terrorists' trucks still smoldered outside the front gate. The Osprey landed in the courtyard next to two others that had arrived before them and the EARF marines all shuffled out and quickly assumed stations at various points in the compound. Steve stepped back onto the courtyard and it felt like his first time there. The area reeked of gunpowder, smoke, and dirt. Several shiny black body bags lined the outer wall by the gate, which was manned by several marines from Manda Bay. Two more body bags were next to the embassy building, surrounded by marines.

"Who is it?" Steve asked as he walked up to the group.

"Fargo and Phelps," someone said. "Explosion got 'em."

Fargo was a cheese dick. Steve wouldn't want to ask for anyone from his squad to get hurt, but if he had to pick someone to take one for the team, it was Fargo by a marathon. A hulking cocksure juggernaut, Quentin Fargo was a fourth-generation marine, and made sure that everyone around knew that legacy made him special. Superior. That, and his preposterously muscular frame. There wasn't a marine in the squad that could best him physically. They all tolerated his shtick because he could practically bench press a tank, rocked at hand-to-hand combat, and feared nothing.

But Milo? Steve's stomach twisted in knots. He couldn't believe it. His best friend. Gone? A scrawny five-foot-six, Milo Phelps was the least likely marine in the squad, even less so than Steve, who was muscular, but not much taller. Milo's accuracy with a scope was his hallmark. He was an Expert — the best shot in the squad. Steve was accurate with a rifle, but wasn't close to the level of consistency that Milo could maintain. A point that Milo reminded him of at regular intervals, just like a good friend should. In turn, Steve pointed out that Milo lacked the dexterity to peel potatoes and was less imposing than the weekly laundry cart in boot camp.

I should have been there, Steve thought. His heart and brain waged war, debating whether he could have made a difference at all if Milo had truly died in the explosion. He had only been gone two hours, but he missed so much. Steve looked on from behind the crowd, forcing back a tear and struggling to swallow the wad of guilt lodged in his throat. A far larger group had coalesced to the side of Fargo's bag. Only a trio of mourners stood beside Milo's. It was easy to tell them apart. Fargo's stretched and rippled, straining to fully contain his muscled girth. Milo's had room to spare in all directions. Steve joined the group by Milo and covered his mouth to hide his quivering lips.

After a few minutes lost in thoughtless contemplation, Steve walked around to the back of the building to look at the results of the explosion. A huge crater exposed the top three floors of the building. Grisly fingers of blackened metal twisted out from the building as if reaching for more lives to claim.

A brusque hand grabbed Steve on the shoulder. McNamara. "You did good today, corporal. Got the ambassador out just in time."

Steve bit his cheek as he looked around at the results of the day and fidgeted with the rifle strap over his shoulder. *I didn't do shit*, he thought. He looked between the hole in the building and the rear wall, which was twenty feet high. "Looks like they attacked the front gate. Any idea where the RPG came from?"

McNamara shook his head. "Not yet. Hopefully, the camera footage will tell us something. EARF is going to handle the investigation. Let's organize a search and secure the building. I imagine we'll be closed down for a while."

The next few days were abuzz with activity as the embassy was stripped of anything of value. More marines from Manda Bay had arrived and took care of almost everything. Steve and the others from the embassy security detail were given only a few menial tasks. Nothing to take his mind off what happened. The embassy security guard had lost two of their own. Steve wasn't even there to help shoot back. Couldn't help search for his best friend when the fight was over. Useless.

———

Steve gasped as his focus returned, gazing wide-eyed at the mound of rubble. "Abby!" Steve yelled, then grabbed his mic. "Abby, what happened?"

Seconds passed. Silence.

"Abby?"

"I'm—"

His heart skipped.

"I'm okay." She coughed over the radio. "Just slipped. Stupid shoes." More coughing. "I should have worn boots."

Steve wiped the sweat from his face and breathed a sigh of relief. At the moment, he didn't care if she had stumbled upon a cache of a million survivors sitting on top of the lost gold of the Aztecs. His mind was only on her. He wasn't useless. He could do something. Steve jumped into the pile of rubble and began to climb.

Abby's mic was still open. "Oh. Thanks. Hi, I'm Abby. Steve, I'm actually down in the pocket now with two survivors. Can you help me get them out?"

"I'm on my way up. Are you okay? Are you hurt?" he asked into the mic.

The moments it took for her to respond seemed like eons.

"Good enough. A few cuts here and there. Suppose I'll have to pay another visit to Dr. Eddie."

"I'm ready at the trailer when you are," Eddie said, chuckling over the radio.

Steve grumbled, suddenly wishing he had the ability to give others exquisite pleasure.

"Shine your flashlight up so I can see where I'm going," Steve said to his mic.

Moments later, shafts of light shot up through the debris. His anticipation grew with each grasp of broken concrete or step onto a steel girder. His heart pounded. The physical exertion wasn't trivial, but his pulse raced because Abby was buried beneath this twisted wreck.

The giant mess of steel and concrete suddenly heaved and groaned, sounding like Godzilla rousing from a thousand-year slumber. *Shit!* he thought, picking up his pace. The rubble shifted beneath his feet like scree on a mountainside. The ruins of the mall shifted and screeched again.

"Abby!" Steve yelled.

"We have radios, Steve," she calmly scolded over the radio moments later.

Steve grinned. The wave of warmth from her true words paled in comparison to the radiant affection for her that warmed his heart.

"I'm almost there," he said into his mic.

Indeed, he was close to the spot where she fell. The debris was becoming thin. Each handhold and foothold had to be tested for stability. *She's fearless*, he thought as his progress slowed. When he found the lip of the opening, he pulled out his palm light and aimed it into the hollow space beneath.

"Hey," he said, smiling and panting a little.

Abby and two more teenage boys were standing in a small alcove, miraculously free of jagged steel or hundreds of pounds of concrete. They were eight to ten feet beneath Steve, each covered with dust, cuts, and bruises.

"Hey yourself," Abby said, smiling back, shielding her eyes from the glare off his light. "Think you can reach if I boost them up?" she asked.

Steve got down on his stomach, which wasn't a comfortable proposition given the sturdiest position was over the edge of a steel I-beam. He reached in and scooted as close to the edge of the beam as he could.

"Let's try," he said. "Can you both climb yourselves down once you're out?"

The young men each nodded.

Abby and one of the boys hoisted the other up to Steve's hand, and Steve pulled him up over the edge of the beam. While not a workout warrior like Ben, he was grateful that he had managed to keep most of the muscles he had developed in the corps. Steve guided the first teen down to safer footing, then made his way back up to the opening.

The second lad hesitated. "Maybe you should go first," he said to Abby.

"Nah, I'll be fine. Your turn," she said. They found a spot where she could help prop him up and he could get a foothold on some steel where Steve could reach. The boy quaked like Jell-O as he reached for the outstretched hand. Steve gave him a confident nod, then grasped his arm and pulled him up.

After the second teen was safe, Steve clambered back to where he could see Abby. "Okay, you're up." But as he said it, he realized he had no safe way to reach her. He stretched his arm out. "Any way you could jump up and grab my hand?"

Abby attempted a feeble jump off a protruding steel beam, but didn't get close. "Ya know, I was joking about that WNBA contract."

Steve chuckled. He reached in further, risking his stable foothold. "Here, try again."

On cue, his foot slipped. He tumbled headfirst into the alcove. Abby attempted to soften his landing, but they both slammed into the floor of concrete and metal.

"Ow. Shit!" Steve rubbed his head where it had met a disagreeable plate of steel.

Abby bounced up more quickly. She dusted herself off and helped Steve to his feet.

"My hero!" Her grin gleamed in the wan glow of her palm light on the ground. She swatted his hand off his head and replaced it with hers, caressing the rapidly growing bump that would no doubt hurt for days. "Any damage?"

Her other hand rested on his chest. He wondered if she could feel the thunder of his heart. She could reach in and pull it out if she wanted. He brushed a hand through her hair.

"I'm just glad you're okay," he said.

Steve leaned in and kissed her. It was passionate. Urgent. And she broke it off way, way too soon.

"Agent Palmer!" She said, taking a step back. "Don't we have work to do?" Abby grinned from ear to ear.

He slowly closed the distance between them as she backed herself against the wall of debris separating them from the parking lot. He stepped in close and put a hand around her back. "Yes, we do."

They locked lips again. Eager hands explored. They pressed against the steel behind her. The structure creaked and they stopped to look around their private room of rubble. After a few seconds of silence and shared shrugs, their grinning mouths found each other once more. Steve closed his eyes and melted into their passion. He would do anything for this woman.

Then her lips tore away from his. She screamed.

Steve opened his eyes and she was gone. The floor beneath her had given way.

"ABBY!" he yelled.

Nothing. The hole was dark.

He reached for his mic. "Abby! Abby! Are you alright?"

Steve's pulse raced at triple time. He fumbled for Abby's light on the ground and shone it down the hole she fell through. She was sitting up and holding her head.

He exhaled.

"Abby?" he called to her.

"Fuck. That sucked." She swept the dirt from her hair and wiped her bloodied face on a sleeve, then looked up at him. "Eddie's gonna get tired of me real quick."

"Hang on, I'm coming down."

"Wait—" she started, but then shook her head. "Be careful."

Steve found a strong handhold to lower himself through the hole, hoping his sweating palms would behave. He clambered down the fifteen feet to reach Abby on a rough slab of concrete. *Tough as nails*, he thought as he knelt down and inspected a cut on her forehead.

"Are you okay?" he asked, reaching his arms around her.

She sighed, hugging her arms around his. "Better now."

The structure groaned again with movement.

"Think we can climb out of here?" he asked.

"I have a better idea." She reached for her radio mic. "Everyone, clear away from the debris pile by the truck. I'm gonna toss a mountain top."

"What?" Steve got to his feet.

"Any size, any distance, remember? I could lift this whole thing if I wanted."

"Abby, that's… insane."

"Yeah, well, you can use *your* insane ability to tell me if I'm speaking the truth."

His eyes widened with the realization. She was right.

"Everyone clear?" Abby asked into the mic.

"We're good," Bailey responded. "Everyone's on the other side of Bessie from the pile. Give it hell."

"Light, Aziz!" Abby snapped to Steve.

He gave her a quizzical look.

"Fifth Element?"

Steve shrugged.

"Dude! You drop a perfectly fine Battlestar Galactica quote and you haven't seen The Fifth Element? Turn in your nerd card!"

Here they were, dozens of feet beneath the rubble of a tornado-torn mall, and Abby was calling him out on his nerd-cred.

"After we get out of here, we are totally watching that movie together," she said, dabbing at her cut with a hand.

He smiled. "I could do with a movie." He shone the light up at the structure.

Abby walked the edge of the hollow they were in until she found a spot she liked.

"Wait. What's to stop all the stuff above us from just falling down on our heads?"

She smiled. "If I do it right and lift right here, it'll all get picked up for a moment. If I let go quickly, the whole structure on top will just fly away into the trash can."

"That's the bravest little trash can I know."

She giggled. "Okay, here goes."

Abby lifted a large metal beam that bore the weight of everything above them. The mass of rubble supported by her delicate hands screamed bloody murder as it was wrenched away with impossible force from the surrounding debris. In an instant, it was in the air. Abby sported a triumphant smile. He could see the sky. A few desperate stars poked through the lingering storm clouds. Bessie's headlights were on them again, and both watched as the massive collection of steel and concrete floated through the air to join Abby's mountain of debris on the parking lot.

"Oh no," Abby said.

Steve saw her too. Gigi was ogling Abby's handiwork on the wrong side of the trailer, and didn't have a radio on.

"GIGI!" they both yelled, but too late.

The debris smashed down into Abby's mountain with a crash. Large hunks of rubble tumbled down the sides in all directions. A sizable boulder of concrete rolled straight at Gigi. It slammed into her and clattered to the ground next to Bessie. "Gigi!" Steve and Abby yelled again.

Steve hit his mic button. "Gigi's hurt! Get to the other side of the trailer! Now!"

"Let's go," Steve said, grabbing Abby's hand.

They scrambled down the debris. He tripped and stumbled, focusing his gaze on Gigi's motionless body, instead of his footing. *Shit. Shit!* he thought.

The others had surrounded Gigi by the time Steve and Abby got there. He breathed a huge sigh of relief as he saw her sitting up and rubbing her arm, not looking entirely flattened. "Gigi, are you okay?" Steve asked.

Gigi massaged her bloodied shoulder through a jagged hole in her shirt. "Peachy. Did anyone get that on camera?"

CHAPTER 32
BOUNCY

Gigi stripped down to her underwear and took stock of her injuries in her floor-to-ceiling bathroom mirror. Her left arm was badly bruised up and down, the image of an angry stormfront of purple and blue clouds. It looked very much like it had just been smashed by a hunk of concrete. It hurt to move, but she raised the injured limb over her head. She grimaced.

"That's just fucking great."

At least she already had her A-Space All-Stars audition out of the way. She didn't know how well she did — talent evaluators rarely gave decent feedback during an audition, but with these bruises all over, her file would have gone straight to the reject pile.

She poked at her ribs and winced. Eddie had repaired as much of the damage as he could; those few minutes were a pleasurable blur. But the reach of his R-Skill as a medical treatment was evidently limited to lacerations and abrasions. The wide and deep contusions on her left arm, ribs, and thigh would probably be there for weeks.

And oh, how she wished she had a camera running on her at the time. Surely, getting squashed under a hunk of tornado-torn building and bouncing right back up from it would help to get Bouncy one step closer to a household name. If only there had been footage.

More humiliating than the bruises was that Abby, after nearly killing her, still was seen as the hero of the disaster recovery. She rescued ten people. Gigi only got to be the victim.

Her phone buzzed. A text from Mom.

"Sorry sweetie, we're out at the lake this month. I thought we told you? Dad and I are entertaining some clients right now, but I'll call later, okay? Glad you're alright!"

Gigi sighed. Her mom couldn't even be bothered for thirty seconds to call and offer some parental comfort after a near-death experience. Typical. No doubt they'd also be too busy to call later. Just par for the course with her folks. Gigi would manage recovery just fine on her own, as she had throughout most of her gymnastics career. The sympathetic conversation with her mom would just have to take place in her head.

"Ow." Gigi stretched gingerly, observing how her body moved. The entirety of her left side was sore. Negotiating pain was something with which she had ample experience as a competitive athlete. She wasn't bothered by it in the slightest. If nothing else, it would be a constant reminder the next few days of the need to stand out in the face of increased local competition for accolades.

She treated herself to a fruit-only smoothie with raspberries, bananas, strawberries, and orange juice. Then she poured a hot bath with some CBD-infused soaking salts that smelled like a detonated potpourri factory. She flipped the spa jets on, then pulled the rest of her clothes off, save her twin layers of socks of course, and stepped in for a rejuvenating soak.

"Ow! Shit."

The water was quite hot, and the injured tissues were a choir of stinging protest. She forced herself in, ready to let the hot water and CBD work their magic. While not one to ever consider an illegal substance, she was happy to try the CBD oils her coach had recommended years ago. Miraculous stuff. It quickly became part of her recovery routine after any injury. She'd have some tincture too before going to bed.

Gigi closed her eyes and ran her hands over every inch of her body, sore or not, and worked the heat from the water into her tissues. Her mind relaxed, the essential oils in the salts — eucalyptus, lavender, and pink grapefruit — having the desired effect of melting her tension.

Then her phone buzzed, vibrating off the edge of the mottled sand-colored marble bath enclosure and clattering to the floor. She picked up the phone to see a small chip in the corner of the screen.

"Ugh." She was only mildly perturbed, as she welcomed any excuse to go to the mall and shop. A new phone would be a fun diversion tomorrow after work. The text was from an unknown number. She rolled her eyes after discerning it was from Abby.

"Hey Gigi. Ben gave me your number. Just wanted to apologize again for the accident and make sure you're okay. Is there anything I can do to help?"

"The nerve," Gigi said.

As if there was anything the bad-attitude teenage foster kid could do. Abby had already unwittingly disrupted Gigi's focus plenty enough. She didn't need to be tended to like a convalescent.

"I think I'm better off with you miles away," Gigi texted back, feeling no need to be diplomatic about her desire to not be anywhere near Abby. Except maybe to use her as a punching bag next Wednesday.

Abby did not respond, but her interruptive text still had the unintended consequence of pulling Gigi from her meditative relaxation. Instead of finding calm, she replayed the events in Frisco over in her mind. Perhaps the worst thing about the incident was that she was rendered the hapless victim. An innocent bystander. Just one more reminder that Abby's presence on the team regularly threatened to turn Gigi from rising star to sideline reporter, and that was a position in which she had no interest. The bath was doing its job again though, and after a short while, the repetitive waves of the spa mixed with the relaxing aromas of the salts had her in calmer spirits.

After her bath, Gigi swallowed a couple drops of CBD tincture and popped some Advil. She heated a prepped meal from the fridge for dinner — grilled chicken, cubes of sweet potato tossed with olive oil and herbs, and asparagus. She made a small fresh salad of avocado, heirloom tomatoes, thinly-sliced shallots, and spinach, tossed with a little vinaigrette. As she ate, she scrolled through her social feeds, pressing 'Like' on posts from well-wishers that had responded to the series of posts she made on the drive home. Other than an exact catalog of the extent of her bruises, the post was light on details, referring to the incident simply as a nondescript 'workplace accident'. One follower suggested she contact OSHA or better yet, sue her employer, which gave her a smile.

"I know, right?!" she replied to the tweet.

As expected, the thorough stretches she did before going to bed did nothing to alleviate the pain and tightness she felt the next morning. There was nothing to do about it but work through the inconvenience, using it as fuel for motivation.

"All part of the price of fame," she told her bruises in the mirror as she began her morning exercise routine.

The team was to convene at Warehouse 11 that morning. Everyone would get to enjoy a respite from what had turned out to be an atypically stressful prior day. Gigi made sure to get to work early. Not only to convey the image that she was far above using the injuries sustained as an excuse to be late or absent, but also to engage with Ben before yesterday's hero Abby, and her chauffeur Steve could. That the two of them appeared to be hitting it off only added insult to Gigi's actual injuries. Not long ago, she too had her eyes on Steve. But he didn't have a way to turn off his honesty, and it turned out that wasn't an attractive thing.

Rice was in his office in gym clothes, toweling off from his workout. Like her, he spent a good deal of effort staying in shape, and, like her, it showed. And she liked that. She walked across the inner expanse of the warehouse to his door as fast as she could without drawing his attention, hoping to take in his physique up close before he got dressed. She'd make small talk about his workout routine. Hopefully that'd keep him out of the suit for a few moments. But how to put a halt to Abby's unintentional knack for getting attention?

Never shy to flaunt her body, she now had a second and maybe even third reason to do so. She pulled off her University of Texas sweatshirt and pants and tossed them in a heap outside her boss' door, then went inside wearing only her white sports bra and gym shorts, plus an array of bruises to show off.

CHAPTER 33

THE ADJUSTER

BEN TURNED to see Gigi strut into his office half-naked and covered in ugly bruises. He started to turn his head out of decency, but then realized she meant for him to see her like this. "Woah. That looks terrible, Gigi."

She smiled at him. "It's not a big deal." She made a point to stretch her lithe arms and legs to show that she was, aside from all appearances, unaffected by the accident. Despite her effort, she did not at all look unhindered.

"You seem to be in pain. Why don't you take a day or two off to recover?"

Gigi scoffed. "Whatever for? I'm fine."

Ben tilted his head. "Seriously. It's practically an off day here anyway. All we have going on are reports on the events at the mall. Go home. Relax."

She shook her head. "And miss all the fun?"

"I'm glad you're finding reports so enjoyable," he said, wondering where the conversation was going.

She closed the door, leaving them precariously alone. Then she moved close to him. Far too close to be comfortable, given their equal states of relative undress. Gigi put a hand on his bare shoulder.

"Someone's gotta keep an eye on her out there. Might as well be me. She's reckless, and her R-Skill is powerful. That's a dangerous combination."

Ah, Abby, Ben thought to himself as he breathed an internal sigh of relief to find Gigi was merely angling for deference over her perceived competition for attention. That she had been affected by Abby's arrival was plainly evident. He should have anticipated it. Gigi's personal quest to attain social media relevance was practically all-consuming.

Not that he would mind an entanglement with Gigi. She was attractive, well-off, and most of the time, quite personable. For her sake, he hoped that personality was her genuine self, rather than a well-honed persona, crafted merely to pursue fame. Ben attributed her vainglorious pursuit more to the staunchest innate drive that some have to be recognized by their peers, rather than a conscious analysis and agreement of its actual value to society. But perhaps being twelve years her senior, his own perspective was merely swayed by generational bias. He used social media only sparingly to follow the goings of his friends and family back home in Minneapolis.

None of that had to do with the appropriateness of a direct report being behind closed doors in his office, wearing only her underwear and he bare-chested and sweaty. He shrugged Gigi's hand off and stood to move to the door. She slid in front of him, holding the door closed and brushing her barely clothed, well-toned butt against the front of his gym shorts. An unwelcome fog began to cloud his reason.

"Gigi, that's… that's not appropriate." Ben raised his hands in protest, but grazed her hips with the motion. By the end of the contact it was practically a caress as his fingers touched the skin above her shorts before he got control of them.

"I agree. That feels very inappropriate, Agent Rice. I was referring to the fun we had as a team, but I wouldn't mind a little of *that* kind of fun with you too."

The encounter had lurched in the very direction he had hoped to avoid. She turned and pressed herself against his bare chest. The touch of her skin against his set fire to his manhood.

"This is a bad idea."

She put her hands on his stomach. "I think a worse idea would be to turn down an opportunity to fuck a gymnast."

Her touch was electric. He wanted to resist, but the decision-making center in his brain had already shut down in deference to the one in his pants screaming for control. She pulled his head down to meet hers and stretched up on her toes to force the connection with their lips. He gave in. As far as he knew, they were the only two at the warehouse that early, but he broke the kiss to close the window blinds and lock the door.

———

After a thoroughly pleasurable and, frankly, exhausting hour of Gigi testing the limits of his physical fitness and libido, they stopped to rest. Ben immediately felt guilt gnawing at his conscience. He knew better. He also knew he possessed an R-Skill that would allow him to implant any scenario in Gigi's head to escape any personal or professional consequences that could arise from an ill-advised workplace encounter. And it was of the worst kind, that between superior and subordinate. He *knew* better.

Gigi stood and stretched her arms high, making show of her shapely breasts as she smiled at him. She bobbed around looking for her clothes, they having been tossed to a wall somewhere in the excitement of imminent congress. Both he and Gigi were willing participants, that much he knew. Maybe this was a culmination of some mutual attraction he had been ignoring for months. The guilt still gnawed. Gigi showed no signs of remorse, smiling and playfully searching behind furniture for her underwear. He knew if he let it, this encounter could turn into a regular occurrence. That by itself wouldn't necessarily be a bad thing. He could use the outlet, and sex with Gigi turned out to be a special kind of workout. His body tingled. His pulse still throbbed with echoes of pleasure from the exertion. No doubt it would get in the way of the team's work at some point. Things would get weird, opposing sides would form, and he was, at present, more married to work than anything else. Did he want it to continue with her? The short, but difficult answer was no.

He was going to have to use his ability to handle the situation here. He hated himself for it. After Rachel broke off their engagement when he told her about becoming an Adapted, he at first had used his R-Skill to change her mind. But their relationship at once had become a falsehood, and day by day, he found less and less to love in it. He couldn't change her character, only her short-term memory. It took less than a month for him to understand that what they had before he became an Adapted couldn't be regained. He practically lobotomized their last months together out of her, and felt like a hollow ass as he gave her the idea to leave him and move out so that he could keep their condo. After that, he swore to himself not to use his ability to affect others' romantic perceptions of him. But here he was, about to do it again.

"So, that was indeed fun. I forgot all about my bruises there for a while." Gigi had found her clothes and was eyeing Rice up and down as he started to get dressed.

"Yeah, that was something," he said, lamely.

But what to do about Gigi? He looked at her, and almost longed to see what would happen if he proposed they go another round or schedule an encore for later. It would be a disservice to her to erase her memory of their passion. Also, a disservice to him, as an eager participant, and by his estimation, successful in satisfying her. The rest of the team couldn't know about it, though. He stood and dressed, then leaned down to kiss Gigi, who had perched herself on his desk to watch.

"I really enjoyed it. I hope you did too," he said.

"Hell yeah. You really know how to use this thing." She rubbed him through his slacks. "I'm already looking forward to next time."

"Right." Ben sighed, exerting himself to avoid becoming more excited than he already was. He stretched his neck and popped the willing joints. "I think we can agree we enjoyed ourselves, but this was a one-time thing. We don't need to speak of it or mention it to anyone."

Gigi cocked her head and clicked her teeth, then ran her hands up his shirt and pulled him in for one more kiss. "Yeah, that's probably for the best. Too bad, for both of us."

He opened his office door. Bailey was typing on a laptop at the lounge table. She tossed Rice a glance of hello with a nod, then went back to whatever she was working on.

"So," Gigi said, walking closer and speaking low. "Are you sure she shouldn't be sent to the island? I mean, she's already killed one person, and nearly killed me yesterday."

Ben rolled his eyes. "I'm certain, and I'll thank you to keep such opinions to yourself. Accidents can be prevented, surely. I'll have a talk with her."

He looked out into the warehouse and saw Bailey peering in at them.

"I'm glad you weren't seriously hurt," Ben said to Gigi, loud enough to be heard by anyone else outside. "Those are some bruises."

"Yeah, me too," Gigi said, stepping out of the office and grabbing her sweatshirt and pants from the floor. "They should heal up in no time. Though, I think I will take you up on your offer to go home and rest today."

"Good." He watched her pull her sweatshirt and pants back on, and already yearned to be helping her out of them again.

CHAPTER 34
BOUNCY

GIGI GLOWED on the inside as her Tesla drove her home. She had worked her way into Ben's personal sphere. Didn't matter that they wouldn't become an item, even for a little while. They now had a history. She had an advantage over anyone else on the team and would be able to influence him in a way the others couldn't. She smiled to herself. It was only a matter of time.

She hadn't planned on enjoying it so much though. *Damn*, she thought. It was a shame they wouldn't have sex again. She knew it, but didn't know why. He had enjoyed it. She did as well — hell, she still tingled. Gigi ran her hands over her body remembering the way he made her feel. Moments later, her phone buzzed and pulled her out of the reverie with a text from her bestie, Kendra.

"Hey girl! How are you feeling after yesterday?"

"Hey K, whatcha up to? I'm taking the day off," Gigi texted back.

"Cool. Wanna hit the mall?"

"Yeah, I'm game to get my shop on."

"Great!"

"OMW meet me at the Apple store in thirty."

Gigi knew that rest would be the best thing for her battered body. But hanging with Kendra and shopping would lift her spirits far more. Plus, the cracked corner on her phone was already vexing her. She instructed the Tesla to take her to their favorite mall and the car's autopilot software swiftly changed lanes to head to the proper exit off the highway.

———

NorthPark Center, considered by many North Texans to be the best mall around, was a spotless structure of white brick walls and polished-to-a-shine dark concrete floors. It was full of meticulously maintained flower beds, sculptures, modern art, and loaded with high-end luxury brands. The kind whose clientele were still busy with private tennis lessons, hot yoga classes, and Montessori preschool carpools at this time of day. The mall was mostly empty per usual for a weekday morning, except for the Apple store, which, for whatever reason, was always absurdly crowded. Gigi bought a new iPhone and got a store tech started on transferring her data. She followed Kendra around the store as her friend browsed the workout accessories. The store tech barely acknowledged Gigi, but had hungry eyes for Kendra. Annoyed, and concerned the tech wasn't doing what he was supposed to be doing with her new phone, Gigi suggested they head to the women's room at Neiman Marcus where Gigi could show off her bruises.

"Oh my God Geeg, that looks terrible!" Kendra exclaimed as Gigi pulled her sweatshirt and pants off.

"I know, right? I told my boss Abby is too reckless. She can't have much rope left after this."

"I'm surprised she's still there. Why did he even hire her? Sounds like a pain in the ass."

Gigi shrugged. "I think he means well, but she's annoying as hell. It was fun beating her up at the training session. All she could do was tackle me. No self-control. I'm sure Ben wanted her for her R-Skill, it's pretty impressive. But still…" She trailed off, frowning at the bruises in the mirror.

"You'll be fine in no time," Kendra patted Gigi's back. "I don't know anyone that works as hard on their body as you do. Look at those abs!"

Pride radiated through Gigi like the heat from a good soak in a hot tub. An honest compliment from Kendra was as rare as a cool breeze in the North Texas summer. Her friend didn't know Ben though. "You should see my boss," she said with a chuckle, pulling her pants and sweatshirt back on

"Oh yeah? Details!"

Gigi's fingertips wiggled as she remembered the rigid contours of Ben's stomach. She sighed at the thought that she wouldn't get to touch them again. "He's ripped. Gorgeous."

Kendra laughed. "Wow. Would you— you know, if you got a chance?"

A wide grin broke across Gigi's face as they left the bathroom. "Oh yeah, I totally would." *Again*, she thought, unable to speak the word aloud. She let loose a satisfied sigh at the memory of Ben's naked body pressed into hers. It was the only commentary she could make on their workplace tryst. She usually would share all the juicy details of any hookup with Kendra, but today's was a secret she couldn't bring herself to share.

The two friends wandered around the mall, floating from store to store like butterflies unsure what kind of luxury nectar they had a taste for. After they stopped by the food court for smoothies, they headed to Nordstrom where Kendra pressed for details of Gigi's A-Space tryout while they tried on various outfits.

Gigi beamed. "I thought it went great. I was bouncing all over the place, doing flips and twists. I saw a couple mouths gaped open."

"Fun. Sorry I missed it. Had a last-minute shoot to do."

"Yeah, would have been nice to see you there." Of course, Kendra wasn't going to show up. "The evaluators liked that I had national competition experience and almost made the Olympic team."

Kendra raised an eyebrow over a rack of designer dresses. "C'mon. You weren't that close. Weren't you like the tenth alternate?"

And just like that, Gigi's twin swells of pride and satisfaction lost their air. Leave it to Kendra, supposed best friend, to take the wind out of her sails with absolutely zero intention. She wasn't about to admit that her best ranking was fourteenth, and instead found her most offended scoff and let Kendra have it.

"It's higher than you ever got. You didn't even qualify for nationals."

Kendra shrugged, holding a yellow sundress up to her shoulders and smiling at a mirror. "I never loved it like you did."

Gigi buried her face in a different rack of dresses she had no interest in and grumbled at her inability to get under Kendra's skin. Would it kill her to show at least a little reciprocity in their friendship in some way? Every aspect of their relationship was always uphill. "You could have made it," Gigi said, head still hidden in the clothes.

"Thanks. Maybe."

Not a chance, Gigi thought. She extracted her head from the dress hideout and turned to a different rack.

"What else did the evaluators say?"

"Like you even care," Gigi mumbled to herself.

"What was that?"

"Oh, just the usual platitudes," Gigi said with a shrug. "Awesome job, in great shape, you know. They liked that I worked for RADSA, though they all seemed pretty disappointed I wouldn't divulge any inside information on the team or the Adapted we've interviewed."

"Yeah, I still don't get that."

Gigi turned to face Kendra, who had looked over at her. "Well, aside from the ridiculously strict non-disclosure agreement we all signed, I kind of agree with it. If an Adapted doesn't want to be outed to the public, why should we? Let them remain in the shadows. More room for the rest of us to shine."

Kendra's eyes widened. "Shine?"

"You know, one less name for me to compete with. You too, Miss Won't Tell Me Her R-Skill."

Kendra busied herself with another dress in the mirror. "You'll see it soon enough."

"What do you mean?"

"Production for A-Space All-Stars begins in six weeks."

"I… don't follow — wait. How do you know that?" Gigi darted over to her friend and grabbed her arm.

Kendra bit her lip and shrunk into her shoulders.

"Oh. My. God. Kendra! You're on the show? Why didn't you tell me? You couldn't hook me up?" Gigi's blood began to simmer with a caustic mix of anger and jealousy.

Kendra shook her head. "Nope. I can't talk about it. We all signed a ridiculously strict non-disclosure agreement," she said, miming Gigi's words with air quotes.

Gigi rolled her eyes. "Fuck that! Spill it!"

"I can't!" Kendra pulled her arm away. "Seriously. And before you ask, I talked to LeAnne about getting you in and she said you didn't have the right look. Maybe if you can come up with something special to get A-Space's attention, she'd consider it."

Gigi staggered back. Her stomach twisted with outrage. "Not the right look? *Fuck her!* Is it my height? My nose?"

Kendra moved toward Gigi, who stepped back in turn.

"I don't know. You know how agents are. They act like every word out of their mouths not spent making money is time wasted."

"Ugh!" Gigi stomped a foot and threatened to throw her smoothie cup at her traitor of a friend.

"I'm sorry!" Kendra held out her hands to deflect any flying smoothie from her face. "At least you had a great audition? You could still get in."

Gigi considered dousing her friend in her blend of kale, carrots, lemon, and wheatgrass. But, aside from a waste of a good smoothie, it was the kind of attention she had always avoided. Negative stuff. She knew herself, and knew that she could always prevail by being the best she could be. While that hadn't completely worked out for the Olympic trials, she still had faith in her ability to achieve her dreams doing things the right way. And that certainly didn't include making a mess of a C-list local celebrity in the middle of Nordstrom in front of dozens of security cameras and more than a handful of nearby shoppers with phones (and cameras) in their hands.

"We'll see. I'm not sure I even want to do it," Gigi said. She would have given Steve a whopping headache with that lie, but it would pale to the pain radiating in her side after she had prepared to throw the cup. Ben was right. She should have gone home to rest. And that was a convenient excuse to bail on Kendra. Gigi dramatically grabbed at her side, wincing and gasping for effect.

"Geeg, are you alright?"

"I think I better go home and rest. See ya."

"Oh, okay. Text me later."

Gigi turned and left without even acknowledging her friend's request. She would, of course, but for once wanted Kendra to be the one on the waiting end.

CHAPTER 35
THE ADJUSTER

"YOU CAN PARK ANYWHERE HERE, BAILEY," Ben said to the intercom.

"Alrighty," Bailey replied.

He felt the heavy weight of Bessie more and more as it rumbled over the washboard gravel until coming to a complete stop. For an ordinary driver, Bessie would be a problem to back out of the narrow path they had followed, but he knew it would pose no challenge to Jo Bailey.

"Want me to come with you?" she asked over the intercom.

"No, this one's skittish, apparently. I'll see you in a bit."

Ben grabbed a tablet and headed out the back door. He jumped out and inhaled a breath of hot, but fresh, air. The area around Dallas and its first three layers of suburbs was essentially solid concrete, aside from parks, golf courses, and lawns. The air quality wasn't awful, but usually had a grungy scent of smog, hot or no. After the suburbs, the development faded quickly, leaving open prairie, farmland, and the occasional pocket of forest. A dense stand of oaks and pecans lined both sides of the drive. The canopy extended well over the road and provided some relief from the midday summer sun. But there was no escaping the heat, even in the shade, and today was a hot one, no mistake. The forecast was for a ridiculous high of 110 Fahrenheit, and that was before the heat index. Ben decided comfort was better than image, and tossed his jacket in the back door of the trailer before heading down the drive, thinking Abby's habitually-worn baseball hat wasn't so bad an idea.

He checked the signal on his tablet. Five bars. Having lived through the early days of wireless, the vast reach and strength of the latest generation networks were nothing short of impressive. He reviewed the details for the interview subject as he walked. Brix LaFontaine, 43, formerly of New Orleans, relocated to the Dallas area after Hurricane Katrina. Spotty employment history, currently no employer shown. R-Skill unknown, though the 'Recruit?' box was checked. RADSAnet's reach was remarkable; it could parse the tiniest shreds of pertinent text from social media or news sites and come up with an endless list of Adapted to interview. Not once had the system suggested a candidate that wasn't Adapted.

Around a bend in the road stood a ramshackle house nestled under a canopy of trees. The front door had visible gaps above and below. A window on the side of the house looked pilfered from a junkyard. A black mid-80s Chevy Trans-Am, complete with a sweeping firebird decal on the hood, sat parked in front of the house.

More unusual than stepping into this little time capsule were the structures surrounding it. Evidently, Brix was into gardening. A monstrous glass greenhouse towered above the home from behind. Ben couldn't see the front of it, but it had to be nearly ten times the square footage of the house. Two long rows of raised garden planters lined either side of the house as well. Far more care went into the construction of the gardening plots than the house; they were neat, square, and well-maintained. He marveled at the scale of the operation. It had more than enough growing space to provide enough fruit and vegetables for a family to live off of.

Except, everything was dead. Half the raised boxes were bare earth. The other half had gray, wilted vines and brown leaves baked to a crisp by the summer sun.

All the natural vegetation around the garden plots and house was dead as well. Trees, shrubs, grass. All brown and gray. Lifeless. As Ben surveyed the gravel clearing around him, the scene was far more reminiscent of a dreary day in January, instead of a sweltering one in late August. Hardly any of the trees around had leaves, and most of the grasses and bushes down the path were just as lifeless. North Texas wasn't immune to long stretches of drought, but the area had enjoyed strong seasonal rains that spring, so things should be reasonably green. It had to be related to the man's R-Skill.

Ben made his way to the house and knocked. The loose planks of wood that comprised the door shed dry dust with each rap of his knuckles. The structure seemed a century out of place. It would be awfully drafty during winter, which could get plenty cold on occasion. After a half a minute of waiting with no answer, he knocked again.

"Mr. LaFontaine?"

"Unless you brought a giant check, I'm not interested!" a voice called from within.

Ben stifled a laugh. "I'm afraid I'm empty handed at the moment. But I thought we might talk for a few minutes. My name is Ben Rice, I'm with the Radiologically Adapted Dangers to Society Administration. RADSA. It is our understanding that you've become an Adapted recently, and I'd like to interview you for our records.

"Fuck that, G-Man! You ain' sendin' me to no fuckin' island!"

Ben wiped the sweat forming on his forehead and loosened his tie. "That is most definitely not why I'm here. Part of our mission is to develop patterns of emergence and look for commonalities amongst R-Skills."

"Do what?" The voice was thick with a creole accent, but there was a frailness to it, like the man was much older than forty-three.

"Abilities, Mr. LaFontaine. The official designation for them is R-Skills. We look for any similarities between abilities that develop between people within a certain proximity." Ben thought he was talking way over the door's head. "In case any patterns can be found. Do you mind speaking face-to-face? Your front door is quaint, but I would like to meet you."

No response came.

"Mr. LaFontaine? Brix?" Ben knocked again.

Again, nothing.

Ben walked around the corner to a window and peered in between the torn, yellowed curtains obscuring most of the glass. A pair of dirty, bare feet rested atop a frayed wicker footstool in front of a television. Most of the screen was obscured, but he thought it might be a game show - The Price is Right, maybe. He went back to the door and knocked again.

"Could we talk for just a minute? Then I'll be out of your hair."

Nothing.

Ben sighed and raised his voice. "Let's talk, Brix. It won't take long." He knocked again.

Still, nothing.

The itchy tingle of pressure in his joints urged him to force the issue with Brix. It would be so easy. He admonished himself for even considering forcing someone into an interview, and turned to walk back to Bessie, resigned in defeat. On the way back, he recalled Director Gustafson's recent scolding about his team's head count. He dialed Steve.

"Hey Ben, what's up?" Steve answered.

"Are you free to help with an interview?"

"Uh, sure. I was just taking Abby home."

Ben bristled at that, given that he had mindlessly written Abby a large check as a signing bonus to get a car for herself. Not that he cared about his budget. They had funds to spare and he had his own special way to get more if he really wanted to. But there was also the matter of the open mic night Steve and Abby held atop the ruins of Stonebriar mall. Ben hadn't brought up their workplace indiscretion to either of them yet, but would need to soon. *Hypocrite,* he thought. His tryst with Gigi was a far more grievous lapse in judgement, despite the fact he had adjusted away her ability to use it to cause problems for him.

Still, he thought Abby's verve might be just what he needed to break through to Brix. "Bring her too, she may help. Grab some pizzas and beer. We need to win this one over with some bribery."

Steve laughed. "Alright, send me the address."

Ben hung up and texted Steve the address, which, if not for Google Maps, would be impossible to locate. He noted the gradual increase in living vegetation as he got further and further from the house.

Bailey was inspecting Bessie as Ben approached. "Hey. How'd it go? Ready to get out of here?"

Ben shook his head. "Not yet, I didn't get far with him. Steve and Abby are coming over with pizza."

"Nice."

He gestured up and down the dusty drive. "What do you suppose would make someone want to live all the way out here in a broken-down shack of a house?"

Bailey raised an eyebrow. "Is he making meth?"

Ben laughed. "Not that I could tell. Looks like he was doing a lot of gardening at one point, but everything's dead around the house."

"Maybe he got tired of this heat. Yeesh!"

"Yeah." Ben wiped the sweat dripping off his forehead.

Bailey glanced up and down the drive. "I suppose if I didn't want to be bothered by anyone, I might find seclusion like this comforting." She inspected the nearest tire on Bessie, checking the tread. "The world is a big place, there's bound to be a few with the right combination of brain cells out there that don't want to be part of society."

"Yeah, the kind with an Anarchist's Cookbook in the kitchen."

Bailey looked at him with a shrug. "Why stick around? It's not like we get to everyone on the list."

Immediately, Ben's mind went to the checked 'Recruit?' box in Brix's RADSAnet profile. He wasn't ready to give up yet. "I don't know. Something seems a little off." He checked his watch and pointed to the trailer. "Let's get out of the heat. Steve and Abby won't be here for a while."

Ben took the opportunity to squeeze in a quick workout in his office and a cool shower to shake off the heat. He was at his locker in just a towel when the back door to the trailer opened and Steve and Abby climbed in, one with a case of beer, the other carrying a pair of pizza boxes.

"Woah! Sorry, Ben," Abby said, ogling his chest for a moment before averting her eyes. "Geez, I guess I know who to call when I need to hand wash a sweater."

Steve raised an eye behind Abby's back.

Ben laughed "No problem, my fault. I thought you'd take longer to get here. I'll get dressed and then we can go see Mr. LaFontaine." He grabbed some spare clothes from his locker and went to his office to dress.

The four set off on the gravel drive towards the run-down house. A series of loud pops came from around the corner, followed by numerous cracks and a thudding impact on the ground. Then another. And another. The team picked up their pace, and after rounding the bend, came to a massive pile of dead trees blocking the road.

"Well. That's… new," Ben said.

"That wasn't here before?" Bailey asked.

Ben shook his head.

"This guy really doesn't want to talk to us," Steve said.

They checked the edges of the blockage, but there was no easy way around.

"Mind moving these, Abby?" Ben asked.

"I'll go grab a trash can from Bessie," Bailey said.

"Thanks. Don't want the pizza to get cold!" Abby said.

Bailey ran back to Bessie and retrieved a small wire mesh receptacle from the trailer. She set it to the side of the gravel drive. "There ya go."

"Okay, stand back," Abby said, grinning. She eyed the trash can for a moment, then hefted the largest trunk of the pile over her head as if it were made of Styrofoam.

Ben shared an impressed look with Steve. The trunk had to weigh as much as a car. Despite having seen it in action after the tornado, to see a feat of strength like this close up, especially coming from one so slight as Abby, was nothing short of amazing.

She tossed the trunk like a basketball at the trash can. The dead tree crashed to the ground, flattening the wastebasket with a thud. Shards of smaller dead branches flung off in all directions. Abby went to lift another tree and it came up without resistance. She made quick work of the rest of the roadblock, tossing each dead tree aside with ease.

"I must say, that's handy," Ben said as they approached. "It's no disaster rescue. But still, very impressive."

Abby blushed. "How was he gonna get his car out?" she asked, admiring the Trans-Am parked out front.

Ben shrugged, then knocked on the door. "Mr. LaFontaine, it's Agent Rice again. I've got a few of my teammates with me, as well as some beer and pizza.

"What?" the man inside shouted. The door swung open. "Can't you leave me in peace?"

Brix LaFontaine was the very image of death, personified: ashen skin, sparse threads of colorless hair, sunken red eyes with pupils an impossible shade of tan, and so gaunt he was unsettling to look at. His sweat-stained undershirt and filthy khakis only worsened the man's appearance.

"Mr. LaFontaine, are you well?"

Brix coughed. "Don't it show?" he asked, holding out his atrophied arms and moving forward as if to grab everyone for a grotesque, contagious hug.

The team instinctively took a step back.

Brix laughed between coughs. "Don't worry, it's not catching. It's my damned ability."

"Mind if we talk about it?" Ben asked.

"Eh… only if you tell me how you got past all those damn trees." Brix said.

Abby stepped forward, looking a little sheepish with a raised hand. "That was my doing."

"You moved my roadblock? Good Lord, how?" Brix asked.

"It's my R-Skill — ability, as you called it." Abby said. "I can lift anything that's garbage and throw it at a garbage can. Apparently, dead trees count as garbage."

Brix furrowed his eyebrows. "Adapted, eh? Figures the gub' would put them to use somehow." He ran a hand through his thinned hair and smacked his lips. "And what about you, little one?" He looked at Bailey.

She tossed him a frown. "I can discern the most efficient path between two points."

Brix scoffed. "And what good is that for?"

Bailey folded her arms. "I drive a giant semi-truck through traffic with ease. Among other things."

"Ah," Brix said, not looking impressed.

"I can tell when people are speaking the truth," Steve said.

"Bullshit," Brix laughed.

"Try me. Say two things, one of them false," Steve offered.

"Okay. I hate the government, and I want you all to leave!" Brix stepped back into his shabby house and slammed the door.

"Was that two things? Or just one?" Abby asked.

Steve was rubbing his forehead. He stepped up to the door. "Mr. LaFontaine, you definitely hate the government, but you most certainly do not want us to leave." He stepped back.

After a moment, the door swung open again. He looked wide-eyed at Steve. "Call me Brix. I bet you're a hoot at drinking games."

Steve smiled and shook his head.

"They're all Adapted, just like you Mr. LaFontaine," Ben said.

"Speaking of that… mind telling me how you came to know about my ability?" Brix asked.

Ben held out his tablet. "The artificial intelligence that runs our database put together a profile on you and suggested our team pay a visit. It collects data from a wide variety of sources."

Brix shook his head. "And people say I'm crazy when I tell them the government is always watching. C'mon, let's get that beer in the cooler." He led them inside. "Sorry for the mess, wasn't expecting visitors."

The house was a disaster inside, which was no surprise. Trash spilled out of a garbage can. Empty water bottles lined the area around his recliner. A layer of gray dust covered nearly everything.

Brix took the case of beer from Steve and made some room for it in his refrigerator. A large water filtration mechanism sat on the counter next to the fridge.

Abby set the pizza boxes down and opened them up. Brix reached for a slice of the supreme pizza. "Watch this." He picked off a thin piece of green pepper. It shriveled in between his fingers, turning from a delicious roasted green to sickly gray. After a few moments, he flicked it in the air where it became a thin cloud of dust. "I destroy plant matter."

"Woah," Abby said, mouth full of pizza.

"Bigger things like trees take longer, and stay together better. But then there's this." Brix pulled a red onion off the slice and stuck it on his tongue. Like the green pepper, the onion shriveled into gray dust. He spat it out and wiped his tongue on his shirt. "Tastes like shit. I can't eat fruits or vegetables anymore."

"Oh man," Bailey said.

"Is that why you're sick?" Steve asked.

"Yeah. I saw a doctor a couple times, but they say there's not much to be done for it. Just take an assload of vitamins and fiber supplements. Oh. And eat meat."

"That doesn't sound so bad," Abby said.

Brix coughed. "Well sure, if you're not vegetarian. I can't stand meat! I don't have the money for that, or the various supplements I'd need. I'm a man of simple means. Before this I got by just selling produce from my greenhouse and eating only the fruits of my own labor. Now that's all gone to shit." Brix looked at the floor with a frown.

Ben moved to the fridge. "Can I get you a beer, Brix?"

"Eh. Not a fan. Was all about clean livin' before this happened to me." Brix gestured over his withering frame.

"Could you even drink beer?" Steve asked Brix, cracking open his own can.

Brix shrugged. "I think so. Seems if the plant gets processed enough my ability doesn't work on it. I could eat the crust of the pizza, but not the tomato sauce. Don't ask me why. I can't even wear cotton underwear. And don't get me started on my polyester sheets!"

Ben took a sip of his beer, then cleared his throat. "Forgive me for being blunt, but you'd rather wither and die here than change your diet?"

Brix just shook his head.

"Why?" Abby asked.

That made Brix chuckle. "I'd rather die on my own terms than get shipped to the island. I'm not going to be a prisoner for the rest of my life."

"But you're not going to Island-A," Ben said.

"Ah. Agent Rice, you've got the faith. I don't. I don't trust this system your government has put together." Brix gestured air quotes with his fingers. "The Dangers to Society list? Please. What happens if I decide to go out for a walk and trip into someone's prized begonias? Suddenly I'm a number five on your fucking list because I've ruined some rich asshole's landscaping. Then comes some bullshit witch hunt? No thank you. I will not live my life in that kind of fear."

"Are you a number five?" Steve asked.

"I don't fucking know. Does it matter? My touch decimates plants. I could be a three, five, or six, depending on whose sanctimonious normie ass is judging me."

The withered man's interpretation irked Ben. The reaction was nonsensical. Sure, plenty of people didn't trust the government, for any number of reasons. But President Phelps had bent over backwards in his pursuit of pro-Adapted policy changes. Sending Adapted to Island-A was a choice of last resort.

Abby put her half-eaten pizza down on the box. "I kind of see your point, Brix. We're trying to help out there, but if it's not something you can turn on or off, maybe it's better if you stayed out of view."

Brix shrugged.

Ben looked at Abby with surprise. "What if I offered you a job?" he asked Brix abruptly. "Pending a background investigation, of course. You could help us provide assistance to other Adapted."

Brix could hardly contain his laughter. "Fuuuuuck that, G-Man."

"Come on, we can help you." Bailey said from atop a stool.

"I wouldn't take a government job for all the barbecue in Texas, little one," Brix sniped. "I don't care about joining the Adapted club. I don't need to work for the man, just so I can afford to shovel meat in my face to stay alive. Y'all can go be on A-Space and have a grand ol' time. I have no interest getting in bed with RADSA and shipping people off to the island, nor do I desire to become a lab rat for some prick scientist in Washington."

Ben scowled behind his beer can. *What a waste,* he thought. His joints ached and he was ready to move on. "We won't stay any longer. Thanks for speaking with us."

"Sure. Thanks for the pizza," Brix said. "I don't mind the cheese, at least."

Ben and the team said their goodbyes and shuffled off down the dusty path back to Bessie.

"I can't believe he doesn't want help," Bailey said.

Abby shook her head. "I don't know. Is it worth exposing himself to the public eye? I'd be worried about him bumping into the wrong close-minded asshole."

"That could cause a PR problem for all of us. The RADSA team that had to ship one of its own to the island? Could you imagine the shade of red on Gustafson's face? Scandalous!" Steve said.

Ben walked in silence and gnawed on his thoughts. Here was an

Adapted that had a significant R-Skill that could use a well-paying job and healthcare. And he was going to refuse because of a lack of trust in the government? Risk his own health because of an aversion to meat? It was all so… inflexible. Unappreciative. And his 'Recruit?' box was checked.

"You guys go on. I think I'll give Brix a business card in case he changes his mind," Ben said.

Bailey laughed. "I know this is Texas an' all, Ben, but that is a *serious* waste of paper."

Ben nodded and turned to walk back to Brix's house. He knocked on the door again and Brix opened the door, with a full scowl on his face.

"Look, Mr. Rice. You seem like a nice enough fella. But I've already told you what you need to know. Now leave me be, or I'll go dig out my rifle and put away my manners."

"I just thought I'd leave you a business card, in case you change your mind."

Brix began laughing, but quickly erupted into a furious bout of wet, garbled coughing. He brought forth two mouthfuls of phlegm which he unceremoniously spat at Ben's feet.

"Or needed help." Ben looked at the creamy yellow globs on the ground and grimaced. "You don't sound well, Brix."

"I'm fine," Brix said, gasping for air. "Now you be a good boy and go shovel the president's shit and leave me alone."

Brix stepped onto his spit with his bare feet, then patted Ben on the shoulders. As his hands touched Ben's shirt, the linen disintegrated, exposing the flesh beneath. Brix ran his hands down the front of the shirt, making twin trails of bare skin. When he reached Ben's belt, Brix giggled, then stepped back into his shack while shaking his head and closed the door.

Ben stood there, dumbfounded. The newly opened panels of his shirt billowed in the steamy southern breeze. The scalding sun sliced into his bare skin, but his blood ran hotter. Brix was a little unhinged. Maybe even a danger to someone, if left unchecked.

Aching joints begged for release. Ben's own tension filled their capacity with potential. He rolled his neck to release some strain, and when the first vertebra popped, followed by the second, he acted by instinct.

Ben knocked on the door. Again, Brix opened it, scowling.

"For the last time, I don't want your damn business card."

"No. You want to accept that job offer."

CHAPTER 36
LUCKY

"MY FELLOW AMERICANS," Phelps began. "I am here to announce the detection of two more Dark Objects. They will impact the planet within the next few hours. Both appear to be of the same composition as the Korean UDO and the two that splashed into the Pacific last week. The good news is that both are far smaller in size and should again pose no threat for a long-term global impact."

The president paused for water and scanned his teleprompter.

"At present, both appear headed for unpopulated areas in Egypt and Iran. We have already made requests of those governments to avoid an ill-advised military response to the objects. We hope they will allow them to descend unfettered. I will again publicly beseech President Abbas and President Korami to exercise restraint. Nuclear weapons have no effect on the UDOs. Do not risk the health of your citizens and the planet at large by engaging in futility."

Let's see how they react, he thought. He took another sip of water and continued.

"To everyone listening to this around the world, I ask that you keep the safety of our fellow humans in your thoughts, hearts, and prayers. We have survived a far larger impact than what these two UDOs will generate. We will survive again."

. . .

"That was the president in his press conference earlier today," the CNN reporter said. "Again, to recap for those of you just tuning in, two more Unidentified Dark Objects have impacted the planet today. The first touched down in the desert west of Cairo, Egypt. No casualties or damage are expected. The second UDO was far smaller, and impacted at an industrial complex outside Tehran, Iran. Iranian officials said the facility was a petrochemical plant and that casualties are expected to be few, but rumors have swirled that it may have been the site of a new clandestine nuclear weapon facility. So far, no indication of radiation has been detected." The reporter tapped on the tablet in front of him. "Okay, let's take a commercial break, and then our panel of scientific experts will debate the significance of two new UDO impacts and what it could mean for the future. Stay tuned."

CHAPTER 37

THE SLEUTH

STEVE SET his beer down and tried in vain to shake the pain from his head. The press conference had begun innocently enough, forgiving the sheer lunacy of nigh-undetectable interstellar objects crashing into the planet. Today marked the fourth and fifth such UDOs. Each announcement caused panic planet-wide. But in Steve, they caused wonder. Where are they coming from? What are they made of? Will there be more?

At first, Steve attempted to search for the truth through his own words. His inner nerd had thought it might be a sign of intelligent extraterrestrial life. Horrifying as the prospect would be that such alien life would be communicating with and/or attacking Earth via behemoth objects. He wished he could lean on his R-Skill to just utter the truth of things, but his own limitations on speaking the truth were confined to things that he actually knew about. He'd be able to say the UDOs were created by aliens, even if they weren't, right up until the point when that truth was revealed through actual observation of their actual source. But there were so many wondrous possible explanations the reaches of space could hold.

That wonder was obliterated when President Phelps spoke. There was truth to his words. Two UDOs were headed for Earth. Indeed, two UDOs came. But only one crashed into an unpopulated area. The president was wrong. His words were false. Was it a lie?

An unsettling pattern had developed. The chief victims of the UDOs were long-time adversaries of the United States. North Korea, China, and now, Iran. Was it possible the president knew the second would crash near

Tehran? If so, why would he lie about it? If not, why were they able to correctly predict that the first would crash in the desert near the Pyramids of Giza and be so wrong about their prediction of the second? Steve wondered what Milo's opinion of his father would be now.

The muted news coverage showed pictures of a black-as-night sphere sticking out of the dusty sands near Cairo like an enormous scarab. The Egyptian President was talking on screen next to the pictures. The closed-captioning translation relayed his and his entire country's relief that their national treasures and colossal tourism magnets weren't damaged.

"The president knew the UDO would crash near Tehran."

Steve frowned.

"The president didn't know the UDO would crash near Tehran."

He chewed on his cheek. He couldn't guess the truth out of thin air. The president hadn't spoken the truth. But what could Steve do about it?

His phone displayed no new messages. Abby hadn't responded to his last text; he had asked what her reaction was to the press conference. He didn't want to seem overly eager by pestering her with messages, but he longed for her company. And her lips. The chaste goodbye kiss they shared when he dropped her off was nothing short of altogether too short. Seems she was patient. He would be too. She'd no doubt have a down-to-earth perspective on his conundrum. He picked his phone up and read over their prior conversation, mostly over Gigi's injuries and subsequent cold shoulder to Abby. Though his heart radiated a yearning to connect with her, Steve set the phone down and forced himself to wait until morning. He was her ride, after all. They'd be sitting side by side in a few short hours.

The news coverage cycled into replays of already-shown clips, so Steve turned the TV off and headed for bed. The familiar, concerted routine of cleaning up the kitchen, washing up, brushing teeth, and tidying his bedroom did nothing to settle his apprehension. Something was lurking beneath the surface of what the president was telling the world. He knew it.

As he tossed around in bed, his racing mind fought off the welcome peace of sleep. Could he uncover the truth? The list of seemingly random facts about salt he had uncovered scrolled through his brain. It used to be used as currency. Nearly half of the salt produced every year in the United States was used on roads. Canada combined salt with beet juice to de-ice their roads. The federal government had awarded many contracts for salt products over the years, for everything from military use to national stockpile storage. None of what he uncovered seemed to validate his concern over the president's speech covering trade with China.

Unable to relax, he flipped on A-Space Tonight, hoping for some levity from Kristen Brently. But the featured guest was again Dr. Norman Pruett, there on his seemingly weekly appearance to talk about the science behind the UDOs. He would have plenty to talk about, with four recent UDO impacts, and the continued acceleration of Adapted emerging across the country and the world.

Steve's interest held strong, but fatigue from the momentous day caught up to him. His mind wandered between UDOs, Dry as Late July, and Abby's sweet, soft lips. He dwelled on those the most.

Dr. Pruett made his entrance, and immediately began talking about the UDOs that crashed into Egypt and Iran, using words like 'unpredictable', 'undetectable', and 'nonconforming'. Steve was half asleep, when his consciousness was ripped back to the foreground with the mention of radiation.

"I'm not certain we'll discover what kind of facility was destroyed near Tehran. There is absolutely zero detectable radiation present, but then that seems to be a pattern with the UDOs." Norman said.

The studio audience rumbled in hushed murmurs until Kristen waved them down.

"Was there radiation from the aircraft carrier?" the host asked.

"Again, zero radiation present," Norman said.

"That seems odd, given we know that was a nuclear-powered ship."

"Indeed," Norman said. "But as we saw with the Korean missile strike, the compound that the UDOs are made of seems to be able to absorb a remarkable amount of radiation. In hindsight, it's almost like the North Korean nuclear warhead never launched."

"That's wild. So how does the radiation go from the UDOs to the people that become Adapted? 'Cuz, you know, with traffic as bad as it is these days, I wouldn't mind sprouting some wings and just flying myself around."

The audience roared as the host jumped on top of her desk and flapped her arms.

Norman craned his head back, laughing. "Wouldn't we all? That's a great question Kristen. We are still working to uncover how that's happening."

It was a great question, but finally fatigue tugged at Steve's eyes. He turned off the TV, and hoped he'd dream of all the possible ways super-human abilities could develop. Instead, he dreamt of Abby.

————

"That's fucking nuts," Ben said, casually sipping the Starbucks Steve had brought in for him. "Like an extraterrestrial attack?"

"I have no idea!" Steve said. "It sounds insane to me too, but at this point it's a possibility. What's the likelihood that we get hit by five of the same dark objects within a couple years? Pretty damn low I'd say."

"I say they're all just chunks from a larger thing that broke off. These last few took longer to get here because they were smaller?"

Steve rubbed his head as pain sparked behind his eyes. "Nope. If that was the case it seems impossible they'd all just happen to hit Earth. The planet isn't in the same position relative to the Sun now as it was when the first one hit."

Ben shrugged. "Like I'm one to hypothesize. I hardly passed my science classes."

"Speaking of science, Norman Pruett was on A-Space Tonight again yesterday, and it sounded like he wasn't even sure the radiation from the UDO was the source of the Adapted anymore. I fell asleep watching it and haven't even been able to wrap my mind around that one."

"What else could be affecting people to cause Adapted? The air?"

"I don't know. Maybe. Maybe it's something we don't even know how to measure." Steve took a long slurp from his coffee and wished he hadn't put so much sugar in it. He frowned. "The thing that really bugs me about all this is that the president has things wrong."

"Politicians speak untruths all the time. Sometimes unwittingly. It's not like he'd be the first president to be manipulated by special interests or his own cabinet."

"Yeah, but about this? He was wrong when he said both UDOs were headed for unpopulated areas. And a bullseye on a moving ship? Seems unlikely."

"You're putting an awful lot of faith in our ability to accurately predict where these things are going to strike."

Steve's frustration simmered. Ben was being so dismissive. "It's not an isolated thing! When he was talking about the new agreement with China, almost all of it was false. True, there was a new agreement. True, he took part in negotiations. But *none* of the exports he mentioned were correct, with exception of one."

Ben tapped away at his keyboard, apparently only half-listening. "Which one?"

"Table salt, of all things. My point is, I can see how he could get some details wrong in a speech. But all of those? And he was there! He had a hand in crafting the agreement."

"Huh."

Steve looked at his boss and had to fight back a scowl. How could he be so disbelieving? This was his R-Skill talking! Infallible.

Ben shrugged again. "I find it highly unlikely anything untoward is happening. Maybe there's some aspect to the accuracy of your R-Skill that we don't yet understand?"

That sent Steve's blood to a boil. "Come on! If you were an Adapted you'd understand. I just *know* how it works. It's in my DNA. I know when people speak the truth. When they lie it's a fucking dagger behind my eyes. There's no mistaking it."

"Steve," Ben said, stretching the joints in his neck until they popped. "Relax. I just don't believe President Phelps is anything other than a politician. He's got all manner of other agendas going. If you want to spend your brain cycles thinking about this fine, but don't waste my time on it, please."

And with that, Steve felt better. And he knew he wouldn't bring it up to Ben again. It was a good idea, since Ben wasn't receptive in the slightest. Steve was wasting his own time too.

"I've talked to Director Gustafson about your concerns a little, and she thinks we should investigate your R-Skill a little further. I have come to rely on it a great deal, and we don't want to be making decisions based upon your reactions if the basis of our understanding regarding them is suspect."

Steve shifted in his chair. "Investigate... how?"

"Frannie has dispatched an agent from RADSA's science division in DC to come talk with you. A psychoanalyst or some such, I think. She says he'll be able to get to the bottom of what's going on."

That didn't sound good at all. Psychoanalyst? Steve wasn't crazy. He knew himself. He knew what his R-Skill was about, what he could and couldn't do. He grasped the arms on his chair and squeezed. "I don't think that's really necessary."

"He's already on his way, this Agent Orton. We'll see him tomorrow."

Ben scanned Steve's body and raised an eyebrow. "Don't worry. There's nothing wrong with you. He's just coming to make sure there isn't something else about your R-Skill we don't know yet."

True. And False. Steve bit his tongue to mask the pain from Ben's second statement. Ben was wrong about Agent Orton's purpose. Was it possible Ben was lying too? Steve couldn't fathom how much he didn't believe that. He needed time to think. Alone. He stood to leave.

"Before you go," Ben said. "I wanted to talk to you about Abby."

Steve drew in a short breath.

"I, ahem, overheard the two of you on the radio the night of the tornado. You both did a world of good, but Gigi nearly died out there. We can't afford distractions."

Steve avoided looking directly in Ben's eyes. His guilt over Gigi's injuries and near-miss had barely subsided. At least Abby had been able to move past it fairly easily. She always seemed to be able to focus on the good things in life. He loved that about her. He loved more than that about her. His heart swelled as he thought about her compassion, her smile, her eyes, her lips. Then he shook himself out of it. He had discipline. He'd be able to keep things professional at work. It wouldn't be a problem.

Ben cracked his knuckles. "Pursuing a romantic relationship with a coworker is a bad idea."

Steve's heart hit the floor. It was the truth.

CHAPTER 38
THE ADJUSTER

"WHAT ARE YOU DOING?" Ben asked himself in the mirror.

He toweled off the last few droplets of water from his shower and admired his physique in the mirror — of him, that at least was real to others. Simultaneously he cringed at the sight of the ugly scar on his face. A constant reminder of what he was doing to those around him. The more he used his R-Skill to alter others' minds, the worse he felt about it.

It felt like cheating.

Wasn't it? he thought.

It's not like he chose this. Becoming Adapted wasn't something most people asked for, given the widely unpredictable and sometimes awful R-Skills that could develop. Would anyone else with his ability use it any less than he had? It's not like he was robbing banks or rigging elections with it. There were many who would. Or worse. All he was doing was trying to help.

"But why?"

After hearing about what happened on the bridge with Zeke, Ben gave Abby, Gigi, and Steve all the verbal accolades he could muster. He meant them too, but they all rang hollow inside him. He was just acting the part. He thought being in this position would make him care. Hell, he thought he already did care. About the Adapted. Life. But now, he wasn't sure. More and more, doing anything of substance seemed to require his special brand of cheating. All the grind, the work, the effort of enduring the human condition had been supplanted by the sheer magnitude of his R-Skill. Had he been the one on that bridge talking to Zeke instead of Abby, he would have just popped a joint or two, uttered a suggestion, and the young man would have instantly been convinced that life was worth living and he should come off the edge. It would have been easy. Effortless. Over in seconds. And he probably wouldn't have even gone.

He smiled to himself about his instincts regarding Abby. At least he was right about her. She cared. She didn't hesitate. According to Steve, Abby practically pulled him and Gigi out the door as soon as they saw the news bulletin.

Today, though, was a new threshold. Brix LaFontaine was starting his new job with the team. He'd accepted the help of a dietary consultant to get his body healthy, and after a few days of targeted nutritional supplements and finding unexpected joy in eating meat, he was raring to join the team and make a difference for the Adapted. And it was all a lie. Ben's lie. The actual Brix was no fan of the government. Or meat.

As the eye surrounded by scar tissue in the mirror looked back at Ben with disapproval, all he could do was shake his head. At least by being attached to the team, they could keep Brix out of trouble and assuage his irrational fear of being shipped to Island-A.

Ben walked to the kitchen of his spartan condo, in a new high-rise not far from the American Airlines Center near downtown Dallas. After starting a cup of coffee brewing, he looked out of the window that had a nice view of a little park ten stories below. What he saw made the hairs on the back of his neck stand up. Ordinarily, at this time of morning, a regular group of friends doing yoga and some locals walking their dogs would be the only occupants of the park. Instead, Ben saw a swarm of people holding signs and pumping fists at someone yelling at them on a small platform. He raced to the television and turned on the local news. The bright yellow alert banner across the bottom read "Angry Protest Outside Adapted Home".

A massive lump choked his throat. He tried to gulp it down with no success. Ben turned up the volume.

"...the alleged Adapted's R-Skill is supposedly on the RADSA list of abilities too dangerous for civil society. This would mean that, if confirmed, the alleged Adapted would be sent to Island-A in the Atlantic." The morning news anchor's style screamed Texas, with a cascade of bleached blonde curls spilling over either shoulder, artificially white teeth, and a tan that dermatologists could only shake their heads at. She fingered a sheet of paper in front of her. "This one is number four on the list: Abilities that alter or deny others' free will."

The blood in Ben's veins turned ice cold.

"What the fuck?" He moved back to the window. "They know? How could they possibly know?"

His heart raced, but he was chilled to the bone.

"The person that reported this to us had this to say," the news anchor said.

Ben turned back to the TV and instantly breathed a sigh of relief. The video replay showed a handsome young Black man on a city street, talking with a reporter. The yellow tag at the bottom of the screen read "Ex-Boyfriend of Adapted" and in smaller lettering beneath that "Devontae Stokes".

"We were at the mall eating lunch," the young man began, speaking eagerly and too close to the reporter's microphone. "I told her I wanted to break up. The next thing I know, I'm walking laps around the food court with my pants and underwear down at my ankles! I couldn't pull them up or move my hands to cover my, uh, crotch! I was humiliated! I looked over at Nona, and she was laughing hysterically. Then she just grabbed her things and took off, and I couldn't hide myself after she was gone."

"She made you do this?" the reporter asked. "With her R-Skill?"

"Yeah, she's one of those Adapted alright." The young man looked directly at the camera with anger in his eyes. "Send them all to the Island, I say!"

What were the odds of two people in the same block with a Number Four R-Skill? Ben shook his head as he walked to his nightstand for his phone. He sent a quick email to Director Gustafson to let her know the situation, then used the urgent messaging app she had given him to text the team to check the news and get downtown as soon as they could. By the time he had emerged from his closet with his coat and tie on, Bailey had responded she was already en route with Bessie.

"ETA 10 mins," her text message read.

He smiled. Bailey was a rock. So reliable. Travel mug of coffee in hand, Ben headed out to see what could be done at the park.

———

Down on ground level, the air hummed with tension. The park was half a block away and on the other side of his condo building's entrance, but the noise was raucous. The instigator's mostly unintelligible voice could be heard over a bullhorn between roars from the crowd. Ben briskly walked towards the corner and saw several people running across the street toward the protest. All young men, all white. He frowned and picked up his pace. The Adapted populace had largely replaced people of color as the focal point for bigoted minds. While that was some relief to Ben, it was no comfort to know that the same hate he himself had felt many times in the past was now directed at people no more responsible for being Adapted than he was for being Black. If only he could use his R-Skill across a wide group of people. He would be able to quell the flames of unrest in an instant.

He rounded the corner and immediately winced as he was blinded by a bright light shining right at his face.

"Sorry." A voice said.

Ben shielded his eyes from the light and saw in the corner of his eye a Channel 5 camera man picking up a tripod stand with a large circular light on top. Ahead, four police cars had blocked road access to the park. He twisted his neck until one of the joints popped, and he altered the impression of his face for the pair of people in front of him.

The cameraman's wide eyes that were staring at Ben's scar returned to the tripod. "Stupid kids knocked it over," he said.

A young woman holding a Channel 5 microphone at her side also dropped her look of surprise. "Excuse us," she said curtly, walking over to Ben. "We're on the air in less than two minutes. Come on Victor!" The reporter was a tall, attractive Latina woman with curly, medium-length dark hair filled with blonde highlights and a yellow pantsuit almost as bright as the ring light. She bent down to help raise the tripod.

"Gimme a minute, sheesh. They bent one of the legs," Victor said, pounding away at the aluminum tube with his fist.

"Sorry," the woman said, standing to face Ben. "I'm a little on edge. This is my first breaking news segment."

Ben smiled, then popped his shoulder.

"Relax. You'll do great," Ben said.

Immediately, her nerves settled and the worry in her forehead smoothed into calm. "Thanks. I'm Camila Rios." She extended her hand.

"Ben Rice." He reached for her hand and shook it gently. Her skin was soft and velvety. He missed the feel of a woman's skin.

Camila's eyes smiled at him for a moment, then grew wide. "Wait, you're..."

"Yeah. Regional manager for RADSA." Ben nodded.

"Thirty seconds, Cammie." The cameraman had managed to bend the tripod leg back into shape and was settling a large video camera onto his shoulder.

"I have *got* to talk to you later. Can we do an interview?" Camila asked.

Ben gave her a card from his inside coat pocket. "Sure, call me." He wouldn't mind talking to her again. She was pretty, and his self-imposed moratorium on romantic pursuits was growing tedious, and a bit hypocritical given his dalliance with Gigi. He pointed towards the park and flashed a smile at her. "I've got work to do. Break a leg."

"Thanks," Camila said. She turned to the camera, swiped the hair on her face behind her ears, looked at the camera, and spoke into her microphone.

After nodding to Victor just before they went on air, Ben walked over to one of the police officers monitoring the scene on the street and introduced himself. The officers were just there to keep traffic off the road and respond if things turned violent. That notion was worrisome. Some of the early protests after the emergence of the Adapted had become prickly. A few broken windows here and there, some graffiti, a burning effigy in a yard. Ben shuddered at the thought of the hundreds of people in the park descending from boisterous protest into violent rioting. And he knew nothing of this Nona girl the angry victim on TV referenced. As he walked towards the park, he logged into RADSAnet on his phone and checked for any local points of contact with that name, but found none. Not surprising. Anyone with a reported Number Four R-Skill would get red-flagged immediately for capture and transfer to the island. Ben wondered how many other Number Fours out there were like him, hiding in plain sight, using their ability to avoid detection. Then he wondered how many were abusing the power. *One is one too many*, he thought.

"Even one is too many!" a voice bellowed over a bullhorn ahead.

Ben's heart skipped a beat at hearing his own thoughts repeated aloud, but the park and protesters came into view and his attention was immediately drawn to the two people on the platform egging on the crowd: Jeb and Delilah Dewberry. Ben recognized them immediately and clenched his teeth. Hard. The situation was more perilous than he expected. Jeb and Delilah were the proud and vociferously outspoken creators of FIGHT — the Foundation for the Integrity of God's Human Triumph. FIGHT began as an online haven for Internet trolls looking to fan the flames of hatred over the Adapted that were just emerging after the Dark Object's impact.

After President Phelps created RADSA, FIGHT became the de facto voice of protest and instigator of unrest every time and anywhere RADSA was espousing harmony and calm. After the Pope's unfortunate and well-televised emergence, every organized religion openly accepted the Adapted as part of God's plan. But there were many rumors that some hyper-conservative sects were privately funneling support and money to FIGHT and other organizations like it. Some suggested it was the new, modern-day racism. Which was funny, since classic, old-timey racism was still a thing, though albeit somewhat lessened of late. The advent of the Adapted gave those with angry souls something new and shiny to hate.

The Dewberrys, according to the latest RADSA report on contrary social media trends, were recently released from their third stint in prison for inciting lawlessness at their FIGHT rallies and protests. *These two sure get around*, Ben thought. Jeb was the rumored brains of the pair. He wore his customary ensemble: an orange T-shirt beneath blue overalls and a blue and white University of Florida ball cap. Tufts of graying blond hair poked out from all sides of his hat, and his face was darkened with a few days of stubble. Jeb scratched at the sides of his face constantly. Delilah was all bubbles and sunshine, when not spewing hate into a microphone. She wiggled up and down on her toes, causing her platinum blonde curls to bounce and her disproportionately large fake boobs to jiggle. Seems she embraced the eye candy role, given the majority of the FIGHT followers were young men. She wore a snug white shirt split down the front to show off her shiny, red push-up bra, and cut-off denim shorts.

Jeb and Delilah had spent a few nights in jail after a protest they led outside a popular hundred-year-old bar in Portland, Maine turned into a riot. Half a dozen storefronts were vandalized, and several cars torched by the end of a well-rehearsed night of lamentations by the Dewberrys over the deviation of society from God's plan. Adapted were a taint, the work of the Devil, and it was incumbent upon the unaffected to fight back against the infection threatening to undo all of God's good work. All this after a poor Adapted emerged while half-drunk at the bar, and in his alcohol-induced stupor, couldn't stop himself from screeching through the harmonic frequencies of every piece of glass in the space. The mirrors behind the bar and in the restrooms—shattered. The floor-to-ceiling windows covered in chalk marker with a local artist's homage to lighthouses—destroyed. The stained-glass rosettes set in the original wooden front door—obliterated. Every glass, tumbler, and bottle, full or empty. All burst into pieces.

The young men who had trampled Camila's light stand were at the back of the crowd, pumping fists into the air. Two of the four of them had handguns carelessly holstered over the waists of their jeans, and one of those two kept putting his hand on the weapon every few seconds.

Ben attempted to choke down the lump forming in his throat. "Shit."

The raging debate over openly carried handguns in Texas washed over his mind. Years back, the state legislature passed a law changing the long-standing concealed-carry policy into license-to-carry. But it was commonly referred to as open-carry. Over time misinformation had convinced the easily persuaded that open-carry meant anyone could bring a firearm wherever they wanted. Gun-related crime had increased somewhat since the law was changed, but not nearly as much as many had projected. Ben hadn't formed an opinion on the law, or gun ownership in general as he had little interest or experience with firearms. He had only hoped he wouldn't have to arm himself and his team, and instead let their abilities shine when called upon, which was RADSA's general philosophy. But all it would take to change his mind (and likely the stance of the entire RADSA organization) was someone on his team getting hurt by a handgun under his watch.

He thought back to the Portland riot that earned the Dewberrys a few days behind bars. No one was seriously hurt during the violence, but two store owners were sent to the hospital with cuts and bruises after attempting to discourage the rioters from vandalizing their shops. Ben worried things were about to turn much worse here. He could feel it in his joints, the large ones each throbbing with dull, radiant pain, each ready to release its tension to fuel his R-Skill. He feared for his team, and himself. And for the poor girl Nona sheltered somewhere inside the condo building across the park from his own. She was probably scared out of her mind. He looked up to the right at his window ten stories up, then looked over at Nona's building and again found it incredible two Number Fours lived so close together.

The young man fondling his gun had slipped a finger inside the trigger guard and looked like he was about to pull out the weapon. Ben ran up to him and popped his knee. He tapped the guy on the shoulder to get his attention. "There's a trash can over there. Forget your gun." He pointed.

The young man nodded in immediate acceptance and jogged over to dispose of his gun. Ben repeated this with the other guy, who also tossed his weapon into the trash without a second thought. Both returned to their spots and resumed their fist pumping and yelling, none the wiser.

Ben moved along the back of the crowd to one corner to get a better look at the podium.

"I'm stealing all the thunder. Here you go, babe," Jeb said as he handed the bullhorn to Delilah.

"Thanks, babe," the diminutive woman said. "Alright! Gimme an F!"

"F!" the crowd yelled.

"I!" Delilah barked.

"I!" the crowd responded.

"G-H-T!" Delilah screamed.

"G-H-T!" the crowd cheered.

"I'm gonna tell you what FIGHT means to me!" Delilah shouted into the bullhorn.

Ben felt his phone buzz. A text from Director Gustafson waited. "I hope you're on top of this situation."

He frowned, not liking the idea of being under the watching eye of the director. "I'm here, team en route. On it." He texted back.

There had to be nearly three hundred people in this crowd. Could he use his R-Skill to convince them all to leave at the same time? Ben didn't think so. The most he had altered simultaneously was a room of five people. And that was a *small* room without distractions. And there was the not-insignificant matter of obscuring his face. No. He could approach Delilah right now, but she was mostly a cheerleader.

"FIGHT is my voice in a freaky, fucked up world of radioactive meteor mutant monsters!" Delilah barked into the microphone, twirling on stage.

The crowd roared.

Her husband was truly the mouthpiece of FIGHT. Ben's best shot would be to connect with Jeb off stage and convince him one way (or the other) that RADSA would handle the situation. It would be the truth. If Nona indeed had a Number Four R-Skill, Ben would have no choice but to send her to the island. Unfortunately, Jeb headed off the stage in the opposite direction into the crowd and ducked out of sight seconds later. Ben would have to wait for him to come back and approach him on stage. Frannie probably wouldn't mind seeing RADSA break up a FIGHT rally on live television.

"FIGHT defends the Lord's plan for humanity!" Delilah yelled.

The crowd roared.

"Who here is ready to FIGHT?" Delilah barked.

The crowd roared.

"FIGHT for God!" Delilah reached for the sky and honked the loudspeaker's over-loud horn.

The crowd roared.

"FIGHT for yourself! For your fellow man!" Delilah screamed.

Nearly everyone had their fists in the air at this point. More than several had guns in their hands. Ben grumbled at his luck, then busied himself covertly convincing anyone he saw with a weapon to dispose of it in a trash can. He stopped counting after he reached double-digits.

CHAPTER 39
THE SLEUTH

STEVE SAT in his idling car, as nervous as he could ever remember being. The day's heat had not yet begun to swell, and the Camry's air conditioner was at full blast. Yet he was sweating. His coat and tie, usually worn from the time he left his apartment until he got home, lay in a disheveled heap on the back seat. He watched the stairwell for Abby to keep his mind off the day to come. The sight of her would no doubt brighten his pensive mood. But for as much as he anticipated her company on the drive to work, he dreaded what he was going to have to tell her.

Beyond his worry about Abby, or the UDOs, or the president's press conferences, he had Agent Orton on his mind. He hated psychologists, therapists, and the like. This, a product of his post-embassy emotional non-trauma that the Marines' counselors kept insisting could surface later in his life and needed to be discussed to prevent any lingering effects. But he knew himself. He didn't have PTSD over how his friend Milo died. It was just plain, old-fashioned survivor's guilt. The high of having a tiny role in helping Milo's father get elected president had worn off long ago.

He did have a problem. At least, that was the stance of RADSA's director. Agent Orton would investigate Steve's R-Skill's capacity and limitations. Such a waste of time. Steve knew himself. At least he thought he did. Not once had he questioned what his R-Skill was telling him about something. Every Adapted he had ever met had a similar unwavering understanding of the nature of their abilities. As far as Steve was concerned, the president was wrong about the dark objects. He *had* to be. But was he lying?

Abby loped down the stairs from her apartment, and Steve inhaled a sharp, pleasant breath of cold, conditioned air. She waved at him as she jogged to the car. He was falling for her. That much he knew. Just how far he had already fallen was yet to be determined. But he knew it was a bad idea. He had to tell her.

She opened the door and slid into the passenger seat. "Jesus, Steve! Are you keeping a side of beef in here?"

He laughed.

"I think I'm gonna need a jacket." She put her hand on the door handle.

"You could use mine," he said.

"Oh, okay. But…" She looked at him with a raised eyebrow that would make Spock proud. "You do not appear to be wearing one."

He reached back and pulled his suit jacket to the front. The tie tumbled to the floor. "Sorry. I'm a bit out of sorts this morning."

She pulled the blazer on, and he was immediately a little more taken with her. The sharp lines of his jacket echoed the stark definition of her jawline. With her Rangers hat and a yellow Nirvana t-shirt, the addition of his jacket gave her the look of a hip Silicon Valley tech founder. It was a good look. In the corner of his eye, he caught her pulling the collar of his coat to her nose. She inhaled deeply, closed her eyes, and smiled. That she could have the same interest in him as he did in her was thrilling. It melted his concern over the RADSA agent coming to analyze him. At least, for the moment. Instead, it bubbled up his apprehension over putting a stop to what was blossoming between him and Abby.

"When's the last time you had this cleaned?" Abby asked. She was looking at him with a smirk on her pretty face.

"Uh. That's fresh from the dry cleaners," he said, getting the car moving.

"Oh. So that's what I'm smelling."

His head suddenly sparked in pain.

"It's not bad." She took another sniff, this one deliberately audible. "Maybe I should get my clothes dry cleaned." Again, she smirked.

No doubt, she was enjoying the scent of his cologne in the jacket. Steve rubbed his head, wondering if she had just intentionally set off his R-Skill in a flirtatious manner. *That* would be a first. He wasn't sure he'd want a lot of that, but wouldn't be surprised if Abby turned out to be a button-pusher extraordinaire.

He shrugged. "I'm not much of a fan of the chemical odor."

"Must be something else then." She wrapped her arms across her torso and shivered. "So, what's got you so hot and bothered, Agent Palmer?"

"I'd rather not talk about it."

"Hmm." She studied his placid face. "I guess not."

But was that true? He just said it, so it must be. The introduction of this expert from RADSA HQ called into question the true nature of his R-Skill.

"Not even a little?" Abby raised both her eyebrows and smiled.

In that moment, he wanted to spill his guts. But he didn't want to let on that there may be unknown limitations to his ability, lest others try to test them or take advantage of him. "Well, maybe a little." That much was true. "Let me ask you. How confident are you in your understanding of your R-Skill?"

She gave him a puzzled look. "Like, what I can and can't do with it? I dunno, pretty confident I'd say. I guess I never thought about it much. When I emerged, I just knew. Ya know?"

Steve unintentionally pursed his lips.

Abby caught it. "It's not the same with you? I— I thought it worked that way for all Adapted."

He let out a frustrated sigh. "I don't know. I thought so too. How would you feel if there were unknown facets to your R-Skill?"

She shrugged. "I guess we would just come across those as we use our abilities. Not much else to do about it. This first step would be knowing you had more to learn about what you can or can't do."

Steve stomped on the brakes to avoid colliding with the large truck stopped in front of them. The car quickly lurched to a halt. "Crap, sorry."

"You're a bit—"

"Distracted," he said. "I'm meeting with an agent from RADSA HQ today."

She reached over and tugged at his ear affectionately. The physical contact hit him like lightning. "Abby!" he gasped, gripping the steering wheel.

She jerked her hand back. "Sorry."

"It's a bad idea." He blurted out the words.

"What is?"

"Us."

She looked at him with those pale blue eyes, which seemed at once darker and cloudier than before. "Oh." Abby's eyes betrayed a moment of hurt before she turned to look out her window.

Steve sighed and admonished his indelicacy. "It's not that I don't…"
She said nothing.

"We just can't," he whispered. "It's a bad idea."

After a moment, Abby drew in a loud breath and huffed it out. "It's okay, Steve. I get it. You've got your duty thing turned on. Workplace relationship training, yada yada."

That wasn't it at all. His head scorched with pain from the false statement. This wasn't his sense of duty talking.

"I'll be okay. We'll just be friends," she said. The disappointment was plain on her face, but she didn't press the issue.

He nodded appreciatively, but couldn't say a thing. What had he just done? Every fiber in his being wanted to walk back everything he had just said and rewind to the moment when they were kissing each other goodbye in private after the team had adjourned following the tornado rescue. Every fiber, but one, apparently. The one that made decisions.

The conversation dropped like a hammer. He was glad to be past the worst part of the morning, having to call things off with Abby. He didn't really want to, he hoped she knew that.

"Okay, this is awkward," Abby said abruptly, making show to rub her eyes like she was trying to get an irritant out. "Let's get back to the other topic. Why is this guy coming to see you?"

Steve's heavy heart quickened, having leapt from one torment to another. "I can't say it," he blurted out.

"Say what?"

"I can't say why he's here."

"Agent Rice didn't tell you?"

"No, he did."

"I'm confused. So, you do know why he's here?"

"Yes. But I can't say it. It's not true." Steve ran a hand down his face and shook his head. "I can think it, I just can't say it."

"That's… weird. So, Ben was wrong? What's it like to have words you just can't say?"

"Frustrating."

"Are you feeling alright? Are you sick or something?"

"Yes and no."

"Could there be something wrong with your R-Skill?"

"I don't know."

"This agent is here to figure that out?"

"That's what Ben said. I just can't say it." Steve frowned.

"Well," she folded her arms amid thought. "What would it hurt to talk to him? Maybe there's something to the idea that as Adapted we don't fully understand the nature of our R-Skills, and just have a general idea. I mean, it'd be pretty useful if I could lift things that weren't explicitly considered garbage, or could toss stuff into a dump truck or something larger. I don't think I can, but do I really know if I don't try?"

"Have you tried?"

"Sure. It got tedious at the construction site to wait for them to empty the dumpsters every ten minutes. Didn't amount to much, but that's okay."

He stared ahead at the road.

"C'mon, experiment some. Maybe you'll help advance Adapted scientific understanding."

Steve's frown was unaffected. "I suppose."

Abby shrugged. "It can't be as bad as typing up interview reports all day."

He knew that much was true, and it brought a smile to his face.

Suddenly, both his and Abby's phones beeped at the same time with a similar alert to the one that woke him the night of the tornado. She picked hers up and read the message.

"Oh shit! Steve, we need to turn around. There's an anti-Adapted protest downtown."

CHAPTER 40
GARBAGE GIRL

"I CAN'T BELIEVE THIS," Abby said. Nerves of worry prickled her spine.

"Let's get in there before the protest turns into a riot," Steve replied. "C'mon."

They raced from the side street where Steve parked his car in front of two police cruisers blocking the way into the park. Bessie was idling inside the cordoned off area. Either Bailey had talked her way into getting an officer to move his car, or, more likely, she had negotiated the big rig through the narrow gap between one of the parked cruisers and the live oak trees that dotted the sidewalks.

Bailey, clad in a bulky black vest with RADSA emblazoned on the front and back in bold, light blue letters, stood by one of the front tires, and was just barely taller than it. She waved the two of them over urgently. "Here, put these on," she said, handing Abby a vest. It wasn't the utility vest they wore while searching the debris after the tornado. Abby's eyes grew wide when she realized what it was.

"Kevlar. Yeah," Bailey said. Her eyes darted down the path they were about to take towards the park. The grim look on her face read she didn't want to go. "Ben said there were guns out there. Better safe than bullet-ridden."

Steve shrugged and pulled his vest on, tightening the Velcro straps at the sides in one swift motion. Clearly, he had worn something like it before. The look on his face was placid.

In contrast, Abby felt like she was about to pee herself. They were about to go into an angry protest where guns were seen? She wasn't qualified for this. She wasn't trained for this. Her hands shook as she struggled to pull the vest on.

"Here," Steve said, lifting the vest up then taking her Rangers hat off.

Abby blushed as she managed to pull the vest over the vital organs that were suddenly on her mind. Steve helped tighten the straps on the sides. The fact that his hands lingered on her didn't help matters. His touch set her heart aflame, just after she had spent the better part of the morning tamping out that fire. He had told her that they were a bad idea. She understood that a workplace romance was ill-advised. But, damn it, it wouldn't have stopped her. Steve's opinion on the matter seemed to have changed overnight. At least part way. He was hesitant when he said it in the car. There was something still there. She could see it in his eyes. And feel it in his fingers.

"Well, at least you look halfway official now," Bailey said to Abby. "You gotta get a uniform."

"Or a suit," suggested Steve. He handed Abby her cap.

Abby put the hat on with a scoff. "Over my dead body."

Bailey jumped up and popped Abby in the middle of her Kevlar vest. "Not today!" She frowned, but gave Abby a wink.

"Let's go," Steve said.

Abby pushed thoughts of Steve out of her mind for a moment and scanned the street for their teammates. A pair of police officers stood at either end of the blocked off street, and there was a news crew at one corner. "Should we wait for the others? Or more police, or something?"

"We may not have that kind of time," Steve said. "C'mon."

The three jogged away from Bessie, towards the protest and potential bullets. Abby ran track in high school; she wasn't any good, but it kept her fit enough and out of Bonnie Kim's hair three afternoons a week. With the weight of the bulletproof vest strapped tight to her chest, each breath she drew seemed thin and inadequate, like the end of the first 5k she ever ran at school.

Bailey carried an extra vest for Ben. "I got it," she said when Steve offered to carry it.

The noise of the crowd swelled as they grew closer. Abby couldn't remember her heart racing any faster before.

"Ain't she great, everyone? Alright folks," a raspy voice bellowed over a bullhorn from the park ahead. "Del and me are gonna take five. Your boy

Colin here will go through this week's list of people like *you* that have been victimized by vile Adaptabominations!"

The crowd roared in anger.

"Thanks Jeb," another voice boomed. This one had a deep, rich baritone rumble, worthy of radio.

"Oh man," Steve said, picking up the pace of their jog.

"What?" Abby asked.

"Jeb and Delilah Dewberry," Bailey answered, huffing. She struggled to keep up with the much taller, longer-legged Steve and Abby.

"Wait." Abby stopped running and folded her arms across the RADSA lettering on her vest. "FIGHT is here? Shouldn't we wait for the FBI or a SWAT team or something?"

"This is *our* territory, Abby," Steve said. "We're RADSA. The president created our organization to handle affairs related to the Adapted, good and bad." He walked up and cupped her elbow. "It's a bad day. You'll be okay. We all will," he said, smiling.

The touch of his hand was gentle, and thrilling. And confusing, given that he had pretty much called a halt to any further progression of them as an item. And it did nothing to soothe her nerves. She gazed at the dark pools of his eyes and wanted to believe him. He only spoke the truth. But he wasn't a psychic.

Bailey looked back and forth between them with a raised eyebrow. They caught her looking and she nodded towards the park. The three rounded the corner of the building blocking the view of the park and were met with the backs of dozens, maybe hundreds of people staring up at the podium where a tall man with an unkempt mop of gray hair was flourishing his hands at a young African-American next to him.

"Okay, friends of the FIGHT, our list of brothers and sisters who have been victimized begins right here, with our very own Devontae Stokes," the deep voice on the bullhorn boomed. The crowd cheered. A few stragglers sneered. One late voice called out "Nice dick!" in reference to the incident at the mall.

The crowd roared with laughter and applause.

Steve frowned. "I thought I recognized that voice."

"Who is he?" Abby asked.

"Colin Jockery. He had a kitchen sink talk radio show on 89.9. Until the Dark Object struck and the Adapted emerged, it was pretty entertaining."

Bailey climbed up on top of a park table to see the podium. "Now he just reads tabloid headlines regarding the Adapted and makes wild, uneducated accusations. He's critical of us, but I didn't think he was part of FIGHT."

"Well, that's great," Abby said. "Where's the pro-Adapted media when you need them?"

"Head over to A-Space," Steve said flatly.

"Oh. Right." Abby rolled her eyes. Social media had never held her interest much, and she put even less stock in the nascent go-to site for all social things by, and related to, the Adapted. "Gigi's probably in a live chat right now on her drive here."

Steve said nothing but nodded his head with a disapproving frown.

"There's Ben," Bailey said, pointing to another corner of the park. She hopped down from the table and the three went to meet their boss.

"Devontae has been violated, friends. *Raped*, if you will, by a mind-controlling Adapted named Nona living upstairs in this very building," Colin barked into the bullhorn, pacing around the podium and gesticulating in the air. "As you are aware, mind-control is on the list that gets you sent to Island-A! The Radiologically Adapted Dangers to Society Administration's list!" He thrust an angry finger at a window in the condo tower. "She is a danger to society! She must go! She must go! She must go!" Colin honed the crowd's fervor into a raucous chant.

Abby put her fingers to her ears. The park was surrounded on all sides by condo towers. The angry chanting, compounded by the reverberations off concrete, brick, and glass bordered on deafening. Which was saying something, considering how many rock concerts she had been to in her life.

"Then there's Vela Kura- uh, Kurajowashi?" Colin said into the bullhorn. He peered over his glasses at an index card. "Am I saying that right? Kura-joo-wishi? Something like that. Eh, don't matter."

The crowd grumbled.

"Vela's from Newport Beach, California, folks, and recently a widow. Poor thing. If you're watching, Vela, our hearts go out to you." Colin paused to allow the crowd to clap or something, but little happened. "She used the money from her late husband's life insurance policy to buy their dream golf course retirement home. And on Monday, her lawn guy Manuel blew it over with a *cough*! Should he stay?"

"NO!" The crowd roared. "He must go! He must go!"

"I hadn't heard about that one," Abby said to Steve. "Is it true?"

Steve nodded. He gazed intently at Colin, with his lips a grim flat line.

Abby imagined Manuel, just scraping out an existence by mowing lawns for those fortunate enough to retire on a golf course in California.

"I think that one's a Number 3 on RADSA's list. What do you think? Is he a danger to society?" Colin asked.

The crowd roared again.

The list of Island-A worthy R-Skills was covered in one of her training videos, but Abby knew them by heart. She imagined most Adapted did, for fear of having to defend themselves one day from RADSA showing up at their door. Number 3 was 'uncontrollable destructive projections that threaten the safety of others or their property'. Was the loss of this woman's retirement home worth sending poor Manuel to Island-A? Abby's heart broke at the idea. She knew the same fate awaited Nona upstairs, but she didn't want to think about it.

"They all are!" Colin bellowed, reaching for the deepest, rumbliest registers of his voice.

"This guy straight up sucks." Abby swatted Steve on the shoulder as they jogged. "I can't believe you used to listen to him."

"Yeah, me too," Steve said.

"Hey gang," Ben said as Abby and Steve reached him at the back corner of the crowd by Nona's condo building. Bailey caught up a few seconds later and handed Ben his bulletproof vest.

Three cops had taken position outside the building's entrance to discourage anyone from barging inside. The way the middle officer kept looking over at the podium and slightly nodding gave Abby the impression he'd rather be in the crowd.

"And on Tuesday," Colin began again.

Ben slid on the vest Bailey was carrying.

"What are we going to do?" Bailey asked.

"We need to talk to the Dewberrys and get them to end this before it goes south," Ben said. "We have to get Nona out and on her way."

"To the Island, you mean." Abby folded her arms and frowned.

Ben nodded with resignation on his face. "We have to, Abby. It's part of our job."

Yeah, the shitty part, Abby thought. She gave Ben a stern frown, but he turned back to watch the stage without responding.

"Poor little Lily Marple of Mrs. Marple's Bakery in Oskaloosa, Iowa," Colin barked. "She was *robbed* in broad daylight by a masked hoodlum that blasted her face with spaghetti from his fingertips. That one's a Number 5, I'd say. Should he stay?"

"NO!" The crowd cheered. "He must go! He must go!"

"They can't send someone to the Island for that!" Abby gasped. "Jail maybe."

"Yeah," Ben said. "That one wouldn't qualify."

"At least the guy won't go hungry in prison," Abby said, chuckling.

Bailey elbowed Abby in the thigh.

"He made that one up," Steve said. He was wincing and had a hand over his forehead.

Abby touched his shoulder and gave it a squeeze, and asked him with a look if he was okay. Steve nodded and smiled at her with those same gorgeous dark eyes. He sure didn't look at her like he wasn't interested anymore. They'd have to have a longer conversation about the appropriateness of pursuing a relationship, because right now she was ready to quit her job if that's what it took.

The bodies in the crowd right in front of them started jostling, and along the edge of the building, the Dewberrys emerged, with a handful of burly bodyguards in black T-shirts and pants.

"Alright, alright! Thank you! We love you too!" Jeb shouted to no one in particular. "We'll get back up there in a few minutes."

Delilah was signing autographs and posing for selfies.

A wry smile crossed Ben's lips. "Well, that's lucky. Let's go."

The bodyguards held the crowd back as the Dewberrys approached the condo door. The three officers closed ranks and stepped forward.

"Tenants only," the shortest of the three said. He was of Latin American descent, with short buzz cut black hair, clean shaven, and a little pudgy for a cop. He had a gold bar on each shoulder, where the other officers had none.

"I just need to take a piss, officer," Jeb said.

"Do you have a key card?" the lead officer asked.

Jeb put his hands to his hips. "Fuck no. Come on, I had like six Red Bulls this morning!"

"Well, you should have held your hate rally somewhere else, Mr. Dewberry," the officer said, folding his arms across his chest.

"Hate?" Jeb said in protest, taking a step towards the officers with his hands outstretched and a smarmy grin. "We preach nothing but love for the Lord's work here! I quote John 1: 'He gave the right to become children of God, to those who believe in His name: who were born, not of blood, nor of the will of the flesh, nor of the will of man, but of God.'"

The short cop rolled his eyes. The other two looked at each other and shrugged.

"The hell does that mean?" Abby looked at Steve. He shrugged.

"Come on, sugar," Delilah said, pulling at Jeb's arm. "I think I saw an outhouse by the street."

Jeb looked as if he wanted to pick a fight with the shorter cop, but then he caught eye of the RADSA team approaching.

"Well, well, well. Finally here to save the day! Look hun', RADSA." He waved his hands in the air like an inflatable tube man. "Woo-hoo. La-de-dah!"

"Mr. Dewberry," Ben said, popping his neck joints and glancing at the cops as he walked up to the pair. "Mrs. Dewberry. I am Agent Ben Rice, North Texas regional manager for RADSA." He reached out to Jeb for a handshake, but was not taken up on it.

Delilah looked at Ben in horrid disgust. "RADSA put *you* in charge here? Gross. Are you gonna give us all some hugs and warm cookies, Ben?" Delilah spat on the ground. "It's spooks like you that keep the filthy Adapted in our towns!"

Abby balled her fists, ready to put her sparring sessions with Gigi to practical use.

Ben smiled. "Not today, Delilah. We're here on business." His tone grew less civil. "As you know. There are people in your crowd with weapons. You can end this now before things turn violent. You already know the fate for Ms. Kagai upstairs."

The dour expression on Ben's face was unusual. Abby had never seen him so unsettled.

"A drop in God's bucket, Agent Rice," Jeb said. "You may get her out of here and off to one of God's tropical paradises, the lucky bitch. You may get the next one that is on your so-called list. But sooner or later, one will slip through your fingers and kill innocents." He stepped right into Ben's face. "Rest assured, *Agent* Rice, the day that happens, I'll be on your doorstep with this very crowd calling for your head on a platter. Every one of these monsters you defend is a disgrace in the eyes of the Lord. It's only a matter of time before you fail and we start taking matters into our own hands."

Abby's blood went cold. For the first time she wished she was back at the construction yard chucking garbage. She looked to Steve for his reaction, but he was staring with grim intent at Jeb.

"If you have a problem with our nation's laws regarding the Adapted, I suggest you take it up with your senator from Arkansas. Or write a letter to the president," Ben said.

Jeb scoffed. "Fat load of shit, that'll do us. He sleeps with the Devil, that one. President Lucky my ass."

"We ain't leavin', ugly," Delilah said to Ben with a curiously repulsed look on her face. "Go and get your prize, don't let us stop you." She waved her arms at the crowd. "We'll give her a big goodbye when she comes outside to leave." She spat on the ground again.

Ben frowned and took a step back, wiping his hand down the front of his face and stretching his knuckles with audible pops.

"Hey guys," Gigi said as she jogged up to the team, wearing her tight blue and pink uniform underneath a light blue tactical vest. "This is, uh, wild." She snapped some photos with her phone, then slid it into a pocket on her leg.

Zeke trailed in right behind her, struggling to get his vest strapped on as he ran. "I don't believe this!" he said.

"Gigi, Zeke. Welcome to the fun," Steve said.

Abby waved at Zeke and smiled apologetically at Gigi. The gymnast shrugged and smiled, as if she was tickled pink at her next opportunity for social media fame and had completely forgotten that not long ago Abby had nearly killed her with a hunk of tornado-torn mall.

"Now what?" Bailey said, huddled close to Steve and Abby.

"We can't make them leave if they don't want to," Steve said. "The cops have to break this up, and that will only happen if they're breaking the law."

"Alright!" Colin's deep voice bellowed again over the bullhorn. "Let's get Jeb and Delilah back up here!"

The crowd cheered.

Ben's eyes darted between the Dewberrys and the crowd, and his expression grew angry for a short moment. Then a wash of calm came over him and he straightened his back, rolled his neck and popped his shoulders.

"Actually," Ben said, looking at Jeb. "I think there's an announcement you were going to make."

Jeb's eyes sparkled. "Right you are!" He grabbed Delilah's hand. "Come on babe, you won't believe this!" The two turned and headed back to the stage, bodyguard detail in tow.

"What's that about?" Steve asked.

Ben turned his back to the team and said nothing. He walked over to the short police officer and said something, cracking his neck joints in the process. The policeman nodded and started talking into his radio shoulder mic.

"Let's go up to the stage," Ben said. "I'll get up there if I have to. I don't want to bring Nona out with this crowd here."

"We can't bring her out the street door?" Bailey asked. "This building has an exit sixty-two feet from Bessie."

"Yeah, I wouldn't do that," Gigi said.

Everyone looked at her in surprise.

"The street is full of people now," Gigi said. "Cops too. They have the entrance to the park blocked off. Good thing I wore my outfit, or they probably wouldn't have let us get our vests."

Ben shook his head. "Doesn't matter. I want to break this thing up. These people are never going to leave us—" he paused. "Or the Adapted alone. Come on." He caught up to the last of the Dewberry's bodyguards and pressed through the crowd behind them. The rest of the team followed.

As members of the crowd noticed their RADSA-emblazoned vests, Abby saw a wide spectrum of expressions on their faces: surprise, relief, anger, and disgust. She bumped into shoulder after shoulder, and her mind again turned to the safe isolation of the construction yard.

Jeb hopped back up on stage, followed by Delilah. The team stopped at the edge of the platform. Ben folded his arms. Bailey hid between Steve and Abby against the brick condo wall. Gigi popped her bubble gum and pulled her phone out to record the show.

"Here they are!" Colin yelled, handing the bullhorn back to Jeb.

"Thanks buddy, keep up the good FIGHT here in Dallas! I hope you're all tuning into Colin's radio show on—" he stopped to speak to Colin. "89.9FM, morning drivetime every weekday!"

The crowd cheered.

"So, I've got a fun surprise for y'all," Jeb said, pacing the stage. "But before I do that, I'd like to point out that our friends from RADSA are here." Jeb splayed an open hand towards the team huddled in front of the corner of the stage.

A cacophony of boos rained down. It was the loudest response yet.

Jeb hit the horn button on the loudspeaker. "Now, now, they're gonna conduct our friend upstairs to her destination on Island-A. But before they do, I'd like to say that I am an Adapted too."

The crowd began to cheer, then trickled into a quiet hush.

Jeb was smiling, standing front and center of the stage. He stretched out his arms and washed himself in the attention he had garnered. "It's true! I used my mind control powers to convince poor Delilah here to get her ridiculous boob job." He waved a hand at her. Delilah's eyes nearly fell out of her skull.

At once the crowd erupted into a frenzied rage. Shouts and boos filled the park space and reverberated up the walls of the surrounding condo buildings. Delilah gaped at her husband. Her eyebrows were mashed together in pained confusion.

"Shit!" Ben barked, looking nervously at the crowd.

Abby's heart raced. She wanted to leave. With Steve. She'd drag him out. Job or no job, staying put was nuts.

Steve hid his face in his hands, seemingly overcome by the noise.

Jeb gnashed a cheesy grin at the crowd, arms still outstretched.

A loud shot rang out. Red mist fanned out from the back of Jeb's head. Then his body crumpled to the stage. Delilah screamed. The crowd exploded into chaos as everyone began to flee the scene. Aside from the locked condominium doors, the only way out was the street entrance. Protesters pushed and shoved, bumped and collided, looking for the right way to run. Three more shots rang out and the crowd collectively ducked. Shards of broken glass cascaded from a fifth story window and chittered on the stage.

"Holy crap!" Abby exclaimed.

"Condo door, now!" Ben yelled, pointing.

The slim corridor along the wall they had followed to the stage was now choked with a bedlam of frantic humanity. Abby grabbed Steve's hand and followed behind Zeke, Ben, and Gigi. The team inched along the wall, back the way they came towards the entrance. Every step was slowed by a new frantic body in the way. Gigi slugged a fat protester in the face who came up to confront them. For once, Abby was glad Gigi had a great right hook. The sight took her mind off her racing nerves, but only for a moment. The crowd was tumultuous. Over the panoply of shouting and screaming, Abby thought she heard Delilah wail on stage behind them and wanted to take pity on her situation. But she was far more concerned about her own hide at the moment.

Ben pressed in front of the group as they reached the officers holding protesters back with raised batons and pepper spray at the ready. He craned his neck as he approached the short officer. "Let us inside!"

The officer nodded, rushed to the door, and waved a key card at the reader. The team shuffled inside and the cop slammed the door behind them. Abby finally let go of Steve's hand, unable to even revel in the moment of it. Her pulse had never raced higher.

A protester got too close to the door and the cop hosed him in the eyes with pepper spray.

"Everyone's here," Bailey said, checking herself for bullet wounds and breathing a sigh of relief. She walked a circle around the group, inspecting everyone's vests.

"What the hell just happened?" Abby asked, panting.

They all shook their heads. Steve massaged his temples. Ben looked like he had seen a ghost.

CHAPTER 41
BOUNCY

"WE JUST SAW that guy get shot in the *fucking* head!" Gigi said to no one in particular. Half-stunned, half-thrilled, she couldn't believe she had just witnessed a cold-blooded murder in person. She was in the middle of the action! And it was all on her phone.

The team caught their breath in the atrium of the condo building's park entrance. All but Gigi, of course. She was the thoroughbred to the rest of the team's pack mules. Each of the others exchanged nervous glances, in obvious distress over having front-row seats to a bloody murder. It was all she could do to keep her hands off her phone.

"I—" Ben stammered. His hands were on his knees, like he had just lost a family member or someone just as important. "I can't believe it."

Zeke's eyes were about to fall out of his head. Abby was almost in tears. Bailey *was* in tears. Steve, stoic as ever, merely had his resting bitch face in effect.

"We should get Nona out of here," Steve said.

"Bessie too," Bailey said through a teary sniffle. "Who knows what the rioters will do to her."

Ben continued to stare at the floor.

Why was he so affected? Gigi was somewhat at a loss as to the teams' reactions after watching Jeb die. *A colossal pain in RADSA's collective ass was just removed from the chess board, people!* she thought. Sure, to see homicide in person was quite spectacular, but she had seen more graphic violence on *Law and Order: Crime Lords* on NBC last night. Though Gigi wasn't surprised with Abby. The wimp.

"Ben?" Steve said after a long silence.

With a long, restorative inhale, Ben regained his composure. "Yeah," he sighed. He cleared his throat. "Yeah."

Ben led the team to the reception desk and asked for Nona's condo number. The receptionist resisted, but after Ben gave her his business card and her eyes grew wide at it, the team headed for the elevator and unit 404.

Gigi stole into a corner at the back of the elevator and waited for everyone's eyes to face the metal doors. She whipped out her phone and texted her friend Kendra. "Girl, call your agent quick. Tell her I've got front and center video of the FIGHT dude getting shot. I want an exclusive with A-Space!"

Seconds later, Kendra texted back. "OMG GIRL WHAT??? Calling now!"

Abby grumbled. Gigi slid her phone back into her pocket, sensing a conversation coming.

"Do we have to do this?" Abby asked.

Gigi rolled her eyes. The newbie had made her distaste for Island-A known on every occasion possible in her short time on the team. By now she had to understand that the list, the Dangers to Society List, was immutable.

"Yes, Abby," Ben replied, an unusually harsh impatience in his tone. His face still lacked its usual tan color.

What was eating at him? Gigi wondered.

"But, couldn't she join the team or something? I mean, sure, she fucked up there in the mall with that guy, but whatever happened to second chances? Or a fair trial?"

Steve butted in. "She's going Abby. Either we do it with as much care and compassion as we can muster, or the national response team comes in, probably with an armed escort."

"This sucks," Zeke muttered, staring at his shoes. "I'd much rather be digging people out of rubble."

Abby looped her arm around Zeke's and gave it a squeeze. Gigi stifled a chuckle at Steve's raised eyebrow.

The elevator stopped on the fourth floor, and the team moved down the hall to Nona's condo. Ben raised his hand to knock, then hesitated. He looked around at the team.

"When I took this job, I took an oath to uphold the charter of RADSA and abide by the D2S list." He scanned the group again. "We all did."

He met each of their eyes and waited for the other to nod. When he looked at Gigi, she nodded quickly. She didn't care that this Nona person was going to the island. Rules were rules. Abby was last, and waited the longest before nodding. Her eyes were fixed on the floor and the grimace on her lips reached nearly that far.

"Now, let's do our jobs." Ben knocked.

Of course, Nona didn't answer.

Gigi felt a buzz from her phone.

It was from Kendra's agent, LeAnne Clarke. A tingle of excitement flittered up her spine.

"Gigi," LeAnne's text began, "I've spoken with a rep at A-Space. They don't want your video. 'Not their thing,' they said. But TMZ and some others are champing at the bit for it. Already emailed you the offer from TMZ. Sign and send it back if you want to accept. They won't negotiate, but since you're not officially repped by me, I won't take the usual 10%."

Then the tingle of excitement up her back warmed into a radiant glow. She got the text she had been looking forward to seeing for a long time. "I want to represent you. Have also emailed you the standard company contract. A-Space did say they had some more openings for their reality show filming here soon. They want some Adapted with physically impressive skills for the show. I think you'd be a great fit. Money's good, exposure would be off the charts."

Gigi barely contained her screech of joy. A tiny squeak escaped her clenched teeth.

Ben shot her a quizzical eyebrow, then knocked again. "Ms. Kagai, please come to the door. My name is Benjamin Rice. We're with RADSA."

Moments later, a muffled, threatened voice screeched from the condo. "Go away!"

"Ms. Kagai, you understand the seriousness of the situation. Either you come willingly with us, or an armed team will come and pull you out by force. "

Gigi wasn't paying attention. She sent LeAnne a quick "I'm in!" text, then looked over the TMZ offer. She rolled her eyes. Pages upon pages of fine print. Like she was going to read all that. She added her digital signature to the form and sent it back to the agent. *Her* agent! Then she sent the video. She didn't even care what happened to it, or about the money. She had that to spare. It was the access that it had granted. When she gave up competitive gymnastics, the momentum of her career, the treadmill beneath her feet, had stopped. A big OUT OF ORDER sign hung around her neck for all to see. Now that noose was lifted. The treadmill had started and would soon begin to pick up speed. She had momentum again. It was exhilarating, just like the first time she had the best aggregate score at a gymnastics meet when she was fourteen. It was then she felt she could really compete with others at the highest level. Gigi had that same feeling again.

Ben knocked again on Nona's door. Harder, this time.

Abby stepped up and pushed him out of the way with surprising brusqueness.

"Nona, my name is Abby. Abby Alstrom. We can help you. Help us understand what happened. Let's get your side of the story." Abby looked at Ben, who glared back at her with arms folded. "Then we'll worry about what comes next. We just want to talk for now."

Gigi rolled her eyes. Nona booked her trip to Island-A the second Devontae Stokes' pants dropped to his ankles. Bailey patted Abby's back. Steve smiled but shook his head. Ben chuffed in surprise when Nona began to unlock her door.

The team all peered expectantly as the door slowly swung open. Behind it stood a young woman, about the same age as Gigi. Dark skin, black, curly hair cut short with a thin streak of red dyed above her right ear. She wore an overlarge Southern Methodist University sweatshirt and jeans. Her face was awash with tears.

Nona said nothing, just turned and walked back into her condo.

Ben turned to Bailey. "Wait out here Jo. Protocol Four. Steve will lead us out."

"Gotcha," Bailey said with a nod to Ben, then Steve. She leaned up against the wall and pulled a small spray can from her belt.

Protocol Four was the procedure put in place when the team encountered a potential Number Four Adapted. A team member was to wait separately, armed with a spray form of the Truex gas used during interviews. In theory, it decreased the chances of the Adapted using their R-Skill against the solitary team member if they were attempting to escape. Steve was designated to lead the team out, and Protocol Four indicated that if someone other than the designee left first, then everyone was to get the spray.

Ben led the team inside, where they found an open concept kitchen and living space. Bright lights, huge windows looking down to the park, modern furniture. The living area featured a large L-shaped white leather sofa facing a big TV and a triangular glass coffee table. A number of Adapted magazines were splayed on top. Nona slouched at one end of the sofa, crying.

Gigi pulled her phone out and started recording again. Ben gave her a look, but they typically videoed all of their interviews. Why should this one be any different?

"Thank you, Ms. Kagai. As I said before, my name is Ben Rice, North Texas regional manager for RADSA. We have seen evidence that you possess an R-Skill on the Dangers to Society list." He pointed at Steve. "This is Agent Palmer. He is an Adapted and can tell when people are speaking the truth. Are you an Adapted?"

Nona shrank at the question. "Yes."

"And your R-Skill, your ability, gives you command over other people's free will? Make them move involuntarily?"

Nona looked at the team. Tears streamed from her eyes. "Yes."

"That is Number Four on the Dangers to Society list. It is my duty to inform you that you are required by the United States Government to immediately relocate to the facility commonly referred to as Island-A, per the Adapted Act."

Nona buried her face in her hands.

Ben continued reciting lines from the training video on apprehending D2S listers. "Please refrain from using your R-Skill. Be advised that now your ability has become public knowledge, any attempt at escape will only delay the inevitable and may incur criminal charges as well."

"Don't I get some representation or something?" Nona asked.

"No," Ben said. "Per the Adapted Act, those with confirmed R-Skills on the Dangers to Society list are required to be immediately sent to Island-A. There is an appeals system on the island, but to my knowledge, there haven't been any Adapted that have returned to the mainland yet."

Abby punched him in the shoulder. "Geez, lighten up." She then made a beeline to sit next to Nona who had a massive wet spot on her sweatshirt from the tears. She put an arm around her shoulder and patted meaning-less reassurance with her hand. "Can you tell us what happened?" she asked.

Nona recounted the afternoon at NorthPark where she forced Devontae to show off his family jewels to the unsuspecting food court patrons. Evidently, he had nothing to be ashamed of in that department. She had developed her R-Skill months ago and was afraid to use it for fear of being caught. But he had made her so mad. He was dumping her for someone else and had the audacity to have the other girl in earshot two tables over.

"Did you use your ability on Jeb Dewberry down there?" Steve blurted out.

Ben's mouth gaped open, and he raised a hand to stop Nona from answering.

She looked up and her tears flowed. "No," she peeped.

Steve nodded.

"The shooter?" Ben asked.

Nona shook her head. "My R-Skill only has a range of about thirty feet. I've been up here all morning."

Steve nodded again.

"Alright," Ben said.

"I'm fucked," she said, hiding her face back in her hands.

Abby attempted further consolation, but Nona was lost in her sorrow.

Gigi eyed the SMU Law School diploma hanging on the wall. *You fucked up, alright,* she thought. All that effort down the drain.

"What happens now?" Nona asked, looking up at Ben with tears in her eyes.

"Well," Ben moved towards her a step. "You'll need to pack the things you want to bring with you. The island is well-supplied with clothes, books, electronics, and things to do. You'll have a furnished place to stay. It's not a penal colony."

Abby was shaking her head at Ben. For once, Gigi agreed with her. Ben's bedside manner sucked.

"For now, pack just what you can carry." Ben stopped to look at his watch. "You'll probably be on a plane before dinner. Any remaining items can be sent to you, but space is indeed limited. We can make a list of things you want shipped and box them up later. Someone from the RADSA head office will contact you to handle your property affairs, bills, mail, etcetera."

———

While Ben, Zeke, and Abby helped Nona pack her things, Steve and Gigi sat on the sofa and waited. Gigi had catalogued everything in the condo so that it could be appropriately dispositioned by a relocation specialist from the home office. Mostly clothes, a bicycle on the patio, plus the usual furniture and electronics. She did have a curiously large collection of Pokémon cards and several large stuffed animals that she said Devontae had won for her at the State Fair last year.

"Can I bring the cards?" Nona asked.

Ben said that he didn't know the particulars on what was and wasn't allowed, but would check on it. He figured they would be okay to be shipped.

For those with an R-Skill on the D2S List, RADSA was dispassionately firm in sending those individuals to Island-A. But they did go out of their way to delicately handle the person's belongings, real estate, business affairs, and relations. Probably Pokémon cards too.

Gigi checked TMZ's website, but her video wasn't up there yet. It hadn't even been an hour since she had sent it, but she figured it wouldn't take long for them to jump on it. They had other clips from people in the crowd, but all of them were from the post-shooting chaos. She pulled up LeAnne's contract and began reading. The TMZ one didn't matter, but she figured it would be prudent to read the details for the important one.

"Whatcha reading?" Steve asked, looking over at her from the other end of the sofa. "Anything new about the situation downstairs?"

Gigi shrugged. "No. I got an offer of representation from an agent this morning. Reading the contract." She didn't like telling Steve the news first, but it's not like she could tell him something else and he probably wouldn't let it go if she said nothing.

"Oh," Steve said with a 'what-the-hell-Gigi?' kind of tone. But then he seemed to appreciate what the news meant to her. "That's... actually really great. I'm happy for you. You've been after that since I've known you."

"Thanks." She smiled. He hadn't known her all that long. She'd been after this her whole life.

She sent a tweet, stating she had exciting news coming up and to stay tuned. Then she checked her number of followers and saw she had gained two hundred overnight, without even doing anything. A fresh tingle of excitement tickled her skin.

"Eddie's downstairs," Steve said looking at his phone. "I'll go get him."

"Actually, we're about done here," Ben said, walking back into the living room with a metallic pink suitcase in tow.

Zeke came out next with another large suitcase, followed by Nona and Abby each with bags over their shoulders. Nona's face streamed tears.

Abby's looked like she had done some crying too. *Wimp*, Gigi thought. Poor Zeke looked like he was about to throw up.

They had been in the apartment nearly two hours and were finally about to leave. Gigi was eager to clock out early and go visit her new agent. She stood and looked down at the park through the window. The local authorities had gained control of the area and cleared out the FIGHT protesters. Only a few remained, huddled in groups with one or more officers. One set surrounded a news reporter in a bright yellow suit. Another set appeared to be giving statements to the police. On the stage, she saw Eddie standing next to the Dewberry's bodyguards, and Delilah of all people.

Nona bid a tearful farewell to her home, then the group headed for the door.

"Soup of the day?" Bailey asked when they came out.

"Broccoli and cheese," Steve said, nodding and satisfying Protocol Four.

Bailey nodded back, then led them to the elevator. The ride down was quiet. Solemn. Only a tinkle of metal broke the silence as Nona handed her keys over to Abby, who patted the poor woman on her back again.

"We'll take good care of everything," Abby said.

Ben wanted to thank the police officers who were at the door for their earlier assistance, so they exited the condo building through the park doors. He shook their hands outside. "Thank you for your help," he said to the short officer, whose name was Garcia. "Any leads with the shooter?"

Gigi was a little surprised by his tone. It was that of small talk or obligation, not concern or interest. Officer Garcia said there had not been any arrests yet, but with all the eyes and cameras around, it was only a matter of time. He also thanked Ben for handling the Nona situation and they exchanged business cards to keep each other abreast of new developments.

"This is all your fault!" a frantic voice screamed from the stage. Delilah jumped down from the dais and ran towards the team. Her bodyguards and Eddie lumbered after her.

Abby, Steve, Bailey, and Zeke closed ranks around Nona. Ben stepped forward to meet Delilah, holding up his hands. Gigi pulled her phone out and started recording.

"You made him say that!" Delilah bellowed, thrusting a shaky finger in Nona's direction. Like Nona, her face was covered in tears, as well as a nasty gash down her left cheek. Blood ran down her neck and stained much of her white shirt. It gave her the look of a direct-to-video B-movie horror heroine.

Ben pumped his hands. "Mrs. Dewberry, I'm so sorry for what happened." He paused for a long breath. "We know Nona was not involved with what happened to your husband."

"Bullshit!" Delilah yelled. Fresh tears streamed down her face.

Ben pointed an impatient finger at Steve. "*He* is an Adapted. His R-Skill allows him to tell when people are speaking the truth. We've already absolved Nona of any involvement."

Delilah looked between them with desperate pain in her eyes. "Somebody must have made him do that!

"What makes you so sure?" Steve asked.

Gigi raised an eyebrow. Whenever Steve spoke up, he sensed some truth out there needing to be unearthed.

"Because he didn't make me get my boobs done. I did that before we met." Delilah sobbed, then winced as she touched her face.

Steve nodded at Ben, who frowned.

"What does that mean?" Abby asked.

"He faked it to rile up the crowd," Bailey said, folding her arms.

Steve put a hand to his forehead and flinched. "No," he growled. "Someone else made him do it."

"Wait," Abby said. "That would mean—"

"Another Number Four was here," Ben said, shaking his head. "Gigi, start a profile for an unknown Number Four." He spoke through clenched teeth. That was weird. This whole scenario really got to him it seemed.

"Ow!" Delilah barked as one of her bodyguards, who was attempting to dab a cloth at the bleeding wound on her cheek.

"Mrs. Dewberry," Ben said. "Eddie here can fix you up. He's an Adapted too."

Delilah looked across the team with a disbelieving harrumph. "All of y'all are Adapted. Fucking figures!"

All but Ben nodded. Steve's face was contorted with confusion.

Eddie stepped up to Delilah, holding his thumb up to her face.

"Wait," she said quietly, putting her hand on his arm.

"Better let me fix it *amiga*. A cut like this will need stitches and leave a scar," Eddie said.

Delilah looked at the ground for a moment, then gave a solemn nod.

Eddie smiled at her, then pressed his thumb to the top of the cut.

Gigi smiled. She knew what Eddie's touch felt like. Delilah's eyes were about to roll into the back of her head. Except they didn't. She started crying again.

"It's not working," Eddie said, frowning. He lifted his thumb and attempted again from the bottom of the cut. "What the hell?"

"It won't work," Delilah sighed.

"What's wrong?" Abby asked.

Ben growled. "She's an Adapted too."

Gigi had to contain her laugh. Hilarious! TMZ would pay through the teeth to have that revelation on video. All of the protests, riots, social media confrontation. It was all a ruse.

"What's your R-Skill?" Ben asked. His fists were clenched, knuckles so white his bones looked ready to burst through his skin.

Delilah's bodyguards all took a healthy step back from her.

"I," she sniffed. "I resist what other Adapted can do to me. That's why he can't fix my cut."

Her loss, Gigi thought as Eddie stepped away.

Ben looked at Steve, who was nodding with half a smirk on his face.

"Jeb was too, wasn't he?" Ben asked.

Delilah paused, then nodded. "He could breathe underwater."

The bodyguard with the cloth tossed it on the ground at her feet. "C'mon guys, she's finished." The burly contingent abandoned her without another word spoken.

Delilah picked up the cloth and pressed it to her cheek. The look on her face as she shook her head indicated she understood her entire world had just been upended. "That's just great," she said, watching the bodyguards walk away. "We had a great thing going, Jeb and me. Then you lot show up and it all goes to shit."

Another text came in from LeAnne. Gigi stopped recording to read it. "Gigi, can you put me in touch with Abby Alstrom? I just went over the footage of her on the bridge with that suicidal guy and I think she'd be great for the show on A-Space too. Do you have any clips of her using her ability?"

Like a broken dam, the swell of excitement that had been welling up inside her all morning emptied. Did LeAnne actually want to represent Gigi, or was she merely an access point to get to Abby? Gigi gnawed at the inside of her cheek to keep herself from screaming.

"Let's go," Ben said, turning to the team. "Take care Mrs. Dewberry. I imagine the brass at RADSA will have some more questions for you." He started walking towards the street entrance.

"Get that cut patched up quickly, *chica*," Eddie said. "You don't want it to get infected. That'll just make the scar worse."

Delilah scoffed. "At least I won't look as bad as him." She nodded towards Ben.

Ben spun around. "What?"

Delilah screeched at Ben through snot and tears. "Your face is hideous!"

CHAPTER 42
THE SLEUTH

AND THEN STEVE'S mind broke. An overwhelming surge of shattering pain split his brain. He screamed and toppled to the sidewalk.

"Steve!" Abby rushed to his side.

At least he thought it was Abby. He hoped it was her and figured it would be, but all he heard was his name. No intonation. No inflection. Whoever it was had their hands on his back, he could barely register the sensation. Hands to his temples, he pressed his head together. It felt like the two sides of his brain were pulling themselves apart. At the center, a cataclysm of nervous electricity firing between warring halves of gray matter.

He had just heard a truth. And yet, it was something he knew was false. Ben's face was hideous. His R-Skill knew it. He knew it. Yet, he also knew Ben's face was handsome, chiseled, and rugged. Flawless.

"What's happening?" a soft voice asked.

He looked up through watery eyes at the huddle of faces peering down at him. Gigi's: shocked. Bailey's: worried. Nona's: scared. Abby's: beautiful.

Then there was Ben. He didn't want to look. His colleague. His friend. One of the most dedicated, reliable, honest, and — he wasn't ashamed to admit — handsome men he knew. That man's face was a lie. It had to be.

Steve braved a glance to his left where he knew Ben had to be standing. His mind seared in abhorrent dissonance. Again, the right half of his brain attempted to secede from the union with his left in violent cognitive disagreement.

He screamed. The desperate roar of his voice did nothing to quell the thousand thousand dissonant violins screeching in his head.

Another hand went to his back. Then another.

"We have to help him. Get him to a hospital or something!" Someone spoke. He couldn't tell who.

Then another voice came.

"Steve. Forget what Delilah said. You'll be okay."

The violent tumult in his head began to fade.

"Maybe the Number Four is out here somewhere messing with your head."

Pain.

"This morning has been exhausting. Get some rest, then you'll forget everything that happened here. You'll be okay."

Steve was tired. So tired. He managed to stand, pulling his body through the fog of crushing fatigue. He wiped his face with sweaty palms. "I'm—" he stammered. "I think I'll be okay. It's over. I'm—"

"What happened Steve? Is the other Number Four out here?" a voice to his right asked. He looked at Abby. Her hat was off and her face was twisted with worry.

"No," Steve answered. That had to be true, because he answered Abby's question. But new turbulence began to stir in his mind. A distant rumbling of the calamitous thunderstorm his brain just endured. He wouldn't go there again. Never again. He had had enough pain.

"I— I need to lie down. I'm tired," he muttered.

"Let's get him back to Bessie," Bailey urged.

"Or a hospital!" Abby said. "He just had a stroke or something." Her insistence that he get care was unnecessary, but heartwarming. He would be okay. He knew it.

CHAPTER 43
THE ADJUSTER

WHAT HAVE I DONE? Ben thought.

The group made it back to Bessie and the truck began rolling to Warehouse 11. Ben struggled to maintain his composure as he gave everyone meaningless tasks to keep them busy while he parked Nona in the interview room and used his ability to prevent her from using hers. Desperate for isolation, he slammed his office door shut and flung himself into the nearest chair, banging into the wall and knocking his mirror to the floor. Splinters of shiny silvered glass went flying. "Fucking damn it!" He kicked the mirror frame, dislodging the rest of the fragments all over the small room.

How could he have been so stupid? Of course the secret of his face would come out. It was only a matter of time. And how could he have been so unlucky? To come across the one thing that would expose him that he couldn't fix. An Adapted-proof Adapted. Anyone else— hell, *everyone* else, he could adjust their reactions to seeing his face, a picture of it, or someone's else's description of it. Had he thought of it, he could have prevented Steve from discerning the truth about it by altering his perception of comments like Delilah's.

"Maybe I deserve this," he chortled, face in his hands. He could feel the texture of the scarring, the lifelong wound he would never escape. The pits and crags of his flesh felt deeper than ever.

He had just sent Jeb to his death. Ben didn't pull the trigger, but he essentially signed the execution order. *Why were there so many damn guns at that rally?* he thought. And he'd probably get lauded for what happened. Any second now, he expected to get a call from Director Gustafson for not only bringing in Nona peacefully, but being on hand for the utter decapitation of the FIGHT organization. *If only she knew,* he thought. Someone else may try to take up the mantle, but he figured it would wither and die sooner or later. But there would always be another one.

The death of Jeb Dewberry would hang on his heart for a while, but he'd get over that. The man was a complete tool. It was what Ben was having to do to his team to keep his secret safe that ate away at his soul. He never wanted to be so dishonest with them. His team. His friends.

A watery eye looked up at him from one of the shards of mirror on the floor. He picked up the largest piece and stared at himself. "You should be on that plane to the island, right next to Nona." He tossed the shard to the floor and shook his head. "Fuck."

CHAPTER 44
THE SLEUTH

"TELL ME WHAT YOU REMEMBER," the man across the black Formica table asked.

Steve finally felt himself after a night of dreamless, void-black sleep. Aside from the hole in his memory that covered most of the prior twenty-four hours, he felt fine. The others had told him what happened yesterday. No one lied. Gigi even showed Steve a brief video of him screaming at the top of his lungs. He hadn't known he could scream so loudly. The only weird thing was that no one could recall what Delilah had said to trigger his outburst.

Jeb Dewberry was dead. Steve had actually read that on the Internet before the team had given him their own versions of what happened. He couldn't believe it. Steve had offered Abby a ride to work, but she inexplicably declined for the first time since he'd known her. He had wanted to get the straight truth from her during the commute, but she insisted on giving her recap with the rest of the team. Uncharacteristically sheepish of her.

Nona Kagai was on her way to Island-A, if she wasn't there already. When a "lister" is marked for transport to the Island, RADSA doesn't wait around. A military transport is arranged and on site within hours, and the subject is given little time to wrap up personal matters before being disengaged from society. For the rest of their lives, as far as anyone knew. Maybe they'd find a solution to reverse the unfortunate R-Skills. He himself had dreamed of such a thing on more than one occasion. Some people could be rapid-fire liars.

He slumped in his chair and thought of Nona, alone with her thoughts as she was torn from her life. A wave of remorse made him shudder. By all accounts, she was a nice girl who had just gotten mad after an unexpected breakup. How many other scorned lovers in the history of romance had gone out of their way to embarrass the object of their affection after said affection was officially refused? Embarrassing someone was not looked kindly upon, but generally not against the law either. Unless it was done with an R-Skill. Slim difference.

"Agent Palmer?" the man asked. "Steve?"

"Sorry," Steve said, pulling himself back to the table. "Just collecting my thoughts."

Ben and Abby had gone to interview Delilah again. And it seemed another Number Four Adapted was out there as well. Gigi was scouring news and social feeds for any clues. What were the odds?

And why would Delilah and Jeb work so hard to sow the seeds of discontent against the Adapted if they themselves were in the club? He supposed they thought a staunch anti-Adapted platform like FIGHT was the best way to prevent a trip to Island-A for themselves, not that either of them would have been candidates. Some people just don't trust the government.

"Take your time," the man said.

Steve looked into the man's eyes. Agent Carleton Orton. The very man he dreaded meeting yesterday. Orton, and by way of him, Director Gustafson, RADSA, and Ben were all worried something was amiss with Steve's R-Skill. Yesterday's adventure in the park was incontrovertible proof of such. But it was Steve's questioning of the president's press conferences that had brought Orton here. Something about that seemed off.

Steve frowned and rubbed his forehead, searching for a memory of the pain his teammates had told him he was in. It still felt like he was only recently recovered from a righteous headache. "I don't remember much," Steve said. "Just running into the park with Abby and Bailey. After that, it's a foggy haze until this morning. Then back to normal."

"Well, I guess it could be worse. From what Agent Rice told me, you were in considerable pain there for a few minutes. Maybe it's a good thing that you don't remember."

"Maybe."

Orton was ex-military, like Steve. He could tell. Not a Marine though. The man across the table looked like a linebacker for the Dallas Cowboys, and emanated the smug, misplaced superiority of Army. Ranger maybe. Not a regular grunt. Like Steve, Orton wore a suit. But his was black, top to bottom, including his shirt. And a bit baggy, to provide room for the man's overly muscular frame to move around. A short flat top of blonde hair crowned his sun-drenched face. The two white circles of pale skin around his eyes indicated he spent a lot of time in the sun with sunglasses. Or in a tanning bed. Olsen had three wicked spiderweb-shaped scars, two on his forehead, and one on his right cheek. Possibly from shrapnel. However he got them, the scars told the story of someone with combat experience.

And this man was now a psychologist for RADSA? He looked more like the type to fall into private security service after being discharged.

"Where did you serve?" Steve asked, hoping to turn the conversation away from himself. He pointed to the scars on Orton's face. "Combat?"

Orton gazed at Steve. Aside from a lone raised eyebrow, the man's face bore no expression. "Uh, we're here to talk about you, Agent Palmer." The man shifted uncomfortably in his chair, then fidgeted with his tie the way someone does when they haven't worn one in years. "We can get into my history another time." Orton moved in his seat again, searching for the mythical comfort zone of the completely uncomfortable plastic teal chairs. "How about some coffee? I saw a Keurig out there. I know I could use a cup."

The thought of anything in his stomach made Steve want to retch. "I'll just have a water. There's some in the fridge by the coffee."

Orton frowned. "Are you sure? Some caffeine might help get the old brain juices flowing. Increased blood-flow. Dilated capillaries. Eh?"

Steve considered for a moment, then acquiesced. Orton turned and left the room. It was odd being on this side of the table. He hadn't ever sat there before. Steve was the second person to join the North Texas team after Bailey, and Bessie wouldn't come along for another few weeks. He had spent hours in the chair across the table though, interviewing Adapted, making notes on all aspects of their lives, detailing R-Skills like regenerating fingers (who would want to test that one?) and accurately gauging the actual expiration date of food (the printed date on the packaging was almost always complete bullshit).

He rubbed his face in his palms, hoping some recollection of what happened yesterday would come back to him. He could feel it in there, somewhere. It wasn't gone. Just… masked. Something else amiss with his brain. Unearthing the president's press conference untruths regarding the

Dark Object was bad enough. But now he had evidently witnessed a murder, helped send a number four packing, and doubled over in excruciating pain. He couldn't remember any of it. Steve was to the point where he actually hoped Orton could find something wrong with him so they could have something to try to fix.

The burly RADSA agent elbowed himself back into the interview room with a cup of coffee in each hand.

"You take cream in yours?" Orton asked.

Steve shook his head.

Orton placed a compostable paper cup of black coffee in front of Steve and sat back down with the other cup, a creamy tan.

Steve put the cup to his nose and inhaled the steamy clouds of nutty bold aroma wafting off the surface. Smelled like one of the darker roasts. He wasn't a fan.

Orton reached for his cup and downed a hearty gulp, then sighed.

A slight tinge of pain in Steve's head reminded him he'd gone over twenty-four hours without caffeine. His body craved it. Depended on it. The little demon in his head reached out to the cup with invisible hands, urging him to feed the need once again. Steve gave in. He took a sip. Then another. Then one more.

Orton massaged his fingertips against each other before clapping his hands. "Alright," he said, looking at his watch. "Where were we?"

———

"So," Orton continued, checking the time on his watch. "Let's move to some baseline statements to gauge your reaction. As I understand it, falsehoods cause you pain?" he asked.

Steve nodded. He stared at the door behind Orton, wishing it was the hatch of a cargo plane. He'd happily jump without a parachute right now.

"Do you think you could rate the sensation? Like on a scale of one to ten?"

"Sure."

"Good. Let's try this. The Texas Rangers are the best team in baseball."

Steve shrugged. "Zero. My R-Skill doesn't react to opinions."

"Okay. Three plus four is eight."

Steve winced. "Five."

"Dallas is smaller than Fort Worth."

Again, pain. "Five." Steve rubbed his forehead.

Orton took a slug of coffee from his cup, licking a droplet off his lips as he lowered the cup.

"Phelps will win the next election."

Steve shook his head. "I can't tell the future. But I imagine that he will." He held back his frown, but his stern eyebrows had minds of their own.

"Not a fan?" Orton asked.

"He's alright I guess."

Orton chuckled and checked the time again.

"Have somewhere else to be? I'm happy to end this." Steve said.

"I do, but we need to get to the bottom of things. Determine if your R-Skill can be trusted right now or if there's something truly amiss. Let's try some more. Red and green make blue."

Steve sighed, bracing for another sharp stab of pain behind his eyes. But when it came, the sensation was just pressure, like someone pushing his head around with a single finger. Not pleasant, but not bad. It hurt, but not like it should.

"Two."

Orton nodded and scratched something unintelligible on a small composition notebook. "Hmm. Okay. The Texas State Fair is in December."

Nothing. The fair took place every year in September and October. It should have felt the same as saying three plus four equals eight. A cold shiver ran down his spine. Up until that second, his faith and under-standing in his R-Skill had never wavered.

"Zero."

"Well," Orton said, sipping his coffee and scribbling in his notes. "That would seem to indicate something's amiss, wouldn't it? Isn't the fair in October?"

"It is."

Orton downed the rest of his coffee and turned a page back in his notes.

Steve looked at his own cup. Maybe he needed to wake up more. Maybe the shock from yesterday still had his wires crossed. He took another sip. The dark roast danced across his tongue. His taste buds cried out in bitter protest.

The man across the table ran his thumbs across his fingertips again, looking at each with amusement. Then he smiled and sighed. "Okay, let's see. I am an alien."

Steve laughed. There was a little pain, but not much. Not as much as there should have been. "One."

Orton smiled. "So, I'm human."

Steve nodded, though he felt a little pain again. The pain? He straightened up in his chair. He never had experienced a false positive before. His R-Skill was officially haywire. He downed his coffee. Hopefully the caffeine would do him good. "I need some more coffee," he said. "You?"

"Thanks, I'm good."

Steve rose and left the room. Outside in the Bay, Gigi was at her station. Brix and Zeke were sitting in the lounge, working on laptops. Abby was out buying a car, of all things. She wouldn't be asking him for rides anymore. He already missed the anticipatory tingle of seeing her bound down the steps from her apartment. The moment she got into his car in the mornings was the best part of his day.

He blinked and shook his head out of daydreaming about Abby. More caffeine. He set his cup under the Keurig and found a doughnut shop variety he liked. He leaned back against the wall and waited while the machine prepared its liquid bounty.

"Since when do you take cream and sugar in your coffee?" Gigi asked. She raised a dubious eyebrow at him from her station. "Back when we, uh dated — if that's what you want to call that one evening, you said you liked it black."

"Still do," Steve said, folding his arms as a fresh, nutty aroma from his cup permeated the air. He tapped his fingers on his biceps, as if the gesture alone would urge the Keurig into a gallop. Gigi was alright in small doses, but in his fog, he wasn't prepared to handle her today. Then, a thought occurred to him. "Why do you ask?"

She shrugged, then turned back to her monitors. "I saw that Orton guy put some in both cups he took in a few minutes ago."

Steve clenched his teeth. He no longer needed caffeine to wake up. His blood boiled. In an attempt to maintain composure, he tried something he thought he'd never be able to do again. He lied. "Oh. He drank both of those himself."

The first reaction to those words he had was of utter joy. The ability to tell even the slightest fib had been lost the moment he became an Adapted nearly a year ago. He had lost his previous job after being unable to lie his way out of being late. Instead of a flat tire, or feeling sick, or an obscure religious holiday, he had simply overslept after accidentally turning off his alarm. He was incapable of saying anything else. That boss was a jerk anyway. Ben wasn't. Actually, Steve didn't know what Ben was.

Now he was truly in the dark. Orton had drugged him. The man sent here by RADSA — by the director herself — had drugged him, in order to impede his R-Skill. The implications were wild. All after he simply discussed the president's press conferences with Ben. Ben! Was he part of this? It hardly seemed possible, but he couldn't know for sure with his R-Skill unavailable for who knows how long. Why had Orton brought in only one cup with creamer? The Keurig beeped. Steve dutifully retrieved his cup and looked at it. Orton had dosed himself with the same stuff. It was in both cups. Steve felt like there was a joke about Sicilians and land wars in Asia to be made, but he was in no laughing mood. Would the stuff coursing through his veins, impeding his R-Skill, do anything to an ordinary human? Or…

Steve's eyes grew wide. *Orton's an Adapted too,* he thought. He had checked his watch multiple times, a little too interested in his fingertips. The implications had gone from wild to scary. He looked at the interview room door, imagining the shadowy silhouette of Orton crouched with a pistol and silencer. A panther waiting to pounce with a double-tap to the head as soon as Steve walked back into the room.

Straight up murder didn't seem too likely, given the lengths to which Orton had already gone. Something else was afoot. And at least, if Orton was indeed Adapted, and indeed had just given himself the same treatment he had given Steve, then the blocking effect on the R-Skill wasn't permanent. Which was a relief, despite the ominous cloud of conspiracy darkening the already dark interior of the Bay. Despite the rush he got from being able to lie again, he didn't feel himself. His faith in always knowing the truth was a part of him now. It was the pillar of his moral high ground. And he was desperate to understand what was going on. Some truths had been revealed, not the least of which was that he wasn't safe. He needed to get out. But first, he needed answers. He sucked in a huge breath, fixed a goofy smile to his face, then strolled back into the interview room, coffee in hand, to eke the truth out of Orton.

CHAPTER 45
THE ADJUSTER

"YEAH, YEAH, I'D LIKE THAT," Ben said to his phone. "No cameras, though. We try to keep a modest profile."

"Sure, "the feminine voice on the other end said. "It'll just be the two of us."

"Great. See you this evening."

Ben set his phone down and smiled. Camila Rios, the cute reporter from yesterday had just asked him to drinks and an interview. He needed an outlet. Some human interaction that wasn't all about work. Sure, she'd want to ask him all about the riot and Jeb Dewberry, but he thought he'd be able to steer the conversation away easily enough and keep it focused on RADSA's mission. And if not with his wit and charm, then he could always convince her the other way. *Stop that*, he thought. *You're going down a dark path.*

He cut his self-admonishment short, and daydreamed about what she'd be wearing. She was cute in that yellow number. *Man, I need to get laid*, he thought. He was stressed, and sex was his favorite form of stress-relief. The ill-advised tryst with Gigi had broken free the dam of carnal urges he had held at bay since leaving Rachel. Months and months of self-imposed isolation, full of self-pity and a determination to not use his R-Skill under any circumstances. That steely determination turned out to be wet noodle-strength. Ben was weak.

He thought back to that unexpected morning with the gymnast. For a short moment, he had regretted altering her mind so that she wouldn't pursue him again. It would have been just as easy to install the instruction in her brain to simply never tell anyone. He could have controlled the time and place. He could have had that outlet. It — *she* was there for the taking. She was down the hall right now. For another short moment, he considered asking her into his office and undoing the mental obstruction he placed in her to halt any future advances. *It would be so easy. I could adjust anyone that gets curious,* he thought.

He looked up from his desk to the empty white space on the wall where his mirror should have been. Despite the void, he could see his critical eye, wreathed by grotesque, purple scar tissue. It stared back at him, pierced deep into his soul, and saw it darker. Blacker. He wasn't keeping the promise to himself. An affair with a subordinate. The incident with Jeb Dewberry. He had even brainwashed Brix into joining the team, something he had said he would never, ever, do. *Fuck,* he thought. *What the fuck are you doing, Ben?* He didn't know the person sitting in the chair behind his desk, but he didn't like him very much.

His door rapped loudly with an absurdly long seven knocks. The jarring noise shook Ben from his self-reflection and stirred motes of adrenaline in his blood. "Yes," he said, standing.

The door swung open, and the bulky form of Agent Orton rumbled in, followed by Steve, who had an atypical smile on his face. They sat.

"So, I think there is definitely something going on in there with Steve," Orton said, tapping at his forehead with a meaty, hairy index finger. "Science regarding R-Skills, as you know, is still a work in progress. We don't even have a solid handle on whether ordinary pathogens affect Adapted in the same ways they do humans. He may simply have a virus, or some kind of bacterial infection."

Ben looked at Steve, who simply smiled and shrugged.

"Or," Orton said. "This could be a natural evolution of his R-Skill. Maybe they go away after a time. Maybe the UDO radiation is clearing his system. He could have eaten a Whataburger and strained too hard on the toilet afterwards. There's so much we don't know. So many variables."

"What should we do?" Ben asked.

Orton held his fingertips together. "Well, for me, I'd say his R-Skill is not to be relied upon in the short term. There may be periods where it seems back to normal, and others where it's batshit crazy. Who knows?"

Steve raised his eyebrows and pursed his lips, though he still seemed to be smiling.

"I think we should have him up to DC to see our docs. Run some tests."

The idea of the team being apart had not ever entered Ben's mind. "Maybe he should just wait it out a bit? Get some rest? No need to burden the taxpayers."

Orton folded his arms. Bulging biceps strained against the sleeves of his navy blue jacket. "Well, I think you're all going. Heard through the grapevine you're gonna be honored by Frannie for how you handled the protest yesterday."

Honored? What? Ben thought. A lump of guilt throbbed at the back of his throat. "First I've heard of it," he choked out.

Then his phone rang. He knew who it was without looking at the screen. "Director Gustafson," Ben said as he put it to his ear. "Sure," he said after a moment.

He turned on the speaker. "I have Agent Palmer and Agent Orton here in the office with me."

"Good. I just wanted to have some other ears on the line when I said congratulations. The president is very pleased with the way you handled the situation with the protest. Your involvement helped expose the Dewberrys as frauds and FIGHT has been disgraced. And you peacefully relocated a Number Four. No small feat, that."

The lump of guilt in his throat swelled until Ben couldn't breathe. What had he done? He got Jeb killed, that's what. And nearly broke Steve's mind with careless and incomplete modifications to his perception. It was Abby that had kept things from escalating with Nona, not him. "Thank you, Director," Ben said, struggling to cough out the words. "It was a team effort."

"That it was, but it's *your* team. You should be proud," the voice on the other end of the phone said.

Ben raised his eyebrows and looked at Steve to elicit a reaction from him. The smile was gone. And instead of the stoic calm he usually carried on his face, he had a furious scowl.

What's that about? Ben thought.

"I'd like to invite you and the whole team to DC. Show your faces. Shake some hands. Do an interview or two. Maybe even meet the president."

Ben shuddered. "Wow, that's… We'd be honored." His blood ran cold. Ben sat stunned with the realization that in the very near future, he'd have to use his R-Skill on the president of the United States himself to continue to maintain the image he was protecting. The lie. He had put it to far more use than he had ever intended and was about to cross a serious line. Could he get out of it? How would Frannie react if he declined the invitation? Would it impact his career? His team's? Did he even have a career here? His very presence in this chair — on the org chart — was a lie. The walls of his small office pressed in on him.

"Great. So, Carl. How's our friend Mr. Palmer faring? The president was especially keen to meet you, Steve," Director Gustafson said over the speaker.

Steve wiped the frown off his face, but his cheeks were flushed when Orton looked at him.

"Well," Orton began. "Physically, he appears fine. No worse for wear after yesterday's incident. But there is an issue with his R-Skill we're going to have to study further. I think this trip to DC is a great opportunity to have him visit our science labs and see what they can determine. Ideally, it will resolve itself on its own, but you never know with R-Skills."

Ben stole another glance at Steve. The scowl had returned to his lips.

"Good. All the same, I'd like for you to follow Ben's team around and observe. Don't forget your other errand as well," Frannie said.

"Sure thing," Orton said.

"Let's plan on your team coming up in a week or two, Ben. I'll have my assistant get with you on the timing and we'll see if we can get on the president's schedule," Frannie said.

"Sounds good. Thank you, Director." Ben hung up the phone and wanted to chuck it through the wall. How was he going to fix this?

The crackle of Bailey's rugged voice came over the intercom. "We have arrived at Agent Orton's hotel."

Ben pressed the intercom button. "Thanks Bailey."

"Well, that's my cue," Orton said, standing. "I'll get my other errand taken care of this evening and see you all tomorrow. Let me know where you're meeting and I'll tag along."

Ben rose and shook Orton's hand. "Sure."

"Congrats again," Orton said, smiling.

Ben forced a smile and nodded.

Steve stayed in his chair. Orton patted him on the shoulder as he left the room.

"So, what do you think?" Ben asked after the door was shut.

Steve looked at the door with the corner of his eye, then slowly brought his gaze to meet Ben's. Those dark eyes, eyes Ben had come to respect and trust, now told a story of betrayal. A pain that went far deeper than that his R-Skill inflicted upon him. Seconds passed, and Steve said nothing. He just sat there. Analyzing, like he was wont to do. Staring. Peeling off the manifold untruths Ben had layered on his mind.

He knows, Ben thought.

Steve cleared his throat. "I think he drugged me."

Ben spat the coffee in his mouth back into his cup, narrowly avoiding a Simpsons-worthy splatter all over his desk. He couldn't swallow anything. "What?"

"My ability. It's completely haywire now."

"But he said there was an issue."

"Yeah. I can lie now."

Ben straightened in his chair. "Why would that indicate anything? That limitation is part of your R-Skill as much as your ability to know the truth."

"I couldn't until he slipped something into my coffee a little bit ago."

"He what? Steve, this is approaching paranoia. First the stuff with the president, and now this?"

Steve glowered at Ben. "Tell me a lie."

"I don't—"

"Lie to me." Steve folded his arms.

Ben hesitated. *Something small*, he thought. "I didn't work out this morning." He worked out every morning, without fail.

"Something I don't already know isn't true."

"Oh. Okay." Ben paused. "My favorite sport to watch is football."

Steve shrugged. "What is it really?"

"Hockey. What does that prove?

"My favorite sport is hockey."

"So…"

"My favorite sport is curling."

Ben tilted his head.

"My favorite sport is competitive pie eating." Steve's face was belligerent.

"What does this prove?" Ben wasn't hearing anything that supported this crazy theory. How could RADSA be behind this?

"Gigi said she saw him put creamer in two coffee cups. Only one had creamer in it. He asked which one I wanted, then drank the other. They were both drugged."

"I can't imagine that is what actually happened. He's here to help you."

"At the behest of an organization that's the passion project for someone who has been publicly lying about the UDOs, amidst a myriad of other things."

The breakfast in Ben's stomach churned. He trusted Steve. It hurt to see him so off the rails like this. Ben's joints ached, urging him to pop one and just fix the problem. One little adjustment and Steve wouldn't worry about any of this silly conspiracy stuff anymore. He summoned restraint, and stood to start a fresh cup of coffee from the machine behind his desk.

"The thing that's most upsetting about all of this, all of these lies," Steve said with a fresh coolness to his voice. "Is that you're an Adapted too."

CHAPTER 46

THE SLEUTH

THAT'LL WAKE HIM UP, Steve thought.

It was the truth. He didn't need his R-Skill to know that.

Ben turned to face him. The blood had drained from his cheeks, and his mouth was agape.

After a second of stunned surprise, Ben tried to shrug off the comment. "You know I'm not."

"Yes, you are. Has to do with your face. I don't remember much about yesterday. This morning, after I talked to the others, I pieced it together. But only after Orton drugged me and… unhooked my R-Skill. I think I had some latent fear of triggering another reaction like I had yesterday."

Ben folded his arms in a disapproving stance, but was staring off into the empty space on the wall above Steve's head where he thought a mirror had been.

"It's interesting you've not told me your perspective on what happened. From what the others have said, Delilah yelled something at you, something about your face, and that's what caused my breakdown. Also strange that nobody can quite remember what she said."

The coffeemaker dinged, which seemed to snap Ben back into the conversation. He held out his hands in supplication.

"Okay. *Okay*. You're right. I am an Adapted, like everyone else here."

"You're the other Number Four, aren't you?"

Ben rushed into his chair and talked in a hushed tone. "No! No. I…

have a scar. On my face." He gestured over the left side of his face. "My R-Skill lets me alter the perception of others about me. That's it."

Right about now, Steve was desperate to have his R-Skill back. He got absolutely no impression of whether Ben was telling the truth or not. That he had been lying all this time about it and had gotten around Steve's R-Skill sniffing it out was concerning.

"Show me," Steve said.

Ben slumped his head down. He craned his neck until a couple of joints audibly popped, then looked at Steve.

"Oh. Shit."

"Yeah," Ben said.

One side of his boss' face was clean shaven and perfect. The other side was a Lovecraftian maze of tan and purple scar tissue. A stark dichotomy between cover model and alien experimentation.

Ben slumped his head again.

"How?" Steve asked.

"My ex-fiancée." Ben's eyes were wet with approaching tears. He closed them. "She tossed a pot of boiling water at me when I told her I had become an Adapted."

"Wow. That's... I'm sorry."

"Yeah."

"Why not just tell us? I don't think anyone would care."

"I..." Ben stammered. "I don't want it to come out. Vanity, I guess."

"You have to tell the others."

"I can't." Ben wouldn't look up at him.

Steve stood up. "Then I don't want to work here anymore." He left the room and slammed the door before Ben could respond.

CHAPTER 47

THE ADJUSTER

THE DOOR CLATTERED SHUT with a loud amalgam of rattled aluminum, fiberboard, and black polycarbonate paneling. To Ben, it was the resounding fracture of a thousand panes of glass. His carefully woven stained-glass mosaic of deception now a million colorful shards skittering to the floor.

He could have fixed it. He could *still* fix it. There was no statute of limitations on his ability to correct past mistakes. But he didn't want to be that guy. Be the manipulative Number Four that validated his R-Skill's place on the Dangers to Society list. At this rate, he'd wake up one morning and just decide to punch his own ticket to Island-A and be done with it. Drink mai tais and avoid the Adapted that got sent there last month with a mouth full of piranha teeth and the ravenous appetite to match. But what to do now?

He rubbed his face and felt the scar. A pool of writhing eels under his touch. Ben sighed. "Time to come clean." *At least a little,* he thought.

He punched the intercom for Bailey. "Jo, could you join us in the Bay? I have an... announcement."

"Ooh, mysterious. I'll be right there," she squawked over the speaker.

Ben downed the rest of his coffee and headed for the Bay.

"Hey everyone," Ben called as he emerged from the hall past the bunkroom door. "Come join me in the lounge for a minute. I… need to tell you something."

Abby, Brix, and Zeke were already sitting on the black leather sofas with their laptops. Abby wore her usual ensemble, featuring a badly faded black Alice in Chains t-shirt and white jeans. Brix and Zeke sported new jumpsuits courtesy of Eddie's craftsmanship. Brix's uniform featured cascades of leaves on his arms and legs that faded from green to gray. Zeke's jumpsuit had radiating concentric white circles sewn into the sleeves. He did not look thrilled with it. Gigi, in her spectacularly form-fitting jumpsuit, immediately sprang up from her station and padded over, followed by Eddie, who wore his own jumpsuit with twin trails of crimson piping up the sides.

"I dig the new threads, guys," Ben said, acknowledging each of the uniforms with a point. "They're great, Eddie. When will I get mine?" He smiled, knowing no superficial expressions could mask the trepidation that crawled under his skin. His dread over what he was about to say. To reveal. To undo.

"Sorry boss, Adapted only!" Eddie said with a grin.

The rear door opened and Bailey bounded inside. Ben looked across the bay and caught Steve's eye. He was standing at his locker.

"Yeah, about that..." Ben said. His heart flew like a midnight street racer avoiding the cops.

Eddie threw his hands up. "Okay, okay. You can have one too."

"No, that's not it..." Ben looked around the room. At the team. *His* team. At all the damage he had done. He wiped the sweat from his palms on his pants, and decided to start with the good news.

"First, let me say that Director Gustafson has invited us all to Washington to be recognized for how the protest was handled. The president is pleased, as am I. So... well done, all."

The lounge was a sea of half-smiles and raised eyebrows. They knew it. This was akin to being praised in class for getting a C+.

Ben sighed. "We'll do that in a week. Now—"

He stopped to suck in air and hopefully some courage. "Now, I will give you an apology. I have kept something from you, and I am greatly embarrassed and ashamed for it. I know each of you, and should have been a better manager — friend even."

The smiles in the room were gone. All eyes wide. Eyebrows on alert. Steve took up a spot closer to the lounge and leaned against the wall, arms folded across his chest and a furious scowl painted on his face.

Ben sighed. He could do this. He closed his eyes and opened his mouth, but couldn't find the words.

"Ben. What is it?" Abby asked after a too-long silent moment. "We'll understand."

She *would* understand, wouldn't she? Abby's boundless compassion was her true gift.

Out with it, Ben thought. He blurted. "I am an Adapted, too."

The air in the room was so heavy it could have been measured on a scale. Ben could almost chew it. The thunder from Bessie's diesel engine rumbled like an approaching squall line.

"What?" Gigi squawked through a crack in her voice. Her eyes screamed betrayal.

Ben sighed again, glancing around the room with heartfelt supplication in his eyes.

"I have an R-Skill. I've kept it from you. I've… used it on you. All of you."

Abby's pale skin had turned bone white to match her pants. Gigi now looked more confused than upset. Brix scratched his head. Zeke measured the others' faces as if needing input on how he should respond. Eddie and Bailey exchanged headshakes. Steve continued his death stare.

"What did you… can you do?" Abby asked.

Another sigh slipped from Ben's lips. "I have a scar. On my face. My ability allows me to change how you perceive the way I look. I've used it to hide my scar from you."

Abby covered her mouth.

"All this over a scar?" Gigi scoffed. "How bad is it?"

"It's…" Ben grasped for more air. "Unpleasant. To the point where I believe it would affect my ability to lead this team or your interest in staying on it."

The team exchanged silent glances. Ben couldn't tell how this news was received.

"I want—" Abby stuttered. "I want to see it."

Ben hadn't planned on that. He hadn't thought this through. What would come of peeling off one layer of deception while staunchly holding fast to the deeper, darker secret?

"C'mon, Ben," Bailey said. "It's us. Your team. Like you said, your friends."

"It's not pretty," Ben said.

"Out with it, already," Eddie prodded.

Ben sighed. He closed his eyes and rolled his neck around, popping his joints. The tension was released. His power surged, flying through his veins at the pace of his racing blood. Each mind in the room was there to be changed. To be controlled. He could undo all of this… damage in a split second. They would never know.

He wiped away tears. But somehow found the fortitude to push away the temptation to repair all of this. To hide again. To cheat. He stretched his mind and removed the mental mask he had stretched over the others' perception of him. Of his face. His shame.

The other mask would remain.

Ben opened his eyes to see six stunned faces. Steve's scowl had been reigned into a simply disappointed frown.

"It's…" Zeke said. His omnipresent smile had vanished.

Abby's hand covered her gaping mouth. "You… you're…"

Even you can't sugarcoat this, Ben thought.

"Hideous," Gigi said, popping the tension-filled hot air balloon in the room with all the subtlety of a bazooka.

"I know," Ben said. His chin slumped to his chest. How would he be able to lead the team after this? How could he even look any of them straight in the eye anymore?

"Wait," Brix said. "You can alter your appearance — like shapeshift? Could you change into Batman? Or—"

"Go invisible?" Zeke added, with some surprising enthusiasm.

"Those would be Number Seven on the D2S list," Bailey said. Her frown approached Steve's in severity.

Ben shook his head. Fresh lies were waiting to be woven. At least Steve's R-Skill was off the table. For now. "I can't go invisible. Or shapeshift. It's… subtle. I can just change how you perceive my body. My own skin. If a camera recorded me, it would capture my scar in all its purple majesty." He left out the part where they still wouldn't see his scar on a screen if he had adjusted their perception. The less they thought his R-Skill could do, the better.

"This sounds kinda close to a Number Four thing, Ben." Eddie stroked his dyed-black goatee and narrowed his brow.

"Very close," Steve added from behind the group.

"It's not!" Ben held out his hands. "I'm sorry. I'm sorry I hid this from you. I… don't know what else to say."

The entire Bay fell quiet. Even the droning rumble of Bessie's engine had diminished to a distant hum.

Abby broke the silence. "Why?"

Ben opened his mouth to puke out another bullshit excuse.

"Why did you *lie* to us?" Abby pleaded.

"I'm..." Ben looked at the faces around the room. Faces he trusted. Faces he loved in their own valuable way. Faces he needed in his life. The truth would hurt more than the boiling water that started all of this did.

"Because I'm weak," Ben said.

"What?" Gigi asked, toying with the pull on her uniform's zipper.

"I'm weak! Vain. Prideful. I've hid from this for over a year." He pointed to his face. "From everyone. I didn't want to live a life where the first and last thing anyone thought about me was about my scar."

"This sucks," Brix said. "I don't even know why I'm here." He stood.

Ben's eyes grew wide as he realized his error. While unwinding the veil in Brix's mind regarding the scar, he had also undone the motivation laid into Brix's mind to want to be part of the team. The placid, complacent demeanor was gone. Now replaced by the same revulsion at the idea of him working for RADSA he had back at his shack last month when Ben first offered him a job.

"I'm out," Steve barked. The tendrils of ice in his voice turned everyone's head.

Ben's heart sunk to further depths. The hope he had clung to that coming clean might change Steve's mind just got kicked in the balls.

"Anyone else want to help me uncover what's really going on at RADSA?" Steve asked.

Brix laughed. "Now *that* actually sounds fun."

"Yeah, it does," Eddie added. His eyes were fixed on Ben. Each streak of blood-red vein in his eyes blazed with resolve.

Brix stood. "Fuck this shit." He tossed his laptop aside and pointed a thumb toward the rear door.

"Anyone else?" Steve called. He stared straight at Abby.

But her gaze was fixed on Ben. Full of hurt. Confusion. Sadness. She swallowed and reset her face. There it was. The compassion. A slight smile, a soft laugh. The very pillar of Abby's influence on the team was still unchanged. Despite what Ben had done. He hadn't ruined her.

"I'm staying," Abby said. She kept her eyes on Ben.

Zeke looked between Abby and Steve, then to Ben. "Me too."

Gigi shrugged and nodded. Of course she wouldn't care that much.

Bailey stomped her foot. "Someone's gotta pilot this rust-bucket. I'll stay to drive y'all around." She swung a short, but furious finger at Ben. "But I am *not* happy about this Benjamin K. Rice. We are going to have words."

Steve clicked his tongue. "I guess this is where we get off." His eyes stayed fixed on Abby for a lingering moment, then he turned and walked out the rear door.

Eddie and Brix followed.

Ben could only watch. Still, he could fix this. Set things back to the way they were. He shouldn't. He wouldn't.

The door slammed shut. A final gavel on the cosmic judge's ruling over Ben's transgressions. *Guilty.*

Head drooped low, he rubbed the good half of his face, massaging in the shame. "I'm… so sorry." He couldn't bear to look up and meet their stares. Instead, he gestured to his scar. "Can I… hide this again?" Through to his core, he hoped. Hoped to nestle back into the warm comfort of the lie.

A gentle hand grabbed his arm. Abby. She shook her head. "Ben. No."

Bailey also shook her head. But instead of Abby's gentle *You don't need to hide anymore* message, Bailey's ordered *Don't you fucking dare.*

Abby looked to the door. "I'm… going to go talk to Steve."

Ben nodded, whispering, "Thank you." That she of all the people could emerge from this intact gave him hope for the future.

Bailey stepped aside to let Abby pass. Then she glowered at Ben, pounding a fist into her palm. "Next Wednesday, I'm gonna teach you a thing or two about setting an example."

Ben stifled a laugh. He hated sparring with her. On the training mats, she was as feisty as a hungry honey badger. His height and size lent him a significant advantage over her, but she was built like a tank and got her shots in. He always wobbled away from their bouts like a newborn giraffe.

Bailey gave him an unexpected wink and half smile, then followed Abby out the back.

Ben looked at Gigi. She gawked back at him. Her face was twisted with confusion, hurt, and something else.

He stammered. "I'll be in my office."

Never had a sixteen-foot walk taken him so long. He turned the corner into his private space, and the small room seemed impossibly huge. Every shiny surface an eye. A room full of stares, waiting to pass judgement on him. He shrugged off the instinct to close the door behind him, and flopped into his chair. Now alone with his thoughts, he found that he had none. He had no plan for this. The after. Assuming Abby would be unsuccessful in changing Steve's mind, his most vital asset had just walked out on him. Because of a lack of trust. *Your harvest is here, Ben,* he thought. "Fuck."

He rubbed his face. The rough surface of the scar was now a three-dimensional topographic map of all his deception - every lie, every sin, every obfuscation he had committed against his team.

Out of habit, he looked to the wall where his mirror should have been. Gigi's head popped into view, hands grasping the door frame.

"Hey Gigi." Ben said. He could see the uncertainty in her face. "I'll understand if you want to go too." He figured they all would eventually.

She pulled herself into view, stepping a foot inside the office. "Nah."

Ben blinked. *Huh.*

"But, I want you to fix that for me." She gestured a reluctant finger toward his scar.

A chuckle trickled out of him. So, she was still Gigi. Not everything had changed. "Really?" Ben asked.

"Yeah. I don't need to see that. I don't care if you have to fiddle with my head a little."

He shrugged, popping a shoulder in the process. At least he wouldn't have to hide the fact he was hiding his face from her.

Gigi's eyes widened as she took in his restored, unscarred visage.

"That's *really* cool." She beamed.

"Thanks."

"Now," she said, kicking the door closed behind her and pressing the lock button on the handle. "Just a few minutes ago I had the sudden notion that us hooking up again wasn't such a bad idea after all. How about some more... stress relief?" She tugged the zipper down the front of her jumpsuit and pulled the entire thing off in the time Ben's stunned heart beat just once. As he drank in her exposed skin now covered only by a shiny blue bra and matching boy shorts, he realized he may have undone far more of the adjustments he'd done on the team than he thought. Would Eddie remember attempting to fix the scar? Was Steve's mind fully untethered? How much more would he have to use his R-Skill to clean up this mess? Just a few more frequent flier miles towards his own trip to Island-A.

But as Gigi sauntered around his desk, sat in his lap, and planted her lips on his, his mind dissolved into the moment. The swell of her breasts against his chest and the feel of her skin in his hands. Her tongue chasing his. The consequences could wait until tomorrow.

CHAPTER 48
THE SLEUTH

NAKED. Exposed. Unreliable. All words Steve thought applied to himself as he scanned the parking lot of the recently remodeled Hilton Anatole not far from downtown Dallas. *What the hell are you doing, Steve?* he thought.

"So, what the hell are we doing, Steve?" Brix asked.

"I want to observe Orton. I don't trust him. But, we need to find a quick way out of here if we need it."

"What's wrong with Orton?" Eddie asked.

"He drugged me. My R-Skill isn't working." Steve said.

"No shit!" Brix said.

"Damn," Eddie said, stroking his black goatee. "The sky is red."

Steve shook his head.

"Well, that's not all bad? Fewer headaches, eh?" Eddie smiled and patted Steve on his back.

"I'd rather be myself," Steve said, keeping a wary eye on the hotel entrance.

Brix and Eddie both nodded.

Steve scratched his head. "We need a ride. Orton said he had another errand to do here. I want to see what he's up to."

"I can help with that," Eddie said, pulling out his phone.

"Let's find some shade where we can watch the doors," Steve said.

An urgent voice called from the trailer. "Steve!"

Steve's heart almost lurched out of his chest. He was at once elated to hear Abby's voice, but also concerned for her safety. Who knew what

Orton was up to or willing to do? Steve was a marine. He could handle rough situations. But Abby?

He turned to the trailer in time to see Abby awkwardly leap off from the door level, à la Gigi, and only narrowly avoid planting her face on the concrete. Abby looked up at him from her crouch. She was not smiling.

Eddie whistled and exchanged a wide-eyed look with Brix.

"What are you doing?" Abby barked.

When she called his name, Steve's hopes soared that Abby had changed her mind and decided to join him. But the I'm-gonna-punch-you look on her face told a different story.

She walked up and slugged him on the arm. "What are you *doing?*" she pleaded.

"Ow!" Steve rubbed the spot she hit. "What's right, Abby. Something's going on. Orton drugged me — deactivated my R-Skill somehow. I'm not sure, but I think Ben may be involved. He's hiding things. Lying."

"Yeah. He's hiding a horrible scar. If you had that all over your cute face and could hide it, you would too."

The flirty compliment gave him pause, but Steve pressed on. "That's not it. He lied about being an Adapted."

"A reasonable precaution to hide his scar."

"But he was able to get it past me. Me! You were in the room. He lied about it, and I didn't catch it."

Abby frowned.

"Something else is going on. Ben lying." Steve looked over at the hotel entrance. "Orton drugging me. Either he's a lone actor, or RADSA is involved too. I can't work for them with all the deception." He grasped her arm. "Come with us."

He desperately wanted her to join him. Until she had stepped outside with that pissed off, yet still beautiful compassion on her face, he hadn't realized his hesitation was gone. Whatever had compelled him to call things off with her had vacated his mind. He'd have to have words with Ben about that the next time they crossed paths. But for now, his mind was only on Abby.

"Please, Abby. Help me figure this out."

"There are others that need our help. Ben needs our help too. I'm staying. Can't you work out whatever this is with him?"

Steve cast a furtive glance at the trailer door. "No."

Abby frowned as she took her hat off and ruffled her hair. "Okay then. Be safe out there, Mr. Sleuth." Her pale blue eyes pleaded with him for a silent eternity before she turned and clambered back into Bessie's trailer. The door slammed shut.

"Well, that was dramatic," Brix said. "I thought you two were going to angry kiss there for a minute."

Eddie chuckled. "You *should* have angry kissed."

Steve wished he *had* kissed her before she left. Angry or not, he longed for the touch of her lips. But as he studied the giant metal frame of the trailer, he was glad to be free of that cage. He looked at Eddie.

"How's our transportation?"

"Good. Fifteen, maybe twenty minutes," Eddie replied. "Hope you don't mind riding bitch," he added with a grin.

"That takes on an entirely different meaning coming from you, Eddie," Steve said.

Eddie bellowed a hearty laugh.

"Wait, what?" Brix asked.

"Gay as the sun is hot, *amigo*," Eddie said.

"Huh," Brix said, barely able to keep his eyebrows from hiding in his hair. "I… would not have guessed."

"Speaking of the sun, can we find some shade?" Eddie wiped his forehead, needing both hands to clear all the beads of sweat.

Steve nodded, pulling off his tie and slinging his coat over his shoulder. "Let's find a spot where we can watch the door. Hopefully your friends arrive before Orton leaves."

Bessie began rumbling towards the parking lot exit. On board were the two most vexing people in Steve's life: Ben and Abby.

After an uncomfortable half hour under a thick live oak tree, three motorcycles growled into the parking lot with all the subtlety of a chainsaw competition. Three middle-aged Latinos dismounted in unison, all wearing matching black leather vests, white T-shirts, and jeans. The back of each vest was emblazoned with a winged red skull, circled by white letters that read *Los Presagios Rodantes de Ruido y Cromo*, which Steve's middling recollection of high school Spanish was unable to translate. Something about wheels, he figured.

The bikers exchanged hugs, grins, and spoke over each other in rapid-fire Spanish. Steve couldn't follow the conversation, but he guessed they were eager to be involved in a little cloak and dagger mischief against the federal government. He turned his gaze back to the hotel entrance when a subtle 'hmm' pulled at his attention.

Brix frowned at the bikers. "It's like tryin' to bob for apples in a gushing river. I can't pick out a single word."

The conversation between Eddie and his biker friends escalated to match the heat of the day. The new arrivals were clearly irritated about something.

Steve laughed. "I don't speak it either. Just a bit of French from my time with the marines."

"*Bien sûr,*" Brix said.

"*Vous aussi?*" Steve asked.

"Steve, I'm from N'awlins. *Je parle Français, naturellement.*"

Steve gave an appreciative nod in return.

Eddie cleared his throat loud enough to jostle the leaves on the live oak overhead. "They were saying we should go inside and confront Orton. Or at least watch him or something that isn't standing around in this infernal heat.

Steve was about to disagree, hoping to stay off Orton's radar as long as he could now that they were in the wind. But then he saw a woman get out of a taxi and head to the hotel entrance. She moved with a wobbly saunter, barely able to balance her top-heavy form on her heels.

"I think that's a great idea," Steve said, unable to process this new entrant to the mystery.

Eddie accidentally began to protest. "We should— wait, you do?"

"Yes. Look!" Steve pointed at Delilah Dewberry. "She's got to be Orton's 'errand'. We need to find out what she's doing here." Steve looked at Brix and Eddie. "Orton knows all three of us. Can your friends do a little recon?"

"*¡Por supuesto!*" Eddie barked orders at his friends. "Keep me posted by phone," he finished.

The bikers eagerly loped off, tailing Delilah into the hotel.

Brix wiped his brow. "Shit it's hot. Gonna visit the gas station over there. Want anything?"

"Something cold," Eddie said.

"Me too," Steve added. "Thanks."

"Why do you think Delilah is here?" Eddie asked as Brix headed off.

Steve shrugged. "Dunno. Maybe she's interviewing for a job?"

"Nah, she's here looking for a new man." Eddie mused.

A spark of pain stabbed the unexpecting nerves behind Steve's eyes. "Ow. Shit." He rubbed his forehead. Either Orton's drug was wearing off, or Steve had simply sweated it out.

Eddie shot him a smile. "Got your R-Skill back, eh? That didn't take long."

A calming wave of truth eased the pain in Steve's head. "Seems so." He wasn't as enthused about his R-Skill's return as he had expected to be. The scant few pain-free hours he'd just had were a comforting return to the numbness of normalcy. At least, as normal as being wrapped up in a government conspiracy could be.

Eddie's phone began playing ZZ Top's 'La Grange' as a call came in. "*Sí*," he answered. "Uh huh." He turned to Steve. "They're in the bar. Orton just slipped something into Delilah's drink."

Steve growled. "Of course he did." He didn't like Delilah, or the bullshit con-job she and her late husband were running on the entire country with their FIGHT organization. So many lies. But she didn't deserve whatever was going on. Orton's subterfuge was on another level. An Adapted, willing to subvert his own R-Skill in order to incapacitate that of another? To what end? "Let's see where this goes. Get ready to go in."

Eddie hung up and waved to Brix who approached with sweating bottles of water in hand. He took a bottle and guzzled it down. "Phew. I could use another of those!"

Steve gratefully took his and gulped down half the bottle, then splashed a little on his face. "Thanks Brix."

Brix nursed his bottle more slowly. "Man. This stuff tastes so much better than what I get out of the well at my house, even after I run it through the filter system a few times."

"Does it?" Steve asked. His gaze darted between the water bottles in their hands as he recalled Ben's instinctive guess when Steve had mentioned Norman Pruett's assertion that radiation may not be the ultimate source of the Adapted phenomenon. Could there be something in the water? Something so undetectable that it could get through all the various filtration mechanisms and chemical alterations water is subjected to before being consumed? It seemed unlikely, but then he wasn't a chemist. He took another sip and simply appreciated the cool refreshment sliding down his throat.

Eddie's phone rang again. He answered, then relayed the report. "She just got up to go to the restroom. Orton followed her inside."

"Ew," Brix said. "This hotel is way too nice for a lobby bathroom hook-up."

A tangle of apprehension in Steve's stomach twisted and pulled. "I don't like this." He drained the last, tepid remnants of his water bottle and crushed the empty plastic in his fist. "I need something stronger. Let's go to the bar."

The hotel lobby was opulent: immaculate marble floors and columns, polished chrome everywhere, manicured topiaries that looked straight out of a Dr. Seuss book, and two towering three-story waterfalls that splashed into reflecting pools on either side of the walkway leading up to the front desk. The air was thick with chlorinated moisture from the churning water, but there wasn't a hint of mold or mildew. Instead, a sweet vanilla-orange aroma tickled Steve's nose. Everything here was clean and austere. Lavish. The government wouldn't foot the bill for a place like this. Well, it *shouldn't*. He had no idea who or what was backing Orton. Gustafson? Ben?

They met up with the bikers at the bar and squeezed into a booth. Everyone ordered a beer, except for Brix who opted for a pricey glass bottle of Icelandic glacier water that cost more than the other drinks combined. The man was apparently into his water.

All twelve eyes were fixed at the hallway to the bathrooms. Orton emerged first, tossing a paper towel into a waste basket. He zipped up the fly in his pants and straightened his jacket. Then he saw Steve.

"Well, hello again, Agent Palmer. I didn't realize you were here," Orton said.

Steve bit his lip. He briefly wished Orton's drug was still working on him so he could bullshit the guy. "I needed a beer," he said with a nod.

Eddie reached a hairy paw around Steve's shoulder. "Said he wasn't feeling great. Who can blame him? I'd need a beer if my R-Skill was on the fritz. Hell, maybe ten beers. I thought we'd grab a few *cervesas* and watch the ballgame." He pointed to the Texas Rangers broadcast on a gigantic television over the bar. "My buddies just happened to be in the area."

Orton raised a curious eyebrow at the trio of burly bikers. "Is that right? Well, hope you feel better Steve. I'm looking forward to continuing our conversation tomorrow."

Steve had to hide his smile. He wondered how Orton would react to the news that Steve was no longer on the team. He hoped Abby would provide him with some inside intel. If she wouldn't, he figured Gigi would for the sheer entertainment value.

"I've gotta get on to my other errand," Orton said with a wave. "Enjoy the game."

Steve quickly gulped some beer, and simply raised his glass at Orton with a full mouth. He watched the agent exit the lobby entrance and make conversation with someone outside while he waited for a car.

"Steve," Eddie whispered.

Steve turned his head and saw Delilah also emerge from the restroom hallway. Aside from her awkward high-heeled gait, she showed no ill effects from her encounter with Orton. It didn't take her long to see him or the others. She turned a deep shade of pink and stormed over to their booth.

"You!" She pointed a furious finger at Steve. "You were there when Jeb was shot!"

Steve nodded slowly and attempted to reintroduce himself as Agent Palmer. But the words wouldn't come out. He simply nodded, then managed, "Ms. Dewberry, I remember. I'm sorry for your loss."

"Fuck you, prick! All of you. You've ruined my life."

Steve attempted to tell her that she and Jeb had done that. Two Adapted heading an anti-Adapted organization? How else could it have turned out but in disaster. But again, he couldn't say the words. There again, something was amiss with the truth.

Eddie had no such trouble. "Delilah, you and Jeb brought that on yourselves. Go wag that finger at a mirror."

Delilah's eyes bulged with fury, and she raised a threatening fist at Eddie. Steve caught a trickle of red running down her elbow. His own eyes grew wide. In a blur, Eddie's three friends were out of the booth and had Delilah restrained.

"Wait, wait, wait!" Steve urged, scrambling out of the booth. He freed her right arm from their grasp and held it up to show her the blood. "Delilah. What happened to your arm?"

She looked at the blood and then to Steve in confusion.

Steve snapped his head toward the front door, looking for Orton. But he was gone.

"Let go of me!" Delilah barked. She wiped the blood off her arm with a cloth napkin swiped from the table, then stormed out of the bar without another word.

"What now?" Brix asked.

Steve rubbed his face. Did Orton just hurt Delilah? That opened an entirely new and dangerous can of worms. Had she injured herself? Were they even in the same bathroom? Steve had no idea, and his R-Skill would be no help in figuring out fact from fiction. He slid back into the center of the booth and slumped his head into his hands. "I need to think."

The three bikers filtered back into the booth and demanded another round of drinks. Eddie was happy to oblige and added a few baskets of wings and fries to the order. Steve gazed through the TV as the Rangers managed to take the lead in the fourth inning on a monster home run. The excitement was lost on him. His mind raced with all the possible motivations Orton could be operating with, and his potential next actions.

After several minutes of staring off into the hidden reaches behind the giant TV, the sudden, piquant aroma of steaming hot buffalo chicken wings yanked Steve's attention back to the table. The three bikers had each snared a basket of fries, and were passing the salt shaker back and forth like it was the last one on Earth.

Eddie pounded down chicken wings and his biker friends happily munched on their fries, while Brix simply savored his pricy bottle of water. Steve found it funny that people put so much concern into the source and filtration of their water, but cared far less about nearly everything else they consumed. Then it hit him. Besides water, what else was pervasive in nearly every prepared food item on the planet, and gleefully added to almost any dish?

Salt.

CHAPTER 49
GARBAGE GIRL

NOT ONCE IN her admittedly nascent adult life could Abby remember waking up for work before her alarm went off. But here she was, alert, sharp as a sushi chef's knife, ready to go. She sat up and checked the time on her phone. Forfeiting almost forty-five minutes of sleep seemed like a travesty. Then she remembered what day it was. Wednesday. Training day.

"Shit."

Abby flopped back down on her stomach and pulled a pillow over her head. *Fucking Gigi.* She was probably cramming down a spirulina and goji berry smoothie having already finished her morning routine of weight training and cardio. The bruises Gigi sustained from the tornado cleanup were healing well and wouldn't stop her from wanting to get in a few rounds of revenge with Abby. Plus, she'd get to interact with her followers on A-Space all the way to work because her stupid Tesla was smart enough to do all the driving for her. Abby groaned into her sheets, then pressed her body off the mattress in a feeble attempt at a push-up. She tried two more and groaned into her sheets again. Her own bruises from the prior training session had barely recovered.

"Maybe I should get limber first." She sighed and stretched her neck.

She rolled out of bed and threw on some shorts, then headed to her living room. The Amazon TV box had a number of free options for beginner yoga. She picked the easiest-looking one, and started it. After a thirty-minute session, her body felt more tenderized than it had after last Wednesday's session with Gigi.

"I'm gonna have to ask Ben to put in a hot tub."

She settled for a long and therapeutically hot shower. After dressing, she checked her phone, hoping for a message from Steve.

A single text message waited, but from her foster sister, Mary. "Abby, I need help. Come ASAP. Don't call."

The last direction was peculiar. She texted Ben that she would probably be a little behind, then grabbed the keys to her new orange Subaru and ran out the door and headed to her foster family's house in Plano.

———

Abby parked in front of the Kims' house, unable to decide which was worse. Driving in morning rush hour traffic, or the idea that she wouldn't be doing it with Steve. She forgot all about both when she opened the front door and the sweet aroma of baked cinnamon and brown sugar hit her in the face. *Mmm, hotteok!* she thought. Abby never developed a taste for most of her foster mom's cooking, but the syrupy, nutty pastry was one of her favorites.

She entered the kitchen with her customary greeting. "Hi Mom, hi Dad."

"Morning!" Walter said, looking up from his phone with a smile.

Betty, with her coffee mug in one hand and tablet in the other, only grunted her acknowledgement.

"What are you doing here?" Walter asked. "Shouldn't you be at work?"

"I'm on my way, just here for the *hotteok!*" Abby said. She grabbed a pastry from the basket on the table and stuffed it in her mouth, then gave each foster parent an uncharacteristically warm rub on the shoulder as she walked past them for a cup of coffee.

"You know, I heard about an accident at Charles & Munck. Some poor guy was—" Walter looked at Betty with wide eyes and spoke through clenched teeth. "*Killed.*"

Betty looked up from her tablet in interest. "Did you know him?"

Shit, Abby thought as memories of Tyson again flooded her head. She faced the coffee maker for an uncomfortable moment to hide her screwed-up face. "No. Must have been a different project. But remember, I'm doing something else now." She poured her coffee, smiled again, and turned around.

"That's right. Sit and tell us about it," Walter said, gesturing to a chair.

"How about another time? I just came to help Mary for a sec. Gotta get to work," Abby said.

Betty scoffed. "Why would Mary need *your* help with anything?"

Abby shrugged. "She didn't say. Maybe it's a boy or something." She glared at Betty for emphasis when she said 'boy'. It had the desired effect of turning her foster mother's face red.

"Mary does not consort with boys! She's too young!"

"I'm kidding!" Abby laughed. "I don't know. Maybe she needs help picking out clothes. Is she upstairs?"

Walter nodded. "Tell her she has ten minutes to eat before we leave for school."

"Will do." Abby grabbed a handful of *hotteok* for herself and Mary and headed upstairs.

"Don't get that on the carpet!" Betty yelled after her.

Abby knocked on Mary's door three times. "It's me."

"Okay," a muffled voice replied.

Abby let herself in and smiled at the unchanged familiarity of her sister's bedroom. Mary was still in bed, hiding under the covers and pillows.

"Hey - what's up? Are you okay?"

"No."

"No... why?" Abby drew out the question as Mary's behavior was quite out of character for the typically forward teen. They had that in common. Their parents no doubt blamed Abby.

"Something happened Abby. Last night."

Immediately, Abby's thoughts went to the horrible things that could happen at night to a diminutive teen just entering womanhood. Her fists tightened and a scowl tightened her face. "Oh my God, Mary. Who did it? Where?" Abby began to daydream about plotting the flying cement demise of someone else.

Mary pulled the pillow off her face and shot Abby a hurt look. "Ew, no. Gross. Like I would get myself into that kind of trouble."

The needles of tension in her spine lifted as Abby breathed a sigh of relief. "What, then?"

"I was in the backyard last night letting Doc out before I went to bed. My stomach started feeling funny, and..."

Abby took a bite of *hotteok* and cocked her head to one side. "And...?"

Mary drooped her head. "Look out the window."

Abby nibbled on her pastry as she walked over to the window that looked out over the back yard. A swath of scorched grass split the meticu-lously-kept lawn in two. The black scar swept from the middle of the yard up the side of the neighbor's fence to a tapered point. "How did that…" Then it hit her. Abby's eyes widened with the realization. She turned to Mary, who was now sitting up in bed, tears streaming down her face.

"You're…"

"Adapted." Mary sobbed.

Abby completely understood Mary's reaction, but could hardly contain her own joy. "Hey, hey. It's okay! I'm Adapted too, it's not a bad thing most of the time. Looks like you can control it. I mean, you didn't burn the neighborhood down."

Mary threw her head in her hands and continued to cry.

"Have Walter and Betty seen it?"

Mary shook her head.

"You didn't cook poor Dr Pepper, did you?"

That brought a short laugh through Mary's tears. "No, the dog is fine. Though I literally scared the shit out of him."

"Ew. Roast dog crap." Abby sat on the bed and put her arm around her sister. "It'll be fine. It's a change in anyone's life, but at least you didn't lose all your bones or cause everyone around you to lose their hair."

Mary resumed her crying. She mumbled through her tears. "I can just hear the RADSA vans pulling up now, ready to kick down the front door and drag me out in front of Mom and Dad."

Abby had to stifle a giggle. "C'mon, they don't do that."

"You don't know what they do!" She buried her head in her hands again.

For a moment, Abby debated telling Mary of her new occupation, recalling her own fiery reaction when she learned Steve was an Adapted during her first RADSA interview. Her sister seemed to be operating under the same misconceptions. "I, uh, actually work for RADSA."

That stopped the sobbing. Mary roared with laughter, as if she had just been told the most hilarious joke in the history of comedy. "You? In RADSA?"

Abby appreciated the levity. A month ago, she would have been laughing just as loudly at the notion. She drew an 'X' on her chest with a finger. "Pizza pie, in my eye." It was the sisters' secret code phrase for the honest truth.

Mary's eyes widened. "No way."

Abby shrugged. "Yeah."

"What do you even do? Throw garbage?"

Abby put her arms akimbo and stood up straight. "No, thank you very much. Well, actually, a little, I guess. But I have other redeeming qualities you know!"

Mary folded her arms. "Name one. It's not your taste in music." She tugged at Abby's faded Van Halen t-shirt.

Abby scoffed. "Well, I'm pretty good at helping you with your math homework when you need it." She pointed at the posters around the room. "You're one to talk about music."

"The rest of the Koreans on the planet can't be wrong. Who still likes Van Halen?"

"Hey!" Abby pointed a stern finger. "There are dozens of us!"

Walter's voice called from downstairs. "Mary! Five minutes 'til we leave!"

"Crap," Mary said.

"I've got this. Get dressed, get your stuff together."

Abby bolted downstairs, then returned moments later with another *hotteok* in her mouth. "I'll take you to school."

"How?" Mary called from her closet.

"I have one of those newfangled things called an auto-mobile. I think they may catch on. A brand new, all-wheel drive, five-star crash rated Subaru. In bright orange." Abby smiled.

Mary stepped back into the room, dressed in a tidy blue and tan uniform. She grabbed her book bag. "You can drive?"

Abby gave her sister a hug and whispered into her ear, "I didn't say anything about being able to drive."

———

"My school is that way," Mary said, pointing to the highway exit passing on their right. "I'm not in high school 'til next year, remember?" She nibbled at a pastry.

"I know. You'll be a little late. It's okay. I wanna see what you can do!"

Fear spread across Mary's face. "But what if someone sees?"

"Don't worry, I know a place."

Abby drove for a few more minutes, then took an exit that led to one of her old Charles & Munck worksites. The lot had been cleared in preparation for new construction, but it wasn't scheduled to begin until next year, so it was just sitting vacant for another few months, obscured by a locked privacy fence. The perfect place to test Mary's R-Skill. Abby led her sister to an unsecured spot in the fence she and Tyson had used late one night several weeks back. They had snuck in to stare at the few stars that could penetrate the curtain of nighttime lights above DFW and do a little penetrating of their own in the open air. Abby shook the memory from her head and pressed her guilt down as far as it could go as she showed Mary inside the fence.

Inside, it was as Abby remembered it: an empty dirt field, now with a healthy scrub of North Texas weeds popping up across most of the four-acre lot.

"Okay, let 'er rip." Abby folded her arms.

"What? How?" Mary shrunk under the expectation.

Abby lent a reassuring hand to her shoulder. "It'll be fine. I'll stand behind you. Experiment. You should have a basic feeling for how it works already. That's what happened for me and most Adapted you hear about. Give it your full force."

"Okay," Mary said, unconvinced. She stepped ahead of Abby, closed her eyes, and inhaled. Her eyes opened. For a moment, nothing happened. Then Mary's mouth dropped open, and a massive column of flame leapt forth, roaring like a concentrated solar flare. It shot out at least fifty feet from the sisters, roasting everything on the ground in its path.

"Holy fuck!" Abby exclaimed.

Mary closed her mouth and the flames dissipated. "Yeah." She looked to the ground, ignoring the small fires that still scattered the now scorched black dirt.

"That is so cool!"

"No, it's not! I'm gonna get sent to Island-A. I know it!"

Abby shook her head. "That's not gonna happen. First, you can control it. That's great. No one has to know if you don't want them to. It's not like the government has a way to track when and where people become Adapted. Part of what RADSA does is catalog new Adapted after reports come out through news or social media. If it's not public, we don't know about it any more than you would."

"Well, I guess that's good."

"Yeah, but get this. My whole team is Adapted! Even our boss." Abby paused to digest those last words. She was still shocked Ben had been able to hide his ability from them this whole time.

"And what does the team do?"

"Right now, mostly catalog and recruit. I've gone out on a bunch of interviews and met some pretty interesting new Adapted. We're authorized to help first responders in an emergency if they ask — like that tornado at Stonebriar Mall last week. I helped pull survivors out of the wreckage.

Mary laughed. "Wow. Were they covered in trash bags?"

Abby shrugged. "Actually, I could lift the rubble. It was amazing."

"No way." Mary looked at Abby with wide eyes for a moment, then turned her head. "Are people like me on the team?"

"Well, no one as young as you. And nobody has an ability like that. We've got a guy, Stitch, who can make a seam out of anything — even skin." She left out the part where the sensation was nigh orgasmic. "Bouncy's feet turn any surface into a super-springy trampoline. Pulse blasts things with this weird energy wave when he kisses them. Blight kills any vegetation he touches." Her thoughts went to Steve and wondered when she'd see him again. "My friend Steve can tell if someone is lying. It's amazing."

Mary folded her arms. "How is any of that useful in an emergency? It's not like you can use those R-Skills to stop a bank robber or something."

"Who knows? But it's cool to have a group of others that are different in the same way you are. RADSA is on the side of the Adapted."

"I guess. What's with those nicknames? Do you have one?"

Abby chuckled. "Garbage Girl."

Mary held a hand to her face to suppress her laugh.

"Yeah. It's growing on me. A little. There's a RADSA computer somewhere that assigns them, it's kind of funny. Steve is called The Sleuth. We don't actually refer to each other with them except in jest."

"Funny." Mary looked at her watch. "I should be getting to school." She turned to walk back to the opening in the fence.

Abby looked again at the burned ground and had an idea. "I think I should bring you to the team! It would be so badass to have someone with some actual firepower to lend a hand."

Mary stopped cold in her tracks. She turned slowly, horrified. "Don't you dare!"

"C'mon! I know these guys, they're not gonna send you to the island! My boss Ben trusts me, and I trust him. I helped recruit Pulse and Blight — Zeke and Brix. Neither of them wanted to come, but I talked them both into it. It's a good group." She then recalled that half the team was technically not even on the team anymore. Hopefully Steve, Eddie, and Brix were faring okay in their search for information about the asteroid. She still had a hard time believing there was some kind of conspiracy at play.

"No, no, no, no, no! What I can do is too dangerous!"

"Not if you can control it, Mary! You could be the ringer we need if there's an actual bank robber that needs a quick flambé to learn the error of his ways."

"I don't think I could do that. And I don't want anyone to know about it! Especially Mom and Dad. They would die!"

Abby could see the look on Betty's face at hearing such news, and thought it very much looked like what someone having a heart attack would look like. She thought Walter would be okay with it, or at least would mask his disappointment for Mary's sake. Mary still looked like she had actually roasted poor Dr Pepper the prior night.

"It'll be great! I bet you'll feel much better after you meet them." Abby walked up and hugged her sister.

"I don't know."

"C'mon, come play hooky with me today. It's training day. You can watch me get my ass kicked by Bouncy."

Mary broke the hug and looked up at Abby in surprise. "Wow. I kinda want to see that."

CHAPTER 50
BOUNCY

MISPLACED OR NOT, Gigi always had confidence in herself. Her family. Her destiny. In her pursuit of gymnastic glory, she always knew that above all, no matter what the other competitors did, what she put out there on the floor or bars or vault or beam was the most important. Not once had she left an event she didn't win feeling like she couldn't have done better to improve her score. The result was always completely in her hands.

So, this experience was new to her. The nervous energy. The uncertainty. *I've got goosebumps, for fuck's sake.* The idea that the path to the success she dreamed about didn't start and end with her. Indeed, it now went through her new agent, LeAnne Clarke.

And that's why she was sitting in LeAnne's office lobby with not one, but two homemade smoothies in hand. *Get off on the right foot,* she thought.

"Hey Gigi," LeAnne said with her tinge of southern lilt after barging through the front door to the office over thirty minutes late. She had the self-important swagger of someone that knew they walked in a higher echelon of society than most. Deep tan, glamorous red hair bedazzled with highlights, Gucci sunglasses, white Versace blazer, gorgeous Louboutin heels. Drenched in some Chanel number that instantly overwhelmed the lobby. And she most certainly did not look concerned over being late to meet with Gigi.

"Hi LeAnne," Gigi said, standing up and holding out one of the smoothies.

LeAnne took it with a quizzical expression. "What's this?"

"My usual morning smoothie. I make them myself." Gigi took a sip of hers and suppressed her frown. The extra time waiting on LeAnne had melted much of the ice and had diluted the flavor. "Kale, lemongrass, spirulina, Greek yogurt - ya know, good stuff."

LeAnne cringed. "Hmm. Looks like you tossed an alien into the blender." Then she shrugged, took a sip, and whistled. "Phew. You take this every morning?"

Gigi nodded with pride.

"Good for you." LeAnne patted her on the shoulder. "I'm sure my cardiologist and you would get along famously."

Gigi laughed a little too hard as LeAnne led her through the inner door and down a hallway covered in pictures of local clients that had made it big in Hollywood. Colleen Wishwood. Brad Brickenbrack. The Blazin' Acres. Gigi loved that band. She didn't even know they were from Dallas.

The lights in LeAnne's office lit up as they approached from the hall. Once inside, LeAnne walked around her desk and tossed the smoothie into the trash.

Gigi refrained from commenting and fixed her gaze straight ahead at LeAnne. She knew her smoothies were an acquired taste. *Could have at least waited for me to leave, sheesh*, she thought.

"Alright," LeAnne began, flipping open her laptop. "Did you talk to Abby? I think it would be a great narrative to have you two, both from RADSA, both with big, visible R-Skills, to play off each other."

Gigi groaned to herself. *The fuck? We're just sitting down and the first thing she brings up is Abby?*

"I did," Gigi lied. Over her dead body would she bring Abby, the girl who managed to unintentionally steal every spotlight possible, into this.

"Great! Carlo de Mille, over at A-Space, will be through the moon. This show is really shaping up to be something spectacular. I'm so glad to have you be part of it. Who would have thought we'd place three from DFW in the cast?" LeAnne pulled a glass bottle of Icelandic water from the small refrigerator behind her desk. She popped a couple pills from the wrong day in her weeklong pillbox into her mouth before downing half the bottle.

"Actually, Abby said she wasn't interested. She's not into publicity. I don't think she even has social media accounts."

"You must be joking. She's nineteen, right?"

Gigi shrugged. She was lying through her teeth and hoped LeAnne wouldn't be compelled to pursue Abby further.

LeAnne clicked her tongue. "Well, that's too bad. Carlo really liked her look."

The smoothie in Gigi's gut frothed. *Abby's look? She's all rough and no diamond. Why was everyone so damn keen on the girl?*

"Okay, let's talk the A-Space All-Stars contract then. I trust you looked it over. Any questions?"

"Actually, yes," Gigi said. She pulled out her phone and scrolled through the document. "So, this weight clause," she said, pointing to a spot on her phone, "I totally get it, but I think they have the wrong number down for me. I'd have to lose ten pounds to make this weight."

LeAnne snickered. The lines around her eyes triumphed over Botox's hold. "You know, not a single girl has sat across this desk from me and not said the same fucking thing. And my answer to you is the same. Get a fucking clue. You want to waltz through the front door of the grand Hollywood party and not expect to tip the bouncer? This is the first, but most certainly not last, price of admission." She casually pointed at Gigi's midsection and muscular arms and shoulders. "You've got some meat there you could lose. For a girl as disciplined as you, I can't imagine it'll be a problem."

Gigi grinned and nodded, but cursed internally over the additional calorie reduction and exercise she'd have to endure to make it happen. She was already as lean as a thoroughbred. *Fucking shit!*

"What else, sweetie?"

"Well, everything else seems great. As you said, the pay is good, the planned events, activities, physical competitions, team-ups, social media touch points — it all seems like my cup of tea."

"Great," LeAnne took another huge swig of water and tapped at her laptop.

"But—"

LeAnne raised her eyebrows.

"I didn't see the objective of the show. It's a competition. What do I get if— *when*, I win?"

The agent cocked her head back and bellowed a hearty "Hah!"

In an instant, Gigi felt as small as a cornered mouse with nowhere to run to escape a fatal feline mauling.

"Dear, sweet Gigi. You won't win. They've already picked the winner. This ain't your show. You're not the star — just a side character."

Gigi tilted her head, not fully grasping what LeAnne said. "But… it's a reality show? A competition?"

LeAnne craned forward and talked low. "And every single reality show for the past decade has had a predetermined outcome, despite what the government will have you believe. You think the producers and network putting the money up for this are willing to leave their ratings and revenues to chance? Well, I mean, there's always the possibility it turns into a complete shitshow and everything goes tits up. But these people are *pros*, with petabytes of consumer data driving their programming decisions. They will craft every detail possible to maximize their investment's potential. The entire sixteen episode run of A-Space All-Stars is practically scripted. Too bad we couldn't get Abby to do it, they had some spectacular stuff planned for her." LeAnne winked after a pause. "You too, sweetie."

At once, the air was gone from Gigi's sails. The swell of pride and accomplishment now lost. This opportunity wasn't ever about her. She was just a checkbox and an avenue to Abby, who some marketing asswipe in Los Angeles thought would help drive up ratings. *Fuck this shit.* Gigi failed to hide her disappointment.

"Hey, don't feel bad. This is your first real gig. Like I said, it'll open doors for you that you don't even know exist yet."

Gigi slumped in her chair.

"Besides, your girl Kendra will be the winner. You can revel in that glory together. I'm sure she won't forget you when she hits it big."

"What!" Gigi's head snapped up. How could Kendra be the winner?

LeAnne sighed with a crude smirk on her lips. "Oops. Guess I spilled that can of beans. Oh well. You would have found out soon enough. I need not remind you of the NDA you've already signed?"

Gigi nodded but her face flushed. Her spandex attire couldn't work fast enough to dissipate the heat raging from within her. "I— this isn't—" She slipped her hand over her mouth to hold in all the invectives primed to escape.

LeAnne coughed in between sips of her water. "Geeg. Come on. You didn't think you'd just roll in there and be the star? It's not a big deal. Hollywood is a game — like Chutes and Ladders. Sometimes when you make a move, you hit a ladder and get to move up a bunch of levels. Sometimes you find a chute and your career takes a hit. For you, this move is just a couple spaces ahead of the starting spot. But hey — you're on the board. You're playing the game." LeAnne gave her a smile that read "You fucking naive waste of my time."

Gigi pressed out a sigh, faking conciliation. "That's all fine." And it was. She understood the game. But Kendra would be the winner? Gigi could already imagine the boost to her best friend's eternal smug sense of superiority. And the nerve to keep it secret! Had she known, Gigi wouldn't have even bothered with the open audition, not that it had done her any good. Of all the morning's disappointments, that's the one that stung the most.

"What… can Kendra do? She hasn't even shown me." Gigi asked after a silent moment.

"I think she should tell you that. You seem pretty put out. I understand. Believe me, I've seen this a thousand times if I've seen it ten. Call up Kendra, have some lunch. You're here *because* of her. She'll talk some sense into you. So much at work behind the scenes you don't know about."

The cloying vapor wafting off LeAnne and across the desk dared Gigi to vomit her smoothie all over the pompous ass of an agent. But she held it down. She'd keep that bile for later.

Gigi stood. "Yeah, I think that's a good idea." She managed to hold her smile and offer gracious thanks before leaving the office. Once in the elevator, she screamed. LeAnne probably heard it. Gigi couldn't care less.

"Hey girl, just saw LeAnne. Let's get lunch!" Gigi texted her so-called friend. "NorthPark at Noon?"

"Sounds great. Already there shopping. See you at Botazzo's at 12."

Gigi got into her Tesla and programmed the nav for the mall. It was all she could do to keep her rage contained. No. She would save it. Let it simmer. And then once she saw Kendra, Gigi would completely incinerate her.

CHAPTER 51
THE SLEUTH

THE BREAKING SUN spat out an endless stream of highway stripes as Steve sped down Highway 80 east of Dallas. He tried to imagine a cohesive picture that included all the random puzzle pieces strewn across the table of his mind. More UDOs. The president's peculiar press conferences. Agent Orton with a means to disable R-Skills. Delilah's bloody arm. Ben turning out to be Adapted and lying about it without Steve catching on. None of them fit.

And then there was the sinking feeling he was letting his dead friend Milo down somehow.

But he couldn't focus on the clues. His mind was only on Abby. Whatever had come over him to suggest that they were a bad idea? The notion was completely gone now. Despite her penchant for joking with falsehoods, Abby turned out to be awesome. His initial impression of her was way off. He would have to apologize to her somehow and hope that she would still be interested.

"So, tell me again why we're doing this?" Brix asked from the back seat of Steve's Camry.

Steve sat up a little straighter in the driver's seat. "One of the world's largest salt mines is an hour from Dallas. It belongs to Morton Salt. They were awarded an unusually large federal contract after President Phelps took office. And you remember what I mentioned about the president's trade agreement with China and salt. Just wanted to go investigate."

Eddie stretched against the passenger door in his sleep, shaking the window with his snoring.

"Yeah, I get that," Brix said. "But why are we doing it at six in the morning?" He yawned and slouched against the seat.

Steve smiled, glad to have at least some company for this little adventure. He wished it was Abby snoring next to him though.

Grand Saline was a tiny Texas town on life support. The main street was lined with empty, run-down storefronts. Neglected paint peeled off every building. Unmaintained brick walls everywhere were on the verge of collapse. Cracked window panes let the heat and humidity in, withering mannequins, furniture, and any other relics left behind. It only needed a lone tumbleweed blowing across the crumbling asphalt to complete the image of economic desolation.

The picture of times long passed was vandalized by pristine blue and gold banners hanging from every other light post. Each featured the Morton Salt "umbrella girl" logo and the classic slogan, "When it rains, it pours".

"Talk about your corporate takeover," Eddie said, rubbing his face awake.

"A huge chunk of the town works there," Steve said. "This place wouldn't exist if not for that mine."

Steve parked in front of the Grand Saline Salt Palace, the local chamber of commerce whose walls were made entirely from salt. "Let's get some history before checking out the plant. I called yesterday and asked if they'd open early for us," he said.

"Dibs on the salt lick!" Eddie said. He jumped out of the car and headed for a massive block of salt on display by the front door.

"Nasty," Brix said.

An older woman named Bonnie Lamar was the only person working the Salt Palace when they entered. An impenetrable helmet of dyed-red curls protected her head, and her 1970s vintage flower blouse and tan corduroy slacks were probably the most fashion-forward outfit in the whole town. She narrated the history of the area's original Native American settlers who were ousted after the Republic of Texas formed. After statehood, the small town boomed during the rail expansion of the late nineteenth century. Of course, the reason anyone was there at all was due to the accessibility of the salt, which was first harvested from brackish marshes. Eventually a massive salt dome was discovered, extending all the way to the Gulf of Mexico, with enough salt for the entire planet for thousands of years. Ownership of Morton Salt had changed hands a few times over the years, but they had operated the mine for over a century.

Bonnie was so happy to have visitors that she gave each of them a sack full of tiny boxes of salt. "Give them to your friends, tell 'em to stop by!" she said.

They all bought courtesy souvenir t-shirts and vowed to send their friends to visit. Steve had to pull Eddie away from licking the building walls as they were leaving. "C'mon, let's check out the mine."

The Morton Salt facility was less than a minute south of Grand Saline's bleary main street. Several parked semi-trucks lined the shoulder of the highway as they approached the turn. Blistered asphalt crackled under the Camry's tires as they turned into the drive up to the complex. A double line of semi-trucks with empty flatbed trailers snaked around the right side of the main building, presumably waiting for their turn to be loaded with salt.

"Busy place," Eddie said.

Steve parked next to the other cars in front of the chain-link security fence, then scratched his head. "I'm actually not sure how to go about this. They stopped giving tours a while ago."

"Pfft," Eddie scoffed. "Just bullshit them, man. Oh wait, you can't do that, can you?"

Steve shot him an annoyed look.

"Have no fear. *Papasito's* got this," Eddie said.

"Nah, I've got this," Brix said as he swung open his door and jumped out.

"Well, that's new," Eddie laughed.

Brix jogged over to a man with a clipboard who was walking the line of semi-trucks, wearing a black New Orleans Saints polo shirt. They shook hands and immediately struck up a conversation.

"I'm sorry," Steve said as they watched Brix chat up the plant worker.

"Huh?" Eddie asked.

"You were right… about Phelps."

"I know. I figured you'd work it out, eventually."

Brix waved at them to come over.

"Still. I could have been nicer about it," Steve said.

Eddie scoffed. "I spent over two years in prison, *amigo*. You've got a feather touch. For a marine."

The wave of radiant truth flushed Steve's pride down the toilet.

Eddie winked at Steve and opened his door. *"Vamos,"* he said, stepping out.

Steve got out and followed Eddie, wishing for the first time since he became Adapted that someone had lied instead of telling the truth.

Brix smiled as they arrived. Next to him, the man with the clipboard and Saints shirt looked to be in his fifties with tan, sun-withered skin and a mop of graying hair.

"Hey guys, this here is Remy Carre," Brix said.

"You know him?" Eddie asked.

"Nah. Just another transplant from Hurricane Katrina. We can sense each other out." He looked at Eddie. "Like a radar thing."

Eddie raised an eyebrow.

"Uh, yeah. So, I told him about the new Adapted we're looking for. Give him your card, Steve. Mine haven't come in the mail yet," Brix said.

Shit, Steve thought as his head spiked in pain. He gave Brix a pained look as he fished out a RADSA business card from his wallet for Remy and shook his hand, which was already sweaty from the heat despite the early morning hour. Steve tugged at his shirt collar, feeling the heat from the sun, and from Brix's charade. His forehead twitched in anticipation of further torment.

"All y'all work for RADSA?" Remy asked with a frown on his face, inspecting the card.

Eddie answered before Steve could open his mouth. "That's right," he said.

"Pretty motley group you have here Brix," Remy said, eyeing Eddie's new yellow t-shirt that read 'I licked the Salt Palace'.

"Yeah, well, the training video says we should wear whatever we think will make the other Adapted we come across more comfortable," Brix said.

"That so?" Remy looked at Steve. "Well, a black suit and tie around here isn't gonna do that for nobody."

"I have a t-shirt in the car," Steve said.

Remy nodded.

Steve jogged back to the Camry and pulled off his coat, tie, and shirt and retrieved the souvenir t-shirt he got at the Salt Palace, featuring the Morton Salt umbrella girl and 'SALTY' in bold yellow letters beneath her. He put it on to the tune of Abby telling him 'I told you so' in his head and was immediately more comfortable. Eddie and Brix both laughed as Steve rejoined the group.

"Nice," Remy scoffed. "Y'all are representin'. I like it. I haven't heard of anyone here turnin' Adapted, but I guess you never know 'bout that stuff, do ya?"

"Yeah," Eddie chuckled. "A handful of Adapted can just pop up in your backyard at any time."

Steve stifled a laugh.

Remy looked at his clipboard and rubbed the sweat from his face. "This isn't a good time. Visitors like y'all need to call ahead. I got my regular job to do ya know.

"It's important that we find this Adapted quickly. We don't want an accident to happen. Some people get very dangerous R-Skills," Eddie said.

"Well, I suppose you can walk around for a bit and talk to who you can find if they're not busy. We're way backed up though. No tours. We don't do tours."

A semi-truck rumbled past the group on its way out of the complex. It pulled a flatbed trailer loaded with pallets of blue and white bags full of salt.

"Ugh, finally," Remy said. "Stupid forklift's been busted since yesterday. We're so damn backed up." He looked at his clipboard and sighed. "Ya know, this is a bit unusual for y'all, but I suppose I can trust you RADSA folks not to get yourselves hurt. I just got no time for you today. Check in with Lou in the office over there and get some hard hats. Don't go pokin' around anywhere there isn't someone working that can keep an eye on you. I can't spare you an escort." He directed them over to a small one-story building on the other side of the fence, then returned to his work with the line of semi-trucks.

Steve chewed on Remy's words as he, Eddie, and Brix made their way to the office. "What do you suppose he meant by 'unusual for y'all'?" he asked.

"Does this look like the kind of place that gets a lot of government visitors?" Eddie asked.

"Maybe OSHA inspectors," Brix offered. "But they're not showing up at seven in the morning in a suit and tie."

They stopped by the car again so Brix could pull on his souvenir shirt as well, a simple dark gray shirt that read 'Grand Saline, Texas est. 1895' in a bold collegiate font. At the office, they collected their hard hats and a few suspicious looks from Lou, a balding middle-aged man who was straining the sweat capacity of his white shirt. He seemed just as frazzled as Remy with the backup at the facility. "We weren't expecting you," and "Got work to do," were all he could grumble at them.

They meandered around the grounds, talking to whoever would spare them a minute. Eddie led the discussion, asking each worker if they or anyone they knew were Adapted. Very quickly, Steve discerned that there was indeed an Adapted working at the factory, as his R-Skill cried foul every time someone replied that there weren't any at the site.

A mid-thirties woman wearing a white Morton Salt polo shirt with the name Tammy embroidered on it was outside for a smoke break when the group bumped into her. She quickly doused her cigarette when Eddie told her they were with RADSA. Her forehead, already slick from the growing heat of the day, added a few more beads of sweat when Brix asked if she knew if anyone at the plant was an Adapted.

"Peck Whitley is," she whispered, craning her head low beneath the cover of the taller men. "At least, I think he is. Used to complain — like constantly, walkin' 'round with a mean mug on his face all the time. Then one day last year it was like a light bulb just came on. Happy as a clam, does his job, makes no waves. Hardly says a peep now. He must'a got a good one. Ability or whatever y'all call it."

Though she was only guessing, the way she ordered her words relayed the truth. This Whitley person was Adapted. The corner of Steve's mouth curled up. "Do you know where we can find him?"

She pointed to an isolated pinkish building with steel siding near the evaporation ponds. "He'll be over there, workin' on the new stuff," she said. "Don't mention me or anything. I don't want him to blast me with his laser eyes or whatever he got."

"Fear not," Eddie said, patting her on the shoulder. "If that's what he got, he'll be leaving here with us."

They thanked her, then headed to the pink building.

"You want to bring him back with us if he's on the D2S list?" Brix asked.

Eddie scoffed. "I left my Glocks at home. I'll be running away from him faster than Tammy!"

Steve laughed, but struggled with what he would do. He still felt inclined to turn in a D2S Adapted to Ben if it was safe. Whether or not he was with RADSA, Steve's sense of duty remained. Though, he didn't relish the idea of his Camry's roof perforated with holes. A tip to the RADSA hotline would also suffice.

Up close, the paint of the pink building shined in the sun, and the metal siding showed no signs of rust like the rest of the plant did. It featured a human-sized door, which was locked, and another scrolling metal door large enough for heavy equipment to move in and out. Steve pressed the doorbell next to the smaller door's card reader and jerked his hand back from an abhorrent buzzing sensation when he touched it.

After a long moment, a tall, dark-skinned man opened the door. He wore a white t-shirt and denim overalls. Atop his cornrow-braided hair sat a pair of golden headphones that glimmered in the sun. "Y'all look lost. Need somethin'?" he said.

"We're with RADSA. Just want to ask a few questions and have a look around," Steve said without thinking.

In the moment the man spent processing the request, Steve realized what he had just said. The truth was, they were all still on RADSA's payroll for some reason. Perhaps Ben hadn't processed the termination yet? That didn't seem like him. He looked at Eddie who was staring back, eyebrows raised. He then nodded towards Steve's back pocket and Steve got the hint. He took out another business card and offered it.

The man's head shifted slightly as he looked at the card for a moment, then he stepped back from the door. "Okay. Come on in. Nice shirts."

Another voice called from deeper in the building as they entered. "Who's that?"

"RADSA!" the first man replied as he shut the door. "Make yourselves at home," he said to the trio, pointing to a small kitchenette with a table and chairs.

Machinery hummed inside the skylight-lit building. Several large plastic bins lined one wall, each filled with white salt granules undulating around a stainless-steel augur. The noise combined with the thick, brackish air reminded Steve of his time on the *USS Kennedy* after the embassy attack. He had spent countless hours standing on the deck, staring off at the endless line of the watery horizon, lost in contemplation.

Towards the far end of the building, the other man inside, a balding mid-fifties individual, also in a white t-shirt and overalls, was filling pink and blue plastic sacks with salt from one of the bins with a shiny shovel.

The man with the headphones grabbed some bottles of water from the refrigerator, then sat down at the table with the group. "I'm Peck. So, what's up?"

Steve sat down at the table and took a long sip of water. "We heard on the grapevine that someone here became Adapted."

Peck looked over at the other worker. "Oh. Well, yeah. Took long enough. Thought it would happen sooner with all that stuff in the air."

"Time for your official RADSA interview!" Eddie said with a grin, waving his hands in the air.

"Okay, sure," Peck said, laughing.

"So, what's your R-Skill?" Brix asked.

Peck smiled and shook his head. "It's the silliest thing. I can put LEGO sets together without instructions. How useless is that?"

Eddie cackled. "Wow, that's a good one!"

Steve breathed a small sigh of relief when Peck told the truth. The man seemed completely at ease talking with them. "I loved LEGO as a kid."

Peck smiled. "My daughter thinks it's a hoot. I was kinda hopin' for some superpowers or shit. Ya know, be somethin'. Still, could be worse. You hear some awful things happen in the news. People getting killed by Adapted at malls and shit. This is a small town, but a safe town."

"Yeah, better off not getting something that could send you to the island, eh?" Brix added.

Peck looked at Brix and raised an eyebrow. "Yeah." He paused to examine Steve's business card more closely. "Wait. So, you're from the North Texas RADSA?"

"That's right," Eddie said.

"Huh," Peck said, looking over at the other man working. "Ya know, I don't really have anything else to add. Need to get back to work."

Steve took a sip of water and could sense the mood shifting. They weren't who Peck thought they were. Had others from RADSA been here? Steve tried to ease the conversation. "So, you could probably build a lot of LEGO sets in a year. How many have you and your daughter put together?"

"Year? It's only been a few weeks. Heath's been longer, but only like three months." Peck said.

Steve shared looks with Eddie and Brix. "We were under the impression it was last year?" he asked.

"Nah you've got your calendar all screwed up. That's when we started here."

"Ah. My mistake. Should have checked our research before driving out," Steve said.

Eddie looked over at the other worker. "That's Heath? He's an Adapted too?"

A bell rang from a console above one of the salt bins, and a light above it switched from green to red.

Peck stood up. "Well, yeah. Listen, I've got work to do. Let me see you out."

"Actually," Brix chimed in. "We should chat with Heath too while we're here. Will save us another trip."

Peck looked at Heath. "Uh, sure. Just make it quick. We've got a quota to fill."

Steve's head barked in pain at the lie. He pantomimed wiping the sweat off his brow to hide his grimace. "Don't let us keep you. We'll say hi to Heath and be on our way."

The buzzer above the bin with the red light sounded again, prompting Peck to dash over and press a button to silence it. He grabbed a sprayer attached to a large, rusty metal drum, aimed it into the bin, and squeezed the trigger. Whatever was supposed to happen didn't, as he shook the sprayer and kicked the barrel a few times, but to no satisfaction. "Hey Heath," he called over to the other man. "I need a new barrel."

Steve huddled close to the others. "Are you guys getting the impression something very odd is going on here?"

Brix and Eddie looked at each other and nodded.

They watched Heath wheel over a new, glossy black barrel, with a monarch butterfly emblazoned on the side. He dropped the barrel in front of Peck's feet. "You can get the next one yourself, LEGO boy."

A small tickle in the back of Steve's mind suggested he should know the company from the butterfly logo.

Peck rolled his eyes and transferred the spraying mechanism from the old barrel to the new.

Heath dusted his overalls, walked over to the team, and shook their hands. "Heath Todd," he said. "What brings you here?"

They all sat back down at the kitchenette table.

"We're just collecting data for the official RADSA Adapted database. And to see how things are going in here," Eddie said.

Peck got the sprayer working and began to douse the bin of salt with pink liquid from the new barrel. Steve knew nothing about the manufacture of salt, so for all he knew this was just part of the process.

Heath stretched his arms behind his head and sighed. "Oh, just fine. Nothing changes in here. You three are the first visitors we've had in a while. With that barrel empty, we've got six left. Should last us a few more months before we need another shipment."

Eddie stroked his goatee while turning to look at Peck. "That's good. So what's your R-Skill?"

"Mine's way better than Peck's," Heath said, laughing. "I can excite the electrons in the air molecules around me. Kinda gives off my own personal Northern Lights. I get laid *so much* because of it."

Steve rubbed his head. Heath wasn't lying about his ability, but he most definitely wasn't getting laid because of it.

"That sounds pretty cool. Can we see it?" Eddie asked.

Heath grinned, and pressed his fingertips together. Small wisps of green, blue, and purple light began to dance in the air around his body.

"Wow," Brix said. "That's sweet."

"That makes *me* want to jump your bones," Eddie added.

Heath snorted, soaking up the praise. He closed his eyes and the swirls of luminescent clouds swelled around him.

Steve covered his mouth to contain his laughter. Eddie was definitely not lying.

"Peck said you became Adapted about three months ago?" Brix asked.

Heath nodded. "Yeah. We knew it was just a matter of time. Peck was more excited to get an R-Skill, but his is so lame. I laugh whenever we bring it up."

The light above the bin Peck was working on switched from red to green and a bell sounded.

"What kind of salt are you making here?" Steve asked. "The blue and white bags we saw on the pallets are for rock salt, but I saw you filling some pink sacks."

The dazzling light show around Heath's skin evaporated into nothing. He craned his head towards Steve with a quizzical look. "Huh?"

Peck approached the table. "These guys are the North Texas RADSA."

Heath looked at him. "Oh. *Oh.*" He looked back at Steve and scratched his head. "It's a culinary salt."

Truth. Steve eyed the monarch butterfly on the side of the barrel. "And what's that you're spraying on it?" he asked.

"Anti-caking agent," Heath said abruptly. "You know, when it rains it pours."

Deception. The man wasn't just wrong, or lying, but lying with the intent to cover up the truth. Just like Phelps had done with the China trade agreement. This was a huge indicator they were truly on to something. But it came with a price. Steve's head screamed in pain. Thick fog descended over his vision. He gasped and doubled over onto the table.

"Woah," one of the workers said. "What's wrong with him?"

A hand patted Steve on the back. "Migraines," the hand's owner said.

More deception. Another dagger behind Steve's eyes. He pounded on the table.

"We'd better get him some fresh air," the voice belonging to the hand said. "Thanks for your time."

"I'm gonna make a phone call, Peck. Show them out," the voice presumably belonging to Heath said.

Steve was pulled to his feet. As he stood, his arm knocked a water bottle over, splashing some cool relief into his face. His vision slowly returned as he and his two companions made their way to the door.

As they stepped out, Peck called from within, "Hope he's okay. Go see Lou in the office if you need an ice pack or something."

Steve turned to say thanks, but his eyes caught on the lettering on the side of the new barrel Heath had rolled out for Peck. Two unbelievable words that further complicated the worst night of Steve's life: Fargo Pharmaceuticals.

CHAPTER 52
GARBAGE GIRL

"C'MON. If you don't want to go see my office, we can do something else," Abby said.

Mary's head drooped. "I don't think I should."

Abby put her hands on her sister's shoulders and attempted to wiggle a little enthusiasm into her. "You look like you need some ice cream. I know I could use some."

Mary looked up and tilted her head. "Abby, it's eight in the morning."

"So?"

"So, I doubt there's anywhere open that actually sells ice cream at this hour. And don't suggest fast food. You know I don't eat that stuff."

"Okay. How about an unreasonably huge breakfast full of carbs and cholesterol instead?"

Mary giggled.

"And *then* ice cream. We can go cruise NorthPark or something. It's not that crowded during the day."

"But my classes..." Mary protested.

Abby scoffed. "I'll text Walter and tell him you're having girl issues. He'll phone in sick for you, no questions asked." Abby smiled, recalling the dozens of times she used that particular routine on her foster father to get out of going to class.

"But Mom..."

"Will understand. Come on, it's not like I'll be able to do this every day for you. Hang out with your big sis."

Mary found a slight smile and nodded.

They stomped out the lingering fires on the ground from Mary's incendiary demonstration of her nascent R-Skill, then set off for a breakfast of eggs, bacon, truancy, and delicate conversation.

An hour ago, when Mary had revealed her ability, Abby felt nothing but excitement. Her enthusiasm was buoyed by an even greater sense of sisterhood than they already shared. Which, by her own estimation, was pretty great already for a cross-cultural foster sisterhood. It might not have worked had their ages been reversed. But being the older, wiser sister had settled and matured Abby in ways she didn't expect. She figured the foster system had hoped it would be a good fit after so many failed attempts to stick her in as the youngest with a larger, more established family. Mary was sweet and gentle. Innocent. Full of the enthusiasm for every day that escaped Abby each morning when her alarm went off. This perspective lifted Abby's spirits any time the two were together. Mary, too, needed what Abby brought to the table. Dogged determination, a healthy dose of skepticism, and an unexpected knack for mathematics. The pair conspired to convince their parents that Mary was a calculus whiz. Abby did her best to make sure Mary had the grades — if not the innate talent — to back that up.

Now, as Abby looked at her sister, all of the can't-wait-for-what's-next, bubbly optimism was gone. The young teen's entire future stood on a precipice.

Mary gazed out of the passenger window, wiping at her eyes. Every so often she sighed.

Abby had to remind herself that she was the one driving and should actually be paying attention to the road. But she kept stealing peeks at her sister. As they sat in silence, Abby understood the dread. She was beginning to feel it too. Mary's R-Skill was a clear Number 3 on the D2S list: "Uncontrollable or wanton destructive force that threatens the safety of people or property."

Even if she had a stranger sitting beside her, Abby would have a hard time making the call to turn that person in for transport to Island-A. She wasn't all that married to the job, though RADSA wasn't without its merits. She got to help a few people. Good pay. Steve. But this was Mary. Her sister. Abby just couldn't do that to her.

Beneath her neatly cut black hair with its streak of purple down the side, Mary's face was pallid. Like she had seen a ghost. A wraith of unattainable hopes and dreams threatened to haunt her for the rest of her existence as she baked away in the tropical sun, fearful of her neighbors and what they could do. Her future up in smoke, like the patch of recently roasted grass in her backyard.

By the time they had reached the nearest breakfast place and Abby had ordered the coronary skillet loaded with eggs, cheese, potatoes and bacon, her appetite was long gone. Replaced by a rancid pit of inevitability that Mary would sooner or later find herself alone in the hold of a military cargo plane on her way to the island. She did her best to put on a brave face.

"It's okay, Mary. You *can* control it, right?"

"I guess," Mary said, nursing her orange juice.

"Then we keep it a secret. RADSA has no way to find out about it if no one brings you forward."

"And you're not going to?"

"I would never do that!"

Mary folded her arms. "Isn't it your job? Didn't your team send that girl with the mind powers to Island-A?"

Abby stretched her neck and held out her palms. "Hey, I didn't want that. I hate the island. It fucking sucks."

"Language," scolded her fourteen-year-old sister.

Abby smirked. "That girl, Nona. She was nice. But she fu— screwed up. She used her ability in public, in a manner that couldn't be confused with anything else but a Number 4." She took a sip of Dr Pepper.

"Number 4?"

"It's the fourth item on the D2S - the Dangers to Society list that RADSA says require relocation to the island."

Mary's eyes grew wide.

"You've never seen it? I figured it'd be part of social studies or something by now."

Her sister shook her head and cringed. "What number am I?"

"Number 3." Abby repeated the line from the list. "But you can control it." She gestured around the mostly empty restaurant. "No one getting cooked here."

Tears threatened to escape Mary's eyes again. "Yeah, but…"

"Maybe a number five. But it doesn't matter." Abby got up and switched to Mary's side of the booth. "We just gotta keep it a secret. You've kept plenty of mine over the years. Please trust that I will keep yours." She put a reassuring arm around Mary's shoulders that evolved into a full-on hug, full of tears, back pats, and sisterly love.

"Thank you, Abby," Mary whispered.

Abby's appetite returned after the pep talk. Mary's not so much, but she did manage to down half her stack of cinnamon and raisin French toast and some bacon. They caught up on the news in their lives. Mary gushed about her K-Pop obsession, Pop-Wing-Flight, a band full of the most beautiful boys she'd ever seen. And they were such great singers! Abby talked about working for RADSA, leaving out the part about how she ended up there in the first place. Bile tickled the back of her throat when her mind briefly turned to Tyson. She forced it down. Abby brought up Steve, described his features in detail, and gushed over the feel of the kiss they shared and that they knew it couldn't go further. And then Steve's departure.

Abby swallowed her disappointment there. Beyond losing a potential love interest, she had lost a friend when Steve left the team. Sure, she liked the rest of the team well enough — well, not Gigi — but she and Steve got along in a way that was rare for her. And she didn't like that he wasn't texting her, but she understood it. Kinda.

"Any boys in your life?" Abby asked, hoping to change the subject.

Mary rolled her eyes. "Please. Boys my age are idiots. I'd rather practice my violin."

Abby laughed, then picked up the check as the waitress dropped it off.

"That's a first," Mary said with a raised eyebrow, stashing her own debit card.

"RADSA pays well," Abby shrugged.

"Yeah, but at what cost? I don't think I could be part of sending people to the island."

An unexpected rise in her pulse compelled Abby to defend her new employer. "They're actually really nice to the other Adapted we meet. Nona was the very first in North Texas to have to go to the island. Some people kinda have to go."

Mary smirked, unconvinced.

"Well, if you won't take my word for it, maybe you'll be convinced with some ice cream."

"I doubt it."

Abby grumbled.

"But," Mary shrugged. "You can use that fat paycheck to buy me off with some new headphones."

Both grinned.

———

At Mary's favorite mall, NorthPark Center, Abby smiled wide at the glistening floors and lush flower beds every few yards down the main corridors. As a young adolescent bouncing from foster home to foster home, she had always imagined herself part of the mall going crowd some day, hanging out with friends until the security guards kicked them out on a nightly basis. But that vision never materialized as she had neither the right social circles nor sufficient funds. And Betty insisted on going with Mary to any mall, so Abby graciously declined most trips. She was eager to make up for lost time with a little retail therapy for Mary, who had shaken her dour mood and was bouncing from storefront to storefront, making a mental list of every shop she wanted to visit. But they were on a mission to visit the always-busy Apple store first.

The girls busied themselves playing with the latest iPhone models while waiting for their turn with a sales associate. Whoever deigned to call these buffoons "geniuses" had never met Mary. She was a bona fide computer whiz. Abby had suggested numerous times that Mary create an app or develop a simple game or something to make some spending money. Mary always replied that her interest in computers and software was in the challenge. She didn't want to end up as a code jockette in a cubicle farm for the rest of her life. Abby couldn't argue with that.

Mary got a new pair of noise-cancelling earbuds. Abby got a pair too because why the hell not? She could afford them now.

"Are you ready for that ice cream yet?" Abby asked after they left the store.

Mary paused in thought. "No, but I could use some new shoes." She had a wry smile.

Abby chuckled. "Girl, you're gonna milk this for all I'm worth, aren't you?"

Mary shrugged. "I'm just trying to figure out who the impostor is that's taken over my sister."

Shoes and workout clothes. Two new outfits Mary would no doubt grow out of in a year. Various face creams from a half dozen places, not that Mary's complexion needed them. They racked up a bill that the pre-RADSA Abby would have choked over. She was feeling a little pinched in her pocket every time she pulled out her credit card, but she thought, *Fuck it. Mary's worth it. I don't mind eating ramen.*

"Okay," Mary said, two hours later and hands full of shopping bags. "I'm ready for ice cream now."

Abby breathed a sigh of financial relief and led her sister to the gelato stand at the corner of the second-floor food court. Mary ordered a scoop each of strawberry and mango sorbets. Abby opted for a cookies and cream milkshake. They found a table and giggled as Mary struggled to settle all the shopping bags into a single chair.

"Abby, thank you for this." Mary again had tears in her eyes, but Abby could tell they were happy tears this time. "I mean, thanks for all this," Mary gestured to the bags. "But also for being here. For having faith in me. My future. It means a lot."

"You're welcome, sis." Abby smiled, fighting back tears of her own joy. "We really ought to hang out more. I'm actually quite a cool person."

"A wardrobe consisting of nothing but rock concert t-shirts doesn't make you cool."

"Perhaps, but it certainly doesn't hurt." Abby banished fake dust off her black Muse t-shirt featuring a multicolored depiction of human brain pathways.

"Today fills your cool meter forever."

"Aw," Abby said. Her tears were close. She reached out for a hug and Mary stood to deliver.

"Ooh!" Mary said, perking her head up.

"What? Something else to top off my cool meter?"

"Yeah!" Mary pointed at a store down the hall. "I want some bath bombs."

Abby gagged. "You like that stuff? I can't stand going in there. I come out feeling like I have to sneeze for like an hour."

"Yeah. So what if I want to smell like flowers and shit? You should try it."

Abby swatted Mary on the shoulder. "Language!"

They finished their ice cream, grabbed their bags, and headed off to visit one last store.

While happy to splurge on her sister today, Abby insisted that if she had to bear the cost of today's retail excess, Mary would have to carry all of the bags. Which she did happily, but not without struggling against the bulk of the straps in each hand. Of course, being the big sister she was, Abby felt obliged to bump into Mary at random intervals, knocking a bag or two to the floor in the process. They both laughed at the absurd joy of it.

Sweet needles of perfume from their destination struck Abby's nostrils from fifty feet away. Full of intensely-perfumed soaps, bath bombs, soaking salts, and lotions, close-up, the boutique was a full-on olfactory assault for anyone walking by, let alone those brave enough to dare enter. The lunch hour had arrived, and with it, a small surge of shoppers now freed from their desks or morning commitments. Whereas the store would have been empty at ten in the morning, it had half a dozen shoppers milling about when Abby and Mary walked in.

Abby fanned her hand over her face. "Oof, how do you stand this stuff?" She sniffed a pink-and-purple bath bomb called 'Evening Lotus' and dropped it back in the crate. "Blech."

Mary cocked her head and stuck her tongue out. "Some people actually like to smell nice, instead of whatever it is you wash yourself with. You do bathe, right?"

Abby socked Mary in the shoulder, who gleefully dropped her bags and started sniffing everything in sight. *After five minutes in here, my nose won't work for a week*, Abby thought. She followed Mary around at a distance, allowing her mallrat sister to shop as she was wont to do. Like a cat in a mouse store, Mary bounced and pounced around, dazzled by each new find. Abby gave up pursuit and returned to the edge of the store, thankful for the faint whiffs of unadulterated air from the mall's central corridor.

"What do ya think of this one?" Mary asked, darting over with a mottled purple brick of soap.

Abby recoiled as it was thrust in her face. "Uh, it's… potent." She pushed the soap away. "Is that… lavender?" she guessed.

"No silly, blueberry macaron."

Abby chuckled and smacked her head. "Of course, what was I thinking?" She was thinking, *I can't tell the difference between any of these!*

"Yeah, isn't it great?" Mary said. She jammed the soap against her nose and pulled in as deep a breath as her small frame could contain. Her eyes crossed and she grinned, like she was swooning over her favorite K-Pop singer.

Over Mary's head, Abby saw a familiar face standing at the entrance at the other side of the store. Gigi. She looked to be in a heated discussion with someone. "What the hell is *she* doing here?"

Mary turned to look, soap still crammed up her nose. "Who?" Then she sneezed.

CHAPTER 53
BOUNCY

"WHY ARE you so bent out of shape over this?" Kendra asked. "I had you pegged for someone a little more savvy to the way Hollywood operates. Are you upset I'll be the winner? You should be happy for me."

Halfway through inhaling the dreamy, nigh-intoxicating lavender scent from a pair of flower-shaped bath bombs, Gigi spluttered, then shot eye daggers at her friend. "Fuck you Kendra, I don't want a damn handout. You know me better than that."

"Sure, but you kinda asked me to," Kendra said nonchalantly, inspecting a block of soap from the crate next to Gigi. "You've gotta understand there's an expiration on your ability to establish a lasting career in Hollywood. I was doing you a favor. You're not getting any younger."

Gigi had to swallow her laugh. Kendra was hardly one to speak about a successfully launched acting career. She was a hand model! Having the face and body for modeling or Hollywood didn't matter if she did nothing with them. The only screen time her face had recorded in the past half year was as a background extra for an LA Fitness gym commercial. She had 1.53 seconds of standing behind the main actors, toweling off fake sweat at a three-quarters profile in tight workout attire. Hardly worth mentioning, though Kendra made sure to mention it to anyone she could. Gigi rubbed her forehead and could feel the lines in her furrowed brow. She'd have to spend extra time on her skin routine this week.

Kendra, standing there with her perfectly tan skin, flowing yellow sundress, and platinum blond locks, gave off the air of supreme disinterest in the situation, or her friend.

"What's with this attitude? I thought we were best friends." Gigi said.

"We are," Kendra said, suddenly seeming more aware of the conversation. "Listen, don't do the show if you don't want to. You won't hurt my feelings. I was just trying to help."

Gigi put her hand on Kendra's shoulder. "All the shit with the show, I get. I do. Maybe I'll still do it." She stepped closer. "But why in the world won't you tell me what your R-Skill is?"

Kendra looked away.

A tinge of worry pulled at Gigi's temple. Maybe Kendra had lied before. "I've got to ask you again. Your ability isn't… on the list, is it?"

Kendra whipped her head around, eyes wide. "No! No, no, no…" She shrugged off Gigi's hand and took a few steps away.

"It's just… not special."

"What?"

"My ability. The R-Skill. It's silly. Superficial, like me, if my therapist is to be believed."

"So what's the issue? I don't see why you can't tell me."

"I can't do anything remarkable." She turned to face Gigi. "Not like you. Or your RADSA friends."

Friends. That was funny. Gigi hadn't ever thought of them in that way.

"You're all so special," Kendra said. "What each of you can do has meaning. Purpose. You're each useful in some way. I was so disappointed after my interview with your boss and he told me he didn't think there would be a place for me on your team."

"Ben interviewed you?"

"I asked him to keep it private. I've been so jealous of your team. Of you, Geeg."

Jealous? Of me? Gigi thought. That was the first time in the two decades of knowing Kendra that she had ever admitted, or even given the impression of being jealous of Gigi. "Kendra, I'm…"

"I can turn my skin… shiny. That's it."

"Huh?" Gigi asked, tilting her head.

"Silvery, like a mirror."

"That doesn't sound too bad. There are so many worse R-Skills out there."

"Yeah, but I wanted to *do* something with it, you know? Join your team. Do something good. Like that Abby girl saving that boy on the bridge."

Gigi sloughed off the Abby comment. Though still pissed at her friend, Gigi bristled with excitement to share a deeper bond. "Can I see it?"

"Here? I'm not… out, yet."

"C'mon, I'm dying to see!"

Kendra gave in and tossed aside the soap in her hand. She angled her hands downward, away from her sides, and put her feet apart. Small blotches of silvery, metallic color began to appear, like she was standing in mercury rain. The effect spread as the little patches coalesced into larger spots, eventually covering the entirety of her skin. Her eyes, lips, and hair stayed the same, but now Kendra was completely silver under her yellow dress. She shone. The lights from the store and mall corridor reflected off the mirror surface. The effect was dazzling. Radiant.

At once, Gigi understood how Kendra would have been pegged to win the stupid reality non-competition. She was beauty incarnate. "It's— you're beautiful."

Kendra's form glistened as she smiled and swayed slightly.

Someone inside the store sneezed.

A massive beam of flame lanced across the store, obliterating everything it touched. It swung wildly, disintegrating chunks of wall, glass, and…

"Kendra!" Gigi screamed.

The column of fire swung wildly and hit her best friend in the chest. Kendra was cut in half. What remained of her arms, shoulders, neck and head flopped down onto the remnants of her lower half, which then crumpled together in a grotesque heap on the marble floor. The shining, metallic color of Kendra's skin vanished, replaced by the usual tan. Except at the edges of her two halves. Those were seared black, completely cauterized and sealed to a crisp. Kendra's eyes blinked once and her mouth dropped open, offering a silent, airless scream. Then she was gone.

Gigi's squeal of horror was short-lived, as she retched a second after it started. Green smoothie splattered all over her friend and the floor. Tears poured from her eyes, and she wrenched her head away from the corpse.

The beam continued its destructive path, narrowly missing Gigi on a second pass on its way to carving a gash through the upper ceiling of the store and through the roof of the mall. Shattered glass rained down on shoppers from three stories above. As abruptly as it came, it was gone, replaced by a timid yelp and a gasp from across the store.

Gigi wiped the tears, snot, and smoothie from her face and looked into the store at the wreckage. The floor was awash with a pastel slime of melted soaps and exploded lotions. Flakes of roasted ceiling detritus descended like snow. A stunned little Asian girl stood at the opposite entrance with her hand over her mouth, staring wide-eyed at Gigi. Next to her was Abby.

CHAPTER 54
THE SLEUTH

THE PICTURE WAS CLEARER. Also profoundly darker. Steve set his phone down on the seat. His empty stomach churned, ready to spew up a phantom all-you-can-eat buffet meal. And it wasn't from Eddie's driving skills.

He chose the back seat for the car ride home, wanting to spend the time investigating Fargo Pharmaceuticals. Desperate fingers tapped away at his phone. Instead of discovering something that would connect the research that Fargo did with salt additives in a benign way, he found what he was dreading: Fargo was into bleeding-edge gene manipulation. There was no mention anywhere that could link Fargo to producing chemicals for salt, or any other kind of food-related substance.

Steve was certain they had just stumbled into how the Adapted were actually being created. It had nothing to do with the UDO or radiation at all, but a chemical added to salt that was used in food preparation. It could be anywhere. Everywhere.

The chemical came from Fargo Pharmaceuticals. And with that, came a direct connection to the president of the United States, under whom the entire Adapted era began. The CEO of Fargo Pharmaceuticals, and the president — two fathers that both lost sons in the military in an embassy attack. The embassy whose ambassador was now the head of RADSA, an agency both Peck and Heath seemed to have dealt with before. When it rains, it pours.

He picked up a Salt Palace receipt and wrote three sentences on the back.

"Brix, read this. Say them exactly like I wrote them," Steve said.

Brix took the slip of paper and looked at it. "Holy shit," he muttered, showing it to Eddie.

Eddie glanced at it, then looked back at Steve, letting the car drift into the rumble strip on the side of the road. "*Amigo.* You know I was just kidding about the president."

Steve rubbed his head, praying the pain would come. "Just read it."

Brix exchanged a look with Eddie, then cleared his throat. "An additive in table salt is what causes the Adapted. Frannie Gustafson knows about the additive. Lawrence Phelps conspired to have his son killed to help get elected president."

Truth. Truth. Truth.

Steve thought he'd feel sick, but the waves of radiant pleasure washing over his brain lifted his spirits. Never before had his R-Skill created such bliss. But it was only momentary. His own personal connection to this was far too close for comfort. Phelps. Gustafson. Maybe even McNamara. All involved in the deaths of Milo and Quentin. The sheer notion of it was too surreal. Beyond that was the problem of how to put an end to the president's scheme. Despite Phelps' popularity, and measurably successful administration, this kind of tyranny could not be countenanced. Steve was still a marine.

His phone buzzed with a text message from Bailey. He took a quick look at it, then the phone and his heart both hit the floor.

CHAPTER 55
BOUNCY

KENDRA WAS GONE. Dead, instantly. Right as they were making a breakthrough that would have finally eliminated that pervasive "is she really my best friend" feeling always lingering in the back of Gigi's mind. That final hurdle of understanding and trust. Obliterated by an Adapted teenager hopped up on luxury cosmetic perfume.

Gigi was so stunned by the sight of her friend lanced in two that Abby had to drag her and the other girl Mary away from the store. The trio carefully avoided the ensuing chaos and swarm of police, then Abby shoved them into a gaudy orange Subaru and raced to Warehouse 11. That the garbage girl stayed so composed was… unexpected. The ride took over half an hour. Not a word was spoken. Gigi was as numb then as she was now, sitting on a sofa watching Abby cry. The shock of what happened locked out any ability to sense anything. All she registered was the memory of the stench. Roasted human flesh mixed with all manner of molten lavender, fig, and sandalwood soaps.

For most people, tears would be falling after losing their best friend. Gigi's eyes were as dry as late July. Too stunned. Too pissed. All that effort put into her friendship with Kendra, gone. They had known each other nearly their entire lives. Now, who the hell would she go shopping with?

But why was Abby so beaten up about it? She sat bawling on the sofa along the adjacent wall, stealing looks at Ben's office door between wails. She didn't know Kendra. And it's not like this was Abby's first dead body.

The door to Ben's office opened, and he stepped out. A deep grimace marred his beautiful face. "Alright. Transport is lined up at Naval Air Station Fort Worth. Mary's escort will be here in less than an hour." He walked over to Abby and cupped her shoulder. "Go check on your sister while I call your parents."

"Will they get to see her?" Abby asked through her tears.

Ben shook his head. "I'm afraid not. RADSA has a strict no-visitors policy for those headed to the island." He checked his watch. "It's about time to press the button again."

Abby looked at him, horrified.

"It's for our safety, and hers. She can come out for a few minutes after she's had another dose of the gas," Ben said.

Abby's face reddened as she turned, defeated, and trudged over to the isolation tank in the far corner of the warehouse.

Gigi's skin rippled with goosebumps as she watched Abby press the big red button, gassing the occupant inside and giving off a warbling, electronic ping that echoed through the warehouse. *That's her sister?* "Holy shit," she muttered.

Abby's most recent stop in the foster system was with a Korean family, but until now it sounded like a joke. Why would Abby put up with such an unusual family pairing? Unless she was utterly desperate. But Abby struck her as someone that always had agency over where her life was headed. Until now.

Gigi gawked as Abby unlocked the door to the tank, then escorted the dazed teenager in her tidy school uniform over to the sofas. Mary flopped into her sister's lap. Abby promptly crumpled on top of her, and they both bawled. These two meant the world to each other.

Every molecule of air left Gigi's lungs. Her mouth hung open. The door to Rice's office slammed shut but barely registered more than a dull thud. Time slowed. With each wail, Abby and Mary convulsed as if they were hit by bullets.

Pinpricks of phosphenes danced in Gigi's eyes as she unintentionally asphyxiated herself. She marveled at the depth of emotion these two felt for each other, developed over just a few short years. What these two had was something she had never known. Not with her parents. Not with Kendra.

She blinked, wrenched her eyes away from the sobbing sisters, and managed to coax her body into breathing again. The gasp of cold air was as good as a slap to her face. Kendra wasn't the only victim here. Her parents and Gigi weren't the only ones to know loss over the incident. Mary was as good as gone. Off to Island-A. Abby had lost her little sister.

A tickling buzz in her leg pocket pulled Gigi from her stupor. She checked her phone for the first time in what felt like hours and saw only two notifications waiting. A voicemail from an unknown number, and a text message asking if she had listened to the voicemail. She put her phone to her ear and heard LeAnne Clarke's voice.

"Hey Gigi. This is my private number. Don't give it out. I heard about what happened to poor Kendra. I'm so sorry for your loss. Um, this may seem too soon, but as you know, the show must go on. I've spoken to Carlo over at A-Space, and, after quite a lot of lobbying, for which I am *very* proud of myself, I've convinced him to offer you Kendra's spot on the show. As in, the top spot, if you catch my drift. Call me ASAP."

Gigi's eyes shot wide open. This was it. The gates to stardom were wide open. And she didn't do a thing to make it happen. She was about to play the recording again when the door to Ben's office opened, and he gestured at her to enter.

"Hey Gigi, let's talk a minute," he said.

She stuffed her phone back in its pocket and followed him inside.

"How are you feeling?" Ben asked after he shut his office door.

Gigi eased into the sofa and patted the seat next to her, working hard to contain her smile.

"Gigi, we uh, can't—"

"Relax, I know. My best friend was just killed, and I just got some life-changing news. I could use a shoulder to lean on."

"Oh. Sure."

Ben cautiously approached the sofa and sat a safe, managerial distance away from Gigi. It lasted all of half a second as she immediately scooched next to him and plunked her head against his muscular shoulder. The memory of her hands exploring every inch of his sculpted arms brought a smile to her face. She welcomed the heat radiating off his body. How great would it be to just tear off their clothes and engage in memory-erasing sex right now? But she knew they couldn't do it again. And she had more important things to think about.

Ben heaved a great sigh. "I can't help but feel I could have prevented this."

She barely listened, lost between her memories of Kendra and visions of A-Space stardom. "Hmm."

"She desperately wanted to join the team. I said her R-Skill just wasn't what we were looking for right now. Very pretty though."

Gigi stared off into the space beyond the door, dreaming of being photographed and interviewed at red carpet premieres. "Yeah. It was. *She* was."

"Yeah."

They sat in silence. Ben's words slowly worked their way into Gigi's consciousness. The red carpet cameras in her imagination all turned from her to point at a shining figure of silver emerging from a limousine. "How long have you known about her?"

"I interviewed her weeks ago. She asked me not to tell you."

Gigi turned to look at Ben. "Why not?"

"Something about not wanting to disappoint you."

Disappoint me? she thought. "Huh." Not once did Gigi ever get the impression Kendra was worried about disappointing her. Over anything.

"I take it she didn't tell you?"

"I only recently found out. She wouldn't show me what her R-Skill was. Not until today. She did, right before…"

"Ah. Sorry. Are you feeling okay? You are very calm, considering what happened."

Gigi closed her eyes, and searched for the right word as she curled her hands around Ben's bicep. "I feel… conflicted."

"Oh."

Wails from Abby filtered through the office walls.

Gigi frowned as she thought of the two sisters outside. "Yeah, she was my friend, and yeah, I'm gonna miss hanging out with her. But… we weren't ever as connected as Abby and Mary out there."

"Family can be like that."

Gigi thought about her upbringing as an only child. Endless nights spent alone with a phone and TV for company. Years full of afternoons abandoned at her gymnastics center to practice nigh-unsupervised while Mom shopped with her friends and Dad played golf with his clients. Her only reliable day-to-day family interaction came from the bathroom mirror.

"My parents treated me like a social status checkbox. I got everything I wanted growing up, except what those two out there are about to lose." She sighed. "Have you ever felt like that about someone?"

"I did. Until she ruined my face."

She smiled at him and cupped his cheek. "Looks perfect to me."

Her phone vibrated, no doubt LeAnne checking in again. Gigi would have to leave the team to do the show. Or take a leave of absence or something. She wouldn't get to see Ben's face. That prospect wasn't awesome. But then, perhaps Ben wouldn't be so uptight about getting together if she wasn't working for him.

He flinched beneath her hand as if he was chewing on words, but none came out. That perfect face, of course, was the product of his tampering with how she perceived his face. That she knew he had done it didn't change the impact of his chiseled jaw, or his muscled frame. A frame she wouldn't mind clinging to at the season premiere of A-Space All-Stars.

More crying washed through the door like the waves of an incoming tide. It dissolved the sandcastles of celebrity building in her imagination.

Gigi sat up and sighed. "I've never known what those two have, and they've only known each other for — what, three years? How does that even happen?"

Ben smirked. "It takes a lot of commitment. I'm surprised you never got there with Kendra. You've always been willing to take on whatever effort was required to get what you wanted. In fact, you've always sought out that work. That's why I wanted you on the team."

"I guess I didn't know what I was missing."

"Well, if you ever get there with a friend or significant other, it's worth it."

As she looked at Ben, she wondered if he and she might ever get there. Probably not. She'd settle for another romp or ten in the sack though. Which she knew would never come.

A fresh peal of crying buffeted the room from beyond the door.

"Poor Abby," Ben said. "I hope she's got some friends to lean on. Her parents told me they don't want to speak to her."

"Ouch." Gigi thought back to the few conversations she'd had with Abby. She didn't seem to have much of a social life at all. Just the Tyson guy whom she killed, a vacant chatroom on A-Space, and maybe Steve, if he was even still around. No friends. Which figured, given the amount of work it would take to build a special bond with someone like Abby.

But then, Mary had done it.

Gigi couldn't believe the words about to come out of her mouth. "I'll make sure she's okay."

His eyebrows raised. "That's… good. Thanks Gigi."

Ben's phone beeped and he checked the message. "Shit. Transport's here already. That was fast." He stood up and offered Gigi a hand to her feet. "You said you had some life-changing news too? What's that about?"

"Oh. It may turn out to be no big deal. I'll tell you later."

She followed Ben out of his office, and texted LeAnne as she walked. "Sorry. Going to have to pass. Have something more important to do."

Ben walked Abby and Mary to where a tan, wedge-shaped military transport was waiting outside. Gigi watched from the warehouse door as Mary was carefully loaded on board. Neither sister stopped crying.

Abby turned her back to the transport as it began to rumble away. Gigi rushed up to her with an emphatic embrace. Abby returned the hug, and being nearly a foot taller, plopped her head on top of Gigi's and sobbed.

Finally, Gigi's tears arrived.

CHAPTER 56
THE ADJUSTER

BEN WAS at a loss for words. Abby's sister was now on her way to Island-A. *Of all the people,* he thought. The four remaining team members sat in a semicircle in front of his desk. Their faces read forlorn, disappointed, confused, and — he didn't even have a word to describe the strange mix of rapture and horror on Gigi's face.

Abby, Bailey, Zeke, and Gigi sat and waited in silence for him to address the colossal dead elephant in the room. Abby had fucked up, badly, and, by extension, the whole team had fucked up. Which meant he had fucked up.

He should be fired for this. Hell, they all should. Accountability had to start somewhere, right? Of course, no one in the room was going to lose their job. He had already taken care of the opinions of the local authorities. The official story was that Abby's sister had just developed her R-Skill, and Abby did the correct thing in immediately bringing Mary to RADSA to avoid further danger to others. Neither Mary nor Abby could say otherwise. Ben had told Director Gustafson the same story. Since she didn't know any better, he didn't feel the need to use his R-Skill on her. The option was there if it became necessary, but he'd been using it way too much lately and was dreading another large-scale disaster like the one he had caused with Steve.

The fact they were in this mess simply made his blood boil. Ben let his anger simmer while he closed his eyes and attempted to summon the right words. His team had already been split in two, and now sat on the precipice of completely falling into the abyss. A black eye for RADSA's reputation and potentially risking the lives of Adapted all over North Texas with their absence. He opened his eyes, and concentrated all of his fury into the loudest, angriest sigh he could muster. Then he stood, padded deliberately in front of his desk, and sat down on the edge. He looked directly at Abby as he spoke.

"We have to be better than this," Ben began.

He let those words soak in. Abby was pale. Gigi's eyebrows curled up with concern. Bailey simply had her arms folded. She'd know the simplest path through the lecture to come would be to just sit there and take it. Zeke sat on his hands, sneaking glances to either side of him for a cue as to how to react.

"I understand that responsibility hasn't always been your thing," Ben said. "But a big part of our job is to protect the community, Adapted or not. Today, we failed to do that job."

Gigi opened her mouth, but Ben snapped up a silencing palm.

"Yes, this failure was the result of an individual's choice." Ben gestured wide with his arms. "But we are a team. And as such, any of our actions speak for all of us."

Gigi stole a glance at Abby before looking at Ben. "Are we going to lose our jobs over this?"

She meant Abby, of course. But the distress on her face told Ben she wasn't rooting for such an outcome. At least, not at that moment.

"No," Ben said. "I've already spoken with the director about the path forward. Our team will continue to go out and do our work."

He was lying. Without Steve in the room, he could. Frannie only knew the official story. As far as she was concerned, Abby did the right thing by bringing Mary in when she did. Kendra's death was merely an unfortunate part of life in the Adapted age.

"If it will help, I can just quit," Abby said, eyes fixed on the floor. "I think that may be the best for the team."

There was the compassion that had gotten them into this mess. In her way, Abby was still just trying to help. The other three looked at her with concern, but Abby wasn't looking up.

Ben shook his head. "No, you can't."

Abby looked up at him, tears and confusion in her eyes.

"You're going to spend the rest of your life making up for this mistake, Abby. But I didn't have to tell you that."

She sniffled and wiped at her tears with her shirt as she nodded once and returned her gaze to the floor.

"No one here is better suited to that than you." He tapped her shoe to get her attention. "Abby, heaving huge chunks of a fallen building is impressive. But your compassion is your true gift. That is why you're on this team. Like with Mrs. Tsai. Your decision to fight for her was, in my view, the right judgement call. We need to be compassionate to every Adapted possible, and I expect you to lead us in that regard for a long time."

Abby attempted a smile, but only managed to look like her cheeks were stuffed with cotton balls.

Ben sighed. "Your compassion is also what got us into this predicament. You — we all — have to be smarter. Myself included." His throat clenched tight on the duplicity, though he spared Gigi a knowing glance, because she didn't know anything about their second indiscretion at the moment. A cool sip of water provided no relief to his shame. "The impact of each and every choice we make reaches far into the unknown."

And now came the point that he was dreading. What other choice did he have? He had the power to put protections into place that would have prevented Kendra's death. His own inaction was as much to blame as anything. He swallowed the lump in his throat and cracked his knuckles. "Do not discuss what happened with Mary and Kendra with anyone but me. If anyone comes across someone with an R-Skill on the Dangers to Society list, you are to immediately contact me. We must serve the safety of our community first, and that sometimes means we will have to send someone to Island-A. It is the reality of our world."

Ben nearly choked on his own hypocrisy. He should be on that plane next to Mary Kim right now if he truly believed the words dribbling out of his mouth. Here he was, a so-called Danger to Society, lecturing others on the importance of sending his ilk to the island. Instead, he twisted his subordinates' minds so that they had no other choice but to comply. Ben looked at each of their faces in turn. He had used his ability on all of them. To help them in some cases, but mostly to protect his own skin. His scar. Now they all could see it, except Gigi by her own request, and it was like he was standing naked right in front of them, awaiting their assessment on all his flaws. With Gigi, he had to fix the post-tryst protections in her mind whose unintentional removal had led to their second ill-advised, but thoroughly enjoyable fling. Which she didn't remember at all now. He would continue to give into that temptation, and it would only lead to trouble. For the rest, how long before one of them ran into someone else he had hidden his scar from, and he'd have to fix another cognitive incongruency? It would be simpler to just go back to the way things were. What would be the harm in hiding his scar again? He ignored the tension-built pressure in his joints and returned to the stern facade he had put on to deliver this disingenuous lecture.

"Capture is the first of the four-Cs for a reason. It is vitally important. Imagine the public outcry of FIGHT — well, what FIGHT used to be — if they caught wind of what really happened to Kendra. We'd have protests outside Mrs. Tsai's tea shop. Parents would demand that Mrs. Taliveras and Mr. Cordday be removed from their school. Denied their livelihoods. Colin Jockery would be on the radio every morning spewing venom at every Adapted he hears about. Us included. The hard work that President Phelps has invested in creating an environment of tolerance and even acceptance of the Adapted could be completely undone if we fail to make a critical choice."

Ben gestured around the room at his team. "We are indeed ambassadors of the Adapted, but we are the first line of defense against Dangers to Society. Now I want you all to go through the RADSA training courses again. Abby and Gigi, I expect your incident reports before you leave for the day."

He sighed as the team glanced uncomfortably at Abby.

"Lastly, Director Gustafson has informed me that our former teammate Steve Palmer has been getting into trouble, including trespassing and violating his confidentiality agreement. I want you all to take some zip-tie restraints wherever you go. If any of you come in contact with Steve, you are to detain him and notify me and the RADSA tip line immediately. Dismissed." Ben said, barely believing the words he just spoke.

The team stared gap-mouthed at him in silence for several uncomfortable moments before slowly rising and filing out one by one. Having to go through a handful of training videos again wouldn't be fun, but as far as punishments went, it was gentler than getting tickled with a peacock feather. No one paused on their way out. All but one looked at him with confusion and bewilderment as they left. Abby just stared at the floor.

His stomach churned with self-loathing. Ben quickly left his office and made a bee-line across the warehouse to the exit to find the nearest bar and a stiff drink.

CHAPTER 57
GARBAGE GIRL

"I'LL BE OKAY."

Abby set her phone down after checking to see if her sister had texted anything else since departing for the island. Mary's practically dismissive last message was now hours old. Every muscle in Abby's body was tense, the tight skin on her face on the verge of splitting. At times like this, she wished she was into drinking or weed — anything to put a wet blanket on her brain as it darted between remorse, rage, fear, and self-loathing. Alas, her shirking of responsibility had never crossed into underage substance abuse. Her recent lapses in judgment were far, far worse. Two dead bodies worse.

Absent any news from Mary, there was nothing else to think about. Steve was gone and hadn't responded to her calls or texts. There was no Tyson to play Xbox with; she always felt unsatisfied playing video games by herself. Watching TV or a movie wouldn't distract her enough to be worth the effort to try. She wasn't looking forward to going to work the next day either. It would be a long time before she'd be able to live down her bad decision.

"Hah." She scoffed at the description. Bad. How much worse a decision could she have made?

She knew better, but Abby couldn't help but think she had missed some crucial decision that could have kept Mary's secret safe. Sure, they could have not played hooky, but then would that sneeze have roasted Mary's entire classroom? Which was worse? Would Mary have sneezed at all had they not gone to that smelly store? Maybe it was the weeds at that construction site that did it, and it was Abby's choice to go there that primed Mary's seasonal allergies and directly led to Kendra's demise.

Abby slunk back into her blue leather sofa and let the vacuum of regret suck her in. So much so that she almost missed the knocking at her door. It was probably her neighbor Valeria wanting help with taking the trash out. Most of the time, Abby found the neighbor's weekly requests nigh invasive, but the single mom's eldest of four, Elena, practically worshipped the ground Abby walked on and she couldn't bring herself to say no. Plus, all she did was heave the trash across the parking lot from the apartment steps. It was still fun to watch.

She opened the door, ready to slip her shoes on, and was instead met by a man in a new black leather jacket and jeans. A man that could use a shave and a haircut. A face with the deepest, most sincere brown eyes she ever had the pleasure of seeing. Eyes she hadn't seen in days. Eyes that shouldn't be there.

"Hey Abby," Steve said, calmly.

"Steve!" Abby said, poking her head out of the door to peer down both sides of the landing outside. It was strange to see him in something other than a business suit. "What are you doing here? RADSA wants you captured. You shouldn't be out in public!"

"I know. But I heard what happened. I had to see if you were okay." He looked over his shoulder down the stairs. "Can I come in?"

Still dazed with surprise and swimming in the dark pools of his eyes, Abby shook some sense into her head. "Yeah, yeah." She grabbed his arm and pulled him inside. "Shoes off. I can't believe you're here. How have you avoided capture all this time?"

Steve smiled, kicking off his sneakers and tossing his leather jacket on the sofa. "You'd be surprised how extensive Eddie's network of biker buddies is. Pretty easy to hide in a motorcycle helmet. How are you holding up, after… everything?"

Any other day, she would have been quick to remark on his t-shirt with the Morton Salt girl on it of all things and the word 'SALTY'. Not today. Not on the worst day she could remember. Steve was the first guest she'd had at her apartment since the accident with Tyson. Technically it was his second visit, but she barely remembered the first and her opinion of him had certainly changed since then. A tiny star of hope poked through the black curtain of dread draped over her heart. Hope that could be snuffed out at any moment if Steve wasn't careful. Abby folded her arms. "You didn't have to come all the way back here to ask me that. You could have just texted."

"Gotta keep my phone off. And you know written words don't do anything for me. I have to see the person talking."

"Riiiiiiight." Abby shifted her weight and raised one eyebrow. "Maybe I don't want you to see me talking."

One side of Steve's face winced. "Riiiiiiight," he mimed.

"Dammit. Sorry."

Steve shook the pain off, attempted a serious face, and pursed his lips. "Okay. Out with it."

"I'm…" Abby stopped when Steve preemptively recoiled, gnashing her teeth. She flung her hands out, then flopped them to her sides. "I'm miserable, okay? Life sucks! I failed to turn a dangerous Adapted in and as a result got Gigi's best friend killed, of all people, inflicted probably millions in property damage, and then to top it off, had to send my own sister off to the fucking island. Rice put me on leave to consider my decision making and commitment to RADSA. How the fuck else am I supposed to feel, huh?"

"Well, let's see." Steve wiped a hand across his face in an attempt to hide a slight smile, obviously appreciative of the honesty. "Guilty, angry, betrayed, disgusted, relieved, aimless — some combination of all those?"

"Fucking despondent, that's what."

He stepped closer to her and put a hand on her arm.

"I'm sorry. I wish I had some sage advice."

His thumb pressed on the bare skin under the sleeve of her black Soundgarden t-shirt, moving slightly side to side, sending shivers down her spine. The sensation was welcome, but surprising. He stared at her with the most sincere, warm, affectionate smile she could remember ever receiving.

She put her hand on his. "I… was under the impression you weren't interested in me."

"I said it was a bad idea."

"And I said I was okay with us being just friends."

"That's also a bad idea."

"Oh." Abby looked at the carpet for a moment as she revisited their last conversation that night weeks ago at the park, realizing that Steve had the habit of choosing his words very carefully. She looked back at him, heart thumping in her chest. "What do you *want*?"

"I want to help you feel better."

Abby rolled her eyes and groaned. "Golly gee, Wally. Are we going out for milkshakes?"

Steve shrugged. "If that's what you want."

"What do *you* want?"

He took a deep breath and looked straight into her eyes. "I want to rip all your clothes off and stress-test your mattress."

Abby's skin flushed under his grip; goosebumps prickled her skin in anticipation. She grabbed his shirt and pulled his face to hers, mashing their lips together. "That might make me feel a little better."

She lifted his shirt off and raised her arms as he removed hers. They kissed again, hands roaming newly bared skin on their way to frantically remove each other's pants. Abby ran her hand across the contours of the front of Steve's tight, unexpectedly chartreuse boxer-briefs and stifled a laugh.

"What?" Steve's eyes showed a hint of concern.

Abby's eyes widened, realizing the implications of laughing when touching a man's crotch for the first time. She put a hand to her grin. "No, no! It's just — I had you pegged for a conservative plaid boxers kind of guy."

"Oh." Steve shook his head with a relieved smile. "Not comfortable in the slightest. As for the color…" He kissed her again as he grabbed her ass, then said matter-of-factly, "It came in a multi-pack. Costs less per pair."

"Good-looking *and* sensible?!" She pushed him down the hallway to her bedroom. "How is it you haven't been snatched up already?"

"Turns out women don't want a guy that's 100% honest."

"Huh." She shoved him down on her unkempt bed and got on top of him, a big grin on her face. "I wonder what my tolerance is."

———

Abby roamed her hand in slow circles across Steve's bare chest. He was spent. She was satisfied and happily distracted. At least for the moment. Despite the exertion, she had only been able to partially shove aside her scrambled thoughts of Mary, Island-A, and being responsible for yet another person's death.

And for all Steve's passion, he hadn't been completely in the room with her either. "There's something else, isn't there?" she asked.

He sighed. "Yes."

"Out with it."

"You're not going to like it."

She sat up and folded her arms.

"You're *really* not going to like it."

Abby raised her eyebrows. "Out. With. It."

"The Adapted were not caused by the dark object. They're being created by our government by adding some chemical to culinary salt. Frannie knows about it…"

She blinked at him, unable to accept the words. "That's… I don't even know—"

"And Phelps had his son killed in a terrorist attack, just to bolster his election odds. It was my embassy. I was there, Abby. I was there when this all started."

Abby's mouth dropped open. All Steve could say was the truth, but he just said the most impossible thing possible.

"No one is going to believe this. Is there evidence?" she asked.

CHAPTER 58
LUCKY

PRESIDENT PHELPS HAD HOPED he wouldn't have to deliver this message but knew it could be a possibility. He put on his serious face as he stepped up behind the podium in the media room at AT&T Stadium, home of the Dallas Cowboys. He was in the area for a summit of local business leaders, but stopped by the stadium to take a tour, enjoy the artwork, and have his ear bent by the team owner, who was desperate to allow Adapted to play professional sports. Instead, the president was about to deliver a shock to the country.

"My fellow Americans, it is my sad duty to inform you that we have detected three small UDOs that are on a course to impact the United States today. As the tracking of these objects has proved difficult, we cannot say with exact certainty where or when they will hit. However, we anticipate the impacts will be east of Trenton, New Jersey, north of Miami, Florida, and somewhere east of Dallas, Texas, not far from here. This will likely happen within the next few hours."

He sipped his water and gazed directly into the camera. "I advise everyone in those areas to seek disaster shelter immediately until we have confirmation of when and where we can expect the UDOs to hit. Be safe out there. Our thoughts are with you."

The president nodded to Evans, his lead Secret Serviceman, and they began to make their way out of the stadium to the helipad where Marine One was waiting to take off and head east.

CHAPTER 59

THE SLEUTH

COLD DR PEPPER fizzed down Steve's throat, bringing a smile to his face in the midday heat. He didn't care much for soda, but Abby's love for the drink had him craving some sweet refreshment in the sweltering sun. Small pleasures could still bring a microcosm of happiness during the darkness of a mind-boggling conundrum.

He sat on his car's hood in the parking lot of the huge Buc-ee's gas station in Terrell, waiting for Eddie and Brix to arrive. Abby was right. The first step to unraveling the president's farce was to get evidence. That meant another trip to Morton Salt.

But Steve's mind was on Abby and her incredible ordeal with her sister. What an impossible choice. Given that duty had been drilled into him in the marines, he probably wouldn't have made the same call she had. But as more and more Dr Pepper crossed his taste buds, he saw her side more and more.

Of course, that was easy to do now, knowing the entirety of the Adapted era was a fabrication. A designed upheaval of the order of the world and the evolutionary progress of humanity. A lie.

He knew he shouldn't, but after he left Abby's apartment the previous night, he texted her with his plan to retrieve some of the Fargo salt chemical as evidence. He turned off his phone before he got near the motel he was staying at. And before he could see her imminent text that would likely question his sanity. He had his own doubts. Did he really think he could expose Phelps? Put an end to the largest conspiracy humankind has ever suffered? His years as a desk jockey in the marines hadn't exactly prepared him for a cloak and dagger adventure.

As he waited in the heat and his drink ran dry, his doubts only increased. But the familiar grumble of Eddie's motorcycle jarred him free from introspection. He had a mission. He would complete it.

Eddie parked next to Steve and patted him on the back as he pulled off his helmet. "Man, that's some crazy shit about Abby. How is she?" he asked.

Steve shook his head. "In her own words, despondent."

Eddie's eyes widened. "No phone, right? You saw her? What happened to keeping a low profile? You shouldn't be driving this." He pointed to the Camry.

"It's okay, I kept it hidden." Steve turned his head as Brix's black Trans-Am roared into the parking lot and lurched into the adjacent parking spot. "And I don't think we'd all fit in there. Did you bring your guns?"

Eddie patted the sides of his vest.

Brix jumped out of his car. "Did you hear?"

Eddie and Steve exchanged looks. "Hear what?" Steve asked.

"The president just announced three UDOs are coming for the United States! Guess where one is headed."

"Shit!" Steve's eyes bulged. "How soon? We've got to get some of that chemical!"

"Phelps said 'a few hours'. Let's go!"

They piled into Steve's car, and he took off, weaving around semi-trucks and running red lights to get on Interstate 20 towards Grand Saline. Only a handful of cars were headed in the same direction. The other side of the highway was thick with traffic fleeing an impending UDO impact. *They're the sane ones*, Steve thought as he mashed the gas pedal.

Every station on the radio had been interrupted by an emergency broadcast, replaying the president's press conference. Eddie and Brix scoured their phones for news or updates, but all they found was uninformed speculative opinions on the 24-hour news sites. Steve threw caution to the wind, pushing his Camry as fast as the engine would take it.

"You do realize we are about to get crushed by a giant space rock?" Brix asked from the back seat.

Eddie gasped. "The UDO isn't from outer space!"

A relaxing calm came over the tension in Steve's mind. More truth. "I can't believe it. Someone out there can create them," he said. "We have to stop this!"

"And how do you plan on getting the chemical? I'm sure Peck and Heath will be happy to see us," Brix said.

Steve looked at Eddie. "The fastest way would probably be to flash some steel, grab a barrel, and go."

"You don't think they're armed?" Brix scoffed.

Eddie shrugged. "If I were them, I'd have bailed the second Phelps said 'UDO headed east of Dallas'."

Hopefully, Eddie was right. They would find out soon enough. He pushed the Camry as fast as it would go. Traffic on their side of the highway had dwindled to just one other car in the distance. Steve exited onto FM17 and headed north. A trio of weathered pick-up trucks rumbled by in the other direction, each loaded down with as much stuff as possible: suitcases, mounds of clothes, a refrigerator, a dirt bike. One had a pair of goats thrown in with three dogs. Not long after, a small car rounded a corner towing an overloaded trailer behind. The trailer was poorly balanced and swerved in and out of both lanes of the road. Steve slammed the brakes and veered into the shoulder of the road to avoid a collision.

Then it struck. No noise. No warning.

A streak of smoldering black sliced through the sky out of nowhere. It careened into the horizon behind the trees. Right toward Grand Saline.

"Shit!" Steve gasped. He clenched his teeth and gripped the steering wheel, expecting to be vaporized any second.

"Dead! We're dead!" Brix squealed.

Eddie made the sign of the cross and began muttering something in Spanish.

A rumble like distant thunder washed over the car, followed by tremors in the ground.

But that was it. Steve opened his eyes. Waves of heat radiated off the car's hood. The tall grasses along the side of the road waved in the summer breeze.

"I think… we may be okay," Steve said, opening his door and stepping up on the tire for a better look.

Thick clouds of dust curled up above the trees in the distance. Nearby, birds chirped and sang as if nothing extraordinary had just happened.

"How are we not dead?" Brix gasped.

Eddie shook his head.

Steve marveled at how improbable their survival was. Morton Salt, whatever was left of it, was only a few miles away. A large object falling from the upper atmosphere should have created a far larger radius of destruction. "C'mon, let's go see if anything is left," he said.

He hopped off the tire, then froze in his tracks as he looked down the road behind his car. The vehicle that had been the last one going the same direction on I-20 was slowly coming to a halt in the middle of the road. A black Chevy Tahoe, with dark-as-death windows. Government issue. He had driven MacNamara around in one a hundred times.

"Fuck," he muttered under his breath.

The others clung to the far side of the Camry as the Tahoe crawled to a stop and the passenger window rolled down.

"Agent Palmer," Carleton Orton said in a pompous, fake Texas accent. "Fancy meeting three RADSA agents out here in the middle of nothing much." He pulled his aviator sunglasses off and used them to point in the direction of the UDO impact. "Some weather we're havin'."

Sweat rolled down the back of Steve's neck. He opened his mouth but found no words. His lack of discipline in using his car and phone may have put them all in grave danger.

Eddie filled the void. "You can cut the shit, Orton. We don't work for RADSA anymore."

Steve gasped as his head sparked in pain.

Orton clicked his tongue. "That true, Agent Palmer?"

We're still on the roster at RADSA. What the hell does that mean? Steve wondered. He looked back at Eddie and shrugged.

"What do you want, G-man?" Brix asked.

Orton leered at Brix. "To keep you three out of serious trouble, Agent LaFontaine," he said, dropping the accent after slowly emphasizing the syllables. "Why don't you all hop in the back seat here so we can have a nice, private chat. I'm sure this road won't stay empty for long."

"Thanks," Steve said. "We'll pass."

He reached to open the door to his car. A burst of flame exploded on the handle. He screamed. Pain seized his arm as he yanked back a hand covered in broken red skin and dotted with yellow blisters. He snapped his head back to glare at Orton.

The RADSA agent and so-called Adapted therapist held out his hand and inspected a small ball of flame dancing between his fingertips. A glib smile stretched his face wide. "That was an order, soldier."

Steve rankled at the insult as he clutched his burned hand.

"I got your order right here, bitch!" Eddie hissed.

Two shots rang out, stunning Steve's ears. Both bullets missed Orton.

One struck metal between the doors, the other nicked the corner of the windshield, causing a spiderweb of cracks.

"Fuck!" Orton yelped.

The Tahoe lurched in reverse. Orton flung his arm forward and a spray of fire stretched through the air toward the car.

Steve hit the deck and under the car saw Eddie and Brix's shocked faces looking at him from the other side. "Get in!" he yelled.

His heart raced. The scorched skin on his hand screamed. They had to get word to Ben. To Abby. All three scrambled into the car. Steve floored the gas and checked the mirror. Orton and whoever was driving were running around each other at the front of the Tahoe, changing seats.

Gravel flew in the rear-view mirror as Steve hit the gas and they resumed course toward Grand Saline, or whatever was left of it. Air knifed in and out of Steve's lungs. Adrenaline lit a fire in him hotter than the one that burned his hand. He was finally in the firefight he had missed as a marine. Another concocted by Phelps and Gustafson. He couldn't let them win this one. Steve reached into his pocket with his good hand and tossed Brix his phone. "Call Abby, tell her we're in trouble."

"No answer," Brix said after a moment.

"Well, text her I guess," Steve replied.

"Lemme see that hand," Eddie said.

Steve hissed through clenched teeth as he peeled his seared fingers off the steering wheel.

"You can heal burns?" Brix asked.

"I've never tried," Eddie said with a shrug.

Above the pain of his hand, a tiny spark lit up in Steve's head. "Ouch!"

"I barely even touched you," Eddie said.

"No. You've tried to heal a burn before. Why would you lie about that?" Steve asked.

"I'm not lying!" Eddie protested.

And he wasn't. The spark of pain in Steve's mind resolved into a calm serenity. Eddie had attempted to heal a burn before and didn't remember it.

As Steve was about to remark on the oddity, the car suddenly lurched as a metallic screech pierced their ears. The serenity in Steve's mind dissolved as his burned hand smacked into the dashboard.

"Dammit!" Steve said. "What the hell was that?" he asked, attempting to shake the pain free from his hand.

"Uh guys…" Brix said.

Just inches from Brix's torso, a sharp point of a white, stone-like substance was poking through the rear seat. They all exchanged wide-eyed glances. The car lurched again as another metallic screech tore through their ears.

"It's the other guy!" Eddie said, craning his head to look out the side mirror. "He's making those spear things! An Adapted!"

"Great. We've got two guys chasing us that should both be on the fucking island," Steve said. "Can you shoot back?"

"Eh, I'd just be wasting bullets. I was never that good a shot," Eddie said.

"Well, maybe just one or two to give them—"

Another of the white spears pierced the rear window, shattering the glass. It plunged through the driver's seat into Steve's back, piercing through his chest just inside his shoulder. Blood began to spread through his shirt. He coughed more up onto the windshield.

"Shit!" Eddie squawked.

"*Encouler!*" Brix yelled.

Steve had no words. The pain was tremendous, but he could still think. Aside from having just sustained a potential life-threatening injury, it was nothing like what he experienced in the park at the FIGHT protest. That felt like the cloak of Death itself had wrapped around Steve's mind. This only felt like Death could be a few miles down the road sipping a sweet tea while waiting for Steve to arrive. He sucked in breath, summoning whatever combat training he had left in his head. His heart raced. He had precious few moments before shock would set in. Secure the location. They wouldn't survive a crash at this speed. They needed a defensive position. He slammed on the brakes and used his good hand to veer onto a dusty gravel drive lined with tall cypress trees. A farmhouse stood not far in the distance.

Time crawled. The washboard dirt road up to the house jostled the car, causing the spear embedded in his shoulder to tear at the entry and exit wounds. Steve clenched his teeth, gasped, and screamed. They reached the front of the house and Steve brought the car to a rough halt as he coughed up more blood.

Eddie leaned out his window and fired off a couple shots at the approaching Tahoe. The enemy slowed their advance and approached at a distance along Steve's side of the car.

Gray tendrils of fog wrapped around Steve's vision as consciousness began to fade. He gnashed his teeth and eased himself off the spike in the seat. "Fuck!" he screamed. His right arm dangled to his side as he got out and hobbled around the front of the car. Eddie and Brix had taken positions on the other side. Steve slid to the ground against the Camry as the strength left his legs. Eddie fired off another couple shots at the Tahoe.

"What do we do now?" Brix asked. He pressed his hands against the wounds.

Steve couldn't even feel the pressure as his head slumped down and darkness closed its grip on his mind. "Hold them off," he said. He thought of Abby again hoping it wouldn't be for the last time. "Wait for help."

CHAPTER 60
BOUNCY

QUIET TENSION HUNG like grimy fog over the urgent roar of Bessie's engine. The dour mood was a stark contrast to the polished, antiseptic interior of the trailer. The external camera monitors at Gigi's station showed empty Texas farmland rolling past at uncommon speed. In the lounge, Gigi, Abby, Zeke, and Ben watched the CNN coverage of three near-simultaneous meteor strikes in New Jersey, Florida, and Texas. Gigi's stomach churned like she was about to go into competition. The news on screen was indigestible. The news that had come hours before from what Steve had told Abby the night before was incomprehensible.

That had set the team and Bessie into motion towards Grand Saline. At first, Ben had said it was to prevent Steve from doing something reckless. Then the president had announced three UDOs were bound for the United States, one in the very direction they were headed. Ben's eyes had grown wide as he admitted aloud the realization that Steve had been right about everything. He had been pacing to his office and back ever since.

Everyone had seemed to forget they were racing towards a date with a deadly space rock, and that was a date Gigi definitely didn't want to be on time for. She almost slipped a sigh of relief as the UDO impacted just as they were exiting the highway.

"This is nuts," Zeke said with his cheek in a palm, staring at the TV.

"We should be there," Abby added, aghast at the footage. "I could help." She looked at Gigi. "We all could. But we gotta find Steve and the others first."

"I hope they weren't at that plant. Any word from them?" Ben asked.

"Steve added his number to the find me thing in my phone, but his last location was at that Buc-ee's we passed," Abby said as she checked her phone. "Shit, it's dead."

Gigi scoffed. *Who doesn't keep their phone charged?* she thought. "Girl. Seriously? Gimme that." She ran it over to her station and plugged it into one of the chargers she had at the ready.

As she got back to the sofa the coverage on screen had shifted to a field reporter on the scene.

"Nolan Guiterrez here reporting to you live from Fruitvale just outside Grand Saline in East Texas, the site of a third UDO impact in the United States today. The grim scene here a little more than an hour east of Dallas. Somewhere between one and two square miles have been completely obliterated. Amazingly, the heart of the town of 3,600 was spared."

The video switched back to the breaking news host. "Are there any early estimates of casualties?" he asked.

"The impacted area was lightly populated, consisting primarily of farmland and cattle pastures. However, one of the area's top employers — the Morton Salt mine — appears to be completely destroyed on the surface. The mining operations are some 750 feet below ground, and the stability of the salt formations could have protected those underground from the impact. Unfortunately, there is, at present, no way to communicate with anyone inside the blast zone, and the mine shaft is presumed to be destroyed. I'm told rescue teams from Dallas are en route."

The team sat up as the news was delivered.

Zeke poked at his phone. "There are salt facilities in Jersey, Florida, and Texas where the UDOs hit. What are the odds of that?"

Abby folded her arms. "About zero. This whole thing just got a lot worse."

"Worse than a UDO crashing outside our front door and a government conspiracy using salt somehow to create the Adapted?" Gigi asked.

"Yeah," Abby stood up. "There's an Adapted out there making the UDOs. What are we going to do?" she asked Ben.

He shook his head. "I don't know. I really don't. We gotta get together with the others and sort out who we can trust. Steve should be able to tell our friends from enemies easily enough. If we can get to him in time."

A chime came from Abby's phone.

They all raced over to Gigi's station. Abby picked up the phone and read the single message: "We're in trouble."

"This is so fucked," Gigi said. "I can't believe RADSA is involved in all of this."

"You aren't kidding," Ben said.

Abby fiddled with her phone. "The location is working. Steve's not far!" She barked an address into the intercom for Bailey. The smooth rumble of Bessie's engine hummed a little louder.

Ben jogged to his office. "Suit up. I want them to see us as a team."

Abby rolled her eyes. "Really?"

Gigi patted her on the back. "I think yours is cute. Kinda fits your 'thing'."

"What thing is that?" Abby asked as she pulled her suit from her locker and put it on. It was the same base blueish-gray with wide, shiny black and green bands down the sides.

"Garbage? I mean, it's a change from rock t-shirts. Change is good." Gigi said, slipping on her uniform.

"Ugh, whatever," Abby said as she started to change.

Ben emerged from the hall to his office wearing a base blue-gray uniform. The trailer started to rumble as Bessie turned onto a gravel road rutted with washboard gulleys. Zeke came out of the bunk room wearing his.

Gigi nodded at him. "Nice!"

Zeke smiled. "Yeah. The look is growing on me."

Abby smoothed the creases on the front of her uniform. "These are so ridiculous. We're one supervillain away from being in a comic book."

"You look good, Abby," Gigi said. She meant it. A little. "Leave the hat off," she added, ruffling Abby's hair.

Everyone returned to Gigi's station to watch the external monitors.

"Hang on!" Bailey interrupted over the intercom.

Bessie lurched hard, throwing everyone to the floor. Gigi tumbled to her side and caught herself with her hands. Next to her, Abby's head hit the diamond plate.

"Ow," Abby said, rubbing her head. Her eyes lolled back and forth.

"You okay?" Gigi asked, pulling Abby to her feet.

"Oh, the lights," Abby said, palming her eyes. "I think I just won a free game of pinball."

"The fuck?" Zeke added.

"Guys, we have gunfire ahead of us, sit tight!" Bailey said through the speaker, her voice relaying uncharacteristic worry.

"Someone's shooting at our guys?" Abby asked. Her thumping heart switched from running on fury to racing on panic.

"And us!" Bailey yelled over the intercom.

A shrill screech of metal tearing apart ripped through the intercom, shortly followed by another.

"Oh Bessie," Bailey's voice complained over the intercom.

"Bailey! You okay?" Ben asked, jumping up from the floor.

"Yeah, but we may need a ride home. Bessie's got a new pair of front teeth. What the hell are those things?"

Gigi hopped back into her chair and played with the controls. She didn't know what to do about rogue RADSA agents, but she knew how to work the cameras.

Ben scanned the screens. "Record everything, Gigi."

She pressed a series of red buttons. "Good to go."

On a side screen, two white projectiles protruded from beneath the hood of Bessie's engine.

"I've seen those somewhere before," Ben said. "Get your vests on everyone." His gorgeous lips twisted with fret.

In that moment, Gigi wanted to hold his hand. Not tackle him to the floor and rip his clothes off, which had been her usual line of thinking of late. No. He needed comfort. She had been able to provide at least a little to Abby when her sister left for the island, and Gigi barely even liked her. She liked Ben. She could make him feel better. But there were bigger things going on at the moment. Maybe they could spend some time together when this was all over.

She tweaked the focus on the cameras to make sure everything was clear. On the main screen, one camera had centered on the front of a two-story rustic farmhouse surrounded by dozens of huge leafy trees. The structure was worn, complete with peeling white siding, broken window glass, and a decades-too-old red shingle roof. Four wooden pillars in front strained to keep the short roof over the porch aloft. Bessie had come to a stop at the back of a wide gravel clearing in front of the house. Two cars were parked out front at separate ends of the house.

"Zoom in on the cars," Ben said.

Gigi directed a camera closer to a black, government-issue Chevy Tahoe, and another toward something that barely resembled Steve's Toyota Camry. The Tahoe was pocked with a dozen or more bullet holes and its windows were shot out. Fifty feet away, the Camry was skewered with huge shafts of a solid white material, each three or four feet long, an inch or two in diameter. The paint was blackened all over.

"Where's Steve?" Abby whispered, peering over Gigi's shoulder.

"Look there!" Gigi pointed to a pair of men crouching on the far side of the Camry, and a third lying on the ground. "I can't make out who that is. Is that... blood?" Gigi's heart jumped up her throat. She recognized Steve's sneakers on screen. A muddy red pool was on the ground beside them. "Oh no."

Abby's eyes bulged and she covered her mouth.

"It looks like Eddie's the one shooting," Gigi said.

Eddie had a gun in each hand and looked far more comfortable with them than Gigi expected. *Skills from his prior life*, she thought. He peeked over the hood of the car and fired another shot toward the Tahoe. On the ground below him, Steve was on his back, one knee bent upward. His shirt was drenched in blood. Brix was kneeling next to Steve, attempting to tend to him, but had nothing to work with. Eddie popped his head up over the roof of the car to look at the SUV. Out of one of the Tahoe's windows, another of the white shafts hurtled across the expanse and slammed into the Toyota, pushing it back against their teammates.

"Jesus!" Zeke exclaimed.

"Oh Steve," Abby whimpered.

On the screen, Eddie retaliated with a shot from each gun, putting a pair of fresh holes in the Tahoe. Even inside Bessie, the sounds were unforgettable. Haunting. Gigi wondered how much ammunition he had left. She looked at Ben who had gone from gorgeously tan to pale white.

"Ben — what's wrong?" she asked.

"I don't believe it," Ben answered with stark incredulity.

The others turned to look at him.

"That... that guy. with the spears." Ben struggled to get it out. "His code name is Javelin. He was sent to the island weeks ago."

"But how is he here?" Gigi asked.

Abby slapped her hands on her hips. "This just gets fucking better and better! RADSA is bringing people back from the island?"

Ben pressed the intercom. "Bailey, can you see who else is out there behind the Tahoe with your binoculars?"

"It's Orton," Bailey replied.

"Agent Orton?" Ben asked.

Another exchange of gunfire and hurtling white spears erupted on screen, followed by thin rivulets of fire from behind the Tahoe that arched across the expanse, scorching the side of the car. The flames couldn't quite reach the three men huddled together on the far side of the, but the situation looked perilous. Gigi's heart pounded. Abby looked like she was about to burst into flames.

"Yep. He's the one with the fire," Bailey replied coolly. "This don't look good, boss."

"Oh my God," Gigi muttered. "Orton is one of us."

"One of *them*," Abby said.

"Unbelievable," Ben said, horrified.

"What are we going to do?" Zeke asked.

"Vests. Now!" Ben barked. He headed to the supply cabinet and extracted a bullhorn. "Stay here. I'm going to stop this."

"How? We don't have any weapons!" Gigi said, throwing a vest over her head, then kicking her shoes off. "I could try to bounce them around?"

Ben shook his head, already at the door.

"Put your vest on!" Abby yelled.

"Don't need it. I have something better." Ben opened the rear door and jumped out.

CHAPTER 61
THE ADJUSTER

TENSE JOINTS THROBBED WITH POWER. Rage. Ben's pulse raced; adrenaline stoked fire in every cell in his body. After he landed outside, he popped every joint that was willing, and bellowed into the bullhorn. "Stop fighting!"

The command rolled over the dusty gravel like the first gust of wind before a summer squall. Eddie's gunfire stopped from behind Steve's ruined Camry. The assaults from the far side of the bullet-riddled Tahoe ceased.

Ben met Eddie's eyes. "Put the guns down."

The biker dropped his weapons.

"Ben," a quiet voice said from behind him.

He turned to see both Gigi and Abby staring at him, mouths agape.

"You…" Gigi started.

"Steve was right!" Abby finished.

He sighed, knowing the complexity of the adjustments he would have to make to cover this up. He cracked his knuckles. "Not now," he muttered through clenched teeth. It came out like a tiger's snarl. He felt like an ass.

Momentarily silenced, Abby and Gigi each took a defensive step toward each other. Ben's stomach churned as he continued to abuse his R-Skill in ways he had never intended. "Get the first aid kit and see if you can help Steve. I've got to deal with Orton."

"Already got it!" Bailey said as she hopped out of the trailer. "I'll tend to Steve."

She and Abby raced over to where Eddie and Brix knelt over Steve.

Gigi gave Ben a sheepish grin and shrugged.

"Stay close," Ben said.

The sputtering rumble of Bessie's damaged engine filled the dusty gravel drive with uneven waves of thunderous bass. Ben drew in a breath to steel his nerves and nearly gagged on the acrid stench of the thick, black exhaust billowing out of the twin exhaust stacks behind the cab.

Gigi followed a step behind and to his right as they approached the Tahoe. "So, um. You didn't use your brain thingy on me when we…"

Ben stopped in his tracks. "What? No. That was… just us."

A smile creased her lips. "Oh. Cool. Cuz I'm totally going to need some stress relief after this."

"Focus," Ben said.

He had to stifle a laugh. Gigi was a master of focus, just on her own needs. As his mind wandered to the contours of her blue and pink uniform and the curves of her cleavage, he recognized the need to master his own awareness. Certainly in the moment, but also in the use of his R-Skill. The whole sequence of events leading up to Steve quitting was his fault. A product of inexperience. His refusal to put his ability to use had prevented him from learning the importance of being completely thorough with the mental adjustments he made in others. So many nuances to manage. A missed detail here or there, that's all it took to get him into hot water. He hoped he hadn't gotten Steve killed because of it.

Two voices bickered from around the side of the Tahoe. Ben cautiously followed along the edge of Bessie's trailer until he could see the two RADSA agents, then popped his shoulders and put the megaphone to his mouth. "Orton. Vaco. Come out here. Keep your hands up where I can see them."

The two agents obediently rose from their crouched position and began walking, both wide-eyed in astonishment.

"That's far enough," Ben said after they emerged from behind the Tahoe.

Orton's face broke out in a huge grin. "Frannie owes me a steak dinner. You *are* the Number Four we suspected had meddled in the FIGHT protest."

"She authorized this?" Ben asked, slowly closing distance on Orton.

The huge agent rolled his eyes and pursed his lips.

Ben snarled. "You can talk, or I can make you talk."

The crescendo of a droning whir slowly knifed its way through Bessie's grumbling din.

Orton's grin grew even wider. "Why don't you get it from the horse's mouth?"

Ben looked to the sky and saw a helicopter approach from the west. As it came closer, he recognized it wasn't any helicopter. It was a Sikorsky VH-92. Drab green paint covered the lower two thirds of its fuselage with white paint above. As it landed, the presidential seal came into view on the pilot's door. Marine One.

The rotor powered down, and the rear stair door folded open. Three men in suits rushed out, followed by a fourth who glided down with a beaming smile, as if he was about to be received by thousands of adoring fans. President Phelps.

Ben's blood ran cold. Why was the president here? Orton had just implicated Phelps in authorizing a violent assault on three of his teammates. The president had just landed in the vicinity of recent violence with a minimal escort, acting as if everything was normal. All in the shadow of a UDO that crashed into a salt mine just a few miles from here. A sick chill sliced down Ben's spine.

The president directed his three Secret Service escorts towards Orton and Vaco, then made a beeline for Ben. The lead secret service agent grabbed the president's arm in protest to hold him back but acquiesced after getting a dirty look for the gesture. As the president approached, he took sips from a blue water bottle featuring the presidential seal. Time moved in slow motion. Suddenly the president was shaking Ben's hand.

"Mr. President? It's… an honor. What are you doing here, sir?" Ben asked.

"Ah, Agent Rice. Just checking in on my favorite RADSA team. I heard you got into a bit of a dust-up out here, and just happened to be on my way to inspect the UDO," Phelps said.

Ben's pulse quickened at the realization the president knew who he was. "I'm not sure it's safe for you to be here. Those two were attacking three members of my team."

"*Former* members, if I recall correctly, right?" the president asked.

"Well, yes," Ben said, surprised.

"That's no matter. They're still part of the family as far as I'm concerned." President Phelps peered around Ben's shoulder to acknowledge Gigi. "Agent Conlan, I believe? I'm a big fan of your videos. Incredible what you can do."

Her cheeks turned scarlet, and she toyed with her hair. "Thank you, Mr. President."

Why does he know so much about us? Ben wondered. The unease in his stomach continued to churn.

President Phelps stepped closer to Ben and whistled. "That's some scar. Were you born with it?"

Ben's heart skipped a beat. He had completely forgotten about his scar, and his prior concern over meeting the president and having to use his R-Skill to hide it. "Uh, kitchen accident. I can… hide it, if you prefer."

The president put his hand to Ben's cheek, like a proud father would do to his child. "No, that won't be necessary."

A wet, tingling sensation came over the left side of Ben's face. The pollen-coated feet of a thousand bees dancing in honey. Phelps withdrew his hand and smiled. "There. Now, where's the rest of your team?"

Ben put his fingers to his face and felt nothing. Nothing, but smooth, ordinary skin. His heart raced, both with excitement and terror at what had just happened. The president had just healed his scar. He was an Adapted too! And no one knew. What would the American public think of an Adapted in the Oval Office?

Phelps patted Ben on the shoulder as he walked past and headed towards the ruin of Steve's car.

Gigi whispered to Ben as they followed. "What did he do to you?"

"He fixed my scar. He's an Adapted!" Ben whispered. As he said the words, he couldn't believe them. Despite the president's alarming presence here, Ben was eternally grateful. He wouldn't have to hide his face anymore.

"You look like the same person to me," she said.

Ben laughed. Leave it to Gigi to accidentally say something profound. Scar or no scar, he *was* the same person inside. He had instigated so much trouble for simply not accepting who he was.

"Let's see who we have here," the president said as he rounded the back of the mangled Camry, and the rest of the team came into view. "Agent Alstrom, Agent Bailey, and Agent Pal— oh. Oh no."

Ben's skin prickled as he watched the president's face contort with anger.

"Is he going to be alright?" Phelps asked.

"I don't know," Abby said, eyes fixed on Steve. "We only just stopped the fighting. Bailey's doing the best she can with the first aid kit."

"Damn it!" Phelps glared over at Orton and Vaco who stood dazed next to the Tahoe, flanked by the three Secret Servicemen. "I told you," the president snarled, "I wanted them alive!" He pointed toward Steve. "*Especially* him!"

CHAPTER 62
GARBAGE GIRL

PRESIDENT PHELPS STORMED a few paces towards the Tahoe and pointed at the lead Secret Serviceman. "You all stay there. Not a word or a step." He took a long drink from his water bottle – which was weirdly un-presidential – then shook his head. "You said you had a handle on them, Evans."

Abby gawked at the president, still shocked to be not ten feet from him. The president's furious reaction when he saw the puddle of blood beneath Steve's limp body was even more stunning. She looked at Ben, who stared at the president with concern. Ben's face had changed. His scar was gone again. *What else has he done?* she wondered, recalling not moments ago he proved he was, without a doubt, a Number Four on RADSA's list of Dangers to Society.

The president returned to the group behind the Camry, closed his eyes and gestured in the air a moment, then clapped his hands together. "Okay kids, we have a minute or so here before shit gets real."

Was President Phelps here to inspect the damage of the UDO? That he would just show up with so small an entourage was strange. More puzzling, he knew who she was. And wanted Steve for something? What was that about?

"Damn it." The president knelt right next to Abby and shouldered her aside to get in close to Steve. "Mr. Stitch — Eddie, is it?" he said.

Eddie looked up with shocked eyes. "Yes, uh, Mr. President."

"You can't fix him up?" The president pantomimed a zipping motion.

The kind of motion someone might make to mimic Eddie's R-Skill if they had read an R-Skill report about it.

The pallid worry on Eddie's face relayed the answer. "I've done what I can… uh, sir." He struggled with the formality of addressing someone in high office. "I closed up the outside wounds with Bailey's help, but I'm no doctor."

"You can't help him?" Ben asked. "Like you did… for me?"

President Phelps shook his head. "Takes a day to recharge. The damn limitations to R-Skills are vexing, aren't they?"

Abby put a hand on Steve's head. "He's so pale."

"We need to get him to a hospital, *now*," Bailey squawked. "He's lost too much blood and may still be bleeding internally."

President Phelps nodded with exasperation on his face. "Do what you can. I'll get some help here." He motioned to the helicopter. Presumably whoever was inside was listening in. He looked at his watch for a few seconds. "Okay everyone, this is going to be loud. Hang tight."

A shrill whistle crescendoed, like a resonant hiss from a leaky air hose. Moment by moment, it grew louder. And louder. Soon, the whistle was replaced by a rumble. The rumble lasted only a short second, replaced by a thunderous crash as something struck the back of the Tahoe, caving half of it into the ground, and casting a huge plume of dirt over the entire area. Orton, Vaco, and the three Secret Servicemen were obliterated in the dusty cloud. The force knocked everyone over but the president. Steve's car slid several feet, pinning Brix and Steve underneath.

"Fuck! Get me out!" Brix yelled.

"Steve!" Abby yelled from the ground. Her heart quickened to see him in further peril. The unexpected trip into the gravel had knocked some late sense into her, and she felt more herself, and at present, at least partly made of dust. She pulled herself up and rushed to the car to attempt to lift it, in the hope that in its current state it would qualify as garbage for her R-Skill. But a quick pull at the bumper revealed it was as heavy as it ought to be. The array of white stone spikes in its side lent disbelief that the car could be salvaged. There wasn't a trash can in sight, so that was likely the problem. Eddie and Ben were trying to pull the trapped men out by their legs, but they were pinned.

"Come on, guys! I can't take this!" Brix said, urgently flailing his legs.

Steve was motionless. He merely groaned.

Abby screamed at Zeke. "Zeke, get your ass over here and try your thing! Gently!"

Zeke was standing next to Bailey and Gigi by the truck, all three dusting their team jumpsuits off after picking themselves off the ground. He raced over, knelt by the struggling legs of Steve and Brix, then pressed his face to the car. The Camry lurched half a foot and dragged its captives with them. Brix yelped and Steve groaned.

"Hold them!" Zeke pleaded.

She grabbed one of Steve's legs, Ben took the other while motioning for the others to assist Brix. Together, the six of them held tight as Zeke repeatedly tapped his lips to the beaten Camry, pushing it inch by inch off Steve and Brix. Both writhed and gasped as the car pressed sensitive body parts into the hard, dry dirt as it moved. Abby gawked at President Phelps, who had stepped back, and was drinking from his water bottle as he watched the frantic struggle. After a tense minute, the car had been moved enough to pull the pair free. Both were covered in dirt and fresh blood from their faces, scratched all over.

"Here, let me see to that." Eddie reached out and began to work on Brix's cuts.

President Phelps walked over and patted Zeke on the back. "Impressive R-Skill you have there, Agent Thomas. I like that one."

Zeke smiled and cringed at the same time.

Ben stood and inspected the president's suit for any signs of wounds. "Sir, are you okay?"

"I'm fine, Agent Rice, thank you." He took note of the team huddled around Steve and smiled. "Quite the motley crew you have assembled here."

Ben looked surprised at the complement. "Uh, thank you sir." He looked over at the smoldering ruin of the Tahoe. "What just happened?"

President Phelps turned to look at the wreckage and seemed completely unimpressed by it. "Yeah, unfortunate business with the dark objects. Small ones are popping up everywhere."

"But..." Ben gaped at the place where the two RADSA men formerly stood, now a heap of strange dark object dust and mangled Tahoe. He looked at Steve, who was in no condition to render an opinion on the president's words.

Abby stood up as an icy chill went down her spine. She finished the thought. "You told them to wait right there."

The president's eyebrows raised. "Ah, that I did. Agent Rice's report did say you were the clever one, Agent Alstrom."

Every hair on Abby's head stood straight at attention. The supervillain had arrived. At least the team was dressed for the occasion. She muttered to the team around Steve, "Guys, this isn't good. Be on your toes." She got back nothing but horrified looks.

"My God," Ben said. "You made the UDO? You made all of them!" His mouth hung open.

The president beamed with pride. "You're looking at Adapted number one."

"You made the UDOs today? And Korea?" Bailey asked.

"That's correct, little Agent Bailey," Phelps said.

"But you killed all those people. Americans too! How could you?" Gigi said with disbelief.

The president ruminated a moment, then shrugged. "An unfortunate means to an end. But let me ask you. Do any of you feel our country — and even the world, is in a better place since the UDO struck North Korea last year? That the stagnating divisions holding back true human progress had finally been weakened?"

The knots in her stomach told Abby where this was going. She looked at her teammates. Some were confused, others looked at the ground. All were silent.

Phelps tapped his chest. "I think it's better. Hell, I *know* it's better. You could measure it any number of ways, but just look at my polling numbers. When's the last time we had a president with an approval rating over fifty percent? Hell, last I checked I was over eighty!"

Abby had to agree with the assessment, and she hated that he was right. After decades of partisan entrenchment, the political gridlock in Washington had eased in the months after the destruction in North Korea. But they weren't exactly on friendly terms with the United States. What cost was the president willing to incur to achieve lasting change? This man killed Americans today. He just killed five moments ago.

Abby balled her fists and took a step toward the president. "And the death and destruction today? Jersey? Florida? Texas? You're killing your own citizens you fucking traitor!"

The president rolled his eyes. "Don't be so dramatic, Garbage Girl." He used her code name with condescension, as if she were actually made out of garbage, rather than a well-paid flinger of it. "Your government has been killing your neighbors directly, and indirectly, since before the Constitution was signed." He stretched out his fingers to count. "Slavery, the climate crisis, MK Ultra, McCarthyism, endless conflict in the Middle East, budget cuts to the FDA, EPA, and CDC. Don't get me started on the gargantuan clusterfucks the last two pandemics were in our country. Millions of Americans dead at the hands of your elected officials, either directly, or indirectly through gross incompetence or willful negligence. The list goes on and on. The problem lies in direction. You give the general public a cause to get behind, something to look forward to, something to fight for, you get agreement. Not everyone, but enough. More than enough. The proliferation of the Internet in the late 1990s is a great example. Everyone was so excited for a connected future, dog food delivered to your front door, streaming music and videos, the entire knowledgebase of the history of mankind at your fingertips. It was great. To lead the way for the world, there has to be a unifying force that lends weight to our combined voice."

Phelps paced in front of the group and waved his hands in the air. "And then 9/11 happens. Ever since, every individual's focus has been so myopic. Fearful. Our country lost its way." Phelps motioned at the team. "All of us, all of this, will give — no, has *already* given — America and humanity a new cause. We now have global survival as a common goal. Regular Joes turned Adapted like Agent Conlan there are supplanting reality stars and social media influencers as our modern-day celebrities and role models. They're ordinary people, made extraordinary. And through it, all the caustic, negative stresses on our society are being swept aside."

The team stood dumbfounded. All but Steve, who looked at the president wearily from the ground through eyes barely opened.

Damn, Abby thought. *He gives a good speech.* But she couldn't let this stand. This wasn't leadership, it was just a new variety of fear mongering, mass murder, and callous megalomania. She took another step toward the president, fists ready to pounce. "Why are you here?"

Phelps stifled a laugh, and looked over at the wrecked Tahoe. "Well, as you can see, good help can be tough to find. I'm dealing with a fair amount of turnover."

"Sure, when you murder them by the handful," Abby retorted.

The president scoffed. "You're one to lecture me about murder, Agent Alstrom."

A huge lump welled in Abby's throat as a vision of Tyson's headless body danced through her mind.

"Besides, I call that iterating," the president said, pointing to the small, blackened crater where five men were standing just moments before.

"What?" Ben interjected.

Phelps sighed. "Island-A, as a dumping ground for the dangerous Adapted, works fine. I'm certain you all don't feel great about it, and that's understandable. It's not my favorite part of the plan. But it's necessary. I suspect it's no secret now to this group that we've been "repurposing" certain individuals to come back to the mainland to serve under me and RADSA. Mostly we—"

Ben lurched forward into a defensive spot in front of Abby. "And you want to 'repurpose' us to work for you?"

The president laughed. "You all already work for me! But no, I would like to try something different."

"Which is?" Bailey asked, stepping up next to Ben, arms folded.

"The program on the island is a work in progress. I'd like to have a team at my disposal that can follow orders, as well as think on their feet. Those guys all had trouble with one or both.

"I'm not interested," Abby said. "You're a fucking bastard, *Lawrence*."

The president chuckled at the disrespect, then checked his watch. "It's not like you have a lot of options."

The whistling noise returned. Everyone looked to the sky, then took cover behind the Camry, huddling around Steve. Then, a thunderous crash as a dark object suddenly slammed into Bessie's cab. Dirt and shrapnel flew all over. The force of the impact pulled the front of the trailer into the ground, sending the rear wheels high into the air. Gravity gradually won the battle and pulled the trailer back to the ground, caving the trailer in on itself. The truck, trailer, and every state-of-the-art console and gadget inside were now crushed into useless scrap.

"Bessie!" Bailey yelled from the ground.

Eddie leapt from his ministrations on Steve and aimed a gun at the president. Abby's eyes bulged, but she found no words to stop him.

Phelps casually lifted a hand. "You don't want to do that, Agent Contreras."

"Why not?" Eddie cocked the hammer.

"Because one, it won't do you any good. And two, then I'll know you're not on my side, and I very much want you — *all of you* — to be on my side."

"Won't do any good?" Abby repeated.

"I am Adapted number one, two, three," he counted his fingers. "I think I'm up to thirteen now. I don't get to use any of them very much, but one thing I most certainly can do is withstand bullets."

"Bullshit!" Eddie said.

"Stand down Eddie!" Ben yelled as the trigger was pulled.

The sound was piercing; Abby instinctively cupped her ears, but the damage was already done. Teammates around Eddie recoiled. President Phelps didn't even flinch. Aside from a fresh bullet hole in his pressed sports coat, there was no trace of any effect on him whatsoever. He thrust his chin out, deepening his smug grin. "As I said… bulletproof."

"*¡Dios mío!*" Eddie said.

"I'll give you that one for free, Stitch," Phelps said.

Ben gnashed his teeth and popped the joints in his neck. "Mr. President, put your hands in the air and sit down."

The president hissed through a grin. "Yeah, that's not going to work either. I have you to thank for that one, Agent Rice. Number Fours always worried me. But no longer, thanks to your uncovering of Delilah Dewberry's R-Skill."

Ben's jaw dropped.

"And now that's out of the way, let's talk future." The president looked over the team, now with less amusement. "Everyone get up."

Abby could barely register the command. The maelstrom in her ears from the gunshot drowned out nearly everything. Slowly, the team rose with varying degrees of reluctance. Abby snuck a look at Steve, who was still on the ground. He was sickly pale, eyes barely slitted open. Propped up on one elbow, he used the other to clutch the area recently repaired around his abdomen. His shirt was soaked through with blood, though he did not appear to be losing any more at the moment. Abby's stomach churned as she wondered how badly torn up he was on the inside.

Phelps folded his arms. "In a few minutes, another helicopter will land here. It'll take Steve to get some medical attention, then fly the rest of you to an airbase to await the next plane out to the island. Or—" he paused to pace. "The plane can take your team to the RADSA facility in Maryland, where you'll all get a bit of local loyalty training. Frannie's been working on it for me. A lighter hand than we use on the island, but I'm hoping it will be more effective since you'll be volunteering.

"And what exactly do you want with Agent Palmer?" Ben asked.

"Hah!" The president laughed. "Isn't it obvious? An Adapted that can tell when people speak the truth? I'm going to give him a fucking cabinet position! Assuming he survives."

Everyone looked back in surprise at Steve.

"If not, a blood sample will do." Phelps took a long drink of water from his bottle, then tossed it to the ground and clapped his hands. "Well, how about it? I'm not going to linger here. I'm the president. Things to do, and all."

Abby's gaze remained fixed on Steve. His eyes were shut, wincing, and his gnashed teeth were bared a little. Then he slightly, slowly, shook his head. She turned to face the most villainous person she had ever met. "What kind of insane plan is this? You're the president, you fucking bastard! You're supposed to be the best of us!" She stormed towards the most powerful person on the planet, Adapted, or otherwise.

Phelps darted backward two steps, pointed a finger in the air, and shouted. "Enough of that!"

A shadow stopped Abby in her tracks. She stared up at a jagged object impossibly hovering mid-air not ten feet above her. *Holy crap! He can make them on a whim. Anywhere.* She watched the black, car-sized object slowly rotate for a moment, then bared her teeth to the president again, but the adrenaline coursing through her blood was no match for the icy grip of mortal fear rocking her nerves. Before she could decide what to do, a flash of blue and pink crossed her vision. Then the ground gave way beneath her for a moment, and suddenly she was flying through the air over Steve towards a stand of tall trees next to the house. Even in the air, she could feel the impact of the UDO as it slammed into the ground. She flailed her legs in a futile effort to gather some balance, but crashed ingloriously into a group of bushes, narrowly avoiding a tall oak. The stings of pain from dozens of lacerations all over only added to the confusion of what just happened.

"Fuck!" she yelled. She fought the clingy branches to sit up to see what happened, only to see the UDO cratered right where she was standing a second ago. And Gigi was nowhere to be seen. Abby's fury was the only thing holding her lunch down. "Oh no," she muttered.

The president clicked his teeth. "That's a shame. I liked her videos." He continued matter-of-factly, as if he hadn't just killed someone. "So, any takers? I'm heading out."

Everyone was still too stunned to speak. Bailey and Ben had rushed over to the UDO, desperately searching for signs of Gigi. She was completely buried beneath Phelps' villainy.

Ben stood, fists balled. "Mr. President, I don't think you'll find anyone here that agrees with what you're doing."

Brix and Zeke scrambled towards Abby.

"Well, that's not much of a surprise I suppose. On to the hospital for Steve then. And Island-A shortly thereafter for the rest of you. I'll see you all soon, fear not." The president turned and began walking towards his white and green helicopter that had just begun to spin up its rotor.

"Are you okay?" Zeke asked Abby as he and Brix approached the bushes.

Brix started grabbing branches, withering them into dust to free Abby from her entanglement.

"Gigi… just sacrificed herself to save me," Abby gasped. She couldn't believe it. What had been a caustic rivalry turned into a tepid friendship, only to have it end suddenly. Abby thought it would have been her to make a sacrifice to help another Adapted. *Oh, Gigi, what have you done?*

"Abby, you're bleeding a lot," Zeke pointed to her forehead.

Abby brought her focus back to the moment. She stood and looked at her jumpsuit, now ripped open in a dozen places across her arms, chest, and legs. The cut across her forehead protested in pain as she wiped at it. "Doesn't matter, we need to stop Phelps!"

"But how?" Brix asked.

"Beats me," Zeke said.

They stood and watched the president. Abby was at a loss. "My sister would come in real handy right now," she said.

"No kidding," Brix agreed.

Some motion in the foreground caught Abby's eye. The door Steve was leaning against fell off of the ruined car, dropping him back onto the gravel from his propped position. She had to save him, which meant they first had to stop the president. Somehow.

The whine of the helicopter's engine spun up and rotor blades began to turn. The president was close to escape. Then she saw it. A pilot was emptying out a trash can at the rear hatch. A wry smile broke the bloody grimace she had been carrying. "Do you suppose he's garbage-proof too?"

Zeke looked back at her in confusion. "What?"

Abby rushed down to Steve's Camry, closed her eyes, drew in a breath, and lifted the ruined car over her head. She heaved it at the helicopter and watched with pride as it silently floated in a graceful arc through the air.

Just as President Phelps ducked inside, the previously uninteresting gold Toyota Camry, now scorched black all over by Orton and riddled useless with long shafts of white stone from Vaco, smashed into the presidential helicopter with a calamitous crash. The blades of the rotors flew off in all directions. The fuselage crumpled inward around the impact of the car. Moments later, the entire twisted heap erupted into flames.

"Boom!" Zeke exclaimed with a pumped fist.

"Fuck yeah!" added Brix.

"Woah, Abby!" Eddie exclaimed.

Ben and Bailey stood next to the UDO that had crushed Gigi, mouths agape.

Abby sighed with relief, then took in the stunned faces of her teammates and gasped as the realization set in. She just killed the president.

CHAPTER 63
BOUNCY

THE MEMORIAL SERVICE for Gigi Anne Conlan, A.K.A. Bouncy, was an audacious celebration of friendship, dedication, posthumous viral celebrity, and naturally, her family's wealth. Despite being crushed by one of President Phelps' lethal rocky creations, some of the electronics on Bessie's trailer continued to function after the impact, including a couple cameras and video recorders. The one tracking Gigi had survived to chronicle the entire spectacle. After Ben had reviewed the footage, he gave permission for Abby to upload it to A-Space. The president's murderous villainy was laid bare for all to see, as was Gigi's self-sacrificial decision to bounce Abby out of harm's way. It was most likely unintentionally self-sacrificial, but she died saving her teammate all the same, and that's the Gigi everyone came to know.

Sharing it with the world was the least Abby felt she could do for Gigi. Within a day, the video had nearly half a billion views. As the veil over the conspiracy quickly lifted, replays approached thirty billion. It smashed records for the most-watched video in human history and put a serious strain on A-Space's server farm.

"Well," Bailey said as the remnants of the North Texas RADSA team stood together in black funeral attire watching Gigi's casket as it was lowered into the ground, "She got what she wanted in the end. How many people get to die the hero and have the world watch the instant replay?"

"I don't think dying a hero is really what she had in mind," Abby said softly, her own heart sinking a little bit lower with every inch of the casket's descent. She and Gigi weren't exactly on best friend terms, but they had at least smoothed out some of their differences, and Abby was glad for that, at least.

Later, the team sat in a corner of the extravagant post-service reception, one of the few times they had been together in the weeks after the confrontation with Phelps. Rice offered boilerplate platitudes as most nursed cocktails, and Abby, being the only one underage, sipped at a Coke Zero on ice. Not a Dr Pepper in sight.

"We've all been through a lot in this ordeal," Ben said, raising his glass to the team. "Injuries, unbelievable stress, self-doubt — the list goes on. But we came through as a team and put an end to what I would call the worst villain in modern history. You're all heroes and should feel proud."

Whatever Abby was feeling, it wasn't proud or heroic. It was more like being an emotional pincushion, constantly jabbed and prodded for inter-views, perspectives, demonstrations of her ability, and book deals. All the while, her mind was only on the debt she could never repay. The friend she had just found, only to lose forever.

Abby took some solace in establishing a non-profit memorial fund in honor of Gigi. It was fed by the sizable earnings from Gigi's now-famous social media library and would be used to help provide resources to foster kids and their families throughout Texas. Gigi wouldn't care for the fund's mission, but she would be elated enough to have more attention brought to her name. Abby would milk Gigi's final fifteen minutes of fame on her behalf. It's what Gigi would have done.

CHAPTER 64

THE SLEUTH

DESPITE HAVING TYPICALLY WORN a suit and tie to work since leaving the Marines, Steve tugged at his solid black tie, desperate for a little relief. The air in the room was thick with judgement. Every single word uttered would be measured for weight, importance, and veracity. Truth.

Steve stood in front of the most famous hunk of reclaimed wood on the planet. It was beautiful: a rich caramel-colored stain with a timeworn patina, and exquisitely carved detailing over nearly every square inch. At the center of the side facing him was a large eagle, with a clutch of arrows in one talon, and an olive branch in the other. The Resolute Desk.

Behind it sat the most intimidating woman Steve had ever met. President Annette Wohlers, successor to Lawrence Phelps. The person that he and his team had a direct hand in putting behind this desk. She took her measure of him without saying a thing.

The president wore typical politician attire: a sharp navy blazer on top of a white blouse and an American flag pin on the lapel. She wore little makeup, but enough to convey that she understood that appearances were important. Her rust red hair was shorn close to the sides of her head, rising in turned curls on top.

After a solid two minutes of standing before her in blood-chilling silence, she simply asked, "How is your recovery?"

Steve straightened his back. The sling supporting his right arm tightened. "Better, ma'am. Thank you."

She leaned back in her chair and folded her arms. "Alright, Mr. Palmer. What the hell am I supposed to do with you?"

Steve fell back on his years of experience standing at attention to avoid giving the most powerful person on the planet a quizzical expression. "Ma'am?"

"You. Your team. The Adapted. Your girlfriend did just kill the sitting President."

An involuntary shiver wobbled Steve's head. He figured President Wohlers would have read up on him, but it was concerning that the file on him showed he and Abby had been an item. He hoped they still were.

Steve took a deep breath. "May I be frank, Madam President?"

She nodded.

"Call it just doing our jobs. We exposed the truth behind the Adapted. We exposed Fargo Pharmaceuticals. We stopped an unstoppable Adapted psychopath that just happened to be the president. He killed untold millions with his R-Skill and had proven in his final hours he had no compunction about using that ability on Americans. How many more would he have killed if we hadn't stopped him?"

President Wohlers tapped on her desk. "Hmm. And, aside from the testimony of your teammates and some grainy video on A-Space, what evidence of this do you have?"

Steve swallowed. "The fact that I just said it. I'm only able to speak the truth."

The president rose from her chair like smoke and shot him a wry smile as she walked to the window. "Ah. That," she said, gazing out over the South Lawn. "I read your file. Your R-Skill is interesting."

The heat in his cheeks could not be forced down. Steve was glad the president had her back turned to him. He also recognized that this wasn't the first president to take an interest in his R-Skill.

"Thank you, Madam President."

She snapped her head to stare directly at him. "Don't thank me yet." The president walked to the front of her desk and stood within an arm's reach. "I was born in Indiana."

The stabbing pain behind his eye forced him to flinch. He admonished his lack of control and grasped for composure. This was a test. From the president.

"You were not born in Indiana."

"My favorite color is pink."

"It is not."

She snickered. "This is almost fun."

Steve bit down on his tongue to halt his in-progress frown.

The president turned to pick up an empty glass from her desk. She raised a very full glass of water to her lips and took a sip.

Steve's eyes widened and he took an involuntary step back. "You're…"

She raised her glass to him. "A member of the club. Yes."

The hairs on his neck stood at attention.

"Now, before you go all half-cocked looking for another presidential conspiracy, let me say this: I had nothing to do with President Phelps' plot. I didn't know about it. I didn't know what he could do."

Steve took a deep breath. Her words rang true. His mounting tension eased.

The president smirked. "That must be something, living in fear of people lying all the time."

"I've… learned to cope with it."

"It's a strange, beautiful, horrible world we live in now. How well would you cope with being surrounded by some of the worst liars on the planet on a regular basis?"

"Ma'am?"

"I'd like to offer you a job."

He had not seen that coming, given that was apparently what President Phelps had intended to do. Steve had no allusions to even keeping his job with RADSA. Frannie Gustafson's connection to Phelps had been unveiled, and now she was tied to his grand scheme. She had vanished moments after Phelps was killed and had not yet been found. The new director, Ayesha Pullman, was rumored to be a glorified government bean counter, and the agency was expected to undergo severe budget cuts and an extreme makeover. He straightened his back again and uttered the only thing he could think of. "I serve at the pleasure of the president."

"Relax Steve, or you'll pop your stitches."

Steve was not about to relax in the Oval Office. Besides, he didn't have stitches. He had Stitch.

"But first, if you wouldn't mind, Mr. Palmer, I'd like one more demonstration of your R-Skill."

Steve gnawed at his cheek to halt the scowl that began to form at the side of his mouth. "Of course."

The president pressed the intercom on her desk. "Send him in."

The door to the executive secretary's room opened, and a tall, handsome man in a suit walked in. One bearing the recently repaired, magazine-worthy face of Ben Rice.

He looked at Steve in surprise, moving to stand next to him. "Madam President, it is again an honor."

Steve was split in two to see his boss here. Friend, at one point. The man had lied. Deceived. And Steve had never been convinced that the reveal of Ben's R-Skill was truly the end of the story. All he had to go on was intuition. His own R-Skill had been incapacitated by Agent Orton at the time.

But then Ben did save Steve's life by showing up in the nick of time and somehow stopping Orton and Vaco. Friend, indeed. And, despite hiding the fact he hid his R-Skill from the team, Ben did his best to represent RADSA and the Adapted.

Like she did with Steve, the president stared at Ben for a long, silent, uncomfortable moment. He seemed even more uncomfortable with the nonverbal assessment. Ben looked at Steve with a raised eyebrow. Steve simply shrugged.

"Agent Rice. First of all, allow me to extend the gratitude of the entire planet to you and your team for putting an end to Phelps' villainy. We have a *lot* of cleanup ahead of us. I want your group to be a part of it."

Ben cleared his throat. "Thank you, Madam President. We are, of course, at your disposal."

She looked Ben up and down again.

"But first, I need to know that I can trust you. So, consider who else is here in the room when you answer my next question."

Steve watched Ben with interest. Rice looked as if he was about to be mowed over by an oncoming train.

"What is the nature of your R-Skill?" the president asked Ben with an air of calm suspicion.

Ben inhaled a short breath. "Madam President?"

She shrugged. "RADSAnet has a file on you. Ex-Director Gustafson added it herself. You're an Adapted. But your file is empty. I'm curious. What is your ability?"

Ben's rugged jawline trembled ever so slightly. The color drained from his face as he stared at President Wohlers.

What is he waiting for? Steve wondered. At once, Steve's mind replayed the string of events that led to him walking off the team in the first place.

And then the unexplained halt to Agent Orton's attack. His gut felt like someone had just kicked him in the stitches.

Steve was about to speak up when Ben stepped forward, pursed his lips, and rolled his neck until the joints popped.

CHAPTER 65
THE ADJUSTER

"I'M NOT GOING to turn myself in. And I'm sorry, but I'm not going to let you turn me in either," Ben said, popping his shoulders.

"Then what the hell do you want?" Bailey sat cross legged in the chair across from his desk, arms folded, eyebrows about to collide.

Ben sighed. "I want you to keep me honest." He wanted a confidante. Someone to plan with. To carefully strategize the best applications of his ability.

"What?"

"I want to do good with this. I can help people. *We* can help other Adapted out there. We could help everyone."

Bailey scoffed.

"I'm serious. I know I got into some shit there being careless. But my intentions were *good*. You must see that."

"All I see is someone fucking around with my head, and I don't like it. Give me one example of you using this ability that wasn't a disaster."

Ben wiped a hand down his face. "I helped Abby."

Bailey squinted at him. "Helped… how?"

"I made sure she didn't get into trouble after the accident at her last job. And I helped her not feel guilty over it."

Dead silence. Bailey's face turned red as an August sunburn. "Jesus, Ben."

He truly had thought he had done Abby a service by clearing any professional and emotional roadblocks for her so she could continue her life after killing Tyson Burrows. But the furious look on Bailey's face indicated another interpretation coming.

"You really do belong on the island. You helped Abby escape legal consequences? Don't get me wrong, she's great. She stopped Phelps for cryin' out loud. But what about the other kid's family? Their need for closure? Hell. What about Abby's need for closure? Processing grief? Accepting responsibility? Growing up?"

"It was just easier…"

"It's fucking cheating!"

"C'mon."

"Who else have you tampered with? The president?"

"You *saw* what I did out there. I saved Steve's life for fuck's sake!"

"Which we're all grateful for. Would he have even left the team and been in that situation if you had been honest with him from the start?"

"You know he would have just turned me in. I'm not going to the damn island, Jo. There is too much at stake for the Adapted for me to just go along with that. I can—"

"Brainwash the world? Make it in your own image? Play God?"

The familiar pressure in his joints throbbed. Bailey's anger wafted through the air to him unseen, fueling his R-Skill's well of power. She had the most even-keeled temperament on the team, and he had brought her to a boil.

"Bailey," Ben said, holding his hands out.

"I don't want any part of this. I quit!"

The situation was slipping out of control. He needed her on the team, Bessie or not. "You can't quit. You can either help me, or I'll just set things back the way they were before you came in here."

"The hell you will!" Bailey hopped off her chair and hoisted it over her head to throw it at him.

Before she could, Ben cracked his knuckles and yelled, "Stop!"

Bailey stood with raging infernos behind her eyes, chair frozen above her head.

He slowly stood. "Put that down."

She complied. The fury in her eyes did far more damage to him than the chair could have done.

Ben sighed. "Fuck it." Since returning from Washington DC, he had tried three times to confide in Bailey and get her to go along with the idea of helping him. Now he had failed a fourth time. He popped his shoulders and knees, and rewound everything in Bailey's head by ten minutes.

Her fury vacated and she blinked a few times as the adjustment set in. "What did you want, boss?"

He walked over and opened his office door. "Go gather everyone up, we've got a visitor coming soon with our next assignment."

CHAPTER 66

GARBAGE GIRL

IT TURNED out that offing the president in the heat of the moment wasn't immediately a popular decision. Bessie's other remaining functional camera had captured the entire field of action, from the initial firefight with the RADSA agents, to President Phelps' arrival and Gigi's heroism. All the way up to the point where Abby hurled the wreckage of Steve's car at a tiny wastebasket inside the presidential helicopter and squashed the bulletproof, but not car-proof, leader of the free world into a bloody pulp. The camera's wide angle wasn't close enough to catch the gory mess but left no doubt as to what transpired.

The joint congressional inquest into what was now being called the Adapted Conspiracy left no stone unturned. The truth came out quickly in front of Congress, thanks in large part to the presence of RADSA Agent Steve Palmer, now serving as a special attaché to the newly sworn-in President Annette Wohlers. Those involved in the conspiracy were exposed, at least the ones Steve had uncovered. Former RADSA Director Frannie Gustafson had been indicted but was on the run. The North Texas team was entirely candid in recounting what happened in front of the farmhouse near Grand Saline, and ultimately exonerated (after significant debate). Abby could barely pay attention during her depositions, instead obsessing over what life was like for Mary on Island-A. She hadn't heard from her sister at all.

President Wohlers, not as popular as her predecessor, nor nearly as large an advocate of the Adapted (which were now known to be unwitting pieces of Phelps' grand scheme for global upheaval), was nevertheless convinced of Steve's utility once his ability had been demonstrated at the team debrief in the White House.

He had given Abby a chaste hug hello and goodbye at Gigi's funeral, but avoided speaking to her beyond polite small talk in the group setting. When she inquired as to why he wasn't responding to her calls or texts, Steve replied "I haven't had a chance to get a new phone for my old number." A very specific response. Abby debated the possible interpretations of it.

The thirst for news and opinion was ravenous after the details of the conspiracy were made public, and the coverage of the Adapted Conspiracy dominated every possible media outlet. Abby had to crash at a new apartment Ben leased for her upon returning to Dallas. She stayed in and only answered the door for food, assuming the posture of being under quarantine. News was hard to avoid. She stayed off social media. She avoided her favorite multiplayer video games. Reading helped pass the time, and she watched sports, though the color commentators regularly digressed into opinion pieces on the Adapted Conspiracy and its varied layers of debate. One news story that caught her attention detailed a local middle school principal turned Adapted that was arrested for sexual assault.

She had reached out to her foster family, the Kims, but like Steve, they weren't returning her calls or texts. She didn't blame them for using her as an easy scapegoat for Mary's assignment to the island. Not that Abby had a hand in the decision, nor would she have been able to prevent it from coming down eventually. Abby suspected the Kims also had strong emotions for what was essentially mass genocide for many of their friends and relatives on the Korean peninsula. Talking to Abby about anything would likely serve to further stir their cauldron of simmering anger. Naturally, those that survived the massacre on the Korean peninsula clamored for restitution and some manner of restoration, as did every distant family member or affected business owner, real and imaginary. President Wohlers offered a very non-committal promise to assign a congressional task force to make recommendations, but no doubt that would be mired in research, meetings, and discussions for quite some time.

Every possible media talking head joined in the debate over whether the American taxpaying public owed the survivors anything. Generally, the feeling on the matter was divided down party lines. Even more debate raged over what the fate of the Adapted should be. The public goodwill towards them had all but evaporated in the absence of President Phelps' consistently positive message and the curtain lifted on his outrageous Machiavellian scheme. For a time, at least, RADSA would continue under new leadership, as new Adapted were still emerging daily. The investigation into the conspiracy had identified nearly a dozen special 'pink salt' production facilities across the country (three of which were destroyed by Phelps before his end), and wide-ranging recalls were issued. The salt had made it all over the globe, and it was going to be hard to convince a country more and more and accustomed to eating out to prepare saltless food at home for several weeks out of concern for safety. Island-A would also continue to operate, much to the chagrin of Adapted everywhere. Though it too was under new management. At least that's what the new RADSA director Ayesha Pullman was saying. And RADSA would keep its acronym, dropping Radiologically in favor of Radically in the name.

The day arrived when Rice texted and said he wanted the team to get back to work. A backlog of new Adapted was waiting, and he had appointed Abby as the lead field agent for the team since Steve evidently wasn't coming back. That was altogether weird, considering she was the youngest. He also asked that she pack an overnight bag with a few days of clothes. Warehouse 11 had yet to be identified publicly as the local RADSA headquarters, and she figured the team would camp out to plan their post-Phelps existence.

Her stomach grumbled as she checked her fridge for something to eat before heading to work. She sighed at the empty shelves and resigned to picking up food on the way. A large yellow envelope flopped to the ground as she opened her front door. The word 'ANONYMITY' was scrawled in marker on it. Inside, she found a dark brown wig, aviator sunglasses, a cream-colored blazer in her size, and an envelope with a small stack of hundred-dollar bills.

She inspected the wig and laughed. "Why didn't I think of that?"

Armed with a disguise, her enthusiasm for hot chocolate and a blueberry muffin suppressed any concern she had for someone recognizing her in public. She put on the costume, then drove over to a popular coffee shop not far from Eleven. Her heart sank when she saw the line almost out the door. Undeterred, she took her place and waited. And waited. Evidently the shop had changed its menu or something because every customer was asking questions. *How hard is it to order coffee, people?* she thought. With the line inching along, it was only a matter of time for someone to eventually recognize her. But everyone's attention was in their phone, tablet, and the occasional book. She shrugged and did the same.

A red-headed barista in a green apron and a coffee bean-laden name tag that read "Korbel" smiled as she approached the register. His well-greased handlebar moustache defied gravity as he cocked his head and said with an excited expression, "Hey, I think I've seen you on TV somewhere."

Still behind the sunglasses, Abby shook her head. "I don't think so. I'll have a large hot chocolate and a blueberry muffin."

"Sweet tooth, eh?" He tapped in the order then snapped his fingers. "I know! You're the new meteorologist on Channel 5?"

"Nope." She handed him a crisp bill.

"Thanks, it'll be right up." He gave her the change, then his eyes grew wide. "Oh! Wait, you're…" He pointed at her and covered his mouth. "Oh my God."

Her pulse quickened. She held up one hand and slammed the change of smaller bills and coins still in her other hand into the tip jar. "Let's assume you're mistaken, and just leave it at that. Okay? I'm only here to pick up breakfast and then I need to get to work."

He leaned back slightly. "Uh, sure. Thanks." After a long pause looking at the laden tip jar, he said, "So… Where do you work?"

"In garbage removal."

The barista stammered as if he was being robbed at gunpoint. "Sounds glamorous. Whatever pays the bills, right?"

"It's more than that. It's important."

"Huh," he said, passing her a piping hot cup and small paper bag with trembling hands. "Have a great day."

Abby nodded her thanks for his discretion and beat a hasty exit, nearly dropping the hot chocolate as she jogged back to her car. She looked at her face in the mirror and didn't recognize herself. The wig was cut in a stylish bob. The sunglasses covered almost half her face. Maybe she just shared a resemblance with some other TV personality she was unaware of. But that would be her last visit to that particular coffee shop, just to be on the safe side. She sighed at the thought of a future laden with wigs, costumes, and single-use-only restaurants.

She scarfed down the muffin as she drove, trying to think of something profound to say to the team when she arrived at the warehouse. How grateful she was for their support. How thankful she was that they were still alive. How proud she was they triumphed against an unbelievably powerful adversary. How glad she was to consider them friends. The exact words weren't coming to her, but she figured she'd wing it as she usually did. When she arrived at the warehouse, the large bay door where Bessie would usually enter was open. Bailey stood at the threshold, waving Abby inside. She pulled in, and parked next to a black SUV she didn't recognize, which was next to Zeke's and Bailey's cars. Abby thought it odd they would be going around as a team without Bessie, but then realized she had no idea how long a replacement vehicle like that would take to procure.

Bailey approached, wearing a new blue-gray team jumpsuit. One side was plain, the other had an intricate weave of red, yellow, and green lines depicting city streets. She gave Abby a big hug on her legs. "Hey, Gigi!"

Abby pushed her back. "What?"

Bailey laughed. "G. G.? Garbage Girl."

The connection had never occurred to Abby. "Funny. Let's stick to Abby, okay?"

"Sure. Nice wig," Bailey said.

Abby hastily pulled off the wig and ruffled her hair into form.

Bailey pointed over to a corner where Eddie, Brix, and Zeke sat at the lounge table with Ben, chatting. They all stood and hugged her when Abby approached.

"I'm glad to see you all," Abby said, shedding her disguise. "Ready to get back to work?"

Ben smiled and patted her on the shoulder. A low din outside slowly grew to a raucous whirring. As it approached, the noise reverberated through the cavernous warehouse. "Sounds like our transport has arrived," he said.

At first, Abby thought it might be a new semi and trailer to replace Bessie. But the noise grew louder, and louder, to the point where she had to hold her hands to her ears to deaden the cacophony.

A large gray military aircraft landed right outside the open bay door in the parking lot, the force of its rotors blowing away anything near the opening that wasn't fastened down. The whine of its jet engines began to decrease, and after an excruciatingly loud and blustery moment, the commotion died completely.

Ben led the team outside to look at the arrival. Abby stared in confusion at the tilt-rotor V-22 Osprey that was now parked right outside her office. She had seen one or two fly overhead during a class field trip to DC a couple years ago, but up close, the thing was massive. A high-pitched whine cut the fresh quiet. Moments later, the rear hatch slowly lowered, revealing a man wearing a khaki flight suit and black aviation helmet. His eyes were covered by an impenetrable black visor and his mouth bore a grim expression.

"Who's this guy?" Abby asked.

The man strode down the ramp carrying a large, overstuffed canvas bag. His jaw, which was covered in several days' worth of dark stubble, trembled as if he was about to bark orders at the team. He dropped the bag on the ground, scanning the team in disfavor. Then a smile spread on his face, and he slid up the helmet visor.

"Hey, everyone!" Steve said, ending the charade with a grin.

The tension in Abby's shoulders from the morning's escapade melted away when she saw him.

Everyone cheered. "Steve!"

Hugs were shared and backs patted.

Eddie gave Steve a vertebrae-cracking bear hug. "*¡Qué padre!*"

"What are you doing here? In this thing?" Abby asked, pointing towards the Osprey.

Steve came up to Abby and offered her a hug. It was longer — warmer — than the last they shared. "Called in a couple favors. I thought after what we went through, we could use a bit of a trip." He leaned in to whisper into her ear as they embraced. "Sorry for being distant. This took some effort to set up. It'll be worth it."

He flashed her that smile she loved and winked before stepping back to unzip the large duffel he had carried off the aircraft. "Grab your bags and get your helmets on, people. We have a dinner date with a Navy captain in Key West at 1800 hours."

"Key West?" Zeke asked.

"But I didn't bring my bikini!" Bailey added.

"Just a refueling point on our way to the island." Steve said.

"Which island?" Brix asked.

"*The* island," Ben said. "Island-A."

Abby stepped back from the group, instantly furious. "What the hell, Ben? You're not taking me, or any of us there!"

Ben smiled and put a hand on her shoulder. "No, no. We're on a special assignment from the president."

"What?" Abby asked, heart still pounding.

Steve put a hand on Abby's other shoulder and flashed his smile. "Let's go see your sister."

THE END

ACKNOWLEDGMENTS

Dangers to Society is a story I cherish.

At the time I began this manuscript, I was reading through George R. R. Martin's 'Song of Ice and Fire' series (a.k.a., Game of Thrones), and I suppose the first acknowledgement goes to him for giving me the template for a compelling, character-driven, multiple point of view story.

Next, I thank Brianne, Lauren, and Sam, my writing friends. Their own wonderful stories are wholly different from mine, but each taught me a lot about character, and the results are in these pages. They also provided oodles of feedback to help me pound this hunk of zany ideas into shape.

Thanks my editor Beverly, who not only found my manuscript's early flaws, but also understood and appreciated the story I was going for.

Thanks also to my friends Kevin and Todd, who provided relevant (non-superpower) insight from their own personal experiences.

I thank my fellow writers at DFW Writer's Workshop, who provided meaningful feedback and consistently tolerate my ebullient energy in the read room. Aspiring writers, go find yourself a group like this.

Again, I thank the Writer's Path program (alas) at SMU, Heather, Kay, Keith, and all my classmates for sharing the ride and their knowledge.

Of course thanks to Minh for her enduring support and Sydney for her enthusiasm of my writing career, which at points exceeds my own.

Finally, thanks go to you, the reader. Without the countless readers out there who support authors, the excuse to dedicate the time, energy, resources, and mental headspace necessary to put together a story this large and complex simply withers away. So by being you, I get to share a little of me. Good trade.

If you've made it this far, I trust you enjoyed #DangersToSociety at least a little. Want more? Leave a review, mention it on your socials, and tell a friend or fifty about it and maybe I'll get to write Volume 2!

ABOUT THE AUTHOR

Matthew Rollins is the award-winning author of Steelwing, Dangers to Society, and other fantasy and science fiction books for various ages. Along with writing fun stories, he enjoys cooking, travel, and video games, all things that are vastly time consuming and pull in opposite directions from writing productivity. Therefore he is one of great internal conflict and can ruminate in place for ages.

Matthew spent his formative years in Loveland, Colorado, developing a life-long love for skiing and the Denver Broncos. He graduated from St. Olaf College in Northfield, Minnesota — look it up, it's a real place! Matthew now resides in the Dallas, Texas area with his wife and daughter, and is always hard at work on the next story.

www.ingramcontent.com/pod-product-compliance
Lightning Source LLC
Chambersburg PA
CBHW070557300726
48975CB00006B/1613